The Wizard

and

The Warrior

Book 2 of the Baramayan Chronicles

Deborah Millitello

Word Posse

Dedication
To my dad, Lyle Franklin Laslie

Acknowledgments
I want to thank my writing group: Laurell K. Hamilton, Mark Sumner, Marella Sands, Sharon Shinn, Rett MacPherson, and Tom Drennan, for all their help and insight. Thanks to my family for understanding my writing obsession. And Carl, you're still the love of my life.

From Word Posse
The Naturalist, Mark Sumner
Sleeping the Churchyard Sleep, Rett MacPherson
Bad to the Bones, Rett MacPherson
Pandora's Mirror, Marella Sands
The Water Girl, Deborah Millitello
Do Virgins Taste Better? and Other Strange Tales, Deborah Millitello
Thor McGraw & the Ice Man, Tom Drennan
Restless Bones, Marella Sands
Fortune's Daughter, Marella Sands
On Whetsday, Mark Sumner
The Angel Share books by Marella Sands
Volume 1: Through a Keyhole Darkly
Volume 2: What the Thunder Said
The Baramayan Chronicles by Deborah Millitello
Book 1: The Mourning Dove
Book 2: The Wizard and the Warrior

Like us on Facebook: facebook.com/WordPosse

This book has been typeset in Fanwood. Titles and headers are in Darleston. Cover art by Danielle Shimchick.

ISBN-13: 978-1-944089-09-2
ISBN-10: 1-944089-09-8

I

Winter mornings in Hixus were usually overcast and mild, although sometimes chilly. Snow this far south was a rarity and a cause for delight among the city's children. But it was so close to spring, there little chance of snow. Overnight, fog rising from the warmer ocean waters had crept into the streets and alleys of the seaside city. By now at midmorning, all but a few misty tendrils were gone, but the air was still damp and cool.

Smoke hung low over the houses. Soot blackened the rooftops and upper stories of most buildings south of the cobblestone plaza down to the dockside warehouses. Even the gold leaf-covered dome of the Temple of Baygor on the west side of the plaza and the green copper roof of the Temple of Baramay on the east side were dulled by a thin layer of soot. The faint cry of sea birds mingled with the rhythmic lapping of waves on the shore, and the aroma of baking bread, salt air, and the ever-present odor of fish permeated the city.

Softly strumming "Tellowee's Lament" on his lute, the Wizard Maren scanned the overcast sky. Pulled by a feeling of disquiet, like waking from a dark dream he couldn't quite remember, he wandered south to Hixus' central market in the plaza. A slight breeze trickled to the north from the sea, and he shivered although he wore dark crimson wool trousers and hat, and a wool jacket of the same shade of crimson over his linen shirt.

He'd just come from the prosperous north side of Hixus from the home of one of the most prominent families in the city. The master of the house had invited

Maren to play and sing at a celebration of his daughter's betrothal in six days. Maren had gladly accepted and had left with a small bag of silver coins.

The market was filled with merchants, peddlers, craftsmen, and sellers, hawking wares to the few customers venturing out in the dreary weather. The aroma of rich roasted meat mingled with the scent of bread baked with honey, candied fruit, and spices. Maren's stomach rumbled, since he hadn't eaten all day, but his uneasiness dulled his appetite.

"Come and see the latest fabrics," called the cloth merchant from his open air stall. "Butter-soft wool and white linen, flowing silk and the finest cotton. Cloth in every color of the rainbow." He scanned Maren from head to toe. "Fine goods," he said, "but a minstrel should have clothes that draw attention. Now I have just the thing for you." He caressed a bolt of dark blue and gold brocade. "Imagine a jacket and hat made from this, and dark blue trousers with gold piping to match. And I know a seamstress who would make you that suit of clothes, fit for a lord."

Maren strummed a chord, smiled, and gave a quick bow. "Maybe for the Spring Fete."

The cloth merchant grinned. "I'll be here." He turned toward a well-dressed woman with a young girl in tow.

"Apples, last of the season," a balding grocer said, holding out a red-blushed fruit to Maren, "wrinkled but sound and sweet. Three for a copper gate."

"Three apples for one copper coin? That's a bit steep. Six for a copper."

The grocer sighed. "But I only have one bushel left, and there won't be any more until next fall. Four for a copper."

"Five. Five apples for a copper."

The grocer held up his hands and gazed at the sky. "How can I stay in business like this?" He looked back at Maren. "All right. Five apples for a copper."

Maren smiled at the grocer and gave him a copper coin stamped with the image of a castle gate. The grocer handed him five apples, one at a time, and Maren stowed four of them in his jacket. The last apple he tossed in the air, caught it, then took a large bite. The grocer hadn't lied. The apple was sweet and sound, and reminded him of autumn mornings and harvest moons, of pies and cider and cozy fires. He ate the entire apple except for the seeds, which he dropped in his belt pouch. *Seeds for tomorrow's apple trees*, he thought. *And cider.*

A group of children crowded around him as he walked down the cobblestone streets, and they begged him for a story. "Maybe a bit later," he said and strummed a verse of "Chellit's Cat" for them. "Now run home before it starts to rain."

"It's not going to rain," a gangly tow-headed boy said.

"Run home anyway." He glanced at the sky. "Run home now."

The children grumbled but scattered quickly.

The wide boulevard called Northway ran from the cliffs at the northern edge of Hixus through the center of the city to the seaside. The houses bordering Northway south of the market square were two- and three-story stone tenements crowded with large poor families, but the road and neighborhood were kept neat and clean. Children played stick ball in the street, and women hung clothes from balconies.

Several taverns and inns, catering to the locals and sailors just in port, were wedged between the houses. The Mermaid Inn, where Maren stayed, was ten blocks south of the central market. Jeral the owner, swarthy and black-haired, opened his front door and swept the doorstep. He'd spent twenty years at sea before he'd married and settled down to run the inn. As large and strong as a Formian bear, he never hired roughnecks to get rid of troublemakers. He could handle up to ten men by himself and often did for entertainment. If he won, he took half the pot. If he lost, he took half, too. The Mermaid's patrons enjoyed watching more than betting.

The taverner looked up as Maren walked by and held up his massive hand in greeting. "Come back later an' have a drink with me," Jeral said.

"That I will," Maren said with a nod. He dug the apples out of his jacket and handed them to Jeral. "Can you put these in my room?"

"That I will," Jeral said with nod.

When Maren reached the docks, he noticed only half a dozen men sitting in front of the wooden warehouses, weathered by sun and sea that crowded the water front. No ships were tied up on the docks. One of the dockhands called to him. "How about a song while we eat our lunch, minstrel?"

Maren glanced at the sea, uneasy, then nodded and began playing and singing "Chellit's Cat." The men tapped their feet in time to the music while they ate smoked fish and bread. At the end of the chorus one of the dockhands tossed him a copper coin. Maren pocketed the coin, bowed, then turned toward the sea, still strumming the tune.

Growing more apprehensive, he walked to the end of the longest pier, its pilings crusted with barnacles and moss, and stared out across the sea dulled by the clouds overhead. White and grey seabirds cried out as they circled and dove for fish in the sea. The lapping of white-capped waves on the shore was like the beating of the world's heart. He loved that sound.

When Maren had left the Wizard's Vale, he'd spent only a half a year in Vorlik, ancient home of Wizards, before he'd wandered south to the great forests of Peltik. He'd lingered there for almost three years before he traveled east to Tukkus, home of blacksmiths, coppersmiths, and the world's finest sword smiths. He'd even learned to form simple tools in one of the many forges in the country. Restless after nearly three years, he traveled back to Peltik then south to Beltrin, home of merchants, farmers, and mercenaries. He stayed there only a few months before he moved on to the Freelands, the wide, wild lands of farms and small villages stretching south all the way to the edge of the Southern Plateau. He'd spent more than five years traveling from village to farmstead. Then he'd come to Hixus on the northern shore of the sea. And he fell in love with the city and had stayed there for nearly ten years.

He glanced over his shoulder toward the city of Hixus. White stone and wooden buildings spread across the wide sloping shoreline all the way to the steep northern cliffs and winding road up to the Southern Plateau. Humans hurried through life in the city, working, playing, singing, celebrating with such intensity. Maren wasn't sure if it was because their lives were so short or because it was the nature of humans to take joy in everything.

The years had passed swiftly for Maren. He was forty-two years old, but for a Wizard he was still very young, since Wizards often lived for four hundred years. It seemed impossible that he'd left his home twenty-two year ago. He had gone back just once, but little had changed there. Except the woman he'd hoped to marry had left for the human lands. But there were still many years for love and marriage and children.

He glanced back at the city again and sighed. Time to move on before people noticed he hadn't aged, before they suspected that he was more than just a minstrel. He turned back toward the sea. *But I'll miss this,* he thought as he gazed at the water. *The sound of the waves that I hear even in my dreams, the salty scent of the air, how vast the sea is – I never imagined anything this majestic when I was growing up in the Wizard's Vale. Maybe I'll travel west along the coast so I can still be near the sea.*

He leaned against a weathered piling and squinted toward the horizon. His dark brown hair fluttered in the building breeze filled with the scent of rain and lightning. The air felt close, almost smothering. He gazed toward the western edge of the city where a rocky prominence jutted out into the bay. He shivered and wished he'd worn his heavy cloak that he'd left back at the Mermaid Inn.

A storm's coming, he thought, his stomach knotted with worry, *but something more. Something...dangerous.*

"Hey, what's that?" called one of the dockhands.

"Where?" a second dockhand said.

"There, right there!" the first one said.

Maren turned toward the wharf and saw the man pointing south. Turning back to the sea, he scanned the horizon. There, southwest of the city, black smoke rose to the threatening sky. Shading his eyes, suddenly he spotted a ship on the horizon, coming closer, closer. The ship was burning!

The wind picked up, nearly blowing Maren's hat off his head. The white caps of the waves grew larger and wider. Maren took off his hat, stuffed it inside his jacket, leaned against the piling for support, and frowned at the sky. Dark clouds thickened in the south and raced toward the seaport. Winter storms were extremely rare on the southern sea, and winter was almost over. But this storm made his skin crawl and his chest tighten.

Finally, the ship was close enough that Maren could see a merchant flag flying from the mast and pennants strung on the rigging: red for "Warning," black and red for "Enemies," and blue and white for "Help." The wind was driving the ship fast, but fire was spreading faster. Maren doubted the ship would make it to port before it sank.

Slinging his lute on his back, he wheeled and ran back to the warehouses and the dockhands standing there. "You," Maren said, pointing at one of the men, "go tell the mayor to send out the city guard! We don't know what kind of enemies or how many we might be facing! Warn everyone you see that they might have to flee to the plateau now! The rest of you, we have to rescue the men from the ship!"

The messenger darted up the street toward the center of town.

Maren turned back to the sea. The ship was closer. Flames rose from all parts of the ship. Some of the sails had caught fire. The ship neared the harbor then turned east and dropped anchor in the bay. Men jumped from the burning decks and swam for the shore.

Maren scanned the shoreline. Just beyond the eastern dock were half a dozen small fishing boats. Beside them, two weathered men had hung nets to dry and were mending them.

"We need those boats," Maren told a dark-haired dock man. "Get them in the water and rescue as many as you can."

The dark-haired man and three of his companions ran to the fishermen. Maren watched as the dark-haired man waved his arms then pointed to the sea. The fishermen turned toward the bay, dropped their net shuttles, and raced to their boats. The four dockhands pushed the other boats into the water, then each climbed into a boat, and began to row for the ship.

As the first sailors reached the shore, Maren and the last dockhand waded out into the cold water to help sailors to the docks. Most were all right, but a few were burned or bleeding.

"Who's coming?" Maren asked one sailor, whose left arm was burned severely.

"Pirates," the sailor gasped, "a whole fleet of pirate ships."

"How far behind?"

"Not far," the man said. "Maybe an hour behind us. An hour at most."

"That's not much time!" Maren opened his belt pouch, took out a small blue jar, and opened it. A wholesome fragrance filled the air as he dipped his fingers in a white salve and spread it on the sailor's burns.

The man winced, then relaxed and closed his eyes for a moment. When he opened them again, he gave Maren a weak smile. "Baramay bless you."

Maren helped him to his feet. "Now help your shipmates! Get them to the Temple of Baygor! The priests will tend their injuries!"

"This way!" the sailor called to his shipmates, and cradling his arm, led them up the street toward the town's center.

The fishing boats landed with dozens of rescued sailors. Maren ran from man to man applying the salve as needed, directing those uninjured to help those who were hurt to the temple. In the distance Maren heard trumpets sounded from the north. The city guard was being called to arms.

The merchant ship was completely engulfed in flames, black smoke billowing toward the dark clouds. A grey-haired man jumped from the ship just before the main mast crashed to the deck, then he swam ashore. Maren met the man in cold waist-deep water, put the man's arm around his shoulder, and helped him to land.

The man coughed and gagged, his lean face blackened with soot, burns on his hands, arms, and face.

"Are you the captain?" Maren asked as he lowered the man to the ground then knelt beside him.

The man nodded slowly. His eyes were glazed with pain, and his breathing was ragged.

Maren took out the salve again and spread it on the man's burns. "What happened?"

The captain tried to talk but started coughing again. Maren took a tiny cloth bag from his pouch, then opened the small wineskin tied to his belt. He sprinkled grey-green powdered callum bark into the wine, whirled it to mix, and held it to the captain's mouth. *Not as effective as callum bark tea,* Maren thought, *but it will help.*

The captain took a swallow, coughed, and took several more swallows. He cleared his throat.

"Pirates attacked us as we were coming out of Stejanik's Bay on the southern continent," the captain said. "All the merchant ships were sailing together. We thought we'd be safe in a large group. We were wrong." The captain coughed again. "We thought we could outrun the pirates since the wind was blowing from the south. But fires seemed to spring out of nowhere, setting the sails alight, running along the ropes and rigging, first on one ship then another. All the other ships burned. The pirates killed the sailors who jumped overboard. I could hear the pirates laughing as they slaughtered the sailors. Laughing!" The captain coughed again. "Mine was the lead ship and we barely got away, but the pirates followed us. They're not far behind us. Strange fires started popping up all over the deck. We'd put out one flame and another would pop up. Thank Baygor we made it this far. I anchored the ship in the harbor. I thought since it's burning anyway, we could use it as a barrier. I know it won't last for long, but it might slow the pirates down. What they'll do when they reach Hixus..." the man halted and shuddered.

"How many?" Maren asked.

"A dozen ships at least."

Maren helped the captain to his feet. "Can you walk now?"

The captain nodded.

"Report to the mayor. Tell him what you saw and tell him the people need to leave everything behind. There's no time to pack. We have to get the citizens out of the city and have the city guards in place before the pirates get here."

"What are you going to do?" the captain asked.

"What I can! Now go!"

The captain nodded and hurried toward the city center.

Maren turned back to the sea and scanned the shoreline from east to west. The breeze was coming in strong gusts, blowing Maren's hair straight back. *What can I do?* he wondered. *And how can I do it without being seen?*

His eyes stared at the rocky prominence at the westernmost edge of the city. He ran along the boardwalk down to the sandy shore, past the houses and cottages and tumbled down shacks lining the western edge of the water front. The tide was rolling in faster than normal, lapping farther inland with each wave. Clouds thickened overhead and a few raindrops began to fall. Maren scrambled over the tidal pools, boulders, and fallen rocks, worn smooth by salt spray and crashing waves, until he had reached the narrow row of rocks sticking out into the bay. Edging around the prominence just enough he was beyond the sight of anyone from the city, Maren searched the horizon.

After a few moments he saw a small break on the sea that grew larger – the mast of a ship, then another, and another, two-masted ships with sleek hulls and full sails, driven by the whistling south wind. Standing with one hand raised to the sky and his other hand outstretched, palm up, to the sea, he said, "By the power of Baramay, who made the earth and sea and wind, *tasrin akelleya taychay barason!*"

The air began to swirl into a sphere in his palm, growing larger and larger. He hurled the sphere toward the masts. A wind rose from the shore, blowing counter to the southern wind, now almost a gale. The ships seemed to stagnate in the tumultuous waves. Rain became heavier, then poured down.

Suddenly, he heard dire voices in the wind speaking dark words of darker power. Sorcerers! There were Sorcerers on those ships! In all his years he'd never been close to a Sorcerer, never had to face one of them. And there were at least two of them with the pirate ships. Could he defeat them? Was he strong enough? "Lady Baramay, help me, please!"

He concentrated on the wind spell, trying to push the ships back, but he felt the will of the Sorcerers pushing against him. He braced himself against the cliff face and shouted, *"Tasrin akelleya makeesa barason!"*

The wind howled toward the ships, swirling like a water spout. As it reached the lead ship, a column of green flame crashed against the water spout, which shattered like a ceramic bowl. Maren was hurled back against the cliff, knocking his breath from him and bruising his right side. Stone ripped through the right sleeve of his jacket and shirt, and cut his upper right arm. He sagged onto one of the boulders and gasped for breath. A wave crashed against the rocks and drenched him. His arm stung and burned. Twisting it enough he could examine it, he saw blood oozing from a ragged gash a hand's width long.

Kneeling at the edge of the sea, he scooped up some water in his hand. With his index finger, he swirled the water in his palm and said, "By the power of Baramay who made the sea and waves and all within, *tasrin rasheek kah barason!"*

The water in his hand began to swirl on its own and turned dark blue. He poured the water into the ocean, then collapsed to the rocks, and watched as the streak of dark blue flowed toward the ships. The blue water grew wider and wider, until it touched the lead ship, circling the ship faster and faster. A whirlpool formed under the ship, turning the ship round and round until it was dragged down into the ocean. The whirlpool grew larger, drawing in ship after ship, pulling them into the dark blue water. Ships crashed into each other, listed on their sides, then capsized. Maren heard men screaming and Sorcerers shrieking above the howling gale as the ships sank out of sight.

Only two ships escaped the whirlpool, but they held course for Hixus. Maren lay on the rocks, nearly exhausted, trying to catch his breath. He tried to push himself upright, but his arms shook so much he couldn't hold himself. He lay still, his cheek against the cold, wet stone. A cold wave crashed against the rocks, drenching him. He gagged and choked on the water that filled his mouth. His throat and chest burned, and the cut on his arm felt as if a heated iron had been thrust into the wound.

"Lady Baramay," he prayed as he sprawled on the rocks, "please give me strength."

Rain began pelting down, stinging like hail, and the winds whipped the sea like a hurricane. The tide rushed in, almost reaching the top of the rocks where Maren lay.

I have to get out of here, he thought, *or the waves will drag me into the sea.*

He crawled across the slick rocks to the cliff face, leaned against it, and gasped for air. Every breath hurt his ribs. Fumbling with the wineskin, he untied it, opened the stopper, and drank the rest of the wine and callum bark mixture. Warmth flowed down his throat, filled his stomach, and radiated through his body. The pain in his ribs eased, and he felt a bit stronger.

Clutching at the rock face, he pulled himself upright, paused, then turned to face the storm. A huge wave was building on the sea, rising well over Maren's head. Lifting a hand to the sky and holding the other palm out to the sea, he said, "By the power of Baramay who made the wind to blow and the tide to flow, *tasrin rasheek hamania barason!*"

The wave kept rolling toward shore like a wall. Maren clenched his jaw and concentrated on the water. Slowly, the wave ebbed and receded until the water barely touched Maren's feet. Holding his hands together palms up, he called another sphere of wind and sent it south. Gradually, the winds calmed to a gentle breeze, and the rain diminished to a drizzle, then stopped though the sky was still overcast.

Maren crept to the edge of the prominence and peered around it toward Hixus. The last two pirate ships had reached the harbor, but one had been driven toward the burning ship anchored there. The masts snapped, and the hull cracked as the pirate ship rammed into the burning merchant ship. Men dove from the wreckage into the water and swam for shore. The last pirate ship had furled its sails and was nearing the piers where the city guard had assembled, sword drawn, arrows nocked.

I can't let the pirates land, he thought. *They'll loot and burn the city, and kill everyone they don't torture and violate. I have to stop them, even if the people of Hixus see me.*

Summoning all of his remaining strength, Maren stood erect on the prominence where he could see the city's shoreline and took his lute from his back. He whispered a word of command and began to play and sing a lullaby.

Pirates crowded the portside of the ship, shouting and cursing, their swords and daggers drawn as the ship approached the pier. Maren sang the lullaby with all his might. The pirates jumped from the ship to the pier and began running toward the guards. Slowly, the invaders stopped shouting and lowered their swords. Their heads began to nod. The guards attacked fiercely, but the pirates barely defended themselves.

Maren strained to keep singing, but his voice was growing weaker. The few pirates still on the ship tried to climb over the side onto the pier, but they yawned and draped over the side, sound asleep. Most of the pirates from the wrecked ship were halfway to the shore when they gradually stopped swimming. One by one they closed their eyes and sank beneath the waves. Suddenly, Maren's voice cracked; he couldn't sing another note. The pirates fighting the city guards seemed to shake off their drowsiness and plunged into the fight with renew intent. But the city guards fought until every pirate was dead.

Maren staggered, barely able to stand. *The city's safe*, he thought as his legs gave way, and he sank down to the stony shelf, exhausted.

2

Shaking with cold and unsteady, Maren pulled himself upright and slipped his lute over his shoulder, using the cord as a sling to support his injured right arm. His hair was slicked to his head, and his clothes were dripping. His boots squished as he climbed down from the rocky prominence and trudged slowly toward the city. The pain in his side was so sharp, he had to halt for a few moments, panting for air. He kept his left hand on the wall of the nearest cottage or warehouse to steady himself as he staggered slowly to the docks, where the city guards tossed the dead pirates into a pile. Unexpectedly, he came upon Jeral, the owner of The Mermaid Inn, wiping blood from his short sword on a pirate's shirt.

"Ya look terrible," Jeral said as he slid the sword back in its scabbard. "Yer soakin' wet. An' yer arm's bleedin'! Were ya in the fightin', too? What'd ya think ya were goin' t' do? Stop the pirates with a song?"

Maren tried to reply but was too worn out. He'd never used so much magic at one time. He felt weak, completely drained. He stumbled and nearly fell, but Jeral caught him. Sharp pain in Maren's chest nearly took his breath away. Pain throbbed from his side to the center of his chest.

"Let's get ya back t' the inn," Jeral said. "Molly'll take care o' ya." Taking Maren's arm, Jeral slipped it around his shoulders and supported Maren. He gasped as pain shot up his arm, and he could barely lift his feet to keep walking toward the inn.

Shouts and cheers rang through the streets. Young boys ran toward the docks while their mothers shouted for them to come back.

Thank Baygor the people are safe, Maren thought.

As they entered the Mermaid Inn, Jeral shouted, "Molly! Molly girl, come here!"

"I'm still packin' things in case we have t' run!" a voice called from an upper story.

"We're not runnin'!" Jeral said. "We beat 'em! But Maren's hurt!"

"Maren?" Footsteps ran down the stairs, and Jeral's wife Molly ran to Maren's side, her green eyes wide, her salt-and-pepper hair braided and wrapped around her head. "Oh, yer bleedin'!" she said, touching Maren's arm. "Ya poor thing! Jeral, ya take him straight up t' his room! I'll get some bandages an' clean water. And what about yerself?" she asked. "Are ya hurt, too?"

"No, not a scratch," Jeral said.

"Thank Baygor! Now get him up t' his room and out o' those wet clothes. I'll be there directly." She bustled off to the kitchen.

Jeral helped Maren upstairs, but each step was agony for Maren. He clenched his teeth to keep from groaning. Sweat trickled down his face, but he felt so cold. When they finally reached Maren's small room, the minstrel sank down on the only chair set beside a small hearth, exhausted.

Jeral ran to the east-facing shutters and opened them, letting in wan light and chilled air. A few embers still glowed reddish-black in the hearth on the south wall. He took a small reed from the mantle, held the reed against an ember until it caught fire, then lit the lantern on the wall hook. "Let's get yer clothes off so Molly can tend yer wound," Jeral said. "But let me take yer lute first."

Maren cringed as he slipped his lute off his back, handing the instrument to the innkeeper. Jeral hung the lute on the chair, then turned back to Maren. Very slowly, Maren slid his uninjured arm from his jacket sleeve and inhaled sharply. Jeral carefully pulled the other sleeve, but to Maren it felt as if someone were stabbing him. With Jeral's help, Maren stripped off the wet clothes and put on a pair of linen underwear before he crawled into his bed and pulled the covers up to his chest. He was so cold, his lips quivered when he breathed.

Molly came through the door with a bowl of steaming water and strips of cloth over her arm, the hem of her apron tucked in at her sizable waist.

"Pull that table over t' this side o' the bed," Molly told her husband, "an' hurry! He's pale as fresh milk!"

Jeral moved pitcher and wash basin from the bedside table to the chair, picked up the table, and set it down beside his wife. Molly placed the bowl on the table, then set the cloth strips beside the bowl. She untucked her apron and took out some herbs and two small jars, setting them all on the table. "I need more light," she told her husband. "Can ya bring the lantern over here? An' fetch another one. An' build up the fire. An' close the shutters! Can't ya see he's shiverin'?"

Molly turned back to Maren. "Now let's take a look at ya." She started to take the blanket away from his chest and arm, but he clutched at the cover. "Why are ya being difficult?"

Maren's face suddenly felt hot, and he felt embarrassed. "I just haven't been unclothed before a woman before."

Molly laughed. "I'm old enough t' be yer mother."

"But you're not."

Molly rolled her eyes. "I'm a healer. Now stop bein' so childish."

Maren cleared his throat and let go of the blanket.

"That's better," she said. She pulled the blanket down to his waist, then gasped. "Yer arm's still bleedin'. An' look at yer side, all bruised an' battered! I'll bet ya got a broken rib or two. Does it hurt when ya breathe?"

Slowly, he nodded.

"That's what I thought," Molly said as she sponged the blood from his arm.

Maren squeezed his eyes shut and clamped his jaws tight, trying not to cry out.

Molly crushed the herbs she'd brought and dropped them into the water, stirring it with her fingers. The fresh green scents of mint, roborant, comfrey, and yarrow filled the room. Dipping the cloth in the water, Molly held the cloth gently against the wound, but Maren gasped at the sharp pain in his arm. Sweat trickled down his face, and he swallowed hard.

"Do you have any woundweal?" he said tightly.

"No," she said, sighing. "Used the last bit I had a week ago. Don't have anything else for the pain."

"I have some," he said between short breaths. "Jeral, bring me my knapsack from the chest."

The innkeeper quickly finished stoking the fire on the hearth, then stood, opened the wooden chest at the foot of the bed, and took out a large dark-cloth bag. He brought it to Maren and set it on his lap.

Moving as little as possible, Maren opened the bag and took out a small pouch. Inside were numerous barks, leaves, and small wooden boxes, and one dark blue jar. "Here," he said, handing Molly several dried woundweal leaves and a tiny piece of grey-green callum bark. "And make a tea with this bark."

"Tea?" Jeral rolled his eyes. "Tea's a drink for old ladies. I'll bring ya somethin' fit for a man t' drink."

"No, it's a healing tonic," Maren said.

Jeral laughed. "Oh, all right then.

Molly took the herbs, then sniffed the bark. "I never seen it before. An' I know healin' herbs. What is it? "

"Callum bark. A very powerful healing medicine. Steep it in boiling water for a short time. It'll heal quicker than roborant."

"All right," she said. "I'll be back quick as I can. Jeral, ya watch him good." She hurried out of the room.

Maren closed his eyes and tried to ignore the misery coursing through his arm and side. He was so exhausted, he could barely keep his head up. *But Hixus is safe,* he thought. *All these people are safe. But why were Sorcerers on the pirate ships? At least they were destroyed before they could reach the city. Why were they coming here? What did they want? And what if more come? Would I be strong enough to defeat them? And should I warn the masters back home?*

By the time Molly returned with a wooden cup and a small bowl, all Maren wanted to do was sleep, but the jagged pain wouldn't let him. She handed him the cup of callum bark tea and began dabbing woundweal potion on his arm. Gradually, the potion numbed the pain in his arm.

"Here," he said, handing her the small blue jar from his belt pouch. "Spread this on my wound, then bandage it."

Molly took the jar, opened it, and sniffed at the creamy white salve. A fresh wholesome scent like springtime filled the room. "Never smelled anythin' like this," she said. "What is it?"

"A healing salve. You only need a small amount," Maren said, then sipped more of the callum bark tea. The warmth soothed his throat. Strength flowed throughout his body. Pain began to recede from his wounds.

Molly spread the salve on his arm and side, then bandaged them. "That's all I can do for now. Ya better rest a bit. I'll bring ya some broth later." She motioned to Jeral to follow her. "I'll check in on ya in a few hours."

Maren watched them go, then drank the rest of the callum bark tea. He felt better but drowsy. He set the cup on the bedside table, lay back against his pillow, closed his eyes, and thanked Baygor and Baramay as he drifted off to sleep.

He woke up as someone laid a cool hand on his forehead for a moment. His eyes couldn't focus on the face bending over him.

"Feelin' better?" Molly's voice said. "Ya think ya might want a bite t' eat?"

Maren blinked his eyes several times until he could see clearly. Molly stood beside the bed, holding a tray with a bowl of steaming broth and a chunk of crusty brown bread. The aroma of the broth made his mouth water. He sat up, feeling a little stiff, but at least his arm wasn't throbbing. His side was still sore, but it didn't hurt as much to breathe.

"Here," Molly said, setting the tray on his lap, then adjusted his pillow so he could sit up comfortably. "Would ya like some more o' that tea from the bark ya gave me? I got plenty o' hot water just in case."

"Yes," Maren said as he broke off a piece of bread and dipped it in the brown broth.

"Don't eat too fast," Molly said. "Might not set well on yer stomach if ya do. I'll be right back with the tea." She turned and left.

Maren took a bite of the bread, sucking the warm broth from it before he chewed the bread. The broth was made from fish, peppery but not too spicy, and flavored with onions, carrots, bay leaf and thyme. He broke off another piece of bread and soaked it in the broth. By the time Molly came back with the callum bark tea, Maren was sopping up the final drops of broth with the last piece of bread.

"Barg's Breath," she said, grinning, "ya'd think ya was starvin'. Here's yer tea." She handed him a wooden cup.

The steaming tea filled the room with a wholesome scent. Maren breathed in the fragrance, which eased the tightness in his chest. Blowing on the liquid to cool it, he sipped the tea, letting the warmth rest on his tongue before he swallowed. Fatigue and pain seeped away as he drank the tea. Strength replaced weakness. He felt his broken ribs knitting together, his bruises healing.

"That's amazin' medicine," Molly said, gazing intently at him. "Color's come back to yer face, and yer breathin' sounds better. Where'd ya get that bark?"

"A long way from here," Maren said, then drank the last of the tea.

"Well, I'd like a bit o' that bark myself."

"I don't have much, but I'll share some with you."

"Oh, yer such a dear," she said, taking the empty cup from Maren. "Would ya like some more broth?"

"No, but thank you."

"All right. You get some more rest." Molly set the cup beside the empty bowl and picked up the tray. "I'll check on ya later." She turned to go.

"Wait," Maren said. "What time is it? What's happening in the city?"

"Everythin's all right. Jeral can come up an' tell ya all about it." She looked at him sternly. "Later. After ya rest." She grinned and left.

Maren lay back against his pillow and turned his head toward the closed shutters. Little light seeped through the slats. *Probably late afternoon*, he thought. Sinking into a comfortable position, he closed his eyes. The tea flowed through his body, warming, relaxing, and lulling him to sleep.

3

Maren woke to the sound of sea birds and laughter and the ever-present splashing of waves on the shore, comforting sounds. The room was slightly chilly and lit only by an orange-red glow from the hearth. He stretched a little, testing his injuries. His ribs were still tender, but his arm didn't hurt at all. Cautiously, he sat up, swung his legs over the side of the bed, and stood up. The floor was cool but not icy cold to his feet. He added some wood to the hearth and stirred the embers until flames began to lick at the wood, warming the room.

He dressed as quickly as he could, although pulling on his boots was difficult and caused his ribs to ache, then picked up his knapsack from beside the bed where it lay and retrieved his small pouch of herbs. Taking out a piece of callum bark, he held it in one hand and reached toward the ceiling with the other. "By the power of Baygor who gives the increase, *tasrin callum enisan ahntahni barason.*"

Cupping his hands together, he watched as a blue mist swirled above them growing larger. When it finally dissipated, his hands were heaped with callum bark. He was a little breathless, but otherwise he felt fine. "A little more callum bark tea, and I should be completely healed," he said to himself.

He put half the bark back in his pouch, then wrapped the other half in a cloth that lay on the bedside table. His stomach growled. "I hope Molly has breakfast ready."

Walking down stairs caused twinges in his side, but he managed to reach the common room on the ground floor without too much discomfort. Jeral was no where in sight, but Molly was talking to two men at a table near the door. The moment she noticed him, she hurried over.

"What are ya doin' outta bed?" Molly demanded. "Yer wounds should o' kept ya laid up for a week or two!"

"I'm much better," he said, smiling. "And I'm hungry enough to eat a barrel of fish."

"Well, that's a good sign, but *I'm* the healer. *I'll* tell ya when yer better."

"Here." He handed her the cloth with the callum bark. "Half of what I have."

Molly frowned slightly. "I thought ya said ya didn't have much."

Maren smiled. "I had more than I thought I did. One piece will make a kettle of healing tea. And if you can't wait for water to heat, you can powder the bark and add it to any liquid. It won't be as effective as the infusion, but it will keep someone alive until you can make the tea."

She gazed at the cloth. "I've never heard o' anythin' that'd heal so quickly. It's almost like..." she paused, her green eyes studying Maren, "like magic."

Maren remained silent.

After a few moments, Molly tucked the cloth in her skirt pocket. "Ya sit down there at the table an' I'll bring ya somethin' t' eat."

Maren sat at the table nearest the fireplace. The warmth of the blaze felt good as it soaked through his clothes to his injuries. He closed his eyes, relishing the heat on his face and hands. He breathed in the scent of old wood, herbs, and spices, comforting aromas. This place had been his home for ten years. He'd miss it -- and Molly and Jeral -- when he had to leave.

Jeral came through the front door, carrying a large basket of fresh fish, just as Molly set a tray with a bowl of porridge, several slices of toasted bread, and a cup of callum bark tea down in front to Maren.

The innkeeper's dark eyes popped wide. "What are ya doin' down here?" Jeral asked.

Maren smiled. "Eating breakfast."

"But ya was hurt," Jeral said, "hurt bad."

"All due to Molly's care."

Jeral looked at Molly, and the two of them stared at each other for a few moments.

"I'm not that good," Molly said softly as she took the basket of fish and carried it to the kitchen.

"So what happened at the docks after you brought me here?" Maren asked as he took a bite of the warm bread laced with raisins and cinnamon, then drizzled honey onto the warm porridge.

Jeral sat down across from him but didn't speak for a few moments until Maren looked up at him. "Lot o' the pirates washed up on shore," Jeral said. "The mayor ordered all their bodies carted up to the plateau an' burned. The ones still alive on the ship were taken t' the dungeon. They'll probably be hanged in a few days. Merchant ships should be safe now." He paused a moment, then said, "The pirates on the ship, they was sleepin'. Sleepin'. How could they just fall asleep when they was ready for a fight? It don't make sense."

Maren started to take a drink of the callum bark tea, pale green-gold with a fragrance like spring showers and delicate blossoms and warm kitchens in winter, wholesome and healing, when he noticed Jeral watching him silently. "Is something wrong?" Maren asked.

Jeral opened his mouth as if to speak, then hesitated. "One o' the guards told me he talked t' some o' the prisoners. The guard said the pirates claim they heard music an' singin', like someone was singin' a lullaby, an' they just couldn't keep their eyes open. They fell asleep right where they was." He leaned over the table toward Maren and whispered, "Tell me true, Maren, was it... are ya... could ya be a..."

"Could I be a what?" Maren asked softly, looking straight at Jeral. "And would it make any difference if I were?"

Jeral sat back and gazed at Maren, then shook his head. "No. Ya are what ya are." He stood and turned toward the kitchen, then looked over his shoulder. "But I thank ya for what ya did." He hurried toward the kitchen.

Maren sat quietly, poured milk on the porridge, and began eating it. *If Jeral knows what I am, others in Hixus will also,* he thought. *And if the people of Hixus realize what I am, an enemy might discover me. I could be in danger, and I could be a danger to this city. I'll have to leave soon.*

That afternoon the mayor of Hixus declared a holiday for a week to celebrate the victory over the pirates. Maren was sought after to attend and play at dinners and dances and parties. His wounds were almost healed by the next morning, and Molly said little when she examined his arm. She just shook her head, studied Maren's face, then left his room.

Seven days after the battle on the docks, Maren wandered through Hixus' central market, strumming his lute in the comfortably cool afternoon. He had slept late since he had been up most of the night playing at the engagement party he'd agreed to on the day of the battle. The sun shone brightly, almost as if spring had already come to Hixus. The city was still celebrating their escape from the pirates, and the market square was crowded with venders and citizens, laughing, dancing, and enjoying the unseasonably mild weather. Everyone hailed him and requested songs. Maren played and sang, until his throat was dry.

He stopped at a booth selling mead and asked for a mug. The robust man behind the counter refused Maren's coin. "I wouldn't be here if not for you," the man said.

Maren halted, startled. "What do you mean?"

"You got the word out that the pirates were coming."

"Oh," Maren said, relieved. "All I did was to send someone to warn the mayor to call out the city guard."

"And that was enough to save us," the man said, "that and the protection of the gods. I won't take your money."

Maren sighed and put the coin back in his pouch. "All right, but next time I'll pay."

The man laughed. "Next time."

Maren sipped the reddish liquid. It was strong, slightly sweet, and held a hint of red currants. He smiled at the vendor and raised his mug in salute. The vender grinned back.

Just as Maren was taking a long drink, a young boy plowed into him, spilling mead all over the two of them. Maren grabbed the boy's arm. "Hold, boy! Where are you going in such a hurry?"

The sandy-haired boy twisted like a snake. He was strong for his size, only coming up to Maren's chest, but Maren held on tightly.

"Let me go!" the boy shouted.

"Hold him!" a man shouted over the crowd. "Little thief stole a loaf of bread!"

The boy almost wriggled free. Maren dropped the mug and grabbed the boy with both hands.

"Did you steal a loaf of bread, boy?" Maren asked.

The boy didn't answer, just tried to wrench free.

Maren pulled him closer and stared straight in the boy's hazel eyes. "Did you steal the bread?"

The boy glared at Maren, but didn't answer.

A tall rotund man wearing a flour-covered apron over his clothes pushed through the crowd with two of the city guards. "That's the boy. He still has the bread stuffed in his shirt. My thanks, minstrel, for catching the thief."

Maren looked over the boy's shoulder at the baker. "How much for the bread?"

"What?" the baker said, looking puzzled.

"How much is the loaf of bread?"

"One copper gate."

Maren turned to the guards. "Hold him for a moment. But watch out. He's as slippery as a greased icicle."

The burly guards each took one of the boy's arms and held him fast.

Maren opened his belt pouch, took out a copper coin, and gave it to the baker. "That should pay for the bread."

The baker looked at the coin, glanced at the boy, then back at Maren. "Done. But he needs to pay for what he did or he'll do it again."

"I agree, but what good would sending him to the dungeon do? I have a better plan, if you agree."

The baker frowned slightly, crossed his arms, and stared at the boy. He turned back to Maren. "What do you have in mind?"

"A moment." Maren held up his hand, then turned to the boy. "Why did you steal the bread?"

The boy struggled uselessly to free himself from the guards but didn't answer.

"Boy, what's your name?"

"Let me go!" the boy said.

"Listen to me!" Maren said. "Do you have a family? People who care about you?"

The boy stopped struggling, his eyes growing wider, a bit of fear in them.

"How will they feel when they hear you've been cast into the city dungeon and sold as an indentured servant for ten years? That's the penalty for stealing."

"No, please! They need me! Don't take me away from them!" The boy sagged in the guards' arms.

"Now, what's your name?" Maren asked.

"Quint."

"All right, Quint, why did you steal the bread?"

The boy looked up at Maren slowly, and he swallowed hard. "My mother is sick and can't work, and we haven't had food for three days, and my little sister is so hungry, she's crying, and we don't have any money so...I took the bread."

"Where's your father?"

"He died at sea two years ago."

"Don't you have any relatives in the city who could help you?"

The boy shook his head.

"And how old are you?"

"Twelve."

Maren studied the boy a few moments, then said, "Come here, boy." He pointed to a pair of barrels beside the jeweler's shop.

The guards holding the boy looked at each other, then at Maren, and finally at the baker.

"Please, trust me," Maren said to the baker.

The baker threw up his hands and nodded. The guards pulled the boy over to one of the barrels and plopped the boy on it. One guard stood behind the boy; the other, beside him. Maren sat on the other barrel, facing the boy. A crowd gathered around to watch and listen.

"Quint, I'm going to tell you a story," Maren said, "a very old story that many here have heard since they were small children, but you need to hear it now. Listen and learn.

"Long ago, before Hixus was this great city beside the Southern Sea, the fortress of Hixus Sentinel stood up there," he pointed toward the cliffs at the north edge of the city, "high on the plateau. It was a great fortress of red granite and black marble, built by masons from the land of Vorlik, masons taught by Wizards. The walls stood taller than seven men, and its towers nearly touched the clouds. It was manned by a company of valiant men called the Southern Watch, and the castle was unbreachable by invaders.

"Generations of men and women dedicated their lives to the task of protecting the northern lands against the southern tribesmen, who were aided and led by Sorcerers. There was no greater honor in all the lands of the north than to be accepted into the Southern Watch, and for many ages there was peace in the north because of the vigilance of those fighters."

Maren leaned toward the boy, looking him directly in the eyes. "But there came a time when among the watch was a great lieutenant, brave, loyal, honored by his fellow officers, loved by the men he commanded. He was tall as a picket pine and swift as a deer. His copper hair shone like fire, and his eyes were as green as spring grass. He was handsome and bold and fierce in battle. His name," Maren paused, "was Radamin."

Someone in the crowd cursed.

"One day when Radamin led a hunting party through the woodlands west of the castle, he became separated from his men. He tried to backtrack, but the land seemed to change into a maze of briar thickets, mires, and narrow canyons. Finally, he realized he was completely lost.

"Tired and thirsty, he halted beside a clear stream and dismounted. He knelt by the stream and cupped his hands in the water when he suddenly saw the reflection of a cloaked figure, face hidden by a hood. Startled, Radamin drew his sword, ready to fight.

"'I won't attack you,' said a deep soft voice.

"Radamin kept his sword in his hand and asked, 'What do you want?'

"'Why, only your help,' the voice said. 'I want you to open the gates to Hixus Sentinel so my army can destroy the Southern Watch.'

"'Hah!' Radamin said. 'You must be mad if you think I'd help you!'

"But the figure only laughed. 'Oh, but you will help me. You see, I have your wife, your four children, and your father in my keeping.'

"Radamin glared at him. 'You're lying! I don't believe you!'

"The figure tossed a small leather pouch at Radamin's feet. 'Perhaps this will convince you.'

"Radamin picked up the pouch and opened it. Inside were three things: a carved bone pipe belonging to his father, a sapphire and gold necklace he'd given his wife, and a golden lock of his youngest daughter's hair.

"Radamin was so angry, he jumped the creek and lunged at the figure, shouting, 'Where are they?' But as he grabbed for the cloaked man, the figure disappeared. Radamin trembled with fear, for he knew the figure was no man but a Sorcerer."

Quint's eyes grew rounds as saucers, and he shuddered. Other listeners in the crowd shuddered as well, and one old man muttered a curse.

"'Oh, they're safe,' the Sorcerer said, appearing on the opposite bank of the creek, 'for the moment at least. How long they stay alive depends on you.'

"Radamin leaped at the Sorcerer, but he disappeared again.

"'You fool,' the Sorcerer said laughingly from behind Radamin. 'You can't harm me.'

"Radamin wheeled toward the sound, but the Sorcerer wasn't there. What could he do? He was a soldier of Hixus Sentinel, a member of the revered Southern Watch, but he loved his family more than his own life. What would anyone be willing to do to save those he loved? Could anyone let his beloved father be killed, his dearest wife tortured, his precious child murdered?" He paused for a moment, then looked at the crowd. "Could anyone watch a beloved sister starve without trying to do something?"

The crowd of listeners was silent. Maren gazed at their faces. Surprise showed in their eyes as if they had never considered how hard a choice Radamin had to make. Maren looked back at Quint and continued the story.

"'Please!' Radamin begged. 'Release my family, and I'll do anything you ask — except betray my friends. I'll be your slave, do whatever you ask! But I can't betray Hixus Sentinel!'

"'I see,' the Sorcerer said softly. 'You'd rather see your family tortured and killed. Is that what you want?'

"Furious and desperate, Radamin slashed the air with his sword, hoping to strike the Sorcerer. Suddenly, Radamin felt a hand on his sword arm but could see nothing. The invisible hand clutched Radamin's arm so tight, he was afraid his arm would break. He dropped his sword and fell to his knees, driven by pain and the power of the invisible hand.

"The Sorcerer reappeared and said, 'Now, do as I tell you or I'll kill you.'

"'Then kill me!' Radamin cried.

"The Sorcerer laughed. 'Oh, no, that is what you want, isn't it? No, I'll kill your family first, slowly, painfully. They'll be in so much agony, they'll beg for death. I can hurt them no matter how far away they are. And I'll make you listen to their screams for days.'

"Radamin tried to pull free, but the Sorcerer's grip grew tighter. Sharp nails drew blood. Radamin screamed in pain. 'I can't betray my comrades!' he gasped.

"'Then you've betrayed your family,' the Sorcerer said. 'Listen.'

"Suddenly, Radamin heard his wife's voice screaming, screaming until she had no breath left to scream. 'Stop!' Radamin cried, bending over until his forehead touched the ground. 'Stop! Please! I'll do anything, anything! I'll do whatever you ask! Just don't hurt her anymore! Please! Please,' he said, weeping.

"The sound of his wife screaming disappeared. The Sorcerer released Radamin's arm. 'There,' the Sorcerer said. 'I knew you'd do what I asked of you.'

"Radamin lay on the ground, sobbing. 'What do you want me to do?' he asked.

"The Sorcerer said, 'Three days from now, you must stand the night watch at the gates of the fortress. At midnight, open the gates. Nothing else. Just a simple thing.'

"'But when will I see my family?' Radamin asked.

"'When Hixus Sentinel is mine, and the Southern Watch is no more,' the Sorcerer told him.

"'And how do I know you'll keep your word?' Radamin asked.

"The Sorcerer smiled. 'I promise you'll find your family waiting for you after the battle.'

"Radamin was hopeless. He knelt before his new master and wept. The Sorcerer stretched out his hand and touched Radamin's forehead. Pain knifed through Radamin head. He screamed and fell to the ground, unconscious."

Maren paused and gazed at the audience. Every eye was fixed on him. Many in the crowd looked troubled, but no one spoke or stirred or hardly breathed.

"When Radamin awoke, the sky overhead was dark. His head ached, and he felt dizzy. He struggled to his feet, staggered to his horse, and mounted.

"'What a terrible dream!' he thought as he rode toward the east. 'I must have fallen and hit my head. Thank Baygor it was only a dream!'

"Suddenly, Radamin hear the deep low voice of the Sorcerer laughing.

"'No dream,' the Sorcerer said. 'You are mine.'

"Radamin felt cold with fear as he rode the rest of the night toward his home. The first rays of the sun crept over the horizon and shown on his house. It was a pile of rubble and smoldering wood.

"'Yes,' the voice in his whispered, 'I have them. Remember, midnight of the third day.'

"Radamin's heart was torn between love and honor as he rode slowly back to the fortress. He arrived as the sunset. Soldiers greeted him with cheers because they'd feared he was dead. He claimed he'd struck his head after falling from his horse, but he assured them he was well. Even so, the captain ordered him to see the physician.

"The physician examined Radamin and ordered him to rest that night. The next day Radamin asked for the midnight watch.

"On the third night, under a sky as dark as his heart, Radamin made his usual rounds. He moved cautiously along the walls, knocked the guards unconscious, and dragged them into the shadows of the parapet. Pulling the great wooden bar from the gate and raising the portcullis, Radamin opened the iron-bound doors to the enemy.

"The tribesmen from the southern plains crept into the fortress, as silent as falcons, and killed all the soldiers except for Radamin. Radamin couldn't bear to watch his comrades die, and he ran from Hixus Sentinel to the cliffs outside. He pressed his hands to his ears, but couldn't shut out the screams of his dying friends.

"'Cursed am I, cursed is my name, and cursed is this sword my hand wields! May this blade draw my master's blood, then mingle it with my own!'

"The screams died, and all Radamin heard was the shouts of the tribesmen. Radamin shuffled to the fortress and saw the tribesmen stripping the bodies of the Southern Watch. Horrified, Radamin fell to his knees and wept. 'I did what you asked!' he shouted. 'I betrayed my friends, my comrades! Release my family!'

"The Sorcerer strode from the slaughter and stopped a few feet from Radamin. 'Of course. They're at your cottage now, waiting for you to join them.'

"'Come with me,' Radamin said. He didn't trust the Sorcerer.

"The Sorcerer smiled. 'Of course.'

"They rode until dawn and arrived as the first rays of the sun reveal a terrible sight. Radamin's family was there indeed, but they'd been impaled in a row before the ruined cottage.

"'Your family, just as I promised.' The Sorcerer laughed, then said, 'And now you will join them!'

"Radamin was mad with rage and grief. He jerked his sword from its sheath, and with a mighty swing, cut off the Sorcerer's head. Radamin walked to the line of stakes, fell to his knees before his murdered wife, and wept. He took his sword, braced it against the wooden stake, and fell on his blade. Just as he'd vowed, his own blood mingled with the Sorcerer's blood.

"Hixus Sentinel was conquered by the southern tribesmen. They tore it down until it was only a heap of stones. But the tribesmen didn't stay long. A strange illness struck them. Not one of them returned to their homes. Some say it was a punishment from Baygor, but I don't believe that. To this day the southern tribesmen have never attacked the northern lands again."

Maren looked the boy straight in the eyes and said, "So if you give in to evil, even in a good cause, no good will come from it. I want you to remember that, Quint."

The boy gaped at Maren and nodded slowly.

"Now, are you strong?" Maren asked. "Are you fast?"

"Yes, sir," Quint said.

"And would you be willing to work to earn money for your family?"

"Of course!" the boy said, glaring at Maren, "but no one wanted to hire me. Said I was too little."

Maren turned to the baker. "Do you have an apprentice?"

The baker uncrossed his arms and rested his fists on his thick waist. "Not now."

"Would you take this boy as an apprentice and teach him your trade?"

The baker's mouth dropped open. "Teach that little thief?"

"I'm not a thief!" the boy shouted. "I just tried to feed my family!"

"With one loaf of bread?" Maren asked. "And how long would that last? A day? Two, if you were careful? What if you could have a loaf of bread every day?"

The boy gazed at Maren for a long time. "How?"

"Work for the baker. You can learn a trade and earn money for your family. And you could run errands and make deliveries to earn extra money."

The boy frowned thoughtfully, then nodded. "I'd do anything to help my family."

Maren turned back to the baker. "If I give you the apprenticeship fee and his mother agrees, will you take him as your apprentice?"

The baker rubbed his smooth round chin. "Apprentices are usually younger than he is. I'd only have him for eight years."

"Ah, but he's also stronger and faster than a ten-year-old."

The baker looked the boy up and down. "Well, I guess so. If he's a fast learner and never steals from me again."

Maren turned to the boy. "No more stealing, agreed?"

The boy nodded.

Maren handed the baker a small pouch with the fee he'd earned from the betrothal banquet. "You go with the boy to speak to his mother and get her consent to the apprenticeship. Treat him fairly and justly. I'll check in on him from time to time."

The baker nodded slowly.

"And you," Maren said to the boy, "do what the baker tells you, learn all you can, and you can feed your family for the rest of your life."

The boy nodded.

"Good. Now go talk to your mother."

The guards let the boy go, and he led the baker toward the south side of Hixus. The onlookers began to drift away. Maren stood up and began to stroll through the market.

"Maren! Barg's breath, it's good to see you!"

Maren turned to see a honey-haired man of middle years. His clothes were dark green, a black-striped fur coat over all. Large hands rested on a thick waist, and a wide grin crinkled his bearded face.

"Klaymar!" Maren's arms barely reached around the man's broad shoulders. "It's been more than two years since we last crossed paths. You seem to have prospered since then."

"Yes." Klaymar patted his silk shirt. "I made a good profit on my caravan through Vorlik last year."

"How's your wife Selene and little Gemna?"

"My wife's quite well, and as for Gemna, she's almost twenty-two years old and quite a woman. She fancies herself a warrior." Klaymar chuckled. "I must admit she's the equal of any mercenary in the Beltrin guild. But will she ever make me a grandfather? Not if she outfights every man who shows an interest in her!"

Maren laughed at the merchant's feigned distress.

"You look well." Klaymar's dark eyes narrowed as he studied Maren. "The years have been god to you. You look no older than when we met over twenty years ago."

Maren smiled. "I think your memory's faulty, my friend."

A group of children, licking honey cake crumbs from their fingers, darted around the two men. The air was alive with laughter as dancers whirled and leaped to the music of flutes, drums, and tambourine. Aromas from food stalls wafted on the unusually warm breeze. People watched jugglers and mimes and puppet shows as they wove their way through the crowded square. And above the merriment was the sound of hymns of thanksgiving coming from the Temple of Baygor. Maren nodded toward the edge of the square and began working his way through the press, Klaymar following.

"Great celebration!" Klaymar said above the noise.

"I'm glad the city council declared a holiday. More call for my talents."

"Hixus certainly has something to celebrate and be thankful for. I was down at the docks earlier, talking with one of the captains. He told me a third of Hixus' fleet had been taken. Most captains refused to sail beyond Landsight. Can't make a profit that way. But at least it's over, and life can get back to normal."

As the two reached an open space, Klaymar gazed at Maren with narrowed eyes. "It's amazing how most of the pirate ships were swallowed by a giant whirlpool and the rest of the pirates just fell asleep. A miracle, one might say."

Maren stared back at him. "One might say so."

Klaymar's voice became a whisper. "I know what you are."

Maren remained silent.

"I've some news you probably haven't heard yet," Klaymar continued softly. "News from Vorlik, news of a Wizard."

Maren started, his eyes wide with excitement. "A Wizard?"

"Yes. Briella Mourning Dove."

Maren's heartbeat doubled. "Please, tell me!"

Klaymar pursed his lips and nodded. Leaning very close, he said, "The Wizard of Vorlik is dead."

4

Maren's throat tightened, his chest knotted, and his vision blurred. "No," he whispered. It couldn't be true! Briella couldn't be dead! She was so young, too young to die. Wizards lived so long, he'd always thought there would time to see her again in a few years or decades. He'd always hoped that when he saw her once more, she'd look on him with more than friendship in her eyes. Now that would never happen.

Klaymar put Maren's arm over his shoulder and slipped an arm around Maren's back. "Come on. We'll talk about this more, but not here. There's a tavern just down the way where we can talk in private."

Devastated, Maren didn't resist as Klaymar led him through the surging crowd. Maren barely heard the laughter and shouts of joy from the people around him. He had to force his feet to keep moving. Klaymar steered him down a cobblestone street on the east side of the central market to the sign of the Salty Sailor. As the two of them entered the tavern, they were hailed by the patrons.

A balding man, wearing a broad apron over his clothes, approached with open arms. "Klaymar! I haven't seen you in almost a year. It's about time you stopped in for a drink. And Maren! Wonderful! Give us a song, would you?"

Klaymar embraced the taverner and said softly, "Later, Ayben. Right now we need a table away from the others."

Glancing at Maren, Ayben said, "There's an empty table between the fireplace and the bar. I'll send a girl over with my finest mead, then I'll see you won't be disturbed."

Ayben led them around the tables, shaking his head and quieting his customers. "No, no. No requests. Maren's nearly worn out his voice and needs to quench his thirst before he can sing again. Let him be. The sooner he rests, the sooner he'll be able to entertain us."

Still too stunned to resist, Maren allowed Klaymar to guide him to a solitary corner. The wooden table was pitted and stained with spilled wine. The puncheon benches were bowed in the middle and worn smooth by many occupants. Maren sat down with his back to the other patrons, leaned over the table, and buried his face in his hands. *It can't be true,* he thought. *Merciful Baygor, please don't let it be true! Too many of our people have died or been killed by our enemies. And why did it have to be her? Why Briella? I thought time might change her mind, might turn her heart to me. All my hopes, my dreams -- gone now.*

He looked up when a serving girl set two large mugs and a pitcher of fragrant mead on the table with a clatter. Klaymar gave her two copper coins. She smiled, then hurried on to other tables.

"I'm sorry, Maren." Klaymar's forehead creased with distress. He poured them both a mugful. "The Wizard — you cared deeply for her?"

"Y-yes," Maren whispered. His hands shook as he raised his mug and gulped some mead. "How...how did she die?"

"About a year after we first met, Lord Clevil of Vorlik and his lady were murdered; their son Bren was kidnapped. Clevil's brother Cordwin took the throne and ruled with the help of a Wizard named Briella Mourning Dove until last autumn. Bren arrived in Vorlik secretly, killed the Wizard, then joined forces with Cordwin to fight a Drambini invasion. Bren's now lord of Vorlik."

"Briella was killed by a human?" Maren whispered, almost too horrified to speak. "How? How could a human kill a Wizard? It's not possible. Not possible!"

"It's true," Klaymar said.

"This Bren still lives? Briella's murderer lives?" Maren said softly, gripping his mug so tightly his knuckles turned white. He needed to feel something solid, something certain, since everything else around him seemed so unreal. "She's dead, and he's still alive?"

"Now I don't know the full story," Klaymar said, "so don't judge him without hearing the whole truth.

"What excuse can he give? What reason could he give for killing her? What evil power did he use to end her life?" Maren took a drink of the mead. It felt cool on his tongue, sweet and flavored with current juice, but it burned down his throat. "Did you ever see her, meet her?"

"I don't know for certain, but I think I did — at the Autumn Fair in Tironza maybe fifteen years ago. Blond hair, blue eyes, pretty."

"She was more than pretty," Maren said. "She was beautiful and kind and compassionate. She was a healer, maybe even better than her great-grandfather Casslin, and he was the greatest healer in a thousand years."

"I don't understand how...why she dead," Maren said. "How did Bren kill her? Was he in league with Sorcerers?" He leaned close to his friend and said, "I'm going to find out, and I swear to you, I will find him, and when I do, Bren will pay for her life with his own."

Klaymar drew back, his eyes wide. Firmly grasping Maren's arm, Klaymar shook him. "Maren, be certain you're right before you do anything. And remember mercy. Isn't that what Wizards believe in? Isn't that what separates you from Sorcerers? Do you want to be like them?"

Maren wrenched away from Klaymar's grasp and leaped to his feet. Bracing himself on his fists, Maren leaned toward his friend. "How dare you compare me to *them!*"

Klaymar grasped the minstrel's wrist and glanced about the tavern. "Maren, think of who you are — and *where* you are."

The room had grown very still. All heads were turned toward Maren. Slowly, he sat down. The other customers returned to their own conversations.

Swallowing the rest of his drink in one breath, Maren wiped his mouth on his sleeve. "You're right," he said slowly. "I'll go to Vorlik. I have to face this Lord Bren and learn the truth from him. I won't have any peace until I do."

"I understand." Klaymar placed his hand on Maren's hunched shoulder. "But it's a long journey, especially on foot. You won't arrive in Vorlik for weeks. Remember, it's still winter in the north. The roads are muddy forty miles north of Hixus. Sixty miles more and the roads are impassable, covered with ice and snow all the way to the border of Vorlik. I barely made it out of Beltrin. The weather's the worst I've seen in many years."

"I won't go by foot."

"By wagon or horse is nearly as bad."

Maren looked up at Klaymar. "I won't use either."

Rolling his mug between his hands, Klaymar studied Maren a few moments, then looked back at his drink. "It's said Briella could become a mourning dove at will. But many things were said about her." He drained his mug. "I probably won't see you for a long time. I'm going west this year instead of north. I'm hoping to find some rare spices and trade goods instead of more turnips, woolens, and grains. Perhaps in a few years our paths will cross again. Far-thell," he paused, then added, "and I hope you find your answers. Baramay give you comfort and peace of heart, my friend."

As Klaymar rose to leave, Maren clasped his hand. "Far-thell. Good luck and Baygor protect you. And thank you for reminding me of who I am."

Pressing Maren's hand between both of his, Klaymar nodded, turned, and left Maren alone.

Maren refilled his mug from the pitcher and stared into the depths of the cup. Despair filled his heart. The memory of the last time he'd seen Briella, twenty-two years earlier, rose before his eyes. On the day he'd left the Wizard's Vale to travel the lands of men, he'd kissed her good-bye gently.

"Wait for me," he'd said. "I love you, Briella. Please, wait for me."

She'd rested her hand on his cheek, distress in her eyes. "Maren, I—"

"No." He'd touched his fingertips to her lips. "Let me hope while we're apart."

Kissing her forehead, he'd left the Wizard's Vale and hadn't seen her again. When he'd returned home for a visit, Amaly had told him Briella had gone to Vorlik for a while at least. Maren had left, disappointed but still hopeful that their paths would cross again since they were still very young. Klaymar's news had destroyed all his hope.

Maren drained the mug and poured the last of the mead from the pitcher. He stared pensively at the red liquid. Briella dead? Not her, not the one he'd loved, not the joyful woman who had made him smile and his heart dance, not Briella! She was little more than a girl when he'd left the Wizard's Vale. Even now she would have been barely a young woman in the years of his people. How could she be dead? And killed by a human? He couldn't believe it, wouldn't believe it, until he saw her tomb.

Trying to numb his grief, Maren called for another pitcher, although he knew his kind didn't become drunk as humans did. He felt so cold and empty, he hoped the mead would warm his heart. As the serving girl brought a full pitcher, several patrons called to him.

"A song, a song!"

"Give us a song, Maren!"

Maren paid the serving girl for the mead, then shot a pleading look at Ayben, but the taverner just shrugged. Finally, Maren rose from his table and shuffled to the bar. Taking his lute from his back, Maren began to strum and sing a favorite of tavern crowds.

> Old Mason's at the barrel again.
> It stood beneath a shelf.
> He filled his mug and sat right down
> To drain it by himself.
>
> Old Mason's at the barrel again
> To drink away the night.
> He breathed upon his greening fields
> And caused a dreadful blight.
>
> Old Mason's at the barrel again
> And sang both loud and strong.
> His wife ran out ne'er to return
> And listen to his song.
>
> Old Mason's at the barrel again
> And filled his mug once more
> And when he'd drained it seven times,
> He slithered to the floor.
>
> Old Mason's at the barrel again
> And tried to drink it down.
> He leaned too far and fell right in
> And poor old Mason drowned.

Soon, everyone was cheering and stamping in time to the lively music, tossing coins at the minstrel's feet.

"The drink! The drink! Give him the drink!" called the laughing crowd.

Ayben provided a mug of dark ale. Obliged to finish it in one breath, Maren gulped the bitter, brown liquid.

The crowd rooted him on, laughing and shouting. "Again! Sing it again!"

Maren repeated the song, then swallowed another ale. This time the drink warmed his throat.

"Another! Another!"

He played "I Sailed to Trammoy," "Chellit's Cat," "The Golden Tree," "The Fish Tale," "The Women of Karn," and others the customers called for, each song accompanied by a mug of ale. After an encore of "I Sailed to Trammoy," suddenly, Maren felt dizzy, cold, off balance, and numb at the same time, unlike anything he'd ever felt before. His legs buckled, but Ayben caught him. The taverner waved off further requests and helped the minstrel back to his table.

Laying his lute on the table and resting his head on his palm, Maren lingered on the edge of coherence, confused. "What happened?" he asked.

Ayben gazed at him with puzzlement. "I've seen that look on hundreds of faces, but never on yours. I'd swear you're drunk."

Raising his head slowly, Maren stared back, eyes wide with surprise. "Me? That's impossible. I never get drunk."

"I know," Ayben replied with a grin. "I've never seen you drunk in all the years you've been coming here. Do you want me to stay with you a while?"

Maren shook his head and immediately regretted it. "No," he whispered, his stomach churning.

Ayben laughed, then said, "Well...if you're certain...but call if you need anything." He rested a firm hand on Maren's shoulder, then hurried back to his other customers.

Drunk? Maren wondered as he squeezed his eyes shut. *How? How can I be drunk? Wizards don't become drunk!*

Suddenly, he felt as if death had touched his heart. A voice whispered a warning that echoed through his clouded mind. He sensed a presence, a power that wanted to crush him. He struggled to rise, lurched toward the door, but crashed into a table and sprawled across the top. He lifted his head and gazed about the room. His eyes refused to focus. His mind was foggy. Blinking his eyes until he could see, he stared at the table's lone occupant.

Sipping a large cup of wine, a hooded man gazed at Maren a few moments, then threw back his head in gusty, hollow laughter. The hood fell back, revealing a boyish face with golden curls, but his eyes were ice blue and ancient. Maren recognized the power in those eyes, knew he faced a Sorcerer, and for the first time in his life, Maren feared he was going to die. Desperately trying to stand, Maren turned the table over and slid to the floor. His head struck a table leg. As his vision darkened, he saw the Sorcerer smile, his lips forming words as Maren lost consciousness.

5

Grimmin finished whispering the words of a spell, then reached down and brushed his fingers across the unconscious Wizard's forehead. "Still alive but passed out," Grimmin said, grinning at Ayben. "Can't hold his ale."

Everyone else in the tavern guffawed.

"Lift him up, boys," Ayben said, laughing. "I'll let him sleep it off in one of my back rooms."

Several customers took Maren's arms and legs and carried him down a short hall to the right of the bar. Grimmin righted the table and called for the serving girl to refill his cup. Giving her a silver coin and a wink, he savored the wine, then stood and stretched and strolled outside the Salty Sailor. He wove his way north through the cobblestone alleys between white stone houses and grand manors until he reached an encampment of six wagons on the outskirts of Hixus.

"Hitch up the horses," Grimmin called to his teamsters as he unclasped his cloak. "We leave within the hour for Drambit."

The teamsters looked surprised, then grumbled as they sat drinking from a barrel of fine Hixus mead. Slowly, they rose and sauntered toward their hobbled horses.

The head teamster followed Grimmin to his wagon. "Master, why are we traveling north again so soon?" the leader asked, running gnarled fingers through his thinning grey hair. "It's still winter up there. The wagons'll bog down in the drifts. It'll thaw in a few weeks. Surely that's early enough."

Grimmin stared at the teamster with eyes as cold as ice. "We leave now."

The leader shivered, backed away, and hurried to join the teamsters.

Climbing into his wagon, Grimmin tossed his cloak onto his narrow bed, locked the wagon door, and sat before a small, mirrored table that held an ancient, black leather-bound book. He caressed the silver runes and symbols on the cover. *The*

Enchiridion Canzet, he thought, smiling, *the first Sorcerer's own manual of incantations, the most ancient spells and secret knowledge, the source of Canzet's power -- mine! Not even Quist has the power to understand its secrets as I have. And if it hadn't been for the binding spell I learned from the Enchiridion, the Wizard might have escaped, or worse, might have attacked me.*

Grimmin opened the tome to a yellowed page near the back and memorized the words written in careful ancient script. Shutting the book and setting it on his bed, he closed his eyes a few moments to focus his mind. He stretched his arms skyward, and with a low but intense voice, chanted,

"Barsallin, Hound of Darkness, see

Thy servant Grimmin; hear my plea.

Chaos' shadow, lend thy might.

Give me power; grant me sight."

Grimmin felt power surge through his body, warming him like strong wine. "Logallah of the Winds, you who were Canzet's wife," he said, "I, Grimmin Slayer of the Inner Circle of Derkhafen, summon you. By the oath you swore to Canzet the first Sorcerer, I claim your aid. Come to me and do my bidding. *Tasrin rakathah logallah apayna doton sah!*"

For a few moments, everything seemed to stand still, as if the world had stopped, then a voice like rustling leaves stole through the cracks of the wagon. "It is an age since I've been summoned by Canzet's oath. I've suffered since he betrayed me, but still I'm bound by my oath. How can I aid you, Grimmin of Derkhafen?"

"I must travel to Drambit," Grimmin said. "Winter hinders me. Bring an early spring."

"Why not transform yourself? Become a bird of the air."

The Sorcerer's fist tightened, and his voice grew as cold as his anger. "I haven't that power, not yet. I can change others, not myself. I must have a clear road. I command you, bring warm winds to melt the snow and dry the North Road."

The voice crept kitten-soft around him. "Spring will come soon enough," she said. "Changing the seasons suddenly would bring chaos. I myself might become uncontrolled and cause much devastation."

"That doesn't matter to me," Grimmin said. "I must reach Drambit. You must help me."

"No," she said.

"Fulfill your oath."

"I won't."

"Yes, you will."

"I can't!"

"Yes, you can! Fulfill your oath!"

"Please, no!"

"Fulfill your oath or Barsallin will cast you still alive into the outer darkness of eternal torment!"

Logallah began sobbing. After a few moments, she spoke again. "I'll do this," she said softly, "but be warned, Sorcerer, I, too, am powerful. Canzet didn't transform me into a creature of wind on a mere whim. He knew I could destroy him and his plans to rule all Baramayan." She paused a few moments. "I loved him," she said, "loved him with all my heart, and my love blinded me to his evil. But I still live while he's only a memory of darkness."

Her voice became sword-sharp and blizzard-cold. "Know this, Grimmin: the time of decision is fast approaching, the great war between Sorcerers and Wizards. I've seen it — a gift from whatever gods there are. Choose your enemies carefully, Sorcerer; they'll show you no mercy. And don't summon me again, or I'll destroy you."

Grimmin smiled at her threat. "I leave in an hour. I must arrive at Abasette Castle within two weeks. Keep your oath. Go before me and open my path."

Logallah departed with a mournful wail.

Staring into the mirror, Grimmin called to his minion in Peltik, Akavar Lifebane, Sorcerer of the Third Circle, distiller of poisons, assassin of lords.

"I come, master," a disembodied voice whispered.

Soon, a scarred, leathery face with hawkish eyes appeared in the mirror. "Master Grimmin," he murmured as his colorless lips revealed yellowed teeth.

"What's happening in Peltik?" Grimmin asked.

Akavar smiled, his dirt-brown hair brushing narrow, uneven shoulders. "Your plan's progressing well, master. There's mourning in Castle Lecida. Lord Merrik died two months ago. The poison was so subtle, no one suspects he died of something other than winter fever. His son Lord Merovan has the fever, too, as far as the physicians can tell. He'll last only a few more days. So many have died from winter fever this year—especially those with even distant claim to Peltik's throne." Akavar grinned. "With Merovan's death, Miria of Drambit will be the only heir to Peltik."

Grimmin smiled, pleased. "Wonderful!"

"As for my other task, I haven't distilled enough potion. I need two more Death's Head moths from the Rensle Steppes."

"I'll summon them for you. Have the potion ready when I reach Lecida in ten days, and you'll be rewarded generously."

Akavar inclined his head but kept his golden eyes fixed on Grimmin. "Thank you, master."

The mirror cleared.

"Now to inform the Circle of my progress," Grimmin said. "Someday they'll all bow to me, even Lord Quist."

Again chanting the incantation, he contacted Wellath Far-Speaker of the Inner Circle.

The black-haired Sorcerer's square face appeared in the mirror. A thin slit of a mouth barely moved as Wellath spoke. "Grimmin. What is your message?"

I have located another of our enemies — the Wizard Maren."

"Have you killed him?"

"No," Grimmin said slowly. "He was a minstrel, too well-known and too visible to kill him." Grimmin paused, then continued bitterly, "Especially since many humans proclaimed him a hero for warning the city about the pirate fleet. I *know* he destroyed the pirates and our brother Sorcerers, even if I didn't see him do it."

"And you *didn't* kill him?" Wellath asked.

"No, I couldn't kill him without revealing myself. But I've done worse than kill him. I've bound his powers. He's helpless."

Wellath glared at him, heavy brows shadowing cat eyes. "You should've killed him! You know the binding can be broken!"

"Not this one," Grimmin said confidently. "The spell was from Canzet's own spell book. The Wizard won't even remember how to do magic. He won't trouble us anymore."

Wellath stared nervously back at Grimmin. "Let's hope you are correct. What other news do you have?"

"I'm ready to begin the next step in my strategy. Within a few months Drambit, Vorlik, and Peltik will be mine. Are the other campaigns going well?"

"Yes, but no one else has accomplished as much as the great Grimmin," Wellath said. "Everyone will be in place soon. Our time is almost here."

"And we'll be the victors. I'll contact you again when I'm lord of the north."

The mirror cleared, leaving only Grimmin's reflection. He leaned back against the side of the wagon. The strain of the summoning had been greater than he'd expected.

I'll rest for the hour before we leave, he thought. *Today, I begin my rise to power, and one day soon I'll rival Quist himself.*

Grimmin woke to hesitant tapping at the wagon door. Rubbing his eyes, he rose and opened the door to find head teamster bobbing nervously outside.

"All's ready, master," the man said. "We can start immediately."

"Good." Grimmin clasped his hands behind his neck and stretched. "I'll travel with you for the first three days, then I'll continue by horse alone."

Grimmin stepped down from the wagon and closed the door. The head teamster bowed, stepped back, and hurried to the front of the wagon. He climbed to the wagon seat, clutched the reins, shouted to the other teamsters, and spurred his team of chestnut mares into motion. Grimmin mounted his pale horse and rode to the front of the caravan.

The road to the top of the plateau wound up the side of the limestone cliffs. It was late afternoon, almost evening, by the time the wagons all reached the plateau and passed the overgrown ruins of Hixus Sentinel. The road north was deeply rutted mud. The horses struggled to pull the heavy wagons forward all that day, occasionally bogging down. Drivers and horses were both exhausted when they camped that night. All night long a south wind blew warm air around the camp until by morning the road was dry and solid though the land on either side was soggy. By the end of the third day, the caravan reached the first banks of snow as they made camp. By dawn the snow was melted from the road. The trail was dry and smooth.

Logallah's keeping her oath, Grimmin thought, smiling. *The Wizard's no longer a threat. Soon all Baramayan will kneel to me, even the Lady Miria.*

He saddled his pale horse, its blue-green eyes the only reminder that once it had been a wild ovrin on the plains near Derkhafen. "Travel as quickly as you can," he told the head teamster. "If the horses die, buy others, but be at Abasette Castle in two weeks. Stay on the main road. It'll be safe."

Grimmin mounted his enchanted horse and spurred it into motion. He galloped past houses shattered by whirlwinds and past bodies drowned by flooding streams, but barely noticed the devastation. His thoughts were only of Miria of Drambit.

Wellath tread down the dark corridors, lit by eerie green spheres set in niches in the walls. He dreaded disturbing the High Sorcerer in the meditation chamber. Quist had been known to punish any who entered without invitation. Still, Wellath was certain Quist should be told about Grimmin's actions, and especially about the Wizard. Swallowing hard and hugging his black woolen robe to him for warmth, Wellath continued down the hall that led into the very heart of Derkhafen.

The doors to the Chamber of Meditation were of polished ebony and carved with the symbol of the sorcerers: The Hound of Darkness — Barsallin the Ravager, who fed on the blood and sickness of men's bodies and on the pain and terror of men's souls; Barsallin, god of shadows, born of the black void while the god Barg sat alone in thought; Barsallin, who was banished by Baramay and Baygor to the inner darkness of Baramayan; Barsallin, deity of evil and ultimate source of the power used by the Sorcerers.

Wellath caressed the image of the Hound of Darkness, dread and desire filling his heart, hoping to find protection from Quist's wrath. He opened the door a crack and peeked inside.

The Chamber of Meditation was twenty feet wide and forty feet long with the double doors on one of the shorter sides. Two rows of arched columns trisected the slate floor and supported the black marble roof. The only light was a yellow-orange fire that blazed before a towering jet-black statue of a ravening hound sitting on its haunches.

Robed in black silk that accented his silver-white hair, Lord Quist sat cross-legged on a black marble dais before the statue. His back to Wellath, Quist chanted as his hands wove intricate patterns in the air. Shaped by his will, the fire became a tree budding fiery blossoms only to disintegrate at Quist's word. Next, the flame formed a great Formian bear with a blazing coat and glowing eyes, a huge beast which tore apart huts and men created from the fire. Finally, Quist shaped the fire into a black empty man-shape with burning red eyes. It seemed to fill the chamber.

Wellath gulped, then stepped into the chamber. "My Lord Quist."

Without looking, the High Sorcerer pointed a finger at Wellath. The black man-shape sped, its maw gaping with a terrifying scream, toward the frightened Sorcerer.

Wellath dropped face down on the slate floor. "I beg you, My Lord, spare me! I bring a message from Grimmin!"

With a slight crook of his finger, Quist recalled the man-shape to the fire pit where it became yellow flame once again. Quist rose and turned to the open door, gazing at Wellath.

"Speak," Quist said, his quiet voice striking the prone man like a blow.

Wellath raised himself to his knees. "Grimmin said his plan is going well. He'll soon control Vorlik, Drambit, and Peltik. Also, he has found another of our enemies and has, um, has..."

"Killed him?"

"Uh, no, My Lord."

"No?" Quist repeated snowflake softly

"Grimmin bound the Wizard's powers."

Quist's steely eyes narrowed, and his jaw tightened. "Bound his powers?"

"Yes, My Lord." Wellath blanched and tried to swallow his terror.

"How did Grimmin learn to do such a thing?" Quist said quietly, almost as if talking to himself. "Where did he find such knowledge?"

Wellath swallowed hard before he spoke again. "Grimmin has learned to decipher the Enchiridion."

Quist's eyes widened, and his jaw dropped. "The Enchiridion?"

Wellath nodded.

"Even I can't read what is written in that book!" Quist clenched his fists. "If the Wizard regains his powers, he'll be more dangerous to us than before! Grimmin will pay for his rashness if this causes trouble for us!"

Trembling, Wellath remained silent.

Quist turned back to the fire. "Watch him. Watch him carefully. Leave me now. See I'm not disturbed again — or you'll die."

Wellath touched his forehead to the floor, rose and fled the room. He ran through the corridors until he collided with a young Sorcerer of the lowest circle. Ordering the terrified youth to guard the Chamber of Meditation, Wellath returned to the polished table in the Communing Chamber, relieved to be away from Quist's presence.

"Grimmin must succeed," Wellath whispered, shivering.

6

Maren woke to the clash of metal and the roar of voices. Pressing his hands over his ears, he tried to block out the painful noise. His head throbbed, and his eyes burned, even in the dark room. His tongue stuck to the roof of his mouth. His throat was so dry, he had trouble swallowing. He stank of ale and sweat and stale urine. As he rose up on one elbow, his head swam, and his stomach lurched, forcing him to lie down again. Suddenly, light stabbed his eyes as a door opened.

"So, you're finally awake!" a voice screamed at him with a vicious laugh. "I thought you'd sleep forever!"

Shielding his squinting eyes, Maren recognized Ayben, standing in the door that led to the kitchen.

Ayben wiped his hands on his apron and smiled cheerfully. "You smell as bad as a ten-day-old fish, and look worse."

Maren winced. Ayben's voice seemed to echo cavernously through his pounding head. "Why're you shouting? Is there a battle out there?"

Ayben snickered. "No, just inside your head. Barg's Breath, you look terrible! If you can crawl out of that bed, I'll have a bath brought in for you. I can't let you mingle with my customers looking and stinking like that. It'd give me a bad reputation. I sent for some of your clothing from the Mermaid Inn so you'll appear decent when you leave."

Ayben's laugh was like rusty hinges. "If I'd known you couldn't handle your drink, I'd have forbidden you to have more than two! I ought to charge you for the room, you've been here so long."

Moving deliberately slow, Maren lifted his head. "How long have I slept?"

"Three days. I've never seen anyone so drunk!"

"Three days!" Maren found it difficult to concentrate. Three days? That wasn't possible. He'd never been drunk in his life. And there was something or someone important he should remember, but what? He wished his head would stop hurting long enough for him to think. "What did you put in that ale? I feel as if I'd been hit with a barrel instead of drinking from it."

Lighting a lantern on the small table beside the bed, Ayben barked a throaty laugh, much to Maren's discomfort. "I'll send my wife in with your fresh clothing, then I'll set your bath myself." Still laughing, Ayben left, slamming the door.

Maren rolled onto his side with his back to the lantern. Three days gone, vanished! Vaguely, he recalled the celebration and Klaymar. That was it! Klaymar had told him something, something important, something about...

"Briella!" Sorrow filled his heart, and he wished he were still unconscious. So many Wizards had been killed by Sorcerers, even his own parents. But no Wizard had ever been killed by a human! How could it have happened?

Maren ignored Ayben's wife when she brought in his clothes. He tried to remember precisely what Klaymar had said. Vorlik, yes, he needed to travel to Vorlik, but a shadow clouded his mind. There were gaps in his life he couldn't remember. Why? He had to find out.

Ayben pushed open the door again, hefting a wooden tub. Inside were several clean towels and a cake of lye soap. "The water's heating," he announced cheerfully as he placed the towels and soap on a three-legged stool. "I'll bring it in a few minutes. Would you like me to have one of the serving girls scrub your back?" He grinned wickedly.

"No," Maren groaned, his head aching. "Just fill the tub and leave me in peace while I die."

"If you're planning to drown yourself, I'll have to charge you extra."

Maren stared sullenly at Ayben. After the taverner left, Maren sat up very slowly, holding his forehead. He swung his legs over the side of the bed, but his feet shrank from the cold stone floor. Bending over and cradling his head, he waited until he heard the heavy trod of the taverner's feet.

Ayben waddled in with a large kettle of steaming water and dumped it in the tub. He left and came back with another kettle of hot water. His wife followed with two buckets of cool well water. When she'd mixed the bath to her satisfaction, she left.

Ayben grinned again. "Are you certain you don't want one of the girls to help you with your bath?"

Maren sent him a withering look. Chuckling, Ayben left.

Trying to move his head as little as possible, Maren stripped off his clothes and threw them in a heap beside the bed. He shuffled to the edge of the tub, stepped in, and settled deep into the steaming water. His head bent, Maren let the steam fill his lungs and redden his skin. He almost slept, lulled by the warmth. With a resigned sigh, he lathered himself with the strong soap. He washed his stringy hair and stubbly face. Foam stung his eyes. He reached blindly for a towel and was drenched by a bucket of cold water. Sputtering, he gasped out a common dockman's curse.

Ayben laughed heartily. "Ah-hah! Now I know why you became a minstrel: your eloquent, descriptive language! You look better after a bath, but not much. I'll lend you a razor; maybe that'll help. Hurry up and get dressed. It's long past noon. I've customers coming soon, and I can't waste any more time on you."

Ayben closed the door behind him. Maren stood up and let the water drain off him before he wrapped a towel about himself. Stepping out of the tub, he rubbed his shivering body vigorously. He put on clean linens, then dressed in the black pants and crimson shirt Ayben's wife had brought him. Woolen stockings, his boots, and leather vest completed his outfit.

Ayben re-entered the room with a thin-bladed razor, a wooden bowl of water, and a towel "to soak up the blood." He offered to shave Maren, who accepted since his hands were still shaking. Ayben finished quickly without nicking Maren even once.

Maren dried his face. "What do I owe you?"

Ayben smiled. "Nothing. You brought in more profit than your weight in beer. Just try not to drink more than you can hold next time."

Maren nodded cautiously, afraid to move his head to much.

It was mid-afternoon when he ventured into the blinding sunlight and surprisingly warm weather, almost as if spring had arrived already. His worn clothing was bundled under his arm; his lute, slung on his back. Shielding his eyes, he shuffled through the stalls in the main square, then turned south down the sloping street toward Dockside. The odor of salt water and fish was especially strong and pervaded everything for blocks around.

The Mermaid Inn's common room was nearly deserted except for two men with the rough, leathery look of sailors. Jeral stood behind the bar, talking with the sailors.

As Maren entered, Jeral looked up and waved a huge hand, then went back to filling two mugs for his other customers.

Maren shuffled across the stone floor to the stairs going up. Just as he started up the first step, Jeral clapped his shoulder.

"Are ya all right?" the taverner asked, worry in his eyes. "Ya been gone three whole days!"

"I'm fine," Maren said softly, his head still throbbing.

"Ya don't look so fine. When ya didn't come back and Ayben sent for yer clothes, I thought ya was leavin' us."

"Not yet," Maren said, massaging his forehead.

"That's good t' know. Ya want Molly t' wash them clothes?"

"Yes. Thank you." Maren handed the taverner the bundle of clothes.

"See ya for supper?"

"Yes. Supper."

"See ya then." Jeral sauntered back to the kitchen.

Maren felt so tired, he had to force his legs to climb the steps. When he opened the door to his small room, he was almost blinded by sunlight pouring through the open window. His narrow bed was neatly made and covered with dark brown woolen blanket, a quilt folded on the end of the bed. The bed looked so inviting. He set his lute on the chair set before a small hearth, then flopped down on his bed. "I have to go to Vorlik," he said aloud. "I need answers."

He just sat on his bed for a long time, staring at nothing but remembering Briella. Maren had loved her since he'd first noticed her playing with his sister Amaly. When and where that had been, he couldn't quite remember, but he'd been just a boy. They'd played tag, skipped rocks, and climbed trees. They'd been companions, playmates, friends. But when they'd grown up, she'd withdrawn from him. She'd wanted his friendship, not his love. So he'd waited and dreamed and hoped that time would change her mind. Instead, time had taken her from him forever.

He shuffled to the wardrobe, opened it, and stuffed his few belongings in a knapsack. On the floor of the wardrobe Maren found a red leather-bound book. It seemed familiar, important, and evoked feelings of power and mystery. Opening the cover, he saw page after page of script in a language he recognized, yet he couldn't read it. He strained to remember. *I should know this. I should,* he thought. He stared at the words, frowning, and massaged his aching temple. *This is my book of magic spells. I've done these hundreds of times. But...I can't remember what to do, what to say! Why can't I remember?*

He scrunched his forehead and concentrated, but the harder he concentrated, the more his head ached. Finally, the pain was so intense, he gave up, gasping for breath. *The Sorcerer! He whispered words and touched my forehead before I became unconscious! What did he do to me? Why didn't he kill me when he had the chance? And where is he now? Am I still in danger? Is Hixus in danger? Do I dare leave? Do I dare stay? Could I do anything to protect the people of Hixus if I did stay? Can I do any magic at all? Can I do something as simple as transform into a bird?*

Transformation was one of the first spells he'd learned as a child. Wizards could change shape almost without thinking about it. He sat very still and tried to change shape into an eagle, his favorite form, but failed. He remembered learning to change shape, but not how to do it. He couldn't even recall how, only a few days ago, he'd multiplied the callum bark so he could give some to Molly. How could he reach Vorlik and find his answers if he couldn't use magic?

At that moment, Jeral opened the door, carrying a cup of steaming liquid. "Molly said ya might need some o' that healin' tea, seein' as yer so pale an' hung over. She thought it couldn't hurt."

Unsteady, Maren massaged his temples. "No, I suppose it couldn't hurt. My head feels as if someone has mistaken it for an anvil and is pounding it with a hammer."

Jeral grinned as he handed Maren the ceramic cup of callum bark tea. "Well, that's what happens when ya have one mug too many."

"And I am leaving Hixus. Tomorrow. Early."

Jeral looked startled. "But ya said ya wasn't leavin' us."

"I'm not leaving today. But I need to leave before dawn tomorrow."

"Oh." Jeral paused a few moments. "Oh. Should I hold yer room for ya?"

Maren stared out his window to the east, the heat from the tea soaking through to his hands. "I don't know how long I'll be gone — maybe several months, maybe more. Rent the room if you have the chance. And wake me early. I'd rather leave unnoticed."

Jeral was silent for a few moments, then nodded. "Anythin' ya need for yer trip?"

Maren tapped his forefinger against the cup. "I could use food for several days, a horse, a waterskin, and several woolen blankets."

"Will do." Jeral started to go, then turned back to Maren. "Blankets? Why ya need *them*?" At first he looked puzzled, then incredulous. "Yer going north? At this time o' year?"

Mare took a sip of the fragrant tea, then nodded. "I have to go to Vorlik."

"Roads are still blocked with ice and snow! Spring may have come early here but not up north!"

Maren didn't answer.

"But, Maren!" Jeral's face betrayed mixed curiosity and dread, then he held up his hands and gave Maren an "It's-none-of-my-business" look. "All right. I'll pack food for the road, four blankets, water skin, a small cooking pot, a tinderbox... don't have one, do ya?"

"I don't think so." Maren couldn't recall for certain.

"A tinderbox then, an' a horse from my stable. Wake ya before dawn. Need anything else before ya leave?"

"Just the clothes I gave you to be washed."

Jeral turned toward the door, then stopped and looked over his should at Maren. "Ya have t' leave?" he asked. "I mean, people'll ask where ya gone. What should I tell 'em?"

"That I felt like seeing more of the world."

Jeral nodded and left.

Maren rolled up his clothes from the wardrobe and stuffed them and the red leather book into his knapsack. He found a rosewood box in the wardrobe and opened it. Inside were a set of silver bracers. Each had an eagle etched into the silver, and sapphires for the eyes. His sister Amaly had given them to him; he remembered that. He'd only put them on once, but they weren't the kind of thing usually worn by minstrels, so he'd left them in the rosewood box. He closed the box and put it in the knapsack with the book and clothes.

He shuffled downstairs to the common room for a meal and sat alone, politely refusing any requests for songs or stories. Maren fixed his attention on his steaming bowl of stew, filled with shrimp, scallops, crab, tomatoes, onion, garlic, and lots of pepper. Between bites, his eyes unfocused, he tried to remember what he'd learned as a child, what had been so much a part of who he was, but the harder he tried to recall what he'd learned in the Wizard's Vale, the more obscure and remote the memories became and pain throbbed in his head. He saw in his mind images of Briella, a vibrant blond-haired girl with kind, blue eyes; houses made of sapphires and emeralds and rubies; groves of callum trees with grey-green bark and silver-green leaves; whirlwinds and whirlpools and green fire; and above all the cold blue eyes of a blond young man, the Sorcerer who'd ensorcelled Maren. The memory of those eyes made Maren shiver.

After he finished eating, he trudged back upstairs to his room and opened the door. Evening shadows filled the room, and the air was still unusually warm. He took a candle from the shelf beside the door, lit it from the lamp in the hallway, then went back inside and closed his door. He set the candle in a holder on the washstand beneath the window.

He stripped off his boots and clothes, folding them and placing them on the chair beside the cold hearth, along with his jacket and cloak. Pulling back the coarse blanket and sheet, he slipped into the comfortable bed and pulled the covers up to his chest. Clasping his hands behind his head, he stared at the ceiling. Memories of Briella, the only absolutely clear memories he had, tightened his throat. "Someone will answer for her death, I swear it!" he whispered. He blew out the candle and drifted to sleep.

He slept fitfully, tossing from one side to the other, waking for a few moments, then sinking into chaotic dreams. Suddenly, someone shook him and called his name. Cracking open an eye, he saw Jeral bending over him with a candle.

"It's near dawn," the taverner said. "If ya want t' leave Hixus without bein' seen, ya gotta get up now."

Maren moaned as he opened both eyes, shook the sleep from his head, and brushed his hair back from his face. "It feels as if I just fell asleep."

"I packed yer supplies and yer clean clothes, and saddled a horse for ya. Breakfast's waitin' downstairs, but ya gotta hurry." Jeral lit the candle on the table beside the bed with the candle he carried, then left the room.

Maren pulled on his clothes, picked up his knapsack, lute, and the candle, then left his room, closing the door as quietly as he could. Tiptoeing down the corridor, he descended the stairs to the common room where Jeral and Molly waited for him beside a table with a plate of eggs and fried ham, buttered bread, and cold stewed fruit.

"Eat quick," Jeral said.

Maren set his knapsack and lute on the table and sat down. He gulped down the food too fast, almost choking.

"Not that quick. Here," Molly said and handed Maren a mug of water.

Maren took a drink and swallowed, but it hurt going down. Finally, his throat cleared, and he could breathe again. He ate the rest of the meal more slowly.

"Time to leave," Jeral said.

Maren slipped his lute over his head and his knapsack on his shoulder. As he turned to leave, Molly gave him a quick hug.

"Ya take care o' yerself," she said. "An' come back t' see us."

"I will if I can," Maren said. "And I know I'll miss your cooking." He paused, gazing at Molly. "You're like my family."

Molly's green eyes welled up with tears, and she dabbed at them with her apron. "An' I promised myself I wasn't gonna cry. Oh, go on now. An' Baygor keep ya safe."

"And Baramay bless you," Maren said, then he followed Jeral as he led the way through the kitchen and out the back door.

The stable yard was quiet. Not even the chickens were stirring. Jeral motioned Maren to follow him across the dark lawn to the thatched stable. Carefully opening the gate to one stall, the taverner led a saddled and packed red-gold mare into the stable yard. He stroked the horse's neck. "Her name's Fraivoly. Good steady horse. She'll take ya far if yer good t' her. There's two bags o' oats for her. I packed twice baked bread, dried meat, and dried fruit for a week in the saddlebags, and the water'll last for three days. There're villages along the way where ya can get more."

Maren grasped Jeral's massive hand. "Thank you. May you always be stronger than ten men." He smiled. "I'll miss both of you. Baramay bless you."

"Ya best go now." Jeral gave him a bear hug and whispered, "Baygor protect ya, Maren of the Wizard's Vale."

When Jeral let go, Maren gave the taverner a half a dozen silver coins, climbed into the saddle, and nudged the horse from the shadowed stable yard to deserted cobblestone streets. The echo of the horse's hooves clacking on the stones seemed to shout his presence as he rode through the empty central market. Shops were closed. Stalls were shut tight. The only creature Maren saw was a brindled cat skulking through the market place. He rode north through the rich sections of town and reached the road that wound up the face of the cliffs just as the sun's first ray shot above the horizon, painting both sky and sea a golden pink.

7

Maren felt uneasy as he followed the road, carved from the cliff face up to the plateau. The higher he climbed, the more tense he became, and he had no idea why. He felt as if eyes were watching him, patiently waiting for... what? Even the horse seemed to sense something was wrong, growing skittish and shying nervously.

As he reached the top, he gazed to the west side of the road. Nearly hidden with vines and brush were the ruins of Hixus Sentinel. A limestone arch was the only epitaph of the Southern Watch, the proud and fierce company of dour men who had guarded the northern lands. Maren bowed his head, remembering the men who'd fought and died there. And he remembered Radamin and the terrible choice the soldier had to make. Maren shuddered, wondering what choice he would have made.

The sun felt warm, much warmer than by the sea in Hixus, and his winter clothes made him sweat. He stripped off his cloak and jacket, rolled them up, and stuffed them in his saddle bag. The air was dead still and close, and smelled as if rain were coming. Clouds gathered in the north and west. The rolling meadows and flat lands lay empty, hushed. Water stood in every gully and covered fields of new grass and sprouting weeds. But the road was dry and solid.

He listened to the eerie stillness, alarmed. He glanced around the silent countryside. Something was wrong. Where were the squirrels and mice and foxes? Why weren't the birds singing? He didn't even hear wind stirring the grass or leaves. It was as if the whole world had stopped living.

All morning and into early afternoon he rode without seeing a cottage or village. Disquiet crawled over his skin like ants. The sky became dark as clouds rolled in; the air, icy cold. He shivered and had to put on his jacket and cloak again. *I hope I find shelter for the night before it rains,* he thought as he studied the threatening sky.

Bits and pieces of memories flickered though his mind, places he'd been, people he'd met, things he'd done, all jumbled and disjointed. He remembered his home and his sister Amaly, but not the last time he'd been home. There were towns and villages he'd passed through, but he couldn't remember when or even where they were, only images of people's faces or familiar houses. The one constant image was of last time he'd seen Briella.

The sun was almost touching the horizon when Maren reached a small village, and he stopped dead still, staring in horror. Cottage roofs had collapsed as if a giant hammer had smashed them. Stone walls had fallen outward as if blown apart from the inside. A flock of dead chickens lay half buried in mud beside one ruined cottage. The twisted bodies of a man, woman, and three children lay beside another house. Everywhere he looked, he saw dead bodies. The stench of death was so pervasive, Maren nearly vomited.

Lady Baramay, what happened here? he thought, his stomach knotting with grief. *What kind of storm could cause so much destruction and kill so many people so suddenly?*

He dismounted and winced. His back and buttocks ached, and his legs felt wobbly. *I haven't ridden a horse in a very long time,* he thought, groaning. He tied a kerchief over his mouth, searched through the wreckage, but found no one alive, just more bodies. His mind was overwhelmed by the devastation. Anguish knotted his chest as he gazed at the destruction in the fading light of the setting sun.

It was too late to go on, but he didn't want to stay there, not with so much death, but he didn't have much choice. He decided to camp for the night as far upwind from the wreckage as possible. Tomorrow — tomorrow he'd bury the dead. He shuddered and led his horse through the center of town.

At the far northern edge of the village he found a cottage beside an uprooted maple tree. Three walls were still standing, and its roof was partially intact. If it rained, at least he wouldn't be completely drenched.

Maren tethered his horse to the downed tree, removed his knapsack, waterskin, and saddlebags, and unsaddled his horse. He started toward the house when he heard a faint cry, a pitiful whimper. He looked around frantically, trying to locate the sound. It came from the ruins of the cottage. Someone was still alive!

His heart pounded as he dashed toward the cottage, dropping his possessions at the doorway. He pulled away broken boards and toppled stones, smashed furniture and heaps of wet thatch, tearing frantically through the wreckage in the waning light. The crying was closer, there, under a pile of cracked timbers. Sweat trickled into his eyes and burned. Splinters stuck his fingers. Jagged wood slashed his palms. He didn't care.

He dragged away the last boards. On the dirt floor lay the body of a young woman, curled on her side, cold, dead for at least several days. Streaks of dried blood radiated from the side of her mottled head, from her nose, her mouth. A look of terror was frozen in her dark, dead eyes.

Maren lifted one of the dead woman's arms and nudged her shoulder back. A dark-haired girl lay sheltered beside the woman's body. The child looked to be less than a year old and wore a torn and filthy gown. She stank of old urine. Maren lifted her from her dead mother's side, and she sobbed against his chest. Her lips were blue; her skin was purple-white and cold. Dark eyes stared up at him; tiny hands clutched his shirt. She was shivering, and she lay limply in his arms, as if too weak to move. Her face and arms looked scratched and bruised, but she wasn't bleeding, no broken bones.

"There, there," Maren said as he pulled his cloak around her and held her close. "It's all right. You'll be all right now. Please, please, be all right."

She felt ice cold. He pulled a woolen blanket from his knapsack, stripped off her torn gown, and wrapped her snugly with the blanket. Maren grabbed his waterskin, sat down beside the wall, wet the kerchief, and washed her quickly. The little girl only had a few scratches; her mother had shielded her against serious injury. Maren wrapped her back up in the blanket and rocked the little girl.

"You poor thing," he said, kissing her forehead gently. "Baygor only knows how long have you been trapped there, all alone. It's a miracle you're still alive."

Her eyes were sunken and dark circled, and she stared up at him silently.

"You must be starving," Maren said, "but how will I feed you? I've water but no milk or cereal. You don't seem to have enough teeth to eat what I do."

He smoothed her hair and tried to warm her hands with his breath. He put the open waterskin to her lips. She tried to drink, but most of the water drizzled from the corners of her mouth. He tried again. This time she swallowed a few mouthfuls of water, then closed her eyes.

You need something more than water, he thought, worried. His eyes widened. Broth! He could make some broth from the dried meat in his knapsack. *But I need to make a fire to warm you up.*

He set her on the ground, slipped his lute off his back, knelt, and scraped together some leaves and dry grass. Without thinking, he stretched out his hand toward the tinder, and halted. The words of the spell to create fire were absent from his mind. He searched his memory for the simple words to call fire, but nothing came to his thoughts. He tried harder and harder, until his hand began to cramp with the exertion and his temples throbbed from the strain of trying to remember. *I have to break this enchantment,* he thought, *but how?*

Finally, he rose, retrieved his knapsack, and took out the tinderbox Jeral had given him. He knelt beside the small pile of grass and leaves he'd gathered before and struck flint to steel until he kindled a tiny flame. Gradually, he added more leaves, grass, and woodchips, then broken sticks and splintered boards until he built a chill-chasing fire.

He looked over at the dead woman; he couldn't leave her there. He wrapped her reverently in a torn blanket, carried her just beyond the cottage, and built a small cairn of stones from the fallen cottage wall. *I wonder what your name was,* he thought as he set the last stones in place. *I swear I'll take care of your child and protect her. May you find rest in Barg's kingdom.*

He glanced back toward the fire. The child lay still as if asleep, huddled in the blanket. *I hope she sleeps for a while,* he thought. *Maybe until I can find some food for her.* He broke off a maple twig as thick as his little finger and stripped off the bark. He walked back inside the ruined cottage and shifted boards he hadn't moved while looking for the child. Scrounging through the wreckage, he found a handful of barley meal in a cracked crock and an unbroken cup. *At least now I have something she can eat,* he thought.

Three sound poles lay together nearby. He used them to form a tripod over the fire, then hung his small iron pot from it and filled it halfway with water from his water skin. When the water began to boil, he sprinkled the meal slowly into the water in the pot and stirred the porridge constantly with the maple twig until the cereal thickened. When the porridge was done, he took the pot off the tripod, scooped some porridge into the unbroken cup, and blew on the cereal to cool it.

Gently, Maren picked up the child. She looked thin and felt almost weightless. Her thumb slipped out of her mouth, and her eyes flickered open. Dipping his finger in the cooled porridge, he held it to her mouth. Her lips parted; her tongue touched his finger. He put it in her mouth. She sucked the porridge off and whimpered for more. He dipped his finger again; she sucked the cereal. It took a long time for her to take all the porridge. When she finished, her eyes drooped, opened, drooped again, and finally closed. The little girl fell asleep almost instantly, too weak and exhausted. She sucked her thumb but still sobbed around it.

He tucked the blanket closely around her and cradled her against his chest. Her lips weren't blue anymore. She felt warmer now. So did he. Strangely, the center of his chest felt warmer than the rest of him, especially when he held the child close. *She's so small and helpless,* he thought. *I'd do anything to keep her safe, protect her from harm.*

"Who are you, little one?" he whispered against her dark hair. "And what am I going to do with you? As much as I'd like to keep you with me forever, I can't — this is no life for a child. I have to find a loving home for you, somewhere. And soon."

The girl moaned in her sleep. Maren rocked her, patting her back in a rhythm of three pats then a rest.

"What shall I call you?" he said softly. "You're small and soft and as cute as a little ground squirrel." He smiled to himself. "That's it! I'll name you Ilette, after the little ground squirrel living in Jeral's courtyard. Yes, Ilette's a good name for you."

Maren placed Ilette near the fire, but not too near. Retrieving his belongings from the doorway, he took out some jerky and twice-baked seed cakes from the saddlebags. *Maybe I'll find a village tomorrow. Surely some kind family will take her in,* he thought as he nibbled a seed cake.

He finished his meal, then banked the fire for the night. Pulling out another blanket from the saddlebags, he lay down facing the fire and covered himself and Ilette. An arm protectively over her, his body curved around her for warmth, he soon dozed off.

The next morning Maren awoke, shivering. The fire had burned out some time in the night. Frost covered the ground. The sky was slate-grey but clear in the southwest, portending warmer weather. *At least it didn't rain last night,* he thought as he stretched.

Ilette lay close to him and sobbed in her sleep. Maren sat up carefully so he didn't wake her. He ran his hand through his hair, shaking the sleep from his head. His body ached all over; he wasn't used to sleeping on the hard ground, or maybe he still hurt from the magical seizure he'd had the day before. He found his tinderbox, started a small fire, and made barley porridge for Ilette. While the porridge cooled, he searched through the ruins and found two shirts to serve as gowns and a sheet which he tore into diapers.

Ilette woke not long after. Her eyes seemed brighter, and she seemed more alert. Maren picked her up and fed her the cereal a fingerful at a time. When he held the waterskin to her mouth, she tried to grasp it while she drank. Maren dampened a cloth and washed Ilette as well as he could, packed one shirt in his knapsack, slipped the other over Ilette's head, and secured a diaper with some twisted fabric. He tied the ends of a blanket together to make a sling, slipped it over his head and one shoulder, and placed Ilette in it. She looked happy and cuddled close to his chest.

Chewing some jerky, Maren rolled up his blanket and tied it with a leather thong. He found a relatively clean rag and poured the rest of the barley meal into the center it. *This won't last long,* he thought as tied up the rag. *I have to find more food for her. Maybe there's more in some of the other houses in the village.*

He shuddered at the thought of going into the houses. He put the tinderbox and barley meal in his saddlebag, then washed his pot and the broken cup and stowed them in his knapsack. Dousing the fire with the last of his water, he slung his lute on his back, left the cottage with his belongings, saddled his horse, and retied his knapsack and saddlebags. Reluctantly, he led his horse back to the center of the village.

The village looked worse in full daylight. Every house had been destroyed. Maren felt sick to his stomach as he gazed about. Men, women, children, old, young, all dead. Ilette was the only survivor. There were too many bodies to bury by himself. He did the only thing he could — dragged them to an open space west of the village and made a pyre. It was nearly midday when he finished. His arms ached from the exertion, and his shoulder hurt from the sling carrying Ilette. At least, she slept during the grisly work, and Maren located a little more barley meal in one of the houses.

He bowed his head and tried to say a prayer, but his throat was too tight with dread. He swallowed hard. When he did speak, his voice was hoarse and choked. "I don't know your names, but you'll be remembered. May you find peace and rest in Barg's kingdom."

With his tinderbox he struck a spark on some dry cloth and torched the pyre. It took a while for the fire to catch on the damp wood and spread. Maren watched the orange and yellow flames build. The stink of burning was even worse than the stench of decay. Turning his back on the fiery pillar of death, he walked back to the village and searched for more food in the empty houses, but found only a few handfuls of meal. He refilled his waterskin from the village well. Mounting his horse was slightly awkward with Ilette in the shoulder sling, but finally he climbed into the saddle and left the ruins of the village.

Maren rode north all day under a capricious sky. A blustery wind calmed suddenly, then just as suddenly whipped up again. An icy rain pelted down for a few moments, then dissipated to sultry sunshine. It was freakish weather and made Maren wary. *This isn't natural,* he thought. *It feels...evil.*

Only the road was dry and untouched by the storms. On either side the land was cut by gullies from sudden snow melt. Uprooted trees, tangled brush, and shattered sheds littered fields nearly covered with water. Drowned sheep lay half-buried in the mire. Even burrowing gophers and moles floated atop their flooded homes. The cloying stench of death tainted the air, gagging Maren.

It was midafternoon when Ilette woke and said her first word to him. "Eat."

He smiled at her. "It's a little early to stop for the night. Let's see if you can eat something solid."

He reined his horse to a halt and felt through the saddlebag until he found a piece of twice baked bread and held it out to her. She grasped it with her tiny hands and gnawed on the hard bread.

"Would you like a song?" Maren asked as he watched her eat. He reached for his lute. When he strummed a chord, she looked at him with wide-eyed surprise. He sang a favorite childhood song.

> Oh, the little grey squirrel,
> He lives up in a tree.
> He hops across from branch to branch
> And loves to be so free.

Tinka tinka tottle dee dee
Tinka tinka tottle dee dee
Tinka rinka biddle tee hee
Tinka tinka tottle dee dee

He saves up nuts and acorns
To eat all winter through.
He works so hard to store his food.
The lesson's there for you.

Tinka tinka tottle dee dee
Tinka tinka tottle dee dee
Tinka rinka biddle tee hee
Tinka tinka tottle dee dee

Ilette smiled, her mouth ringed with soggy bread crumbs, and she reached for the lute.

"I don't think you're ready to play a lute, kidling," he said as he put the lute on his back. He gave Ilette another piece of bread, and she chewed on it happily.

Maren nudged his horse into motion and sang the "Grey Squirrel" song but without the lute. He couldn't play and guide the horse, too.

As evening approached, Ilette squirmed and grew cranky. She rubbed her eyes and whined until her head drooped and she fell asleep. Maren kept his horse to a slow walk so he wouldn't wake her.

By sunset the air had turned chilly again. *I need some kind of shelter for her,* Maren thought as he pulled his cloak tighter around the two of them. He spotted a partially collapsed stone building near the road. A wooden door lay askew off its hinges. A large elm south of the hut was split in two, half lying on the ground. *At least the hut will block the wind,* he thought.

Ilette was still asleep when he halted. Maren touched her cheek and smiled at her. *She's so little,* he thought, *too young to have so much tragedy in her life. I hope I can find a good home for her soon.*

He started to dismount, but froze, feeling rather than hearing someone in the shadows of the cottage. "I feel you, stranger." His eyes searched the darkness for movement. Stretching out his empty hands, he continued, "I'm no threat to you. See, I have no weapon, no great wealth. Why not show yourself?"

Slowly, a figure emerged from the recesses of the half-standing shelter. He stepped with graceful precision toward Maren, bow drawn and an arrow aimed at Maren's heart. Nearly as tall as Maren, though leaner, the bowman wore brown leather clothes and knee-boots, a knife on one hip, a sword on the other. A hood obscured the face, and the voice was muffled as if the bowman's mouth were covered. "Leave, bandit," the bowman said. "This shelter's mine. If you try to take it, I'll kill you, just as I killed your comrades."

"Bandit?" Maren said, startled. "Why would you think I'm a bandit? I'm just a traveler needing a place to shelter for the night."

"Of course," the stranger said sarcastically.

"Would a bandit be unarmed, burdened with a child?"

"A child?" Without lowering the bow even a fraction, the bowman paused a moment but kept Maren sighted. "I don't see a child."

He opened his cloak just enough to uncover Ilette's face, then quickly pulled the cloak back to protect her from the quickly chilling wind.

"Oh," the figure said, lowering the bow. "I'm sorry. I didn't know. Who are you?"

"A man from Hixus."

Ilette whimpered.

"Please," Maren said. "She's cold and hungry. We need a place to stay for the night. Can we share this shelter?"

"I suppose," the stranger said. "What are you doing out here?"

"I'm traveling north. I found this child in a village south of here, completely destroyed. She was the only survivor. I don't know how long she was buried in the rubble of her home, but she was nearly dead before I found her. She's hungry and tired. And so am I."

The stranger was silent for a while, then said, "All right. I suppose bandits wouldn't carry a child around with them. You can stay the night."

"Thank you." Maren dismounted and untied his saddlebags and knapsack.

"Well, man from Hixus, what's your name?"

"Maren the minstrel." He rocked Ilette to soothe her.

The stranger gasped. "Maren the minstrel! Now I know you're lying!"

"Why do you say that?"

"You look about twenty, twenty-five years old at the most. Maren must be at least forty-five to fifty."

Maren stared at the stranger curiously. "And how do you know that?"

"I *know!*"

"Whatever you say, but I am Maren the minstrel."

"Hah! I suppose you can prove it."

"What do you mean?" Maren asked, puzzled by the stranger's reaction.

"There're things only Maren would know, things I learned years ago from my father."

"And who's your father?" Maren asked.

The stranger pushed back the hood and pull down a kerchief covering his mouth. In the waning light Maren saw an olive face surrounded by jet-black hair, bound with a studded-leather band. Eyes and lashes were dark as were arching brows. A low, female voice said, "Klaymar of Beltrin."

Maren inhaled quietly, drawn to her unexpectedly as if he'd known her all his life. His heart danced as he gazed at her. He cleared his throat and said, "Gemna."

8

Gemna's eyes widened. Her jaw dropped, and she started to speak but didn't.

"You are Gemna, aren't you?" Maren asked, staring steadily at her. He couldn't take his eyes off her face. He'd never felt this sudden and intense bond with anyone else, not even Briella. His heart told him that Gemna was his life mate! But that was impossible! She was a human, and he was a Wizard. Only one Wizard had ever married a human, and she'd had to give up her powers and become a human. *No!* he thought. *This can't be! I won't believe it! I can't! I must be mistaken!*

"How--how do you know my name?" she stammered.

"Your father told me about you," Maren said, barely able to speak coherently. "I saw him in Hixus before I left. He said you're a mercenary, good with a sword and dagger, but he didn't mention you're an archer." He paused a moment, his heart beating rapidly, then he continued, his voice barely above a whisper. "He also didn't mention how... beautiful you are."

"Hah! Don't try that with me; too many others have. And how do I know you're not lying about knowing my father?"

Shaking his head to clear his thoughts, Maren frowned a moment. He tried to remember everything, anything about Klaymar. Gazing at Gemna, he noticed a silver chain with an opal around her neck and smiled as he remembered a day in his past. "That opal you're wearing," he pointed to the necklace, "he bought that for you at the Autumn Fair in Tironza the day he and I met for the first time."

Gemna gasped and fingered a chain with a blue gemstone. "That's true. Besides my family, only two others knew about the opal: Shiffin the Jeweler and Maren. You're not Shiffin; I've seen him. But you can't be Maren either. He was maybe twenty-five when my father met him twenty-two years ago. Now I learned my sums from Father when I was very young. Twenty-five and twenty-two are forty-seven, and you certainly don't look that old."

Maren smiled, feeling in control of himself again. "Your father made the same comment. I am Maren, despite my appearance, and I don't lie. Would you like me to sing you a song?"

Gemna's eyes betrayed her indecision. "You know about the opal, so you may be who you claim. I'll accept you for now." She backed through the shadowed doorway of the hut.

Three walls of mortared stone still stood. The eastern wall opposite the door had collapsed. Wooden rafters on that side rested on the tumbled stones. Thatch, which once covered the rafters, was scattered about the ground.

Ilette's tiny hands clutched at Maren's shirt as he followed Gemna into the hut. When his eyes adjusted to the dark, he saw Gemna standing beside her horse, a bay gelding with a white face. The dirt floor was littered with thatch, twigs, and splintered wood. One area had been cleared and ringed with rocks; some thatch and leaves were piled in the center. Kindling was stacked nearby. A bedroll, sack, and Gemna's bow lay near the cleared area.

Maren set his possession near the door. "Can you watch Ilette while I tend my horse?"

Gemna stiffened, then relaxed. "All right. Bring her over here." She took a tinderbox from her saddlebags and struck a spark on the pile of tinder until it caught fire.

Maren knelt beside her, slipped the sling over his head, and handed Ilette to Gemna. The little girl gazed up at Gemna for a few moments, eyes wide, then looked at Maren.

"It's all right, dearling," he said, patting her cheek gently. "I'll be right back."

As he started to stand, Gemna said, "I'm—" She halted, feeding twigs to the tiny flame, then stared at him. "I'm sorry if I misjudged you."

Maren studied her face. There was a tightness to her jaw and a wariness in her eyes that touched his heart. "Something happened to you," he said softly.

She nodded.

"Tell me."

She shook her head. "Not now. Not now."

"All right. I'll be back in a few moments."

Maren walked outside, trying not to think about Gemna. His horse Fraivoly shuffled nervously, barely putting weight on her left front hoof. He lifted the leg. "What's the matter, girl?"

A sharp stone was wedged by mud against the tender skin. Using a broken elm twig, Maren scraped out the mud and stone, gave the mare two handfuls of oats, then led her into the hut. Gemna had a blaze crackling that warmed the cottage. Gemna had the sling over her shoulder and rocked Ilette.

As Maren strode to the fire, Gemna looked at him with a frown. "This baby's hungry! Don't you know anything about taking care of children?"

Maren smiled sheepishly. "Not much. I was doing the best I could. Do you know about children?"

Gemna gawked at him. "Are you joking? I'm the oldest of five children."

Maren rolled his eyes and chuckled. "Of course. I'm sure you helped your mother with your four brothers."

"What are you feeding her?"

"Porridge mostly."

"Is that all?"

"It's all I have. I know she needs milk, but I don't have a cow with me," he said earnestly. "I'd hoped to find a villager to take her in, but you're the first person I've met since I left Hixus."

"Well, we need to cook some porridge then," Gemna said. She rocked Ilette back and forth and crooned to the baby.

"I thought I might add some bits of dried apples to the porridge. Do you think that would be all right?"

Gemna smiled. "I think she'd like that."

Maren unsaddled his horse and unpacked his food and equipment. He tied a tripod and poured some water in the pot. Taking the cloth bag of meal and a wooden cup from his sack, Maren sat down by the fire across from Gemna and waited for the water to boil. He stirred in some meal, then tore up some dried apples and added them to the pot. While the porridge cooked, he watched Gemna play with the little girl, and he was touched by Gemna's tenderness.

How odd, he thought, the warmth in his heart bringing a smile to his lips. *When we first met, she threatened to kill me. Now she's sitting there playing with Ilette like any young mother plays with her child.*

Gemna glanced at him, saw him watching her, and she blushed.

"You're really good with children," Maren said.

"I had to be," Gemna said as she played pat-a-cake with Ilette. "Mother had her hands full taking care of the household since Father was gone most of the time. I had to help out." She paused and made a scrunched up funny face at Ilette. The little girl laughed. "She really needs some warmer clothes."

Maren sighed. "I know. I scavenged what I could from the ruins of her home, but there wasn't much."

"Well, we'll see what we can come up with."

When the porridge was cooked and cooled, Maren took Ilette onto his lap, slid the sling over his shoulder, and finger-fed her the cereal. She ate as fast as Maren could scoop up the porridge and bring it to her mouth. She looked stronger; her skin had lost the bluish tint. Her dark eyes sparkled, and she could sit up by herself.

"A spoon would make that easier," Gemna said, smiling.

"That it would," Maren said, smiling back, "if I had one."

"I'll see what I can do about that." She picked up a broken piece of wood, took out her knife, and started whittling.

Ilette ate all the cereal and drank some water, holding onto the waterskin. Maren wiped her mouth and chin, changed her diaper, then wrapped her in the blanket and rocked her, humming softly. Ilette's eyes began to close though she fought against sleep. Maren smoothed her dark hair, rested his cheek against her forehead. Finally, her eyelids closed, and she nestled comfortably against his chest.

A quiet excitement tingled in his chest, surging with his blood, surprising him. He'd always cared about others; Wizards always did. But this feeling was new to him. *Is this what fathers feel when they hold their children?* he wondered. He wasn't sure, but he knew he'd do anything to protect Ilette. The tale of Radamin the Betrayer came to his thoughts. *Now I know why a man would betray his friends to save his family, his children.*

"Could you make a bed for her to sleep on?" Maren whispered to Gemna. "I have more blankets in my saddlebags."

She nodded and rose quietly and gathered some of the scattered thatch into a small bed. She pulled a blanket from Maren's saddle bags, folded the blanket in half, spread it over the thatch, and folded half back. Maren tried not to waken Ilette as he placed her on the bed and tucked the blanket around her.

A chilly, northwest wind blew through the opening. Maren braced the unhinged door across the entrance to keep out the cold. He crept back to the fire and sat beside Gemna. She handed him the spoon she'd finished carving.

"That should help next time," she said, smiling.

He smiled back. "Thank you. Would you like to share my food?" he asked.

"I have my own," Gemna began, "but I never turn down free food."

Maren handed her some jerky, dried fruit, and a seed cake from his sack. Setting his waterskin between them, Maren ate silently for a while, staring at the dancing fire. Hesitantly, he asked, "The bandits, what happened to them?"

Gemna stiffened. "Bandits?"

Maren noted the tremor in her voice. "Yes, you mentioned them when we met. What happened to them?"

She didn't look up at him. "Why?"

"Curiosity."

"They're dead, all but three of them."

"All but three?" Maren said, astonished. "How many were there?"

Her face became as hard and cold as a stone wall, and she stared at the fire. "There were nine of them." She swallowed hard. "They wanted to share this hut and my bed. I disabused them of that idea." She shuddered and closed her eyes for a moment.

"Did they hurt you?" he asked softly. He almost reached out to touch her arm, but stopped himself.

She shook her head, but Maren wasn't sure she meant it.

"Where are you traveling?" he asked.

Gemna wiped her hands on her tunic. "I'm joining my father. My last commission ended earlier than my employer had thought it would, so I thought I'd travel with Father to the western lands. I've never been there before."

"But he's miles ahead of you. He left Hixus," Maren pause to add up the days since he'd seen Klaymar, "five days ago for the western lands. You'll never catch up to him now."

"His wagons will travel a lot slower than I can alone."

Maren was quiet for a while, then gazed straight at her. "What happened to you?"

She stared at the fire, chewing on some jerky. After she took a drink of water, she cleared her throat. "I'd left a village north of here when I saw the storm rolling in from the south. I almost turned back to the village, but didn't realize the storm would come in so fast. There wasn't enough time to reach the village so I rode straight west and took shelter in some caves I know."

Gemna shuddered. "I've never seen a storm like that. Rain so heavy, it was like hail. Lightening so bright, it nearly blinded me. Thunder so violent, it shook the ground. Whirlwinds dancing all over the land. And the sound – it was like a mad woman shrieking so loud, I clapped my hands over my ears and I could still hear it just as loudly. I couldn't breathe. I felt as if the air were trying to crush me."

Gemna halted, shuddering again. "It went on for a day and a night, then stopped. I left the caves and rode southeast across country to try to save time, but the land was like a bog from so much rain. I stumbled across the bandit camp in a twisted heap of trees and rocks. They tried to pull me off my horse, but I got away from them. Barely.

"I found this shelter late this morning. My horse was so tired from slogging through mud, I decided to stay the night here."

She closed her eyes, her forehead creased, her jaw tight. Silence hung like a heavy curtain between them. "Midafternoon, they came for me. I killed six. The other three fled."

"But you're all right?" Maren said gently.

Gemna opened her eyes and nodded. She gazed at him thoughtfully. "Where are you going?" she asked.

"To Vorlik."

"At this time of year? It's still winter up there. Snow everywhere. Why now?"

"For answers."

"To what questions?"

Maren tried to answer, but no sound came. He cleared his tight throat. "I...lost someone I cared about. I want to know how and why. The answers are in Vorlik." He closed his eyes, bent forward, and rested his forehead in his hand, the memory of Briella threatening to reopen the wound in his heart. Too many of his people had died, killed by Sorcerers. But Briella killed by a human? He couldn't fathom how that was possible. After a few moments, he raised his head, and they gazed at each other silently for some time. Maren was the first to speak.

"You sleep," he said. "I'll take the first watch."

Gemna looked surprised. "Why?"

"Three of the bandits escaped. They might come back."

"But you have no weapon."

"Lend me your knife." He held out his hand.

"All right," she said and handed him the hilt.

"Thank you," Maren whispered. He took the knife then stood. From his saddlebag he pulled another blanket and wrapped it around his shoulders. "Stay close to Ilette so she won't be frightened. I'll wake you in a few hours. Sleep well."

Striding to the entrance, he crouched before the door. Knife in hand, he stared through a large crack into the dark night, alert for any movement.

When he glanced back at the fire, he caught Gemna staring at him. She turned away quickly, wrapped a blanket around her, crawled next to Ilette, and closed her eyes.

9

Gemna woke suddenly, her eyes opening to cold darkness. Something, some noise had wakened her from a sound sleep. She felt for her knife but found the sheath empty. She'd given her knife to Maren! What had happened to him?

"Be still," Maren's voice whispered from near the door. "The bandits, they've come back."

Gemna relaxed, just barely.

Maren motioned Gemna to peek through the wide crack. She joined him, bow in hand, and leaned her sword against the stone wall. She nocked an arrow and crouched beside Maren, poised to fire. A waxing quarter moon bathed the land in faint ghostly light. Her eyes scanned the tangled brush and broken trees for movement.

"I think they've brought friends with them," Maren said. "I put out the fire so they couldn't see us."

"Good. They'll come soon. With no light to see us by, they'll be certain we're sleeping and can take us by surprise."

"I don't think I've ever fought for my life before, not like this." Maren halted, then she felt him clutch her arm. "Please, promise me," he said, "swear that if I'm killed, you'll take Ilette and ride from here as fast as you can."

Gemna started to speak, but Maren held up his hand, then pointed. In the dim moonlight she saw a shadow coming from the west, dodging from one bush to another. A figure crawled across the road. Another moved forward, and another. In all, eight figures advanced toward the hut.

Maren whispered, "Can you sneak out through the back of the hut and position yourself for bowshot?"

"Yes." Gemna returned her arrow to the quiver. She crept to her pack and removed a small vial and a strip of cloth. In the ashes of the campfire she found one glowing coal. Using a charred stick, she scooted the ember onto a piece of wood and returned with it to Maren. "There's oil in the vial," she said. "Pry out the cork and stuff the cloth in the vial, like a lantern wick. When you hear me shout your name, fire the wick and heave the vial at the nearest man. If it hits, that's one less we have to fight. If it doesn't, we'll still have light for me to aim by."

"Sounds easy enough. What about the sword?"

"Well, since you haven't used one before —or have you?"

"I don't think so," Maren said.

"All right, hold it with both hands. Just point it and try to block any blow. Maybe you won't have to use it at all."

"I hope not," Maren said. "Baygor protect you."

She nodded and grasped his arm in the manner of a guild brother. Slinging her quiver over her shoulder, bow in hand, Gemna crept to the back of the hut. She crawled out as quietly as she could into the black shadow of night, crouched beside the hut, and surveyed her surroundings.

The six dead bandits lay to her right, where she'd dragged them earlier, about halfway between the hut and the elm. She dodged cat-quiet to the heap of bodies, dropped to the ground, and scanned for any movement. Seeing no one, she took a discarded sword and dagger, then crept south to the elm. She shouldered her bow, climbed as high as she dared, and perched where she had a clear view of the front of the house.

A bandit had crawled within ten feet of the door.

Arrow poised to strike, Gemna shouted, "Now, Maren!"

Eight startled men, wearing leather armor over tattered clothes, sprang up and looked for the crier. Gemna heard Maren kick the door aside and saw the flaming vial hurl through the night air. One man became a living torch. Screaming, he rolled on the ground, uselessly trying to extinguish the fire. His comrades yelled their rage and charged the hut.

Gemna loosed her arrow, nocked another one, and fired, taking down two bandits before three others stared up at her. Unexpected gusts of wind diverted her next two arrows, just missing their targets. A third arrow caught the leg of one of the men who'd spotted her position. By the time she'd drawn another arrow, one of the two remaining men was climbing the elm. She jumped lightly from the tree and loosed another shaft. The wounded man screamed as the arrow pierced his heart. He dropped to the ground with a dull thud.

Gemna dropped her bow and quiver and drew her hand weapons. The man in the tree jumped down just as his companion arrived. One was tall and hairy; the other was short and had a whitish scar running from below his left eye to his chin. Both looked as handsome as wild boars and just as sweet-tempered.

She used the dagger to parry Scarface while she attacked Hairy and tried to drive the two bandits backward toward the road. Swords rang like a mad blacksmith pounding his anvil. She dodged Hairy's down-thrust and took advantage of the opening in Scarface's defense to nearly severe his neck. Hairy drove his sword through her sleeve, grazing her dagger arm. With an upsweep of her sword, Gemna shunted his weapon aside and rammed her dagger hilt-deep into his chest. She jerked the dagger from Hairy's chest, glanced at Maren, and raced toward the hut.

Maren stood in the doorway, Gemna's sword in his right hand, and faced the other two bandits. One was taller than Maren and much heavier, not fat, just huge. He wielded a double-bladed axe that gleamed like moonlight. The other was a weasel-faced man and carried a battered short sword and dagger. Maren held the door against his left side like a shield.

Splinters flew from the wooden door as Giant's axe bit into the boards. Maren staggered backward. Weasel's sword slashed at Maren, and the minstrel cried out, his right arm limp but still holding the sword. Maren shoved the door against Giant and knocked him off balance. Giant toppled like a cut tree. Weasel slashed at Maren, quick and persistent. Maren's face was lined with pain; his jaw, clenched with strain. With a growling shout, he shoved the remains of the door at Weasel and knocked him to the ground. Both hands on the sword, Maren turned to Giant, who was trying to stand, and sliced him across the mid-section. Giant screamed and clapped his hands over the gaping wound. Blood poured between his thick fingers. His skin paled, and he crumpled.

Suddenly, Ilette cried from the hut. Maren wheeled and started back toward the hut.

Gemna watched in horror as Weasel sat up and hurled his dagger at Maren. "Maren!"

Even as she shouted his name, she knew she would be too late. He pitched forward, the dagger protruding from his back. Weasel rose and strode over Maren, poised to drive his sword through Maren's back.

"You bastard son of a whore!" she yelled at Weasel as she ran toward him. "You have to face me first!"

Weasel grinned and turned to face her. Weasel was good with his sword, but Gemna was better. He grazed her arm. She sliced his shoulder. He scratched her thigh; she gashed his. He staggered. She dove at him. Their swords locked, arms pushing, bodies rigid, trying to over balance each other. Weasel weakened. Gemna pushed him backward. He stumbled over the charred corpse of his companion and fell to the ground. Gemna pounced on him and drove her dagger hilt-deep in his chest.

Dropping her weapons, she ran to Maren. He lay deathly still. Trying not to jar the blade, she slit his jacket and shirt, and bared his back. The dagger was just below his right ribs. If she were careful, she could move him without making the wound worse.

She ran inside where Ilette lay sobbing in her sleep. "Hush, hush now," Gemna said, gently but quickly, stroking the girl's head to calm her sleep.

Locating the glowing coal near the door, Gemna coaxed the fire to life. She grabbed a blanket and ran back to Maren. Inching the blanket under his head, she pulled it downward slowly until his entire body lay on it. She gripped the corners near his head and carefully dragged him inside the hut.

I'm glad I learned more than just fighting at the guild hall, she thought. She was cold and tired, and a little frightened. *I wish I had more healing herbs. Maybe he has some.*

She rummaged through his knapsack and found a small pouch with leaves, bark, and roots. "Woundweal! And roborant! And boneset, valerian, and comfrey." She picked up some grey-green bark. "I don't recognize this. I wonder if it'd help him."

Gemna poured the last of her own water into the pot and hung it over the fire. When it boiled, she scooped out a cupful and tossed in three leaves of numbing woundweal. She swirled the steaming infusion to mix it thoroughly, then cooled it with her breath. After she added roborant, valerian, and comfrey to the pot, she let the liquid simmer. She took bandages from her pack, knelt beside Maren's prone body, and steeled herself for her task.

Thank Baygor, he's unconscious, she thought. She never could stand to hear the wounded scream.

She bathed Maren's back with the warm liquid, and she hoped the roborant had numbed the area enough. She folded a cloth several layers thick and laid it close to the wound, in easy reach. Slowly, she pulled out the dagger. Maren moaned, although he was still unconscious.

Blood ran over his pale skin. Gemna placed the folded cloth on the wound and pressed hard. Her arms cramped. She gritted her teeth and kept pressing. After an interminable time, the bleeding slowed, then stopped. She removed the soaked cloth cautiously, careful not to start the bleeding again, and examined the wound.

It was a clean cut. She dabbed the area with more woundweal tea. From a tiny pouch she kept on a cord about her neck, she took one of her most precious possessions: a steel needle, a gift from her shieldmaster at the guild hall. Dipping the needle and a length of thread into the cup of woundweal, she threaded the eye and began the painstaking task of stitching the wound closed.

Maren never stirred as she drew the needle through his flesh, for which Gemna was grateful. Her stomach was jittery enough as it was. When she'd finished, she sat him upright very gently, wrapped strips of clean cloth around him, tied the bandage securely, then laid him on his side close to the fire. His breathing was shallow; his body, too cool.

I've got to warm him, Gemna thought as she pulled a heavy blanket around him. *He has to take some medicine and liquid, but not while he's unconscious.*

Gemna took her blanket and tucked it around Maren before she tended her own wound. After that, she added more wood to the fire until it blazed like the sun and drove the chill of night from the hut. She bathed Maren's face and lips with the herbal infusion, trying to get at least a little of the infusion into his mouth and hopefully into his body. She sat awake and watched night change to dismal dawn, then to a cloud-shrouded day.

Maren slept uneasily. Dreams of terror and death froze his heart. He saw a raging whirlwind with the face of a mad, weeping woman ravaging the land; murder and treachery spreading from country to country; a fair woman who wielded great power; a shadow hovering behind her, source of her power; a man wearing a silver chain with an amulet shaped like a dove, Briella's amulet. He saw a clawed hand of darkness stretch from the south to crush the world; and above the chaos, he heard the same mocking laughter he'd heard at the Salty Sailor in Hixus, saw the same feral blue eyes that bound his power.

Slowly, he opened his eyes. His body ached worse than he'd ever known it could. He lay on a blanket on his side, facing a glowing fire. Diffuse sunlight filtered through the collapsed roof. The air smelled of rain and smoke and cooked porridge. Gemna sat nearby, feeding Ilette. The woman watched Maren with red-rimmed eyes drooping with fatigue.

He tried to move. Pain shot up his back. He groaned. His lips were cracked; his throat was parched. "I think I could drink a river dry," he croaked, licking his lips.

"Lie still!" Gemna ordered. "I'm nearly finished with Ilette."

"The bandits —what happened?"

"They're dead, all of them. No more have come. I hope we're safe."

Easing into a more comfortable position, Maren noticed Gemna's ashen skin, the dark circles under her eyes. "You look tired."

"Kind of you to notice," she said, her shoulders sagging.

Ilette swallowed the last gulp and smiled at Maren, cereal dribbling down her chin. She glowed with contentment, much different from the hungry, terrified orphan he'd found in ruined village. Gemna wiped Ilette's face off, gave her a doll of knotted rags and a scrap of fabric for a blanket, then she set the girl on the dirt floor.

Stepping around the fire, Gemna knelt beside Maren, a tired look on her face. "Well, minstrel, do you feel like singing us a ballad?"

He tried to move and flinched. "Barg's breath! Have you been kicking me? I ache all over: my back, my arm, my hair. Have I slept all day?"

"It's the third day since the attack." She rubbed her eyes and yawned. "And little sleep I've had during that time." She sighed as she removed his blanket.

To Maren's chagrin, he saw he was naked, though Gemna didn't seem to be aware of his embarrassment. He clutched the blanket to him. He'd been uncomfortable enough when Molly had tended him, but at least he'd been wearing some clothing. The thought of Gemna seeing him without clothes was extremely discomforting.

Gemna gave him a puzzled look and tried to pull the blanket away, but Maren resisted.

"What's the matter with you?" she asked with obvious annoyance.

"I'm, uh, not use to being naked in a woman's presence."

The look on Gemna's face changed from surprise to disbelief to amusement. She laughed. "People from Beltrin have few inhibitions about their bodies. Surely, you learned that from my father. I lived for five years at the mercenary guild in barracks with men and women."

"But I haven't."

She laughed again. "I'll respect your modesty." She pushed the blanket down just far enough to reveal the bandage. "Is that all right?"

"Yes," Maren mumbled, too uncomfortable to meet her eyes.

Carefully, Gemna unwrapped the cloth and gently touched his back. "There's no sign of inflammation or infection. It's healing, but you'll be sore for a long time. You should stay here at least two more days. Now for some medicine."

She turned to the fire and poured some green-gold tea into a cup. Being careful not to spill the tea, she shifted slowly back toward Maren. "Prop yourself up on one elbow so you can drink this without choking. I'll make some meat broth later, but you're nearly out of water. I've already used all of mine. We need to find a well or a stream. Maybe now that you're awake I can go scouting. There has to be a water source nearby."

Maren grimaced as he pushed up on his elbow, tucking the blanket around his lower body.

"Oh, I had to cut your jacket and shirt off to tend your wounds. I repaired them as well as I could." Gemna held the cup of medicinal tea to his mouth. "It's amazing how you undressed yourself while you were unconscious."

Maren looked up at her sharply, only to see a fox grin on her face and knew she was teasing. He blushed. "I'm being foolish."

"Yes," she said, "you are."

"It's just..." he glanced at her and squirmed under her mock-innocent gaze, "it's one thing for you to undress me while I'm unconscious, but quite another to have you staring at me when I'm awake."

Gemna's eyes twinkled mischievously. "I promise I won't stare...too much."

"Your father never told me you were born with a sword for a tongue," Maren said.

He sipped the wholesome tea while Gemna held the cup for him. Recognizing the taste, he looked at her with honest respect. "You certainly know your herbs, but you didn't use the callum bark."

"I've never heard of it," Gemna said with a puzzled look.

"It's with the rest of the herbs. The grey-green bark. Boil a piece with the other herbs. It'll speed the healing and strengthen the body even better than roborant."

Gemna stretched and dragged the knapsack to her. She opened it and searched its contents until she found the herbs. Picking out one piece of the callum bark, she held it out to Maren. "Is this it?"

Maren nodded.

Gemna chewed her lower lip. "Just how fast will it work? I'd like to leave here as soon as possible."

"Just add it to the potion and let it steep for a while. And find the blue stone jar in my sack. It contains a potent healing salve. Spread it on the whole area. Between the two medicines I'll be able to travel by morning."

Gemna raised her brow in disbelief. "Nothing can heal that quickly."

Maren's dark eyes twinkled. "Try it."

Gemna tossed the callum bark into the kettle, then rummaged through the knapsack until she found the jar. Removing the lid, she scrutinized the creamy-white salve and sniffed the wholesome, clean scent that filled the cottage. She scooped out a small amount with her fingertips but still looked unconvinced.

"It works." Maren lay on his stomach, his head resting on his folded arms. "Just rub it —ack! gently, please—on the wound. That's right. Now rewrap the bandage. I promise I'll be fit tomorrow morning."

Gemna gazed at the blue jar, then at Maren. "We'll see." She pulled the blanket over him.

Maren reached out and touched her arm. "Thank you for saving my life," he said, turning his head so he gazed up at her, "and for taking care of Ilette. I don't know how I can repay you."

Her cheeks reddened, and she blinked several times. "Um, just get well. Soon." She pulled away from his hand, stood, took the cup from him, and went back to check on Ilette. She crept back to Maren's side with a cup of the callum bark potion. "If you can keep an eye on Ilette, I'll go search for water. I'll be back as soon as I can. Can you stay awake for a while?"

"Yes. Just be careful," he said. "And come back soon."

She nodded, picked up the two waterskins, and her sword, and left the cottage.

The soothing ointment warmed his back, and Maren relaxed a bit. The pain began to subside. Ilette jabbered as she played with her doll. Maren smiled at her and listened for Gemna's return.

I'll be well enough to leave tomorrow morning, Maren thought. Suddenly, an exciting idea occurred to him. Maybe Gemna would be willing to come with him. It would be very pleasant to have her company. *I don't want her to leave me. She was good to Ilette and handy in a fight. Better than I am,* he admitted to himself. *I could ask her to come with us.* He sighed and shook his head. *No, she probably wouldn't. She was following her father south. She had no reason to come north. But I'll ask,* he thought. *I think I need a warrior to protect me and Ilette.*

He sipped the callum bark tea, watched Ilette, and waited for Gemna's return. And he tried not to think about how much Gemna disturbed and excited him.

10

Gemna woke to the sound of singing and the smoky aroma of sizzling meat. Opening her eyes, she was astonished to see Maren, apparently healthy and strong, fully dressed, turning smoked beef on a spit and humming a tune. Nearby, Ilette sucked and chewed a piece of dried peach while she slapped her rag doll against the dirt floor and cooed happily. Maren looked toward Gemna and smiled.

"Would you like some breakfast?" he asked.

Scrambling to her feet, she hurried to his side and started to pull up his shirt.

"Stop!" He tugged his shirt down, blushing. "Will you leave my clothes alone?"

"All right, but—"

She ignored his protest and pulled up his shirt. A growl rumbled through his chest as she unwound the bandage and stared. She ran her fingertips lightly over smooth pink skin. Only the black thread that she'd used to sew the wound together marked where the dagger had entered his back. Straightening his shirt, Gemna swallowed hard, her eyes wide with awe. "That salve is truly amazing! Where did you find it?"

"My homeland."

"Can I buy some? Every healer I know would love to have a supply of this!"

"The ingredients are difficult to find. Only the most skilled can incant — I mean concoct this salve. I knew one, long ago, in another time. She could make medicines to cure almost any illness or injury. She was..." His voice trailed off, and he turned his face away from her.

"She must have been a very gifted woman," Gemna said, watching him curiously.

"Yes, the most gifted woman I've ever known."

Gemna hesitated. "What happened to her?"

"She...died." Maren sat woodenly, his jaw set and his brows pulled together as if by some remembered pain.

"You loved her, didn't you?" she said, wondering if she dared too much.

He stared at the fire, immobile, not even blinking. For a moment she thought he wasn't going to answer. "Yes," he said softly, "I did."

"I'm sorry," she said.

He just nodded. Using her knife, he cut off a strip of the sizzling meat, stuck it on the tip of the knife, and held it out to her. "Be careful. The meat's hot."

She took the knife and blew on the meat to cool it. "Why are you going to Vorlik?" she asked.

"That's where she died. I need to find out how and why."

Gemna nodded slowly. "I hope you find what you're looking for. Now that you're well, will you be leaving today?" She tore off a bite of the stringy meat.

"Yes." He looked up at her. He opened his mouth as if he were going to speak, then halted and cleared his throat. "You're a mercenary, aren't you?"

"You already know that," she said, still chewing the meat.

"Do you have an employer at the moment?"

She looked at him, puzzled. "No. You know that, too."

"Would you accept an offer from me?"

Gemna stopped short, her tongue poised to lick her thumb. "An offer? From you?" She chuckled. "For what? A nursemaid?"

"No, as my bodyguard."

"A bodyguard?" She chuckled louder. "You don't need a bodyguard. You need a keeper."

Maren laughed, too. "Then take pity on a helpless traveler and his young ward." He reached inside a pocket on his vest and pulled out a small pouch. "I can pay you well for your time." He opened the pouch and poured out a handful of gems and quite a few gold coins.

Gemna stared at the sparkling gems and shining gold. "I thought you said you didn't have much of value."

"I don't really value these things," he said.

"But they help keep food in your belly," she said, her eyes mesmerized by the glittering stones.

"You couldn't catch up with your father. He's at least eight days ahead of you. You don't have a contract at the present. I need protection and am willing to pay you. I'll include all the time since we first met as part of your service."

Frowning thoughtfully, Gemna took another bite of meat and chewed it slowly. Maren was right. She couldn't reach her father now and she had no other offer. For some reason, though, she felt uneasy. She studied him deliberately before answering. "You aren't very adept at defending yourself. I suppose you'd come to a horrible end, and then I'd feel a bit guilty," she said with a wry smile. "Just a bit."

"Then save me from myself," Maren said, smiling back.

Gemna licked the meat grease from her thumb, then wiped her greasy mouth on her sleeve. "What terms are you offering?"

"You're to act as bodyguard for myself and for Ilette, as long as she travels with us, until we reach Tarolin Castle in Vorlik. At that time, if you choose to extend your service, we'll discuss terms. I'll provide food and lodging – if we find any – and pay you ten gold castles and your choice of one of these gems when we arrive at Tarolin. Is that satisfactory?"

Gemna nearly choked. Her normal wages were one gold a month, one or two meals a day, and a patch of ground to throw her bedroll on. *I can't pass this up,* she thought. *I'll never have another offer as good.* "All right. I accept, master."

Maren's face reddened, and he cleared his throat. "I'd rather you didn't call me master."

"Very well, minstrel." Gemna noticed he seemed uncomfortable, almost as nervous as when she'd seen him naked.

"Just Maren, please," he said.

"All right, Maren. My sword is yours until we reach Tarolin Castle. Beyond that, I'll consider." She wiped her knife on her trousers, sheathed it, and stood. "One more thing. In any fight, my word is law. You must follow my orders. All our lives may depend on your instant obedience. Agreed?"

Maren nodded. "Agreed."

"Then we should be leaving as soon as possible." She gathered her things and tied them in a bundle, picked up her full waterskin, then secured belongings to her saddle. She glanced at Maren as he finished his breakfast. There was something strange about him, something she couldn't quite figure out. *But I will,* she thought.

Maren smothered the fire with dirt and poured some water on the dust. He rolled up his blanket, picked up his little pot, and stuffed them in his knapsack. He walked to his horse and started to tie the knapsack to the saddle. "Where did these come from?" he asked, turning to Gemna and pointed at a sword and dagger sheathed in a leather belt tied to his saddle.

"I thought you might need some weapons. I can even teach you how to use them."

"But where did you get them?"

"They belonged to one of the bandits. He doesn't need them anymore. We'd better go." She stood at the doorway and waited for him.

Maren bound his full waterskin and his belongings to his saddle, then fastened his cloak around his shoulders. He slipped the sling over his head, picked up Ilette, and placed her in the sling. He took his horse's reins and turned toward Gemna.

Gemna clasped her cloak around her shoulders and led her horse from the cottage. Maren followed her, they both mounted their horses.

"Where are the bandits?" Maren asked.

"I couldn't bury them by myself, so I dragged them to a gully behind the house, rolled the broken half of the elm tree on top of them, then set fire to the tree. The fire's barely smoldering now, and the ground's too wet for the flames to spread. I think it's safe to leave it."

"I think you're right," Maren said. "Let's go."

The day passed uneventfully. The light wind blew from the south with a hint of rain and a metallic tang in it. Rows of white, shifting clouds occasionally blocked the uncomfortably warm sun. Birds sang in the woods that edged both sides of the road, and small creatures skittered from sight. Maren was glad something had survived the terrible storms.

Ilette dozed most of the afternoon, giving him a respite from amusing her with songs.

"Would you like me to take her for a while?" Gemna asked.

Maren smiled. "Not right now, but thank you for the offer. Maybe when she wakes up."

Trees grew thicker, closer together, bringing cooling shade. The woods smelled of mold and fallen leaves. In a few sheltered gullies, little clumps of snow still sheltered beneath stone overhangs. Light grew dim as the sun descended to the west, and the air turned chilly.

"We'll have to find a place to stay the night," Maren said as he gazed at the fading light. "Are there any villages or farmsteads close by?"

"Not that we could reach before dark," Gemna said.

"Then we need to find a place to camp for the night."

Gemna frowned and stared up the road. "I think there's a clearing just a bit farther, and there's a stream close by."

"I hope there's grass, too. The oats are gone, and the horses need something to eat."

They reached the clearing as the sky darkened to indigo blue and the few feathery clouds turned magenta. The air chilled quickly.

Ilette woke up and patted Maren's cheek. "Eat eat eat," she said. "Eat eat eat."

He chuckled as he reined his horse to a halt and smiled down at Ilette. "Yes, little bird, we'll get you something to eat as soon as possible."

He slid off the horse, holding Ilette protectively, and winced, rubbing his back. "I doubt I'll ever get accustomed to riding," he groaned.

Gemna laughed. "Oh, you'll grow calluses on your backside. Eventually."

Maren groaned again. His legs felt unsteady. "Can you take her for a while?" he asked. "I'll refill our waterskins and walk off some of my stiffness."

Gemna grinned and held out her arms.

Maren slipped the sling off and handed it to Gemna. Ilette kept saying, "Eat eat eat."

"Maybe some bread will keep her happy until we cook some food," Maren said. He searched his saddlebag and took out a piece of twice baked bread. Ilette reached out both hands when she saw Maren holding the bread. She grabbed it and started sucking and chewing on it.

"I'll start a fire," Gemna said as she set Ilette on the ground and cleared a circle of leaves and grass.

Maren took both waterskins and walked down to the stream. He knelt on the bank, wincing; his muscles ached as if bruised. He held the waterskins in the icy cold water until they were full, then sighed. *What I wouldn't give for a hot bath,* he thought, *and a soft bed.*

By the time he returned to the camp, Gemna had staked out the horses in a grassy area north of their camp. She had a good fire going and had set a tripod of branches to hang his pot over the fire. Ilette sat beside her, chewing on the bread. Gemna was slitting one of his blankets with her knife.

"What do you think you're doing?" Maren asked, glaring at her.

"Ilette's wearing only a thin cotton shirt, and she's cold," Gemna said as she continued to cut up the blanket. "I'm making her a dress, some trousers, a cloak, and some boots."

"All right," Maren said slowly, "but why use my blanket? Why not yours?"

"I only have one. You've got more."

"Oh." Maren gazed at her, feeling sheepish. "You're right. I'm sorry. I shouldn't complain. I owe you my life." He knelt and held a waterskin out to her.

Gemna set the blanket and knife down, took the waterskin, stood up, then paused. She smiled as she looked down at him. "I like a man on his knees."

Maren's face felt hot. "I...you..." he sputtered.

Gemna gazed down at him, then nearly doubled over, laughing. "Barg's breath, you should see your face! That's twice I've embarrassed you. No, three times."

"Are you going to make a habit of embarrassing me while we're traveling together?" he asked, frowning.

"Only until you stop blushing." She grinned. "Cook some porridge for Ilette. I'll finish sewing her clothes."

Maren stood, shaking his head. "This journey won't be dull. All right. I'll cook. You sew."

Gemna nodded, still grinning. She went to Maren's horse, opened his saddle bags, and pulled out the extra shirt and diapers for Ilette. Maren just watched, his mouth open.

"Since you're rummaging through my belongings already," he said, "why don't you bring my pot and the sack of meal?"

"Of course, anything to help." Gemna walked back and handed him the pot and sack, then sat down beside Ilette again and started sewing pieces of cloth together.

Maren poured water into the pot and hung it over the fire, then walked back to his horse and unsaddled it. He shouldered his saddlebags & knapsack, then returned to the fire.

He cooked the last of the barley meal. As he fed Ilette, he gazed at her, worried. There was only one more day's worth of dried meat and fruit in the saddlebags. Gemna and he could fast or hunt for food, but Ilette needed milk and porridge... and a loving family. If only he could use his power...but even if he could, he wouldn't in front of Gemna. Wizards didn't work magic in front of humans if at all possible.

He glanced at her. She was sewing Ilette's robe intently. He whispered a grateful prayer that she had agreed to come with him.

Keeping Ilette on his lap, he skewered a piece of hard cheese, toasted it, and spread it on the last two pieces of bread. He gave one piece to Gemna and ate the other one slowly. Gemna handed him the dress she'd finished, took a bite of the bread and cheese, and started on a pair of boots. Maren set his bread down on his knapsack and slipped the dress over Ilette's head.

"That dress should keep her warm," Gemna said as she stitched a double thickness of cloth for the soles of the boots. "But I should make her a shirt to go under it. The blanket is just a bit scratchy. You've got an extra shirt in your sack, haven't you?"

Maren nodded, pulled the other shirt from his knapsack, and handed it to Gemna. She slit the seams and started cutting the fabric.

The sky glittered with stars like diamonds on black velvet. The wind blew cold through the woods. Branches clashed like swordsmen in combat. The fire whipped wildly, its heat dissipating rapidly. Maren dragged a huge log onto the fire. He took his three remaining blankets from his knapsack, wrapped one about his shoulders, and handed the other two to Gemna.

"Use these and your blanket to keep you and Ilette warm tonight. I'll keep the fire going and take the first watch."

Gemna started to protest, but Maren stopped her.

"You watched alone while I was unconscious," he said. "I'll wake you later."

She gave him a tired smile and set aside the sewing. She gathered dry leaves and grass for a bed near the fire, spread one blanket over the leaves, wrapped a blanket around Ilette, and set her on the blanket. Ilette squirmed about, fighting sleep, although she could hardly keep her eyes open. Gemna picked Ilette up and rocked her, but the little girl twisted and resisted lying still.

Seeing Gemna's exasperation, Maren fetched his lute and strummed a lullaby.

Hush-a-bye, my little one,
Rest your weary head.
High above the shining stars
Guard your tiny bed.

Hush-a-bye, lullaby,
Sleep, O baby mine.
Hush-a-bye, lullaby,
Sleep, O baby mine.

Hush-a-bye, my little one,
Close your eyes and sleep.
High above the twinkling stars
Their quiet vigil keep.

Hush-a-bye, lullaby,
Sleep, O baby mine.
Hush-a-bye, lullaby,
Sleep, O baby mine.

Hush-a-bye, my little one,
By your side I'll stay.
High above the gleaming stars
Watch 'til break of day.

Hush-a-bye, lullaby,
Sleep, O baby mine.
Hush-a-bye, lullaby,
Sleep, O baby mine.

Maren continued to strum the lute and hummed the tune softly. Ilette's eyes closed slowly. Soon she was sleeping, nestled in Gemna's arms. Gemna mouthed a silent "thank you", placed Ilette on the blanket, lay down beside the little girl, covered then both with another blanket, and closed her eyes. Maren continued to strum his lute and watched Gemna as she curled protectively around Ilette. There was a gentleness in Gemna's sleeping face that her dark, flashing eyes hid when they were open. A comfortable ache grew in his heart, an emptiness he hadn't noticed before.

The night remained cold and blustery. Clouds covered the stars by the time Maren woke Gemna. "Sh-h-h," he whispered, pointing to Ilette.

Gemna rubbed her eyes, carefully removed the blanket she shared with Ilette, and stood up.

"The fire's burning well," he said. "I've heard nothing but wind and creaking trees, but it's clouded over. I hope it doesn't rain. Wake me in two hours. I want to leave as early as possible. We're low on food, and Ilette can't eat what we have left."

"There's a village little more than a day's ride from here," Gemna said. "If we leave early enough, we can reach it by sunset, I think. And if we reach my home, I know Mother would take in Ilette. She's always wanted another daughter."

Maren lay down beside Ilette. Gemna covered them with the blanket. He watched as she sat nearby, her eyes alert. As he closed his eyes, he felt quiet, peaceful, and more content than he'd felt in many days.

11

Grimmin Slayer galloped along the North Road that wound for miles beneath the towering canopy of Peltik's forest. The sky was nearly invisible overhead. In the shadow of the giant trees, the warm breezes of the flatlands became cool, almost chilly.

Reminds me of Miria, he thought, *so beautiful, so cold. But I know how to warm her.* He smiled to himself, then urged his horse to a canter.

The North Road to Lecida, city of the lords of Peltik, was almost deserted despite its being a caravan crossroads second only to Tironza of Vorlik. As Grimmin neared the city, the road broadened to a wide, stone-paved highway. The late afternoon sky was steel-grey with thick clouds whipped north by a howling wind. The trees drew apart, allowing him to see the walled city. Lecida of the Trees, built amid the creation firs, oldest trees on Baramayan. Each of its four gates was named for the land it faced. Priests of Baygor came to study there at the most prestigious college in the northern lands. Limestone, marble, and wooden buildings housed even the poorest families in comfort and safety.

Grimmin halted at the Beltrin Gate, the south entrance to the city. The granite walls, usually patrolled by squadrons of guards, were nearly abandoned. Huge wreaths of nightshade, black rockroses, and black and silver ribbons hung from the balustrade, proclaiming the death of someone in the royal family. Two gate guards stood arrow-straight, but their eyes were dull with despair. They wore black and silver mourning sashes over their green and gold uniforms.

"Hail, Grimmin," said one of the guards. "What brings you to Lecida? It's early for the caravans to come north."

Grimmin leaned forward and gave them a grin. "I hope to beat my competitors to the best bargains. I'm willing to risk your northern weather for a profit."

The guard glanced about nervously. "I don't know why, considering everything that's happened lately." The guard's shoulder's drooped, and his face became grim. "There's been an epidemic of winter fever, too. Lord Merrik died two months ago, and Lord Merovan, last night. All the house of Peltik is dead."

"And the weather," said the second guard, glancing at the sky. "We've had fierce storms. Whole villages have been destroyed. Parts of Peltik's forests have been uprooted. There's ice and hail and snow one moment, rain the next, rain like I've never seen before. So heavy it gives me a headache. And the winds – they howl like madmen." The guard looked from side to side then leaned closer to Grimmin. "It's unnatural, I tell you. I wouldn't stay in Peltik too long, if I were you. I'm thinking of leaving myself."

"I'm on my way to Drambit, but thanks for your advice." Grimmin nudged his horse through the gatehouse to the city.

Usually, when Grimmin passed through Lecida, the city bustled with people. Merchants, shopkeepers, and artisans plied their wares in the marketplace while buyers bartered or haggled for goods. Children file the streets with laughter. Women called to each other from doorways. Friends met at taverns to share a mug and a song.

Now the streets were nearly deserted as Grimmin rode through the city. The few brave souls he saw had kerchiefs tied over their faces. Fear filled their eyes: fear of winter fever, fear of the killing winds, fear of the unexplained.

Grimmin smiled. His underling Akavar had done well. Terror would make conquest easier.

Winding his way north through the deserted central square to the gatehouse of Castle Lecida, Grimmin noticed the mourning wreaths hanging at the corners of the lintel. Two guards, wearing the black and silver of mourning, stood at the gate. They looked exhausted.

"Grimmin, you come at an ill time," one guard said. "The lord of Peltik is dead as are many of his people."

"So I've been told. I share your grief," Grimmin said, sounding as sincere as he could. "Who rules in Peltik now?"

The guard shook his head. "No one. That is no one of Peltik blood. Miria of Drambit is the closest kin, she being granddaughter to Lord Merrik. Counselor Vairin is regent until Lady Miria can be summoned."

The guards passed Grimmin through the gate after a perfunctory search. Dismounting, he noted how quiet the deserted courtyard was. The door wards were bleary-eyed and pale, as if they'd stood watch for several days straight. Inside the castle itself, weeping echoed through the stone corridors. No one stopped him. No one questioned his presence. He was inconsequential compared to the sorrow that shadowed everyone in Castle Lecida.

He found Akavar scrubbing pots in the kitchen, greasy hair falling over his hawkish face. He straightened, wiped his wet hands on a towel, and brushed his hair from his eyes.

"Hail, Grimmin," Akavar said solemnly. "I've finished my chores for now. Come to my room, and we'll talk." He led the way to a tiny room in the servants' quarters. He lit a small candle and offered Grimmin the only chair.

"Well?" Grimmin said as he sat down.

Akavar's smile came slowly, and his eyes glinted like topaz. "Master, Lord Merovan died of winter fever last night."

Grimmin smiled slowly. "How fortunate for Miria – and for us. And the potion I requested?"

"The moths arrived three days ago, more than I needed." Akavar pointed to the table with the candle. Beside a small box lay a dead moth. Its folded black and white wings formed a grinning skull, which gave the insect the name "Death's Head". Opening the box, he removed a tiny glass vial. "Here it is, master, the potion you asked for. It's undetectable in any liquid. One drop in a barrel causes sleep; two drops will kill. How do you wish to use it?"

Grimmin studied the vial of clear liquid. "I'll discuss that later. Stay here until my wagons and an army of mercenaries arrive within the week. Leave with them for Drambit where I'll be waiting. I'll stay at the Silver Wood Inn tonight if you need me, but I'll be leaving at dawn." Grimmin rose to leave, then turned back to Akavar. "Remember, I'll be the most powerful Sorcerer of all if my plan succeeds. You'll share in my power if you are loyal and obedient."

A look edging close to lust lit Akavar's face. "Thank you, master," he said and bowed.

Grimmin left the distiller of potions and poisons, and made his way to the Silver Wood Inn. He was tired, more tired than he wanted to admit. Paying for a room and stabling for his horse, he ate a quick supper, then went to his room. All night long Miria filled his dreams.

The next morning Grimmin left Lecida through the Hargrim Gate. The ancient trees stood like giant guardians of the road, but several lay twisted and broken on the roadside, reminders of Logallah of the Wind's passing. He rode west all day, through the towering trees of Peltik to the rolling meadows and pastures of Hargrim. Logallah had flooded valleys and shattered cottages. By nightfall, he reached Raiga, stark city of Hargrim's lords. Refugees from the wild storms crowded into the city's environs, tents and blankets covering every gutter and alley. Grimmin stopped for the night, then continued toward Drambit and Abasette Castle.

Drambit was a marginally productive land. After Logallah's passing it was desolate. Many trees were uprooted. Farms were flooded. Livestock was drowned.

Cottages were flattened; barns, destroyed. However, the road was easily traversable, and that was all Grimmin concerned himself with.

The sun was westering when Grimmin sighted the granite towers of Abasette Castle. He smiled to himself, savoring the image of Miria and the power he'd command

Miria stared hopelessly from the tower window of the castle. Icy tears streaked her pallid cheeks then stained her black velvet dress. The tower room was cold. She shivered and hugged her furred cloak about her to warm her arms. Nothing could warm the cold in her heart. She caressed the black schorl and silver ring on her right hand—the ring of Drambini lords, her father's ring. Four months ago Captain Callas had returned with her father's body and this ring, and brought news that her father, Lord Paxell, had died by Bren's hand. She'd always envied and desired her father's power, but she'd loved him fiercely.

For the first few weeks after Callas' return, she'd wept and cursed Bren's name incessantly, prayed all manner of evil upon him, but there was nothing she could do. The Drambini army had been depleted. She had a handful of loyal followers but no way to seek revenge.

Cold anger spilled tears from her red-rimmed eyes. "Bren, you'll pay for Father's murder, I swear. Somehow – somehow, I'll make you pay. I want you to suffer, to feel the hurt you've caused me. I want to watch you bleed to death, but it wouldn't be enough. No — no, it'd never be enough for killing Father. Damn you, Bren! How could you do it? How could you kill him?"

"Your hatred runs deep," a quiet voice said.

Startled, she whirled toward the doorway. Grimmin stood there, cloaked, a hood shadowing his face. He sauntered toward her until he was only a hand width away. He pushed his hood back. Blue eyes stared down at her with such intensity, she retreated until her back pressed against a stone wall. It felt warm compared to his gaze.

"What do you want, Grimmin?" she asked, trying to hide the fear that made her shudder.

His voice was unusually gentle. "Why, Lady Miria, I've come to give you what you want more than anything else: power and revenge.

Miria looked deep into his ice-blue eyes. "Power?" she whispered. "What power?"

He leaned closer, and his eyes narrowed. "Power beyond your dreams. Power that your father only glimpsed. Power to control wind and rain, to make fields grow and trees bear fruit. Power to build and destroy, to heal — and to kill. Power to crush a life as easily as one crushes a worm." He closed his hand slowly into a tight fist.

Miria's eyes widened, and her heart beat faster. "Power to avenge Father's death?"

"Is that what you want?" he asked softly. "Is that your heart's desire?"

She thought of Bren, and rage tightened her chest. "Yes," she whispered. "I would sell my soul to avenge Father's death."

"I have that power, Miria."

"Then give it to me!" she said.

"I'll give you more power than you've dared dream of," he said as his hand brushed her cheek, "but will you pay my price?"

Miria jerked away from his touch. "And what's your price?"

"It's small." Grimmin caressed her shoulder and smiled hungrily. "Marry me."

"Never!" Miria shrugged his hand off, shivering.

He cupped her round chin in his hand. "Never is a long time to wait for vengeance, Miria. I'm offering you unlimited power, command of armies, the rule of at least two lands, and your father's murderer. I'm asking so little in return." He smiled at her. "After all, I'm reasonably handsome, and I can be quite gracious if I choose." Bending closer, he continued in a deep, lusty voice. "And I can stir a fire in you and give you pleasure like you have never known." He released her chin. "You could do much worse. You might have married Bren."

Miria felt cold sweat trickling down her back. Grimmin had always frightened her. "Guards!" she shouted.

"They can't hear you," he said softly. "No one can hear what we say in this room." He held up his bare left hand, spoke a strange word, and showed her what no human had ever seen and lived: his ring, ebony carved like a ravening hound, the Hound of Darkness, Barsallin.

Miria gasped, terror draining the warmth from her body. Tales told to her in childhood by her old nursemaid sprang to mind, tales of shadows to frighten a disobedient child. One word blurted from her lips. "Sorcerer!"

Grimmin nodded. "Yes, Miria, and I have the power you want so desperately."

Jerking her belt dagger from its sheath, Miria drove it toward his chest, fear steadying her hand.

Grimmin was quicker. With a sly smile, he clenched her wrist in a steely grip. "Do you think that tiny weapon could harm me? You know what I am, but you don't understand what it means. I am Grimmin Slayer of the Inner Circle, one of the most powerful of all the Sorcerers."

Murmuring strange syllables, Grimmin stared at the dagger. It began to glow red, orange, yellow, almost white. Waves of unbearable heat surged up her arm.

"Drop it," Grimmin said, his brow furrowed. "Drop it now. Let it go! Quickly!" His eyes widened and filled with fear. "Please! Let it go!"

Miria screamed and dropped the dagger to the floor. Blisters stretched across her palm. Cradling her hand, she sagged against the wall and cried in agony.

"I'm so sorry. I didn't want to harm you," Grimmin said, holding her hand gently. "Why didn't you listen to me? Why didn't you let it go?"

Grimmin pressed his hand over hers. Pain, deeper and sharper than any she'd ever known before, stabbed her hand as blisters broke and his palm touched raw flesh. Then suddenly, the pain was gone, barely remembered. Miria pulled her hand away. It was healed, unscarred. She looked up at Grimmin, more afraid than ever. "How did you do this?" she asked, amazed.

"I have many powers, Miria." His eyes became wide with desire. He pressed close to her and restrained her hands when she tried to escape. "I'm a Sorcerer, but the blood of Sorcerers flows through your veins as well. We are so alike. We want a great deal. And what I want, he paused, "is you, Miria."

Frightened, Miria struggled as Grimmin kissed her neck. "No!"

"Accept me, pay my price, let me share your bed," he whispered and kissed her neck again, "and I'll give you everything you desire. Everything. Anything." He released her hands and touched her cheek with a tenderness that surprised her.

Miria gazed at him, bewildered. "Why?" she asked, trembling. "Why do you want *me*?"

"Why?" He stared straight into her eyes. "Because you are as strong as the hardest steel and as beautiful as the mountains at sunset. You can be cold as the deepest winter, but I feel a passion in you that could burst into flame. Your anger burns like a blacksmith's forge. So does mine. I'll make you a queen, if only you'll take me as your consort. Together, Miria, we can conquer all the northern lands." Slowly, he leaned toward her.

He's going to kiss me, she thought, panic freezing her. For a moment she stiffened, then his lips touched hers lightly, and she felt as if liquid fire ran through her body. She felt bathed in warmth and more alive than she had since before her father's death. Startled by the sensation, she kissed him back until she was breathless. He slid his arms around her and held her to his chest. She wrapped her arms around him and felt his heart pounding. Desire bloomed in her, a hunger she'd never felt before. Not when Bren had kissed her. Not when Bren's friend Malbar had stolen a kiss.

She opened her eyes and gazed deep into Grimmin's blue eyes. *Can I trust him?* she wondered, shivering with delight and fear. "I want Bren to suffer," she said, "and to keep on suffering until he takes his last breath. I want to hear him scream in agony, and I want him to know that I am the cause of his pain, just as he is the cause of my pain. Can you promise me that?"

"Yes," he said softly.

"You swear you'll give me the power to destroy Bren?"

"Yes," he said, caressing her hair, "I swear by the Hound of Darkness."

She paused. "Then, yes, I'll marry you," she said.

With a shout, he swept her off her feet and whirled around with her in his arms until she was dizzy. He set her on her feet again and kissed her passionately hard, and she kissed him back just as passionately.

Grimmin took off his ebony ring and placed it on her left hand. "I am your husband, body and soul, from this day forth until the Hound of Darkness parts us. All that I am, all that I have, I give to you. *Tasrin.*"

Miria gazed at the ring, then removed her ring, the black schorl and silver ring of the Drambini lords, her father's ring, and placed it on Grimmin's left hand. "I am your wife, body and soul, from this day forth until the Hound of Darkness parts us. All that I am, all that I have, I give to you." She frowned, trying to remember the last word he said.

"*Tasrin,*" Grimmin said.

"*Tasrin?*"

He nodded. "It means 'so be it' or 'let it be so.'"

"*Tasrin,*" she said. "Let it be so now and forever."

He swept her into his arms as if she were light as a feather.

Excitement tinged with apprehension pounded in her chest. Miria rested her head on Grimmin's shoulder. *What am I doing?* she wondered. *I've given myself to a Sorcerer, whose soul is as dark as new moon shadows.* But no man ever made her feel so vital, so alive, so... aroused with such a slight touch of his hand, his lips. She wanted him. The idea startled and terrified her, but she still wanted him. She glanced up at his face. *But he is beautiful,* she thought, *very beautiful.*

Grimmin gazed down at her and smiled warmly, tenderly, and Miria's heart fluttered. His eyes were like sapphires set in a lean boyish face framed by golden curls. *So very beautiful,* she thought.

"We must keep our marriage secret," Grimmin said.

"Why?"

"Because it's the only way my plan to destroy Bren will work."

"I can't tell anyone? Not even Captain Callas?"

"No, not yet. Later we can tell him and everyone else. Then we'll have a formal wedding and nuptial celebration grander than has ever been seen in the northern lands."

"But if you come to my chambers," she whispered, "everyone in the castle will know, and the word will spread everywhere."

Grimmin smiled and slowly drew his forefinger lightly down her cheek to her chin. "No one sees me unless I wish it. Go to your chamber. No one will see me come to you, I promise. I will be there soon." He kissed her again, then vanished like mist in the morning sunlight.

Miria's legs felt shaky, and her heart danced in her chest. She had to lean against the nearest wall, she felt so dizzy and lightheaded and exhilarated. She'd married a Sorcerer! And now she would have the power to avenge her father's death!

Slowly, she recovered her composure and began walking down the spiral stairs past the open door of Captain Callas' office. He stood and bowed.

"My Lady, is there anything I can do for you?" he asked, concern in his voice. "You look a bit flushed, feverish."

"No, I'm a little fatigued," she said. "I'm going to my chamber to rest."

Callas bowed again, then sat back down at his desk.

Miria descended the stairs to the Audience Hall and crossed the stone floor to the hallway to her chamber, the one where she'd been born and where her mother had died.

A maid stirred a roaring blaze in the open hearth to drive away the damp cold. She turned as Miria entered and bowed. "My Lady."

"I wish to rest," Miria said. "Leave me."

The maid hesitated a moment, then bowed. "Yes, My Lady." She hurried toward the door and closed it behind her as she left.

As soon as the door closed, Grimmin appeared. He whispered some strange words her in his arms, and kissed her firmly, then he swept her into his arms, set her on the bed, and slipped the fur cloak from her shoulders.

Miria lay back against the satin pillows heaped at the head of her bed. Grimmin stretched out beside her and caressed her face, her throat, and she trembled.

"What are you thinking?" he asked.

"I'm frightened," she whispered.

"Don't be," he said as he kissed her tenderly. "You never have to be afraid of me." He kissed her again.

Fire flowed through her until she thought she would burst into flames. Outside the wind moaned like a woman insane with grief, wild and unrestrained, her voice a hollow scream of madness. A wintry storm beat against the castle walls, snow and ice covering the windows. But inside Miria's room she was warm and content. She gazed up at Grimmin and smiled, putting her arms around him. "I'm not afraid of anything."

Grimmin laughed and took his promised payment.

12

The next morning Maren made a meager breakfast using the last of the smoked meat to cook broth for Ilette. Gemna shared the last of her jerky with Maren, though none of them had enough to satisfy their hunger.

"We have to find a village or farm soon," Maren said quietly to Gemna as he washed out his pot. "Ilette needs food."

"I know." Gemna turned toward the little girl playing with her rag doll. "And she's running out of diapers. I need to wash and dry clothes. If we ride hard today, I think we might reach the village of Delwick. Surely we'll find food there. Tonight, maybe we can sleep in the Dancing Maid Inn in a warm room."

"In a real bed." Maren stretched his back to work out the stiffness. "I hope the horses can make it. All they've had is a bit of grass for a couple of days."

Gemna dressed Ilette in the clothes she'd made. "At least you'll be warm now, kidling," she said as she put a cap on Ilette's head and tied a bow under her chin.

"Thank you, Gemna," Maren said, smiling at Ilette. She did look warm in her new clothes and cloth boots. "You've saved both Ilette and me. We owe you our lives."

Gemna blushed and was silent for a while. "I *am* your bodyguard," she said quietly.

"You're more than that," Maren said, gazing steadily at her. "Much more."

She smiled but said nothing.

Maren nodded and dumped the water from his pot onto the last of the embers, stirred the ashes with a stick, and poured more water from his waterskin onto the ashes. "I better refill this while I can," he said, holding the waterskin up.

Gemna nodded and began rolling up blankets. "I'll have everything packed by the time you get back."

He walked quickly down to the stream, filled the waterskin, and hurried back to the camp. Gemna had all their belongings packed and tied to the saddles. She gave Maren the sling, which he slipped over his head. He picked up Ilette.

"Ready for another ride?" he said, swinging Ilette high above his head. She giggled. He slid her into the sling and climbed carefully onto his horse.

"You're very good with her," Gemna said as she gazed at Maren. "You'd make a wonderful father."

Maren looked down at Ilette. "Who wouldn't be good to her? She's just a dearling." He touched the little girl's nose and made a funny face at her. She laughed. "How could anyone not care for her?"

Gemna climbed on her horse. "But you have a gentleness that few men I know have. Most men take care of their children and love them, but you — I can tell you would give your life for her. And she's not even your family."

He looked at Gemna curiously. "Should that make a difference?"

Gemna considered him for a few moments. "No. It shouldn't."

He gazed down at Ilette, who nestled close to him. "Let's go," he said. "We have a long ride today."

They rode at a trot, stopping occasionally to let the horses drink and eat a bit of the sparse grass they found. Clouds rolled in from the south and drenched them with a cold rain about midday. Maren pulled his cloak around Ilette to keep her as dry as possible. The road became muddy, sucking at the horses hooves and slowing them to a walk. Maren shivered, trying to keep warm, but the air and rain were so cold, his breath was like fog.

"We won't make Delwick at this rate," Gemna said, water running off her hood.

"We have to try," Maren said, worried. "We have to find shelter and food for Ilette, and soon."

"There's a farmstead not too far ahead," Gemna said. "Maybe we could spend the night there. I doubt we could reach any other place today, especially if this rain keeps up."

Ilette tugged at Maren's shirt, babbling "eat" over and over. "We'll eat soon, I promise," he said, stroking her cheek.

Her eyes blinked back tears, and her lips trembled. *What can I do?* he thought. *What can I give her? None of my herbs will help. I need to find something for her.*

He glanced at Gemna and read worry and frustration in her face. Her hand clenched the reins convulsively. "Let me take her for a while," she said.

Maren shook his head, splashing water from his hood. "You're our bodyguard, remember. You can't fight very well with a baby strapped to you. We'll find food for her somehow."

Gemna nodded, then she looked beyond him to the side of the road. Her face brightened, and she smiled. "We may not have food, but I've found something that will help." She halted her horse, jumped from its back, and ran to a sapling growing beside the road.

"What?" Maren called to her as he reined his horse to a stop. "What did you find?"

Kneeling in the mud, Gemna took out her knife and began digging mud away from the base of the tree. "Something I haven't thought of in years, something from my childhood. I didn't know it grew this far south." Rain poured down, but she kept digging and scooping mud from the roots. "My brothers and I used to pick tyneberries near the woods. Sometimes we got hungry and ate some of the berries, but not too many or Mother would be angry." She pushed against the sapling's trunk, and it started to give. She dug away more mud around the other side. "But we found something to satisfy us without devouring all the berries we picked."

She pushed against the sapling. There was a sucking, cracking sound. She dug more mud and pushed the sapling again. This time the tree cracked and gave way, its muddy roots popping from the earth, and she fell face down on the muddy ground. Drenched and covered in mud, she laughed and tried to wipe the mud from her face but merely smeared the mud worse. She cut off the side roots, nearly the thickness of her little finger, and washed them clean in the rain. The roots were light reddish-orange with a papery bark. She held one out to Maren. "Honeyroot," she said. "We sucked on it, chewed on it, and loved it. Maybe it will satisfy Ilette long enough to find some real food."

Maren took the root and sniffed it. It had a slightly spicy and fruity scent. He broke off a piece, stuck it in his mouth, and chewed it for a bit. It was porous, soft, and sweet, almost like an apple pie with a hint of cinnamon. He smiled at Gemna. "This is good. I hope she likes it."

"I hope so, too," Gemna said, catching rain in her cupped hands and splashing it on her face to wash off the mud.

Maren handed the root to Ilette, and she stuffed it in her mouth, sucking and chewing on it with her few teeth. Her eyes widened. She pulled it out and looked at it, then stuck it back in her mouth and chewed on it happily.

Looking at Gemna, Maren smiled. "Saying thank you again doesn't seem enough, but thank you. You're our savior."

Gemna laughed. "Maybe, but right now I'd sell you both for a hot bath, dry clothes, and a warm bed."

"Right now, I might sell myself for a hot bath," Maren said.

Grinning, Gemna tried to rub some of the mud from her shirt and pants, but gave up. She scrubbed at her hands until the only mud left was under her fingernails. She mounted her horse. "Come on. I think we can make that farmstead before nightfall."

She clapped her legs against her horse's side and took off at as fast a walk at the horse could manage on the muddy road.

Maren urged his horse to catch up with her, softly singing the "Star Lullaby" while Ilette chewed on the honeyroot. Slowly, the little girl closed her eyes and slept.

The rain finally ended, and the back edge of the clouds blew over as the sun was nearly touching the western trees. The air seemed warmer. Long shadows stretched across the road, turning the world to charcoal and crimson. Squinting, Maren spotted the tall white roof of a red barn up ahead on the eastern side of the road, nearly hidden by the trees. *Thank Baygor, we made it,* he thought. As Maren rounded a slight bend to the right, he saw the trees ended and wide flat fields stretched to the east, and he gasped.

The barn had a few boards missing from the roof and one window was broken out, but the barn was still standing. Beside the barn were the shattered remains of a large farmhouse. Timbers were cracked and scattered across a wide yard and garden. In front of the house were eight mounds covered with stones. Beside one mound knelt an old woman, her white hair straggling around her sun-browned face. She looked work-hardened and thin. Her dark grey dress was muddy and unkempt. A shovel lay on the ground beside her. Hugging a small crock to herself and rocking back and forth, she sobbed quietly. She didn't seem to notice Maren and Gemna as they rode up and dismounted.

Maren and Gemna dismounted quickly. Taking off the sling, Maren handed Ilette to Gemna and hurried to the old woman's side. "Let me help you," he said, lifting her to her feet.

"No one helped me dig the graves," she whispered in a dazed voice as she clutched the crock to her bony chest. "I buried them myself. My husband, my two sons, my two daughters-in-law, and my three grandchildren, all dead, all were killed by the wind." Her wild grey eyes stared up at the sky. "I was in the barn when the storm came. The Witch of the Winds killed them all. But I was left to bury them, all my family. My grandchildren, gone. No one left but me. No one but me." Her legs collapsed.

Maren scooped her slight body in his arms and carried her past a well and to the barn. Inside was cool, dry, and dark, and smelled of straw and dust and dung. Near the front of the barn he found a stall with clean straw. "Gemna, I need a blanket!" he called.

Gemna came through the wide barn door, leading the two horses, the sling over her shoulder. She put her index finger to her lips and said, "Sh-h-h. You'll wake Ilette."

She let the reins drop, took Maren's knapsack from his saddle, pulled two blankets from the knapsack, and carried the blankets and knapsack to Maren. Using her foot to scoot some straw into a small heap, she spread one blanket over the straw and cautiously placed the sleeping girl on the bed, then spread the other blanket nearby. "I'll stable the horses," she said quietly as she picked up the reins and led the horses farther into the barn.

Maren placed the old woman on the blanket, knelt beside her, pried the crock from her hands, and set it on the dirt floor beside him. He felt her forehead for fever, but she felt cool.

Tears streaked the old woman's sunken cheeks. "She killed them. She killed them all. The Witch of the Winds. I heard her screaming in the storm."

The Witch of the Wind? A memory stirred deep in Maren's mind, hovering just beyond his grasp. He'd heard of her, somewhere. He knew it. A story, long ago, about a woman...a woman changed into wind.

Suddenly, pain shot through his head. He pressed his hands hard against his temples and bent over until his forehead almost touched the dirt floor. His stomach lurched, but he gritted his teeth and forced himself not to vomit.

"At least it's warm and dry in here," Gemna said as she came toward the stall. "Maren! What's wrong?" Gemna asked anxiously, hand on her sword as she glanced around the barn. "Are you hurt? Is Ilette all right?"

He couldn't talk, the pain in his head was so intense.

"Barg's breath! You're as pale as a full moon!" Gemna said. "Are you ill?" She felt his forehead. "Warm but not hot."

He shook his head, panting, and massaged his temples. "I'm tired and chilled," he gasped.

"You don't just look tired. You look like you're in pain."

"I'll be all right," he said.

She got down on one knee and stared at him, her eyes wide. "I don't believe you," she said.

"I can't help that," he said, still shaky.

"At least you didn't wake Ilette," she said as she glanced over at the little girl. Gemna put her arm around Maren. "You're soaking wet. You need to get out of those clothes and into some dry ones, if you have any. I don't want you coming down with a fever." She took Maren's knapsack and pulled out some dry clothes. Kneeling beside him, she untied his cloak and started to take off his jacket.

"Stop, please," he said weakly. "I can do this myself." He clutched the front of his jacket, his face hot with embarrassment. "Why are you always trying to take my clothes off?"

"Habit," she said, smiling innocently.

"And you're just as wet as I am."

She laughed. "Yes, and I'm going to get out of my clothes as soon as I get a fire going. And when Ilette wakes up, I'll get her out of her wet things, too." She stood, grabbed her pack, and started to go farther into the barn.

"Stay back there until I say it's all right," Maren said, pulling off his jacket.

Gemna looked over her shoulder and grinned. "Of course. I wouldn't want to embarrass you again." She disappeared into the darkening recesses of the barn.

Still shaking, Maren tucked the blanket around the old woman. She shuddered and stared unblinkingly at the barn's ceiling. "Gemna," Maren called, "can you build the fire quickly? I need to brew some medicine as soon as possible."

"I will when I can," she called from one of the stalls.

The pain in his head finally disappeared, and he felt better, although his stomach still churned and he was slightly dizzy. Maren took his knapsack to the next stall, stripped out of his wet clothes, shivering in the cool air, and tugged on his dry ones. He hung his wet things over the stable railing and wrapped a blanket around his shoulder. "You can come back now," he called.

She came back to the center of the barn, carrying a rake, and cleared a large circle down to the dirt floor. "There. Now to find wood." She gazed out the door. "I'll be back shortly." She strode from the barn.

He rummaged through his pack until he found his herbs. He measured out roborant, callum bark, and willow bark in a cup, then took out his pot. He gazed at the old woman. *The Witch of the Winds,* he thought. *There's Sorcery in this. I know it!* Pain edged close again. Someone didn't want him to remember. *I have to find a way to break the binding!*

Maren looked up as Gemna came back with an armload of wood, which she dumped on the spot she'd raked. Gathering handfuls of straw, she placed them around the wood, then fetched her tinderbox. After several tries, she struck a spark that caught on the straw. The straw burned quickly, but the wet wood didn't want to burn well. She set up a tripod of poles over the fire. She frowned. "I can't keep feeding straw into the fire to keep it from going out."

"Do you have any more oil?" Maren asked, walking toward her with his pot. "That would keep the wood burning until it dries out." He filled the pot from the waterskin and hung it over the guttering flames, which suddenly went out.

Gemna sighed. "No, but maybe I can find some. And I have to find something to cover that broken window."

She ran to the back of the barn, then came back a short time later. Grinning, she held up a bottle of dark yellow oil and a punched tin lantern. "This should help with the fire." She handed him the oil. "And we can use the lantern for light tonight. I found sacks of oats for the horses, a small kettle, a keg of wine, and a wagon. I wonder where the horses are. And I found a root cellar just outside the barn. There's plenty of food for us and Ilette, too!"

"Wait," Maren said, holding up his hands, "none of those things belong to us. We can't just take them!"

The old woman stirred just then and opened her pale blue eyes. "Take what you will," she said in a crackly voice, staring at Maren. "My family and I have no use for any of it now. No use. No use." She closed her eyes again and seemed to sleep.

"All right, Gemna," Maren said, "take what we need but no more than that."

Gemna nodded and went toward the back of the barn.

Maren poured some of the oil on the wet wood, put a small heap of straw on the wood, and struck a spark. The straw burned fast but long enough for the oil to catch fire. At first the wood smoked, but soon it was covered with yellow flames. Maren poured water into his kettle and added callum bark and roborant.

Just as the potion began to boil, Gemna came running back, carrying something in her hands.

"What's wrong?" he asked anxiously.

"Nothing," she said quietly, showing him a ham wrapped in netting and tied with a rope. "We'll eat well tonight!"

"Where did you find that?" Maren asked as he suddenly realized how empty his stomach felt.

"I went up in the loft to pitch down some hay for the cow—"

"What cow?"

"The one in the stall by the back of the barn, and I found this ham hanging in the rafters." She scanned the area, then stopped beneath a cross beam at the entrance to one of the front stalls. "This will do." She flung the rope over the cross beam, and retied the rope so the ham hung at chest level. "Can you milk a cow?"

Maren stared at her. "I don't think so. Why?"

Gemna gave him a pained look. "I was afraid you'd say that."

"Can't you milk a cow?"

"Unfortunately, yes. I always milked the cows at home, and I hated that chore. I think that's why I became a mercenary. But I don't really mind it right now. At least we have milk for Ilette."

Maren smiled to himself as he watched Gemna search for a bucket and milking stool. Not long afterwards, he heard the cow lowing and Gemna's voice soothing the animal.

Ilette woke up just as Gemna returned with a bucket of fresh warm milk. She held a cup while Ilette drank the warm milk. Part of it sloshed and dribbled down the little girl's chin, but she swallowed most of it. "That's good, isn't it, dearling?" Gemna said as she wiped the milk from Ilette's chin.

Ilette clutched at the empty cup. "Eat eat eat," she said.

"There's plenty more." Gemna refilled the cup and held it for the little girl. Ilette gulped the milk down.

Maren took the kettle of potion from the tripod. A sweet, healing scent mingled with the odor of straw and dirt. Cooling a cup of medicine, he knelt beside the old woman, propped her up, and held the cup to her colorless lips. "Drink this," he said. "It will strengthen you and make you well."

"Why?" she asked, not looking at him. "What is there to live for now? I've lost everyone I loved."

"Please," he said, "drink a little. You'll feel better."

She sipped the tea slowly, but her face remained empty, her eyes vacant. When she finished the tea, she closed her eyes and fell asleep. Maren placed her back on the straw and covered her with the blanket, then felt her forehead. It was clammy and cold. "At least she doesn't have a fever," he murmured. He placed his hand on the side of her neck and felt her pulse. It was weak, barely detectable, and her breathing was much too shallow and slow. The tea should strengthen her, but he was worried. The woman had no will to live. All he could do was keep giving her the tea and pray she would get better.

"I'll see what else I can find here," Gemna said as she stood up and walked toward their mounts. "You watch Ilette. I'll come back with some food, and you can cook us a feast." She grinned and wheeled toward the back of the barn.

Ilette reached for the bucket of milk. Maren pulled her back quickly.

"All you had to do was ask, kidling," he said, smiling. He dipped another cupful, set Ilette on his lap, and held the cup while she drank. "I know, you're hungry. We'll eat soon."

When she finished the milk, he pulled her rag doll from his jacket pocket, and rocked her and sang while she played with the toy. He watched as Gemna climbed a ladder to the hay loft and heaved mounds of hay down for the animals.

"I never thought I'd be pitching hay again," she called down to Maren, her voice echoing through the barn. "Father would have a good chuckle if he could see me." She thrust the pitchfork keep into the pile of hay, then wiped sweat from her forehead. She started climbing down the ladder that creaked with each rung she stepped on.

Maren watched with worried eyes as she reached the halfway point. "Be careful! That ladder doesn't sound too sturdy."

She looked over at him and grinned. "I always am." She skipped rungs and jumped the last few feet to the ground. She studied the ham for a moment, then glanced at the fire. "I need flat griddle or frying pan," she said. "Maybe I can find something in the house."

"It looks very unstable," Maren said as he gazed into the growing shadows toward the ruins of the farmhouse. "Be very careful. You're the only bodyguard I have."

She smiled and walked out into the red-orange sunset. She returned with an iron griddle, a large cast iron pot and lid, and a large wooden bowl and wooden dishes and some spoons. "I found all kinds of things we can use," she said. "I even spotted some clothes that Ilette could probably wear. Couldn't carry everything back at once, though."

Going outside again, she came back with four large rocks. She put three rocks beside the fire to form the sides of a square, then raked in some embers, and placed the last rock down to enclose the square. Setting the griddle on the rocks, she took out her knife, cut a slice of meat from the hambone, and placed the slice on the griddle. Soon the meat was crackling and sputtering. She put the ham on a wooden plate and handed it to Maren. "Eat."

"Later. I need to check on the woman."

"Now!"

Maren took the meat and studied her with an annoyed frown. "You're very forceful at times."

She grinned at him. "So I've been told. I'll be back in a bit."

Maren's eyes lingered on her as she walked away. Finally, he turned his attention back to Ilette. He laughed as she kissed her doll, then pounded it against the blanket, giggling.

Gemna returned with bag of tubers and squash, and a sack of flour. She placed the tubers around the fire, and peeled the squash into the kettle, added a bit of water, took Maren's pot from the tripod, and put the kettle over the fire. She set the pot of medicine beside Maren, then paused. "What's in the crock the old woman was holding?

Maren shrugged. "I didn't look."

Gemna walked to the stall, pried the lid off the crock, and peeked inside. "Yeast! Now I can make some real bread." She hurried back to the fire and knelt beside her little stove. Using the wooden bowl, she mixed some flour with a little salt from her pack, added yeast and enough milk to form a stiff dough, then set it just close enough to the fire to let it rise for a bit. "I'm going back to the house while it's still light enough to see."

Maren watched her walk outside. *She's amazing,* he thought. *She can fight as well as any man.* He chuckled. *Better than me. And yet she can do all sorts of domestic chores. What would Ilette do without her? What would I do without her?* He paused. *Could I do without her? Would I want to?* The thought surprised him, his heart beating a bit faster.

She came back with two gowns, three dresses, a coat, and several diapers, all covered with debris. Shaking the garments free of debris, she held them up to the firelight and nodded. "Now I can change Ilette's clothes," she said, "and I can wash the others. Yours and mine, too. Now if I string a rope close to the fire, I can hang the clothes on the line. Hopefully, they'll be dry by morning."

"And you're going to wash clothes in what?" Maren asked, smiling.

"In a small wooden tub I spotted back by the cow's stall. Here, let me have Ilette."

She sat down beside Maren and held out her arms. He handed the little girl to Gemna. She stripped off Ilette's damp clothes and wet diaper, then quickly pulled on the dry clothes. "There, that feels better, doesn't it, dearling?"

Gemna handed Ilette back to Maren, then said, "Now I'm going to change my clothes." She held up her hand. "Don't worry. I'll change in one of the other stalls," she said, with a cat grin. "You know, for someone who has traveled and has seen so much of the world, you are very provincial in some ways." Standing, she swooped down to pick up her pack and her waterskin, and headed to one of the other stalls.

When she came back, carrying a small wooden tub and a length of rope, she looked scrubbed clean and dressed in clean brown pants and white shirt with full sleeves. She set the tub beside the fire, then strung the rope from the crossbeam where she'd hung the ham to a crossbeam on the other side of the fire.

"There. That should do." She turned to Maren. "How about some food?"

"Yes!" he said. "I'm starving!"

She laughed.

Maren rose, picked up the pot of medicine, and went to check on the old woman. She was still sleeping. Her forehead was beaded with cold sweat, and her skin was pasty white. He felt her wrist. Her pulse was barely perceptible. He poured a cup of medicine and propped her up, but she didn't wake up. "Please, you have to try," he said. He shook her. She never stirred. "Please, wake up. Let me help you!" he said, but she didn't open her eyes. He laid her back down, shuffled back to the fire, and sat down beside Gemna.

She knelt beside her makeshift stove. She pinched off a piece of dough the size of an egg, patted it into a circle, and laid it on the hot griddle. The dough bubbled up, and she turned it over. Soon, the aroma of hot bread filled the barn. She kept making rounds until all the dough was gone.

Gemna put a baked tuber, a spoonful of cooked squash, and a bread round on each of two plates. Filling Maren's cup with wine from a barrel she brought from the root cellar, she held the cup and plate out to him. "Here. I can watch the woman."

"She's sleeping, and I fear she won't wake again." Maren sniffed the aroma and licked his lips. "You eat, too. I'll feed Ilette part of mine."

Calling Ilette to his lap, he took a bite of the bread. It was hot and crusty but tender inside. As Gemna sat down beside him with her plate, he gazed at her with appreciation. "You'll make someone a wonderful wife."

"Hah! Not very likely. I've not met the man I'd give up my mercenary life for."

Maren smiled at her.

She rolled her eyes. "Just because I can cook and milk a cow, that doesn't mean I want to spend the rest of my life doing housework. I like my freedom, and I intend to keep it."

Maren laughed. "I've no intention of chaining you to a stove. Don't you know a compliment when you hear one?"

"Then I thank you for the compliment," she said.

Using the wooden spoon Gemna had carved, Maren scooped some mashed squash and fed it to Ilette. She ate almost half his portion and drank another cup of milk. When she'd eaten her fill, she pressed against him, a contented smile on her tiny face.

Looking up with trusting eyes, she chattered, "Da-da-da-da-da-da..."

Gemna gazed at him tenderly, a gentle smile on her face. "You really would make a good father," she said. "You should have lots of children."

Gemna's words startled him. He held Ilette close and kissed her forehead. Dada -- he'd never been called that. The sound touched his heart, but was bitter-sweet. "You should've been my baby," he whispered, "mine and Briella's."

Gemna looked at him sharply. Slowly, she turned away and finished her food without another word.

Singing the "Star Lullaby," Maren rocked Ilette. Soon, Ilette slept in his arms, but he kept humming and rocking her. He watched Gemna as she washed out the kettle, filled it with water, set it over the fire, and fetched a cake of soap from her pack. She shaved curls of soap into the kettle, then gathered Ilette's dirty clothes beside the wooden tub. Soon the scent of oranges and spices mingled with the musty odor of the barn. Gemna poured the hot soapy water into the tub and mixed in cold water. She washed Ilette's clothes, wrung them out, and set them on a wooden plate. Dumping the soapy water out the barn door, she refilled the tub with clean water, rinsed the clothes, and hung them over the rope.

Maren whispered, "Gemna, can you straighten her bed so I can lay her down?"

Gemna nodded. She knelt on the dirt floor and smoothed the blanket over Ilette's straw bed.

Kneeling opposite Gemna, Maren gently placed Ilette on the bed and folded half the blanket over her. He brushed Ilette's dark hair from her face and stared at her. A melancholy smile darkened his face, and regret filled his heart as he caressed her cheek. "You know, she looks like you, Gemna," he said softly. "Same eyes and hair, same complexion. She could be your daughter." He looked up at Gemna. "You'd make a good mother," he said softly.

Gemna gazed at Ilette and touched her cheek. "Someday, maybe," she said. She gazed straight at Maren for a moment, then quickly lowered her eyes.

"We need to add some wood to the fire," he said, standing. "It's getting chilly. I'll get more wood. Can you do something about covering that broken window?"

"I'll find some way to seal it." Gemna glanced out the barn door. "The wood is stacked beside the barn to the right. It's almost dark. Do you want the lantern?"

"No, I can find my way there and back."

He strode from the barn. Stars shone overhead in the deep twilight as he edged around the side until he found stacked wood. Taking several cords from the top of the pile and dropping them on the ground, he took cords from the next layer that weren't so wet. Loading his arms, he trudged back to the barn door.

Gemna had the window frame on her lap and was slipping an empty feed sack over it. "I need some help," she said.

"I'll be right there," he said. He stacked the wood beside the fire and added several more cords to the flames, then hurried toward Gemna. "What can I do?"

"Help me fit this into the window opening, then hold it while I put shims around the frame to keep it in place. It should hold unless we have a whirlwind."

They picked up the frame and wiggled it into the opening. Maren held it tightly while Gemna wedged wooden shims between the frame and the window. "That should do for tonight," she said.

Suddenly, the old woman groaned. Maren hurried over and sank down beside her. He held the cup of tea to her colorless lips. "Drink this, please!" he begged her.

Her pale blue eyes opened, staring terrified into emptiness. "No, it's too late. I wish only to meet my loved ones in Barg's Kingdom." She looked at Maren, and her eyes widened with perceptive clarity. "I know what you are, Wizard," she whispered.

Maren inhaled sharply. "How?" he asked. "How do you know?"

"You shine with a blue light. I see it as clearly as I see your face." She clutched his hand and struggled to speak. "Remember the Witch of the Winds. She holds the keys of chaos. She has the power of light and darkness. In the final battle, she will tip the balance for good or ill. Remember her."

"But how do you know?" he pleaded.

"I don't know how or why. A last gift from the gods perhaps. My people once lived in the north, in the ancient land of the Wizards. Stories passed down from mothers to daughters say we had the blood of Wizards in our veins, though I don't know if it's true. But it doesn't matter now. I am the last of my family. Remember my words. Remember the Witch of the Winds." Closing her eyes again, she breathed out her life.

Maren rested his forehead in his hand, tears spilling from his eyes. *Merciful Baygor, why?* he thought, his heart filled with despair. *There's been too much death, too many lives lost. It's all so senseless, and I can't do anything to stop it!* Slowly, he stood and walked toward the fire.

Gemna came to his side. "The woman?" she said softly.

He shook his head. "She's gone to Barg's kingdom."

Gemna touched his arm. "I'm so sorry."

He glanced over his shoulder at the stall, tears running down his cheeks, and turned back to Gemna. "I couldn't do anything to save her," he said, frustration tightening his throat. "The medicine cures any ill, but can't cure despair. Without her family, she didn't want to go on living."

Gemna nodded. "I can dig the grave."

"No," he said, shaking his head. "You've done so much today. You should rest. I can dig the grave."

She gave his arm a gentle squeeze and nodded. "Call if you need me."

He lit the lantern and walked to the eight graves. Setting the lantern on the ground beside the eighth grave, he picked up the shovel and began digging a ninth.

He glanced back at the barn. Gemna leaned against the door frame, watching him, hugging herself. Her face was shadowed in the twilight. He stopped digging, wondering if she wanted something, but she didn't say anything. She just stood watching him. Slowly, she turned away and walked back inside.

As soon as he'd finished the grave, Maren trudged back to the barn. The old woman felt pitifully light in his arms. He placed her in the soft earth, smoothed her dress, and straightened her hair. "I don't even know your name, but I'll remember you. If only I had my powers, I could have saved you. If only--" Pain crept up his spine. He forced the thoughts away before the pain became unbearable. There was nothing he could do for the woman now anyway. "May you find peace and rest in Barg's kingdom."

He shoveled the loose dirt over her, tamped it down, and covered the grave with stones scavenged from the ruined house. Lantern in hand, he plodded back to the barn and closed the door against the night wind. He added a few more cords of wood to the fire and sat beside it, facing Ilette and Gemna.

Red-gold light chased shadows around the barn and flickered on Gemna's sleeping face. Her head was pillowed on her arm, a sweet smile on her lips. Strands of hair trailed beside her delicate face. She was beautiful, dark and beautiful.

Exhausted, Maren struggled to his feet and walked toward Gemna. He stood, gazing down at her, uncertain what to do. He'd intended to sleep where the old woman had been but changed his mind. He couldn't sleep in a death bed. Draping his blanket about his shoulders, he lay down on the other side of Ilette, facing Gemna. The fire crackled. The soft breathing of the baby and his bodyguard filled the barn.

Maren touched Ilette's cheek and smiled. He almost brushed the dark hair from Gemna's face but hesitated. He left it alone, pulled the blanket close around his neck, and fell asleep.

13

Gemna woke with the dawn and the lowing of the cow. Maren lay asleep beside Ilette, curled around her protectively. Gemna smiled, counting herself lucky that she had such a kind and honorable master.

Shivering, she rose carefully without disturbing the other two, hurried to the fire, and poked the magenta embers to life. After she'd added more wood, she checked the clothes hanging on the line. All were dry. She dumped the milk from the night before, then went to milk the cow. She patted the cow's brown and white side as she sat down on the milking stool. "It's all right, girl," she said. "I'll take care of you."

She chuckled quietly. *How many times did I say that when I was home?* she wondered. *How many buckets have I filled and carried back to the house? I never thought I'd be glad to milk another cow.*

When she had a full bucket of warm, frothy milk, she set it aside, filled the manger with an armload of hay and petted the cow's neck. She crept out the back door into the cold morning sunlight and ran to the root cellar. She gathered the front of her shirt into sling and filled it with a round of hard white cheese and four apples, then ran back to the barn. Picking up the bucket, she walked back to the fire, careful not to slosh the milk out. She set the apples and cheese on a wooden plate, then poured milk into the kettle and set it over the fire.

Fetching a small bowl of barley meal from the root cellar, she set the bowl beside the fire, peeled the four apples, and chopped them. Some she added to the heating milk; some she put on the griddle. She cut thin slices of ham, and soon had them sizzling on the griddle. She sliced the cheese and placed some on each piece of ham. When the cheese melted and the apples were cooked, she place the ham on bread rounds, heaped on some fried apples, and rolled the bread up.

Maren woke, yawned, and stretched, brushing his dark hair from his face. Gemna touched her finger to her lips, signaling him not to disturb Ilette. Stealing away from the straw bed, he tiptoed to the barn door and opened it a crack. He shivered and quickly closed the door again. He walked back to the fire and sat down beside Gemna. "It's cold this morning," he said quietly, holding his hands out to the fire. "That smells delicious."

Gemna handed him one of the meat and cheese rolls. "Eat your fill. There's plenty. I'll cook some porridge for Ilette. When you're done eating, you can wake her up and feed her."

Maren took a bite, and his eyes widened. He licked the ham broth and crumbs from his fingers, then smiled at Gemna. "You really will make someone a wonderful wife," he said, grinning.

Gemna grinned back. "Not if I can help it." She took a bite of a roll, savoring the sharp cheese and smoky-sweet ham, and set it down on a wooden plate. "There's lots of food in the root cellar," she said as she stirred some barley meal into the heated milk.

"It doesn't belong to us," he said.

"The ones it belonged to don't need it now. We can't let the food go to waste. Besides, the old woman said we could take whatever we needed."

Maren nodded slowly. "That's true."

"No reason we shouldn't take some of it with us."

"And how do you suggest we do that?" he asked between bites. "Our horses can only carry so much."

She stirred the porridge constantly. "But there's the wagon I told you about. We can load it up and harness our horses to it. Your mare's very gentle and will take to harness easier than my gelding, but they should work together well. We won't need to worry about food for the rest of our trip. We can even take the cow with us so Ilette will have milk every day."

Lines creased Maren's forehead as he stared silently at the fire. "You're right," he said at last.

"We can take turns driving the wagon."

Maren frowned thoughtfully. "I don't think I've ever driven a wagon before."

Gemna laughed. "I have since I was ten."

He held up his hands, surrendering. "All right. We'll take the wagon. You can teach me how to handle a team."

"After breakfast, we'll load as much as the wagon can carry. I'll harness our horses. You tie the cow to the rear. There's a tether hanging on the wall beside the stall. We should leave as soon as possible."

"I thought I was the master and you were the hireling," Maren said, his dark eyes twinkling.

Gemna gave him a toothy cat-grin.

Before either one of them could say anything else, Ilette woke. Gemna watched with delight as Maren swept the little girl into his arms and swung her above his head. She giggled, and he did it again.

"Good morning, little bird," he said.

"Eat eat eat," she said.

Maren laughed. "All you think about is eating."

Gemna took the kettle off the fire and spooned some porridge into a bowl to cool, then began taking the dry clothes from the line. Maren stripped off Ilette's diaper and wet clothes. Gemna handed him a clean diaper and clothes from the line, and he dressed Ilette and sat her on his lap to feed her. Gemna watched with amusement as the little girl downed two cups of milk and a whole bowl of the apple porridge.

"She does look like a baby bird," Gemna said, laughing.

"Yes, but she's so much better than when I first found her," Maren said as he wiped cereal from her chin.

"You saved her life," Gemna said.

Maren shook his head and gazed up at her. "We both did."

Something warm and comforting settled in her chest as she looked at Maren, a feeling that reminded her of her family but not quite the same, a feeling that puzzled her, but she liked it. "We should leave soon," she said as she took the last of the clothes off the line and folded them.

Maren set Ilette on a blanket and handed her a piece of bread.

Gemna picked up the bucket of leftover milk and stared at it. "I wish there was some way we could keep this." She sighed, then dumped the milk on the fire.

Maren raked the ashes, then shoveled dirt over them. Gemna and he pulled the wagon to the center of the barn and began loading supplies. They took plenty of food, the wine, tools, dishes and cooking equipment, and two spare wheels.

Gemna harnessed the mare first, then her gelding. The gelding resisted at first. "Enough of that," Gemna said, patting her horse's neck. "It's not as bad as it seems. You'll do just fine."

Maren tied the cow to the back. "Time to go," he said, picking up Ilette and slipping her into the blanket sling. He walked outside and waited beside the door as Gemna guided the wagon from the barn.

The sky was clear and water-blue, but the air was cold. Ilette squirmed in the sling as Maren climbed up beside Gemna on the bench seat. The morning sun shone on nine stone-covered graves before the ruins of the farmhouse. Gemna gazed solemnly at the sad sight. She glanced at Maren. His eyes glistened with unshed tears as he gazed at the graves, too. Gemna touched his arm and gave it a gentle squeeze. He looked at her and nodded, but didn't speak. She nodded back. There was nothing she could say.

She flicked the reins. The mare stared forward, but the gelding balked first. Gemna held the reins firmly but didn't jerk them. "Go ahead, try to get away," she said. "You can't. I won't hurt you. Just get used to the pull of the reins. I'll be patient."

It wasn't long before gelding gave in, and the horses plodded up the road. Ilette laughed as she bounced up and down.

The sun warmed slowly as they rode north. Steep-sided bluffs rose on the west side of the road. Lowland fields and pastures stretched to the east. Gemna saw the bodies of several horses and some sheep in one of the pastures. *Has anyone or anything survived the terrible storms?* she wondered, shuddering.

Just before the sun reached its zenith, they arrived at the village of Delwick, situated at the base of the bluffs. Gemna gasped as she surveyed the destruction. Half the houses had been smashed by the winds. She heard hammers pounding and saws rasping through wood, and saw a group of men constructing a house. Women set food on makeshift tables and stirred several large kettles set over fires. Older children fetched boards and nails for the men, while younger children stayed close to the women.

Gemna reined the horses to a stop before a stone building with a sign proclaiming it the Dancing Maid Inn. A bear of a man stood by the door, wiping his hands on a nearly white apron.

"Sorry," he said as he looked up at Gemna and Maren. "There's no room here, not even in the barn. Too many people without homes after the storm."

Maren nodded. "Do you know the farmstead down the road?"

"Yes," the man said.

"The family was killed by the storms."

The man winced and closed his eyes a moment. "They were good friends," he said softly. "I haven't had time to check on them. We've been so busy trying to rebuild the houses one at a time."

Maren told the innkeeper about how he and Gemna had found the woman and how she had died. "We took this wagon and some food and the cow so the baby would have milk. Are there any relatives of the family that we could pay for the things we took?"

"No," the innkeeper said, "not close. I think there were some distant relatives west of here, but no one close."

"I'd be willing to give you some money for these things. I don't feel right about taking them, but it seemed wasteful to just leave it there."

The innkeeper shook his head. "No need to pay me. You did right by the woman."

"There's a root cellar back at the farmstead, with lots of food in it still," Gemna said. "It shouldn't go to waste either, especially with so many people here without homes."

"Thank you," the innkeeper said. "We could all use some of that food. I'll send a wagon and a couple of young men to bring it back. Far-thell and Baygor protect you."

The weather remained pleasantly cool, the sun bright, as Gemna guided the team northward through the rolling hills and thickets. A few trees were toppled beside the road, but none blocked their path. Gemna noticed only a few dead animals and one area where the road was covered by a mudslide from the hills. Luckily, the mud had dried and hardened enough, Gemna had little trouble guiding the horses through it.

Ilette napped off and on in the sling while Maren sang to her. Gemna enjoyed the music. The sound of his voice was soothing and comfortable, like a warm fire on a cold night. As the sun sank toward the western hills, Gemna pulled the wagon off the road.

"This is as good a place as any to stay the night," she said, setting the brake.

"No villages close by?" Maren asked.

"No, but there's one we could reach tomorrow evening. If it's still standing." She raised her eyebrows. "There's an inn there. A very good inn from what Father said. I've never stayed there myself. I usually don't have enough money to stay in an inn. But since you're paying—"

Maren climbed down from the wagon seat and groaned, stretching his back. "If the inn is still there, I'll get us rooms. I want to sleep in a real bed again."

Gemna grinned. "A little too soft for life on the road, aren't you?"

Maren rubbed his buttocks and winced. "And I thought riding a horse was hard."

She laughed out loud and climbed down. "Only one more night. I'll start the fire and milk the cow. You cook our supper and take care of Ilette."

Maren gave her a sweeping bow. "Yes, master."

Gemna chuckled and went in search of fire wood. She came back with an armload of branches and one good sized log, and started a chill-chasing fire. By the time she had the horses unhitched and staked out where they could feed, and had milked the cow, Maren had soup simmering over the fire in the covered iron pot. Sitting on a blanket between the fire and the wagon, he was feeding Ilette porridge and warm applesauce when she brought the bucket of milk.

"How about some fresh milk, little bird?" Gemna asked. She dipped a cup of milk and handed it to Maren.

Ilette drank the cup dry and chirped for more. Gemna filled the cup and laughed as the little girl drained the cup and demanded more.

"It's a good thing we have plenty of diapers now," Gemna said as she refilled the cup and handed it to Maren. She dipped a bowl of soup and sat down beside him. Steam rose from the soup, thick with carrots, cabbage, onions, tubers, barley, and chunks of ham. She stirred the soup and blew on it, swirling the steam into tiny whirlwinds.

"How far are we from Vorlik?" Maren asked as he held the cup of milk for Ilette.

Gemna frowned thoughtfully. "Let's see. We're still in the Freelands."

"Why are they called the Freelands?"

"There're no lords here. Each village is governed by a citizen council. We have about five more days until we reach the border of Beltrin. Another three to four days from Beltrin to Peltik, and then three to five days from the border of Peltik to the Circle Mountains and the border of Vorlik. Of course, that all depends on the weather." She paused and sighed. "And how long we stay with my family. Mother will try to keep us for at least a week."

"So we'll be traveling together for two to three weeks or more?"

"At least." Gemna glanced at Maren, her heart warmed by the thought of spending her days with him but oddly troubled that it would only be for a month at the most.

Maren smiled as he wiped a milk ring from Ilette's mouth. "It'll be good to finally meet your mother and brothers. I've heard about them from your father over the years, but I've never met them."

Gemna smiled and blew on her soup to cool it. "Oh, you'll like my brothers. They're a rambunctious bunch. But my mother," she paused, cringing, "*she'll* like *you*."

Maren looked at her, puzzlement on his face. "And that's bad?"

"Yes."

"Why?"

"You're a man, and you're not married." Gemna blew on her soup again. "You're not, are you?"

"Not that I know of."

"And you're traveling with me. That will be quite enough for her to talk marriage incessantly."

Maren blinked several times, his mouth slowly dropping open. "Oh," he said.

"Just a warning. She never understood why I became a mercenary instead of marrying one of the local farm boys."

Maren grinned. "I'll be on my guard."

Ilette became fussy, fighting sleep. Maren wrapped her in a blanket and sang a lullaby. Gemna ate her soup and watched as the little girl sucked her thumb and listened to him. Soon Ilette's eyes began to droop and finally close. After a while, Maren placed her gently on the blanket, then dipped himself a bowl of soup.

"Can I have some more?" Gemna asked, holding out her bowl.

Maren smiled and refilled Gemna's bowl.

"You'd make someone a wonderful wife," she said.

Maren laughed quietly, and they both finished their supper.

The sky was crystal clear overhead, filled with stars, and the wind turn cold. They huddled together for warmth with Ilette between them on the blanket, all the rest of their blankets covering them. Gemna closed her eyes for a few moments, then opened them to find Maren watching her. He smiled and whispered, "Good night." He closed his eyes. Gemna gazed at him for a while, then closed her eyes and slept.

The next morning dawned cold enough, Gemna could see her breath. She crept from bed, stirred the embers to life, and added several handfuls of twigs and branches to coax flames from the wood and reheat the soup. Maren woke soon after, but she signaled him not to move so Ilette would sleep. Gemna dumped the milk from the night before, rinsed the bucket out, then milked the cow again. She cooked some porridge in milk and added the applesauce leftover from the night before.

Ilette woke up, and they all had a hot breakfast. Maren changed Ilette's clothes quickly while Gemna washed the dishes and dumped the leftover milk and wash water onto the fire. She rinsed out the milk pail, then packed up all their dishes and stowed them in the wagon. Gemna hitched the horses to the wagon and tied the cow to the back while Maren rolled up the blankets and packed them away, then put Ilette in the sling and climbed up on the wagon seat. Gemna climbed up beside him and pulled her hood up against the cold breeze.

"We'll stay at the inn tonight," she said as she flicked the reins.

They reached the village when the sun was still well above the treetops. Most of the houses were undamaged, including the inn. Gemna pulled up in front of the yellow stone building. A young brown-haired boy darted from the open doorway.

"Rooms for the night?" he asked as he held out his hand to Gemna.

She handed him the reins and climbed down from the wagon. "Yes," she said, "and stabling for our horses and a cow."

"Father's inside," the boy said. "I'll take care of the wagon."

Maren climbed down, his lute on his back and Ilette in the sling on his chest. The boy climbed up and flicked the reins, guiding the horses to the stable next to the inn.

"Let me take her for bit," Gemna said, holding her arms out.

Maren slipped the sling off his shoulder and handed Ilette to Gemna. She slid the sling over her head and followed Maren inside. A wiry man with chestnut-brown hair met them.

"Room for the night for you and your lady and the little one?" the man asked.

Maren's face turned red. "Uh, do you have two rooms and a cradle?"

"No. Only one room left."

"Does it have two beds?"

"Yes. And I think we still have a cradle somewhere."

"That's fine. How much?"

After some haggling, they settled on two buckets of milk — after Ilette had her fill — half a bushel of apples from the wagon, four songs, and one silver coin for a room, two meals, a hot bath, clothing laundered, waterskins refilled, and stabling for the animals. Gemna smiled to herself. Maren was becoming very good at bargaining.

The innkeeper showed them to a small but cozy room with a fireplace and two beds. "I'll have my wife bring the cradle after you've eaten. The bathing room is down the hall beside the kitchen. I'll have your baths ready by the time you've finished your supper." He bowed and left.

Maren took off his lute and set it on the floor, then flopped down on the bed. He moaned as he lay there, his eyes closed.

Gemna stared at him. "Is the bed uncomfortable?" she asked.

"No," he said softly, "it's the most wonderful bed I've ever been in."

Gemna grinned. "Do you think you can climb out of bed long enough to fetch clean clothes for all of us?"

"No," he whispered. "I'm never getting out of this bed."

Snickering, she grabbed his hands and pulled until he was sitting up. "Come on. Clean clothes now, supper next, songs, then a bath and bed."

He groaned again and sighed. "All right. I'll be back in a bit." He stood and shuffled out the door.

When he returned, he had a bag of dirty clothes and an armload of clean ones.

The innkeeper's wife followed him carrying a rocking cradle. "My little ones slept in this," she said, placing the cradle on the floor between the two beds. "Such a pretty little thing." The woman made funny faces at Ilette, who laughed. "She looks just like you," the innwife said, looking at Gemna.

Gemna's cheeks felt hot. She glanced at Maren, expecting to see him grinning mischievously. Instead, she was startled by a warm smile on his face and a tender look in his dark eyes that tightened her chest. She cleared her throat and looked back at the innwife. "Thank you."

"Supper is ready. Come to the common room."

"In a moment. Oh, wait." Gemna took the sack of dirty clothes from Maren and handed them to the innwife. "Our laundry."

Sighing, the innwife gazed at the sack she held and started to leave.

"I can do them myself if you show me where," Gemna said. "I really wouldn't mind."

The innwife smiled at her. "No, but thank you for the offer. Maybe after supper we could talk while I wash them. It would make the time go more quickly and pleasantly."

"I'd like that," Gemna said.

The innwife nodded and left.

Gemna set Ilette on the floor, then took off her cloak and tossed it across her bed. Maren did the same. He picked up his lute, then stopped, staring past Gemna. She turned around to see what he was looking at and gasped. Ilette was standing at the end, holding onto the footboard. She gave Gemna a toothy grin, let go of the footboard, and stood by herself. Gemna clapped a hand over her mouth, afraid she'd startle the little girl.

Maren appeared at Gemna's side. She hadn't heard him move.

"Look at her," he whispered. "When I first found her, she was so weak she couldn't hold her head up. But just look at her now."

"I know," Gemna whispered back. Suddenly, she realized he was holding her hand. Her breath caught in her throat. She looked over at him, but he was watching Ilette, his eyes gleaming. "I, uh, better go milk the cow if she's going to have milk with supper," she said. "I'll see you in the common room." She let go of Maren's hand, grabbed her cloak, and hurried from the room.

She strode out to the stable and checked on the horses before she milked the cow. When she came back with a full pail of milk, Maren was seated at a table in the common room, Ilette on his lap, feeding her some warm porridge. Gemna took the milk to the kitchen where the innwife filled a pitcher and gave it to Gemna along with a cup for Ilette. The little girl sucked down three cupfuls before she was satisfied.

The innwife brought out two large bowls filled with a meaty stew. Gemna inhaled the aroma of beef, carrots, onions, tubers, and sage. She sopped up the rich gravy with slices of warm crusty brown bread, and asked for another bowlful. For dessert the innwife brought out wedges of dried apple pie, still warm from the oven.

"My mother is one of the finest cooks I know," Gemna said, her stomach comfortably full, "but I think you are even better."

The innwife smiled broadly as she stacked the dirty dishes and carried them away.

"How about a song now, minstrel?" the innkeeper said.

Maren nodded and handed Ilette to Gemna, then took his lute from his back and strummed a chord. He began with "Chellit's Cat."

While he was playing, the innwife motioned Gemna to come to the kitchen. Picking up Ilette, Gemna stood quietly and walked to the kitchen.

"We're heating water for your bath," the innwife said, "but I was going to wash the clothes now and I'd love some company. About the only time I get to talk to another woman is on market day."

Gemna glanced down at Ilette, who was squirming and trying to get down from Gemna's arms.

"My daughter would play with her if you'd like," the innwife said, waving to a blond-haired girl about twelve years old. "She's very good with children."

Gemna was reluctant to let a stranger take care of Ilette, but the blond girl came over and played peek-a-boo with Ilette, who laughed and giggled. "All right," Gemna said, letting the girl take Ilette. "I just want to keep an eye on her."

The innwife smiled and led Gemna into a small room off the kitchen. The blond girl followed them and sat down on the floor near the doorway and played with Ilette. Two large tubs sat waist high on a low table. Both were filled with steaming water. Cakes of soap sat beside the tubs. And on one side of the table was a stack of laundry, including the sack of Gemna's and Maren's clothes.

Gemna laughed. "This reminds me of home. With four younger brothers, there was always a pile of clothes to be washed."

"I know what you mean." The innwife picked up a cake of soap and started washing a shirt. "Have you been on the road long?"

"About two weeks."

The innwife stopped scrubbing and gaped at her. "In this weird weather?"

Gemna nodded. "I've never seen anything like it."

"I know. One day it's like spring, then suddenly a winter gale. It's not natural."

"I know." Gemna looked at the heap of clothes. "I could help with the clothes," she said. "I wouldn't mind really."

The innwife hesitated, looked at the dirty clothes, then smiled. "I wouldn't mind the help."

Dipping the clothes in the first tub, Gemna scrubbed them until her knuckles were red and sore and the clothes were clean.

"What's your little girl's name?" the innwife asked.

"We call her Ilette," Gemna said as she wrung out a shirt.

"She really does look just like you."

Gemna cleared her throat. "She's not my daughter."

"Oh," the innwife said, surprise in her voice. "A relative of you or your husband?"

"Uh, he's not my husband. I'm his bodyguard."

"Oh." Her eyes widened. "So she's his child?"

"No, he found her." Gemna told the innwife about how Maren had found Ilette, how Gemna had met Maren, and how they'd come to travel together. By the time she finished, the clothes were all rinsed and hanging on lines to dry.

The innwife's mouth opened and closed several times before she said anything. "That's an amazing tale. So where are you taking the little girl?"

"To my mother in Beltrin. She always wanted another daughter, and I'd love to have a little sister. I know she'll be loved and well cared for at home."

The innwife nodded, then a slow smile crossed her face. She leaned close to Gemna and whispered, "I suppose since you're not married to the minstrel, you won't be bathing with him."

Gemna grinned. "Not tonight."

They both laughed.

Gemna picked up Ilette and thanked the innwife's daughter. The innwife took Gemna to the bathing room, lit by numerous candles. Two large wooden tubs sat on the floor, filled with steaming water. "You might want to take your bath now while the minstrel is still singing."

"I think I will," Gemna said. "I'll get a change of clothes for Ilette and me."

Gemna went back to the sleeping room, picked up clothes, and went back down to the bathing room. Cakes of cream-colored soap sat on a table beside folded towels, and thick rugs lay on the floor beside the tubs. Several chairs stood behind the tubs. Gemna set the clean clothes beside the towels, then stripped off Ilette's clothes. Setting the little girl on a chair, Gemna stripped off her own clothes, picked up Ilette, and grabbed a bar of soap.

The bath water was not as warm as Gemna would have liked, but not too warm for Ilette. Gemna sank down into the tub, holding Ilette. The little girl's eyes grew wide, and she clutched Gemna's neck tightly. Gemna scooped water with her hand and poured it over Ilette's back. Gradually, the little girl relaxed and began splashing the water.

The fragrance of oatmeal and mint filled the air as Gemna washed Ilette with the soap. She rinsed her off just as the innwife appeared.

"I can take her while you finish your bath if you like," the innwife said, holding a towel.

Gemna smiled. "Thank you. I seldom have the luxury of a hot bath on the road. I'd like to savor this for a bit."

The innwife wrapped Ilette in the towel and dried her, then tugged her gown over her head and tied a diaper on. Gemna scrubbed her skin with the soap, then lounged in the water, watching the innwife play with Ilette. *Maybe someday I will have a daughter*, Gemna thought, *and I hope I'll be a good mother.*

Reluctantly, she stood, cooling water running down her body, and she shivered.

"Here," the innwife said, handing her a towel.

Gemna stepped out of the tub, wrapped the towel around her, and rubbed herself dry. Quickly dressing, she took Ilette from the innwife and started to gather the dirty clothes.

"Leave them," the innwife said. "I can wash them, too. They'll be ready by morning. Take a candle."

"Thank you again." Taking one of the candles, Gemna walked back to her room, hearing Maren's voice still singing in the common room.

Gemna built a fire on the hearth while Ilette sat on the floor nearby and played with her rag doll. The little girl started rubbing her eyes and yawning. Gemna picked her up and sat down on the side of the bed. Gently rocking Ilette and patting her back, Gemna hummed a lullaby until the little girl was nearly asleep. Gemna placed her in the cradle, covered her with a soft blanket and quilt, and rocked the cradle slowly with her foot.

Maren came in not long after. Gemna held her forefinger to her lips to warn him to silence. He tiptoed to his bed, set his lute on the floor, and picked up his clean clothes. He stopped to gaze down at Ilette and smiled at her.

"I'll be back soon," he whispered to Gemna.

"Don't wake her up when you come back," she whispered back.

He closed the door without making a sound. Gemna climbed into her bed and nestled under the warm blanket and quilt. The bed felt deliciously soft after so many night of sleeping on the ground. She closed her eyes and fell asleep almost instantly.

The next morning Gemna rose before Maren and Ilette were awake. Dressing silently and sneaking out of the room, she went out to the barn to milk the cow and brought back the full pail. The innwife was bustling around the kitchen preparing breakfast. She smiled as Gemna set the pail on the counter.

"Do you have a basket for the apples?" Gemna asked.

The innwife nodded and went into a pantry. She came back with a sturdy wooden basket. Gemna took it and went back out to the barn. She filled the basket with half the apples from the wagon and carried the basket back to the kitchen.

The innwife smiled. "Fresh apple pie. A nice change from dried apples. The storms damaged the local orchard so we don't know if we'll get many apples next season."

"The storms destroyed many things," Gemna said.

Maren appeared at the kitchen door, holding Ilette.

"Eat eat eat," the little girl said.

They all laughed.

After a hot breakfast, the innkeeper came to settle accounts. "One silver coin," he said, "and you can fill your waterskins at the well out back. We're square on everything else. And thank you for an entertaining evening. We haven't had a minstrel here in ten or fifteen years."

Maren smiled. Gemna wondered if he had been that minstrel.

They filled their waterskins, collected their dry clothes, and packed their belonging. Gemna hitched the horses, backed the wagon from the stable, then tied the cow to the back.

The innwife was waiting outside, holding the rocking cradle. "You might as well take this with you," she said, smiling. "I haven't used it in over ten years, and I'm not likely to use it again."

Gemna jumped down from the wagon seat, took the cradle, and set it in the wagon. "Thank you," she told the innwife. "Baramay bless you."

"And you."

Gemna climbed back on the wagon, flicked the reins, and headed north.

The weather seemed milder, warm day and cool night, almost as if spring were finally coming to the land. Gemna saw a few trees toppled and a few dead sheep, but most of the farmsteads they passed were only slightly damaged or they had already been repaired. They camped by the roadside that night. The next day they reached a large town with a sizable inn. Maren sold one of his gems so he'd have coins to pay for a night's stay. He asked for two rooms, but Gemna pulled him aside.

"It's wasteful to pay for two rooms when one will do," she said. "Just ask for a room with two beds. And we have the cradle for Ilette. After all, how can I guard you if I'm not in the same room?"

Maren finally agreed, but he looked uncomfortable. Gemna smiled to herself.

The next night they camped by the roadside, then reach the town at the Beltrin border. They spent the night in a small but comfortable inn. They crossed the border the next morning. They saw the familiar signs of destruction caused by the wild storms, but it didn't seem as severe, or perhaps the worst had already been cleared away.

In the late afternoon, Gemna turned west from the main road to a well-traveled lane. Beyond thorny bushes edging the lane stretched sodden fields and rolling pastures dotted with cattle. *All so familiar,* Gemna thought. *How many times have I traveled this lane?*

As the sun sank toward the western hills, Gemna spotted a stone house. Several roof tiles and two shutters on the second floor were missing. Remnants of a splintered tree littered the ground beside the door. Smoke rolled from the chimney. Light peeped through curtains.

Gemna reined the horses in front of the heavy wooden door. She jumped down, hurried to the door, and threw it open. Her mother stood there, drying her hands on a towel, looking like an older version of Gemna. "Hello, Mother."

"Gemna!" Her mother threw her arms around her. "It's good to have you home!" She held Gemna at arms' length, then shook her finger at Gemna. "Do you know how worried I've been? With all these storms smashing sheds and downing trees, I was afraid you'd be hurt or worse! But at least you've come to your senses and returned home. And..." she smiled as she looked toward Maren and Ilette, "I see we have visitors."

Gemna blushed as her mother's dark eyes gleamed.

"It's about time you brought a man home, girl!"

14

Malbar was surprised when he was summoned to Miria's presence. He had seen little of her in the past months and not at all in the last two weeks. But he'd heard her crying, weeping for her father. How he'd wanted to comfort her, wipe away her tears, hold her gently until her grief was past. He couldn't, though. She saw no one except Malbar's father — Captain Callas — and her maid. She took her meals in her room or in the tower study that had been her father's.

The tower study — that was where she had summoned him. He climbed the spiral stairs, past his father's office, up to the wooden door at the top of the stairs. Knocking, he waited until he heard Miria's voice.

"Enter."

Malbar slid back the bolt and pushed open the door. Miria sat at the desk studying a map. His father, Captain Callas, stood beside her, pointing at the map. They both looked up as Malbar walked in and bowed.

Miria smiled, looking as radiant as a summer morning. She was wearing a blue dress with silver piping, and her golden hair was caught up in silver netting. Malbar gazed at her, entranced. He'd always loved her, but she'd never looked at him the way she'd looked at Pyccis, their childhood friend. But now Pyccis was Bren, Lord of Vorlik, and Miria hated him. Malbar hated him, too. Now, she gazed at Malbar with an intensity that tightened his chest.

"Malbar," she said.

"Lady Miria," he said, his voice barely a whisper.

"You have always been loyal to me," she said softly.

"Always, My Lady."

She smiled again. "That is why I'm giving you a task that only you can complete. It is dangerous," she paused and a look of concern flickered through her blue eyes, "but you are the only one who can do this for me."

Malbar knelt before her, his heart dancing in his chest. "Anything for you, My Lady."

She smiled again and glanced up at Callas. "I need you to deliver a letter," she said, "a letter to Bren."

Malbar's throat tightened. His hands closed into fists. "Bren?" he whispered. "You want me to go to Vorlik? To our enemies? And deliver a letter to that...that traitor?"

Miria smiled again, but it was a sly smile, and her eyes narrowed. "Yes, I want you to go to our enemies and deliver a letter to Bren."

Malbar stood and shook his head. "I can't," he said, his voice shaking. "I never want to see him again. Ever. Please send someone else. Anyone else. Don't ask me to face him. Please!"

Miria stood slowly, walked around the table, and stood barely a hand's length from Malbar. "You must be the one to go," she said. She reached up and touched his cheek.

Malbar trembled, feeling hot and chilled at the same time. "Please, don't send me there. I beg you."

"It must be you."

"But why? Why me, My Lady?"

She stared deep into his eyes. "Because he will look at you and remember his childhood. Because he will see the friend he once knew."

Malbar turned his face away slightly. "Please," he whispered. "I can't. He betrayed us all. I couldn't look at him without wanting to kill him."

Miria turned his face back toward her. "But you will go to him, won't you, my champion?" She stood on tiptoe and kissed Malbar's lips lightly.

The world seemed to tilt, and the floor seemed unsteady as Malbar tried to keep his balance. His heart pounded in his chest, and his face felt as if he had a fever. Miria had kissed him. *She* had kissed *him*! It was all he'd ever wanted, more than he'd dare hope for! How could he deny her anything? "I will go to our enemies and stand before Bren, for you, My Lady. Anything for you."

Miria smiled up at him.

Dressed in the black and silver surcoat of Drambit's guard, Malbar rode his charcoal horse toward the Circle Mountains and the border with Vorlik. He was accompanied by four soldiers and his squire, who carried the flag of embassy. Malbar gazed up at the flag. The white silk, trimmed in gold and bearing a small silver serpent in one corner, hadn't been used for so long, it had had to be cleaned and pressed before it was fit to tie to the slender staff. The flag nearly glowed.

They'd stayed the night at an inn just inside the Drambini border and left before dawn. The sky was deep blue, and the few clouds overhead were like magenta feathers. The air was crisp but not uncomfortable. The scent of pine needles trickled down from the mountains. It would have been a good morning for hunting ducks, which flew northward in V-shaped flocks overhead. But today wasn't a day for hunting ducks.

Malbar's apprehension grew as he approached the border keep, the grey-stone structure carved from the *mountain. The road into Vorlik passed beside the keep, and no one entered the land without permission from the border guards. Will the Vorlikians let us cross into their land?* he wondered. *Will they attack us even though we have the flag of embassy? Will I be dead before the day is out?* He stared at the snow-capped mountains before him and shivered, but not from the cold. *It might be better to die here than to see Bren again.*

He tried not to think about Bren. That brought too many painful memories, too many things he wanted to forget. He concentrated on hate — hatred of the Vorlikian soldiers who guarded the road through the mountains, hatred of their lord far away in his castle.

Malbar reined his horse to a stop. A dozen soldiers wearing blue and gold uniforms poured from the shadowed keep and stood in the road. Their swords drawn, the soldiers glared at Malbar and his companions. Several Vorlikians started toward the Drambini when another guard strode from the keep and shouted, "Stand fast!"

The Vorlikian guards stopped instantly and came to attention, sword at their sides. "Yes, sergeant!" they all said.

The sergeant strode toward the Drambini but didn't draw his sword. He gazed up at the white and gold flag, then at Malbar. The sergeant's hand rested on his sword, his fingers clutching and unclutching the hilt until Malbar was certain the sergeant was going to attack him. Clearing his throat, the sergeant said, "You come as an ambassador? To Vorlik? From *Drambit?*"

"You can see the flag," Malbar said.

"Why? What would bring you to Vorlik — besides seeking your own death?"

Malbar placed his hand on the leather pouch slung over his shoulder. "I carry a letter from Lady Miria of Drambit to Lord Bren of Vorlik."

The sergeant stared up at him, his jaw tight and eyes narrowed. "You travel a dangerous path," he said slowly. "That flag is the only thing that's keeping you alive right now." He paused. "It might not be enough to keep you alive once you're in Vorlik however. I'll send an escort with you, as much for your safety as ours. I myself will escort you to the Western Guard barracks. Stay where you are." He turned toward the Vorlikian soldiers. "You," he said, pointing at four of the guards, "stand watch over the Drambini. If any harm comes to them, you will answer for it, and the punishment will be swift and harsh. The rest of you, back in the keep." The sergeant strode back inside the keep.

Malbar tightened his grip on the reins, his jaw clenched. *It's not bad enough I have to travel into the enemy's land and face Bren,* he thought, *but now I'll be surrounded by soldiers who want me dead as much as I want them dead.*

The sergeant and eleven soldiers brought their horses from the keep and mounted.

"Let them pass," the sergeant called to the four guards.

They stepped back, glaring at the Drambini. Malbar clapped his legs against his horse's sides to urge his mount forward. Malbar was surprised the Vorlikian didn't disarm him and his men. The border guards stationed themselves one on each side of the Drambini troops, with the sergeant riding on Malbar's left. The sergeant never spoke, but Malbar caught the Vorlikian watching him.

The road climbed up to the tree line, where snow clung to barren rock and the wind was cutting. Each breath tightened Malbar's chest, as if he were breathing ice instead of air. Finally, the road began to descend into Vorlik. Malbar pulled up his horse and gazed at the land below, bright in the early morning sunlight.

"Why are you halting?" the sergeant demanded.

Malbar just stared at the land, green with spring. White flocks of sheep or goats dotted pastures. Dark, rich fields were just starting to green. Orchards were budding and flowering. A sizable town sat at a crossroad. He saw farmsteads and vineyards, and at the far edge of his sight was a great forest stretching to the east. "I've never seen a land so rich, so alive," he whispered, "so...beautiful."

"Yes," the sergeant said, "it is beautiful."

Malbar turned toward the sergeant and saw a look of surprise on the soldier's face. Malbar was just as surprised that he could agree with a Vorlikian on anything. Nudging his horse into motion, Malbar continued down the road.

They reached the Western Guard barracks midmorning. The sergeant dismounted and went inside. Moments later, the sergeant came out with a tall muscular man in a blue and gold uniform. The man stared grimly at Malbar, glancing at the flag of embassy and back to Malbar.

"How many men can you spare for an escort, lieutenant?" the sergeant asked.

The lieutenant just stared at Malbar. "Are there enough guards in all Vorlik to keep these men safe?" he said tightly.

The sergeant frowned as he turned toward the lieutenant. "Sir?"

The lieutenant slowly turned his head toward the sergeant. "I want you and your men to escort the ambassador to Tarolin Castle. I'll give you six more men, and I'll send a squad back to the keep until you return. That should be enough."

The sergeant didn't reply for a while, then he saluted. "Yes, sir. We'll stay the night at the castle and return tomorrow."

Wheeling, the lieutenant strode back inside the barracks.

The sun was nearly overhead before four more guards joined the escort, and they continued east at a steady pace. Malbar noted as much about the land as he could, as his father and Miria had instructed him. The sergeant rode at his side, silent and watchful.

They rode passed through what looked like a hill that had been split down the middle. Malbar looked curiously from one side of the cleft hill to the other.

"It's called the Hills of the Axe," the sergeant said. "Some legends says a giant was chasing a huge snake that burrowed into the hill. The giant took his axe and split the hill in half to get at the snake."

Malbar chuckled quietly. "It must have been a large snake."

"Legend says it'd swallowed the giant's prize bull."

Malbar stared at the sergeant a few moments, then burst into laughter, the image was so bizarre. The sergeant looked startled, then started laughing, too. When they finally stopped, Malbar gazed at the sergeant, surprised that they had shared a joke, surprised and uneasy. *He's my enemy as surely as Bren is my enemy,* Malbar thought. *But if he weren't, if he were a Drambini, we could have been friends, I think.* He tensed, anger filling his heart. No! No Vorlikian could *ever* be his friend! Not the sergeant. Not Bren. Especially not Bren!

Malbar looked away from the sergeant and consciously refused to look at him again. The man was a Vorlikian, and Malbar wanted all Vorlikians dead. That thought sat uncomfortably on Malbar's soul, though he didn't know why.

They approached the town Malbar had spotted from the mountain. He heard the clang of a blacksmith's hammer, the rasping sound of saws, chickens clucking, children laughing, and merchants hawking their wears in the marketplace. Several people were nearby when the soldiers rode toward crossroads. Staring at Malbar and his retinue, the townspeople appeared filled with anger. They called to others, who came running. By the time Malbar reached the crossroad, a large crowd stood glaring at him. One man stepped from the crowd, a sword in his hand, his green eyes like burning emeralds, and came at Malbar.

The sergeant rode between the man and Malbar, drawing his sword. "Halt!" the sergeant said.

"He's a Drambini!" the green-eyed man said.

"He's an ambassador and under my protection. Stand down unless you want to die."

"He's a murderer!"

The sergeant pointed his sword at the man. "I said stand down!"

Slowly, the man lowered his sword. Glaring at Malbar, the man jammed his sword in its sheath, then wheeled and shoved his way through the crowd.

"Go on," the sergeant said to the townspeople. "Go back to what you were doing."

The townspeople dispersed slowly, grumbling in whispers, with bitter glances over their shoulders.

The sergeant sheathed his sword, rode back into position on Malbar's left, and signaled for the escort to continue.

Malbar rode silently, troubled by the sergeant's defense of him. The man had been willing to fight to protect Malbar, in spite of the hatred Vorlikians had for Drambini. Malbar wouldn't have done so much for a Vorlikian.

By midafternoon the group had reached the edge of the forest, tall ancient trees that reached far overhead. A gentle breeze rustled the branches and brought the scent of mold and old leaves and damp earth. Leaves crunched under the horses' hooves sending up a spicy odor. *A nice place for an ambush, especially in summer when the leaves would block out most of the light,* Malbar thought as he glanced from side to side. He paused, breathing in the fresh clean air. *But it could be a place of refuge and solace. I'd like living here. It's peaceful and quiet and safe.* He smiled grimly to himself. *Safe if I weren't a Drambini.*

The late afternoon sun was nearing the western mountains when the woods thinned north of the road until the trees disappeared completely. A wide grassy field stretched north, and in the center of the field was a large blue marble building with a gilded dome. Two-story wings extending south, west, and east; Malbar couldn't see it there was a wing extending north. Gardens and pebbled walks covered the grounds from the building to the road. Several men and women, wearing blue and gold robes knelt silently and worked the soil in the gardens. Others pruned climbing roses on trellises. All stopped and watched as Malbar, his entourage, and the Vorlikian escort rode past.

"What is that place?" Malbar asked the sergeant.

"The Great Monastery and Temple of Baygor," the sergeant said.

"Baygor?" Malbar asked, frowning thoughtfully.

The sergeant turned and stared at Malbar. "Baygor," he repeated. "Baygor the Preserver."

"I've never heard of him before. Was he one of the lords of Vorlik?"

The sergeant's mouth dropped open, and he gaped at Malbar. "You mean you don't know? You've never heard of Baygor? Or Baramay?"

Malbar shook his head.

"How could you not know about the gods who created our world?"

Malbar laughed derisively. "Everyone knows the Hound of Darkness spat out our world into the night."

The sergeant's eyes were so wide, they looked as if they were going to pop from his face. His mouth opened and closed several times, but he made no sound. Finally, he just shook his head and kept riding.

Malbar looked straight ahead and saw a crossroads, and on the northeast side of the crossroads sat Tarolin Castle. The outer walls were of red granite. The castle itself was white limestone, tinted yellow-orange by sunlight. On the west side of the north-south road, tents were being set up. Carpenters hammered a dais together, and men and women set pots of early spring flowers at the base of the dais. Wagons loaded with wood and heaped with food formed a line from the castle to the field. Tents crowded all along the western side of the castle wall.

"A celebration?" Malbar asked.

"The Spring Festival," the sergeant said, "celebrating the return of spring and life."

Malbar shrugged. *These Vorlikians have such primitive beliefs,* he thought scornfully.

Suddenly, there was a cracking sound and a scream. An axle on one of the wagons had broken, and the wagon had fallen on one of the men unloading it. The sergeant started toward the wagon, halted, and looked from Malbar to the castle and back. "Go on to the castle," he told Malbar. "You're safe now."

The sergeant called his troops to follow him, and they went to help rescue the injured man. For an instant, Malbar wanted to follow the sergeant to help, but remembered he was in Vorlik, surrounded by his enemies. Being so near so many of them made his skin crawl. He glanced back at the gathering crowd, then signaled his entourage, and rode toward the castle gate.

Malbar gazed at the high granite walls, lined with soldiers, and his stomach tightened. He heard shouts from the wall, and saw a soldier running along the wall toward the gate house. The closer Malbar came to the castle gate, the more he knew he didn't want to be there. But Miria and his father had insisted Malbar be the ambassador. If Bren were to believe any Drambini was sincere, Miria had told Malbar he was the one. And Malbar would have done anything for Miria, just as at one time he would have done anything for Bren.

Unwelcomed memories of Bren clouded Malbar's thoughts. They'd been best friends once, grown up together in Drambit. Hunting side by side, wrestling in the courtyard, sneaking into nearby cottages to learn of pleasure -- those days were long past. Bren was now the lord of Vorlik, and Malbar's enemy.

Malbar approached the entrance to Tarolin Castle, his guards following close behind. Garlands and wreaths of the first spring flowers hung from the castle walls over the gatehouse. Carts loaded with food and barrels of drink flowed in a long procession from the castle to western field. Malbar was amazed at how prosperous and well-fed everyone seemed to be. The people of Drambit always had the hollow-eyed look of hunger.

At the open gates he was halted by two soldiers, dressed in the red and gold uniform of the castle guard. They drew their swords and glared at him.

"What do you want, Drambini?" demanded a dark-haired guard.

"You see my banner," Malbar said, sitting rigidly. "I'm an ambassador from Lady Miria of Drambit. I have a message from My Lady to your lord, and I must deliver it personally."

"Really?" The other guard stepped dangerously close, his pale blue eyes glaring at Malbar. "I've a message I'd like to deliver to your lady personally myself."

Malbar stared at him as disdainfully as he could manage. "As I've always said, Vorlikians know nothing about civilized behavior. You're barbarians."

"Barbarians! You accuse us of being barbarians?" the dark-haired guard sputtered. "Only last fall you Drambini sneaked across our borders and attacked us! And your kind killed my brother!"

The guards lunged at Malbar from both sides. He drew his sword and dodged dark-haired guard's first blow. The other Drambini rode to Malbar's defense. More Vorlikian guards poured from the castle gate to aid the gate guards.

The second guard's sword clanged against Malbar's. He shoved it away, but he twisted to keep his balance in the saddle, turning his back slightly to the first. From the corner of his eye, Malbar saw a blade flash, sweeping toward his side. Fear shivered through him. He was going to die, he knew it.

As the dark-haired guard's blade fell toward Malbar, another blade deflected it with the ringing of fine steel. Wheeling angrily, the dark-haired guard faced a man, perhaps forty years old, dressed in dark green. Beside him was a red-haired man with eyes as green as Drambini emeralds and wearing a red and gold uniform. "Halt!" the red-haired man ordered.

White-faced, the Vorlikian guards dropped their swords and sank to one knee, speechless.

"How dare you attack an ambassador!" said the man in green, his dark eyes glinting like black diamonds.

"But they're Drambini!" one of the guards said, hatred in every word.

"I don't care if Canzet himself and his Sorcerous minions had come with a flag of embassy, you would be bound to honor that flag! You've disgraced the Tarolin Guard, and the house of Vorlik! Report to the watch commander and have him send two true soldiers to take your places! I'll determine your punishment myself."

The guards hung their heads and said nothing. They picked up their swords, sheathed them, and shuffled toward the barracks.

The man faced Malbar, who held his sword in readiness. The Vorlikian put his sword in its scabbard and bowed solemnly. "I beg your pardon, ambassador. I assure you, they will be punished."

Malbar sheathed his blade, but his hand was shaking. "Beheaded, I hope," he said, trying to hide how unnerved he was by the attack.

The man frowned. "I'll escort you to Lord Bren."

Malbar nodded.

The red-haired man ordered the castle guards back to their posts.

Turning back to Malbar, the man in green said, "If you and your men will come with me, please."

Followed by the red-haired man, the man in green led Malbar and his entourage to the wide front steps of the castle where Malbar and his men dismounted.

The Vorlikian clapped his hands. Several young boys hurried from the stables. "Tend the ambassador's horses."

A blond boy, taller than the other stable boys, took the reins of Malbar's horse. "Yes, Lord—" The boy turned red. "I mean, Sir Cordwin."

Malbar stared at Cordwin. So this was the man who had given up Vorlik's throne after ruling for twenty years. Malbar wondered why Cordwin hadn't just killed Bren and kept the throne. Any other lord would. Malbar certainly would.

"Ambassador," said the man in green, "your men will be quartered and given food, but they will not be allowed to roam through the castle freely. There's too much animosity between our people yet. But I swear they will be safe and well treated. You have my word." He turned toward the red-haired man. "Captain, I leave them in your hands."

The red-haired captain nodded. "Follow me."

Not moving, the Drambini soldiers looked to Malbar.

"They will be safe," said the red-haired captain. "I swear on my life."

Malbar nodded to his entourage. "Go with him, but stay together. All of you," he said when his squire started to protest. Malbar glanced at the two Vorlikians. Oddly, he felt confident that they would keep their word. After all, they could have let the gate guards kill them, but didn't. "Go. I will be safe, and so will you."

"Yes, sir," the soldiers said.

Signaling two guards to follow him, Cordwin led Malbar through the entry hall, up three spirals of steps, and along the torch-lit corridor. Cordwin stopped before a wooden door, knocked, and waited until a voice bid him enter.

Dressed in dark blue robe, Bren sat at a table in his study, reading a book. Light from a window behind him lit the room. On the left wall a limestone and brick fireplace blazed, warming the study. He looked up when Cordwin entered.

"Uncle, I think I finally learned my part for the ceremony, but--" Bren halted, gazing past Cordwin at Malbar. Bren's eyes widened, then tiny lines pulled his brows together. His lips formed Malbar's name but made no sound.

Cordwin bowed. "My Lord, an ambassador from Drambit."

"Malbar." Bren's voice was soft; his blue eyes glistened brightly. "Malbar!" He leaped to his feet, hurried around the table, and embraced Malbar. "I never thought I'd see you again."

For a moment Malbar forgot who Bren was and returned the embrace, almost overwhelmed by how glad he was to see his friend. Bren hadn't changed at all: same dark brown hair, same gold-flecked blue eyes, same lean face. All Malbar's memories, all his life was tied to Bren. His absence was a dark pit in Malbar's soul.

Pulling back, Malbar clasped Bren's arms and smiled at his friend. A gleam of gold made him blink. It was a gold sunburst medallion around Bren's neck -- the symbol of Vorlik. Malbar stiffened, the smile fading from his face. *He's not my friend any more,* Malbar thought, conflict tearing at his heart. *He's my enemy.* Dropping his arms stiffly to his side and stepping back, he tried to keep his tone icy, but he could hardly speak. "I'd hoped we'd never meet again, except in battle."

Bren winced. Slowly, he walked back to his chair and sat down. "Since you didn't want to come," he said slowly, "why *are* you here?"

Malbar opened a leather pouch slung at his side, removed a rolled parchment, sealed with black wax, and handed the parchment to Bren. His hand shook almost as much as his voice. "I was sent to deliver this letter from Lady Miria of Drambit. I'm to wait for a reply."

Bren gazed at him, a long searching gaze, but finally looked away. Malbar wanted to enjoy Bren's discomfort but couldn't. Being near him hurt too much.

Bren took the parchment, broke the seal, and read the letter. His eyebrows raised; his eyes widened. He blinked several times, and his jaw dropped. He cleared his throat, swallowed, and blew out a short breath, then looked up at Malbar. "I'll give you an answer after I consult with my advisors. Until then, you'll be treated as a guest, but be warned: you'd be killed if you leave the safety of the castle. Most Vorlikians hate anyone from Drambit.

"Guards," he called, "summon my lieutenants and advisors to council in one hour. Escort the ambassador to the Green Tower chambers and see he has anything he wants. It's a long trip from Abasette Castle." Bren gave Malbar a sad smile.

Malbar bowed stiffly and left the room, angry that part of him had wanted to return the smile.

After the door closed, Bren turned to Cordwin. "Do you have any idea what this letter says?"

Cordwin shook his head, rigid and alert.

Bren pointed to a chair across the table. "Please, Uncle, sit down."

Cordwin sat but remained rigid.

"I need your advice," Bren said earnestly. "This letter has stunned me, and I don't know what to do. Let me read it to you, then give me your opinion."

Cordwin nodded slowly.

Bren cleared his throat and began to read aloud. "My beloved Bren, I know you never expected to hear from me. Perhaps you don't want to hear from me anymore. Please, at least read this letter, think about it, and remember how much we meant to each other.

"I've been afraid to write. Our lives have changed so much since childhood. As children we were close, and our affection grew even as we did. We pledged our love and swore to marry, but that seems so long ago.

"Bren, I loved you, and I'm sure you loved me. I never knew of Father's treachery until it was too late to warn you. We were pawns, used by him for his ambitious plans. We loved him, and he betrayed us both.

"You must despise me for what my father did, but my love for you is as true as my father's was false. I release you from your vow and hope someday you'll think kindly of me.

"If, by some mercy, you still love me and want to marry me, send word back with Malbar. Faithful as ever, Miria"

When he finished, Bren looked to Cordwin, who scowled and fingered the hilt of his sword.

"Well, Uncle, what do you think?" Bren asked anxiously.

"What do you think about it?" Cordwin said.

"It's a dream I gave up, a hope I thought was hopeless considering what happened. How could she still want to marry the man who killed her father? But now," Bren paused, feeling as if he'd suddenly awakened from a nightmare to find a bright spring day, "now there are possibilities that I thought were impossible." He gazed at Cordwin. "Tell me, honestly, how do *you* feel about the letter?"

Cordwin was silent for a while. When he finally answered, his voice cracked, and new lines marked his face. "I can't believe her. I've too many reasons to distrust the Drambini. They murdered my brother and his wife; they stole you. They caused Briella's death. I can't trust them!"

Bren lowered his eyes, guilt sitting lead-heavy on his heart. "Any more than you trust me," he said, raising his face to gaze straight at Cordwin.

Cordwin started to say something, then looked away. "Sometimes. Sometimes doubts fill my heart. I don't know you yet. It's hard to be certain where your heart lies -- here where you were born or in Drambit where you grew up. I wish I trusted you completely."

"So do I," Bren said quietly. "If I could do anything to earn your forgiveness and win your trust, I would do it. I swear I would."

"I know," Cordwin said. "I know. Sometimes I look at you and see my brother shining through your eyes, and I love you as I loved him. Then I remember Briella, and it's hard not to draw my sword and strike you." He touched the silver dove pendent hanging around his neck. "But how can I remember her and not remember how kind she was, how full of love and compassion? She stays my hand when my anger threatens to seek vengeance. She is the one I trust with all my heart.

"But this Lady Miria — I don't know her. She's a Drambini born and raised. For countless generations her people have hated our people. They have attacked us time and time again. How can I trust her? It's hard for me to judge." Cordwin's voice softened. "Do you truly love her?"

"Yes," Bren admitted. "I have since we were children."

"And you promised to marry her?"

"Yes."

"Do you trust her?"

"I've never had any reason to doubt her."

Cordwin's voice grew softer. "Did you have any reason to doubt Paxell?"

Bren looked away. The pain was still fresh, the wounds still raw. Bren gazed at his uncle. Cordwin caressed a dove-shaped, silver amulet about his neck. Shared grief bound them together, but they couldn't speak of it, not yet. Like a barely clotted wound, they needed time to heal.

At last, Bren spoke. "I love Miria. I always have. I didn't send for her after the battle because I couldn't believe she'd still love me, not after I'd killed her father. She must have thought I hated her because of her father's actions. But if she'll have me, I'll marry her. Perhaps our wedding will end the hatred between Drambit and Vorlik."

"Could this be a Drambini trick?" Cordwin asked.

"I don't know."

"You have the Sword of Truth," Cordwin said. "Use it."

"Call Malbar—" Bren halted. "Call the ambassador back."

Cordwin stood, went to the study door, and spoke to one of the door guards standing in the corridor. "Bring the Drambini ambassador back. Lord Bren wants to speak to him again."

Bren walked from his study to his bedchamber and retrieved a sword hanging in its scabbard on the wall. He carried the sword back and placed it on the desk in front of him. The sword gleamed as if it were filled with light. He brushed his fingertips over his name, etched on the blade, and he remembered the day he first saw the sword – the day the Wizard Briella died by his hand, just after she'd given him the sword.

Malbar appeared at the door. "You sent for me?"

Bren nodded and placed his hands on the sword. Cordwin motioned Malbar to sit in the chair, then he stood against the wall by the door.

Malbar sat facing Bren and stared at the sword. "Are you going to kill me?" he asked.

"No," Bren said softly. "Do you know the contents of the letter you brought?"

Malbar stiffened. "No. I'm just a courier."

"But you know what was in the letter."

"No, I don't."

Bren felt a tingle from the sword. Malbar had spoken the truth. "The letter contains a proposal from Miria. She wants to know if I still want to marry her."

"Marry?" Malbar stammered. "Marry you?"

"And what do you think about it?"

Malbar looked bewildered and lowered his eyes, but his hands were clenched.

"How do you feel about the proposal?" Bren asked again.

"I *can't* have feelings about it!" Malbar said. "It's not my place!"

Bren's fingertips tingled from the sword. He looked straight at Malbar. "But you love Miria. I've always known that."

Malbar clamped his jaw shut.

"You're in love with Miria, aren't you?"

"Yes!" Malbar said. "But she never looked at me the way she looked at you! Never!"

Again the sword tingled. "And is this proposal a plot against Vorlik?"

Malbar glared at Bren. "What else could it be? After all, she's a Drambini and you're a Vorlikian. How could it *not* be a plot? How could any Drambini have true feelings for a Vorlikian?" He stopped abruptly, averting his eyes.

"Is it truly a plot against me?" Bren asked quietly.

Malbar was silent for a long time. "No," he said, his voice so low Bren barely heard his reply, "not as far as I know."

The sword tingled under Bren's touch. Malbar had spoken the truth.

"May I go now?" Malbar asked, his voice trembling. He didn't look at Bren.

"Yes," Bren said, wishing he could recapture the warmth of their friendship, if only for a moment. He knew that could never happen, and that left him feeling empty, as if part of his heart had gone cold. He sighed. "Guards, escort the ambassador back to his rooms."

Malbar stood, turned his back to Bren, and left.

Cordwin closed the door to the study. "Well?" he said. He walked back toward the desk and sat down facing Bren. "What did you learn?"

"He spoke the truth," Bren said.

"Even when he said it was a plot?"

"No, not then. But everything else was the truth."

"Are you certain?" Cordwin leaned crossed his arms on the desk, his eyes narrowed and his face grim. "Are you very certain? So many lives depend on the honesty of that man. His kind has always been deceitful and hostile to Vorlik. Why would that change? How can we possibly believe him?"

"Because as far as the sword can tell, he spoke the truth. And Briella told me it will always know the truth." The instant Bren said Briella's name, he wished he hadn't. The pain in Cordwin's eyes was almost more than Bren could bear.

Cordwin stared at Bren for a few moments, then lowered his eyes. "Then..." Cordwin paused, "you have my blessing, if that's what you want. But be wary. We only know as much truth as the ambassador himself knows." Standing, he walked to the door, then looked over his shoulder. "I hope your trust isn't misguided." He left.

Bren stared at the closed door, listening to Cordwin's retreating footsteps. They'd both lost people they'd loved, but Cordwin's loss was greater. Maybe Miria and he could end the hate that killed so many Drambini and Vorlikians. Bren hoped there'd never be war between them again.

15

Malbar paced the lower floor of the tower apartment. The room was richly furnished in shades of green. A velvet covered lounge and heavy chair set before a small hearth. A square table of dark wood between the chair and lounge held a silver tray with two silver cups. Opposite the hearth, a small writing desk of dark wood inlaid with abalone shell sat beneath stairs spiraling up to the bedchamber. All very comfortable, but Malbar recognized the apartment for the prison it was. Two armed guards stood outside the door to prevent him leaving.

I wish I'd never come here! I wish I'd never seen him again! And how can Miria wish to marry him, after what he did? He killed the man who raised him, Miria's own father! How could she? Bren's a traitor! He turned his back on the people who raised him, on his friends, on me! Malbar clenched his fists. *We meant nothing — I meant nothing to him! How could he betray me? How could he? Someday he'll pay for his treachery, and all Vorlik with him!*

There was a knock at the door, startling Malbar. "Come in," he said.

The door opened, and Cordwin stood there. "May I come in?"

"I didn't know jailors knocked before entering a prisoner's cell," Malbar said, surprised by the Vorlikian's presence.

"Is everything satisfactory?" Cordwin asked.

"As satisfactory as any prison could be."

Cordwin sighed and shook his head. "This is only a prison if you choose to make it one."

Malbar sat down on the lounge and studied Cordwin curiously. "How does it feel?"

"How does what feel?"

"How does it feel to have all that power and authority suddenly taken from you?"

Silent for a while, Cordwin answered in a quiet voice. "I never wanted to be lord of Vorlik. I was only a regent until we found Bren. He's my older brother's son and the rightful heir. I knew that the throne was his from his birth."

"But the power you gave up," Malbar said. "You could've killed him and kept Vorlik for yourself."

Cordwin's steady gaze made Malbar uncomfortable. "You don't understand. I never wanted power."

"You're right," Malbar said. "I don't understand."

Cordwin sat down in the chair and gazed at the hearth, silently. At last, he asked, "You knew Bren well?"

"Unfortunately."

"You were friends?"

"No!" Malbar said as he tried to hide his hurt with anger. "Friends don't turn against you." For a moment, he saw compassion on Cordwin's face.

"It's not easy to forgive, is it?" Cordwin whispered. He stared out the single window in the room.

Puzzled, Malbar wondered what he meant, what hurt marred the lean face, what pain hid deep in the man's heart.

Cordwin looked back at Malbar and cleared his throat. "Food and drink are being sent up. Do you prefer wine or ale?"

"I prefer someone else taste it first."

"If you wish," Cordwin said softly. "I'll drink first and taste your food, also. But know this, Drambit: you have less to fear from me than from anyone else, despite what you think."

Malbar smiled sardonically. "Do you mind if I don't believe you?"

Cordwin pursed his lips. "I see you trust Vorlik as much as we trust Drambit."

A knock at the door interrupted them. A servant girl entered with a food-laden tray and a bottle of wine. Placing the tray on the table, the girl started to open the bottle when Cordwin dismissed her.

Cordwin opened the bottle himself, half-filled a silver goblet, and sipped it while Malbar watched. After eating a spoonful of the venison stew and a crust of thickly-buttered bread, Cordwin looked at Malbar. "Excellent food, and not poisoned in the least."

"But you might be willing to sacrifice yourself to kill me."

"I could have killed you before you entered this castle." The intensity of Cordwin's stare made Malbar so uneasy, he had to look away.

"I don't care what you believe, ambassador," Cordwin said. "But I swear by Baramay that you are safe here. No one will harm you. And I would fight to the death to protect you if anyone *tried* to harm you. So, are you hungry? If not, I'll send this food to someone who is."

"No, leave the food," Malbar said. "If you were going to kill me, a dagger would be much easier." Against his reason, he admired the man.

Cordwin turned and strode to the open door. "You may be returning home very soon, ambassador, but you may visit us again." He closed the door behind him, leaving Malbar staring thoughtfully after him.

He seems like an honorable man, Malbar thought grudgingly. *I could almost like him if he weren't a Vorlikian.*

16

In the council chamber, Captain Daikin, the lieutenants, and counselors were assembled, questioning looks on their faces. All stood as Bren entered, followed closely by Cordwin. Bren had changed into a white shirt, black leather vest, and black pants tucked into black leather boots. The golden seal of Vorlik hung against his chest. He tried to look confident as he strode past the advisors gathered in the council chamber. The room hushed as Bren sat at the head of the long table. Cordwin sat at his right hand; Captain Daikin, at his left.

Bren scanned the faces anxiously. He'd only been Lord of Vorlik for less than half a year, and he still felt unprepared to rule. And his counselors trusted him less than Cordwin did. Swallowing hard, Bren spoke. "I've received a letter from Lady Miria of Drambit."

Whispered muttering broke out among the counselors. The soldiers all cursed.

"My Lord, what does it have to do with us?" Lieutenant Rayvil asked, his dark eyes narrowed and his voice tight.

"A great deal." Reading the letter, Bren watched as astonishment filled their faces. When he finished, he said, "What do you think?"

Everyone began talking at once, many cursing.

"Silence!" Cordwin said, bolting to his feet and glaring about the room. "This is not a tavern! You are counselors and advisors. Behave as such!"

The room quieted instantly, but Bren could see anger and hostility in many of the faces. Cordwin sat back down.

"You can't be seriously considering this!" Rayvil said. "She's a Drambini! That is enough for me!"

Daikin spoke next. "My Lord, our people would never accept this...this...woman as your wife! At least I couldn't! Her father murdered your parents and kidnapped you! He invaded our land and caused the death of many of our soldiers! He nearly killed your uncle and me, too! How can you even consider marriage to her?"

Bren stared down at the table, his shoulders hunched. The burden of his guilt weighed heavy on him, he couldn't speak.

"But Lord Bren has known her from childhood," Lieutenant Linaria said pensively. She turned her hazel eyes toward Daikin. "And he gave his pledge to marry her. Would you have him break his oath?"

"Yes!" Daikin said.

"Can she be trusted?" Lieutenant Loren asked warily.

"Can any Drambini be trusted?" Lieutenant Rayvil asked, running his fingers through his grizzled hair.

"This marriage might end the hostility between our peoples," said Scribe Talison. His sallow face was lined with grief, and his gnarled hands folded on the table. "Hasn't there been enough death and hatred? We've all lost someone we loved; I lost two sons and a grandson. The fighting, the killing must end. This union could be the beginning of peace!"

Confused discussion broke out with many opinions voiced, although Cordwin remained silent. Bren began to feel the matter was hopeless. Finally after several hours of debate, the consensus was an uneasy acceptance of Bren's marriage to Miria. The only dissenting voice was Daikin, who remained adamantly opposed.

"This is a trap, a ruse!" Daikin said. "I don't trust a Drambini any farther than I can throw one — preferably from the top of the highest tower."

"Captain!" Cordwin said. "That's enough!"

"No, it's not!" Daikin stood and planted his hands firmly on his hips. "You've said nothing about this. I want to hear what you think. Tell us, do *you* support this marriage?"

With all eyes looking at him, Cordwin stared down at the table for several moments. Finally, he gazed at the assembled men and women. "I've given Lord Bren my blessing."

Daikin's mouth dropped open as he gaped at Cordwin. "You don't mean that," he said. "Tell me you don't mean that."

"I do and I have," Cordwin said quietly.

Daikin slumped down onto his chair. "Baygor protect us," he whispered.

"I'll send word to Lady Miria of Drambit to come to Vorlik," Bren said. "We'll make the announcement on the seventh day of the Spring Festival. When I receive word of her acceptance, I'll declare an additional week of feasting ending with our marriage."

Daikin stood up slowly. His face was grave, his jaw set. He braced himself on the table, and he didn't look at Bren. "My Lord, I can't be part of this. I can't stay in Tarolin Castle if that woman is here."

"Daikin!" Cordwin said, fear in his face. "The Sword of Truth confirmed the ambassador spoke the truth."

Daikin shook his head, his coppery hair falling close around his face. "Even so, my heart tells me this is a trap. I can't stay here. Please, My Lord, send me to one of the border Guards where I can serve you and Vorlik and still keep my honor."

Cordwin stood facing his cousin. "Daik, please, don't do this!"

"How can I do otherwise?" Daikin said.

Bren was startled and troubled by Daikin's request. Daikin was his cousin, a good soldier, loyal to Vorlik, and respected by all the guardsmen. Bren didn't want to lose a valuable captain and a part of his family. But Daikin was adamant; Bren could tell by the glint in Daikin's green eyes. "Very well," Bren said reluctantly. "You are relieved of your duties in the Tarolin Guard. I'll reassign you to the Southern Guard as second-in-command under Lieutenant Kyris."

"My Lord, you can't do this!" Counselor Kenna said. "Captain Daikin is your cousin and third in line for the throne! You can't send him away!"

"It's by his own request," Bren said, not looking at Kenna. "I will not keep him here against his will." He turned to Daikin. "We'll miss your presence, Captain. Perhaps, in time, I hope you'll come back to us."

The light from the torches cast shadows on Daikin's face, but dismay filled his emerald-colored eyes. "I can only hope I'm wrong, My Lord." Daikin bowed his head, and he strode briskly from the chamber. The other men and women watched reverently as he left, then slowly turned back to Bren, but no one spoke for a few moments.

Kenna was the first to speak. "But who will be captain of the Tarolin Guard?"

"My uncle," Bren said, turning toward Cordwin, "if he will accept."

Cordwin stared at Bren for a moment, then nodded slowly.

"Then all is settled," Bren said.

The advisors and lieutenants rose, bowed to Bren, and left. Cordwin walked beside Bren as they left the council chamber. Neither spoke a word as they crossed the Audience Hall floor to the entrance hall and climbed the three flights of stairs to Bren's chambers.

"Bring the Drambini ambassador to me," Bren ordered one of his door guards. He entered his study followed by Cordwin. Cordwin sat in the chair opposite Bren and stared at the floor.

Taking a sheet of parchment and a quill, Bren wrote:

"My dearest Miria, I wanted to write to you, too, but my guilt stopped me. I remember our love and our pledge to marry. I still love you, Miria. Please be my wife. If you accept, I'll announce our betrothal formally on the seventh day of our Festival of Baygor. Come to Tarolin Castle with Captain Callas and any others you wish to attend the ceremony. Until we see each other face to face, I am your faithful love. Bren."

Rereading the letter, Bren thought of Miria. The memory of her slender form and delicate face, golden hair and blue eyes, brought a tightness to his chest and a warmth to his heart. He could hear her laughter and smell the scent of her perfumed skin. *We'll heal all the old wounds, Miria*, he thought. *We'll unite our lands as we unite with each other, and at last, there'll be peace.*

Bren noticed his uncle's silence. "I'm sorry to see Daikin leave."

Cordwin kept his eyes averted. "So am I."

Bren took another sheet of parchment from his desk and began to write the order of transfer. When he finished, he blew on the ink to dry it. He rolled the parchment and sealed it with red wax and stamped with the seal of Vorlik. "See that this is given to Capt—" Bren halted, then continued, "given to Lieutenant Daikin."

Cordwin stood and braced his hands on the desk, gazing intently at Bren. "Let me deliver the orders myself. Maybe if I speak to him alone, if I can reason with him, maybe I can persuade him to stay. We need him. He's a better soldier, a better captain than I'll ever be." Cordwin hung his head. "I can't bear to think of him leaving."

Bren nodded slowly and handed Cordwin the orders. "It's painful when friends come to a parting of their ways," Bren murmured, his thoughts on Malbar.

"Painful indeed," said Malbar, who stood in the doorway, flanked by two guards. "But the pain is temporary and as easily forgotten as the friendship."

Bren stared at him. He wished they could be as close as they once had been. How could he ever think of Malbar as an enemy? "No, not so easily forgotten."

"You sent for me," Malbar said, his face as blank as a stone wall.

"Here's a letter for Lady Miria." Bren rolled the parchment, sealed it with wax, and handed it to Malbar.

"Are you..." Malbar stared at the floor, "are you going to marry her?"

"Yes," Bren said.

Malbar winced but said nothing.

"You can leave now if you wish," Bren said quietly, "but you'd have to spend the night traveling roads you don't know. That could be dangerous. Or you can stay here, leave at dawn, and arrive in Drambit by sunset. The choice is yours. Of course, I'll send an escort with you either way."

"Neither prospect is pleasant," Malbar said, "but I'll stay the night in the castle. I have your promise of safety?"

Bren nodded, a slight sad smile on his lips, a hollow ache in his heart. "Don't you trust me?"

"No," Malbar said bluntly. "But even if I don't trust you, I do trust him." Malbar pointed Cordwin. "He is an honorable man and trustworthy, even if he's a Vorlikian."

Bren flinched. "Yes, he's honorable and trustworthy," he said quietly, "and much more."

Malbar glared at Bren. "If you've nothing else for me, I'll return to my cell and leave at first light. I look forward to my departure as much as you do, lord of Vorlik." With an exaggerated bow and a grim smile, Malbar left the study.

17

Daikin folded his red-and-gold surcoat and placed it on his bed. His calloused hands lovingly smoothed the uniform he'd worn proudly for nearly twenty-three years. His heart ached with the thought of leaving comrades and friends, especially Cordwin. *Why can't they see this marriage alliance with Drambit is a terrible mistake?* he wondered, worry tightening his stomach. *Why am I the only one who sees it for a deception that will only lead to disaster?*

He opened the small trunk at the foot of his bed that held all his possessions. He pulled out a rosewood box that held his dearest treasures. He brushed his fingertips over the box, then undid the catch and opened it. A red silk kerchief lay folded on top. He took it out and carefully unfolded the silk. In the center lay a lock of his mother's auburn hair, tied with a green ribbon. He barely remembered her face, but he never forgot her long auburn hair. He held the kerchief to his nose and inhaled. The scent of lilac, his mother's favorite fragrance, still clung to the fabric after all these years.

Next in the box was a short dagger with a carved bone handle that had been his father's. He rubbed his thumb along the grooved handle, remembering how his father had used the knife to whittle wooden toys. When Daikin was six, his father had carved all kinds of birds and had painted them in exact detail, then suspended them over Daikin's bed. Daikin remembered how the breeze through his window made the birds seem to fly overhead.

Both his parents had died of winter fever the same year Cordwin's parents had died. Cordwin's brother and sister-in-law, Lord Clevil and Lady Ellisa, had taken care of Daikin as if he were Cord's brother. The two of them hadn't been apart for more than a few days since Cord was eight and Daikin was nine. Now he had no idea how long it would be before he saw Cord again.

Packing several changes of clothes and his few personal possessions in a saddlebag, Daikin glanced around the small room in the castle barracks. He had a room next to Cordwin's in the castle itself, but he seldom used it. For over twenty years since his promotion to captain, the sparsely furnished room close to his men had been his home. He had never thought he would leave it.

As he turned to leave, he saw Cordwin standing in the doorway, his face mirroring Daikin's own despair.

"Daik, don't leave," Cordwin said. "Please don't leave. I need you here, the men need you, and Bren needs you, more than he realizes."

"I can't," Daikin said, his throat tight. "I'm sorry, but I can't."

"But we've never been apart. Who will get me into trouble now?" Cordwin smiled for a brief moment.

"You'll have to do that all by yourself." Daikin smiled back, but there was no mirth in his voice or his heart.

Cordwin held out a rolled and sealed parchment, his hand trembling. Your transfer to the Southern Guard."

Daikin walked slowly toward Cordwin and took it.

"Daik, please." Cordwin's face was filled with loneliness. "Isn't there some way you can stay here?"

Daikin's throat was so tight, it was hard to speak. "I'd do anything for you, Cord. You know that. But I can't stay here and pretend everything is fine. I can't."

"You're the best friend I have," Cordwin said. "My only friend. Don't leave me."

Daikin clasped Cordwin's shoulder. "Do you want me lie to you and to myself? I'm your cousin and friend, and you're like the brother I never had, but I have to be truthful about my fears, even if the truth separates us, perhaps forever. If Bren marries Miria, nothing but trouble will come of it, I'm sure. How can I stay at Tarolin and watch Bren destroy himself and Vorlik? I know you have the same doubts I do. I saw it in your face at the council meeting. Come with me. We can go to the Southern Guard together."

Lines gathered at the corners of Cordwin's eyes. "Don't you think I want to get on my horse and ride beside you? Don't you know how much your leaving hurts?

But I can't leave Bren. He needs me now more than ever, especially if you're right about Miria. I have to stay and protect him. I have no choice."

Daikin clasped Cordwin's forearm. "I know. You'll stand by him no matter what happens. I can't stand by and watch. Who's to say which of us is right?"

"You'll wait 'til morning, won't you?" Cordwin asked. "You don't want to leave tonight."

Daikin glanced out the small window above his bed. The sky was dark and glittering with stars. "I could reach Yarrow in an hour or two, if I left now. A night at the Singing Wheels Inn might be very pleasant, especially with some fine Yarrow wine." He tried to smile, but he couldn't.

Cordwin embraced his cousin fiercely. "Be careful, Daik. May a friend guard your back."

Daikin felt as if winter breathed down his neck, and he shivered. "May you not die alone."

They stood silently, arms around each other. Daikin wished he could find the words that would convince Cordwin to come with him, but Daikin knew there was nothing that would draw Cordwin away from Bren's side. Finally, Cordwin pulled away and gazed at Daikin.

"Baramay protect you and keep you safe, Daik. I pray that you are wrong and that you'll come back soon." Wheeling, Cordwin left.

Daikin stared at the doorway, feeling desolate and dejected. *Baramay hold you in the shelter of her hand, and Baygor protect you from harm,* he thought. *Will I ever see you again?*

He slung his saddlebag over his shoulder and walked from his room toward the mess hall. The day watch was still lingering over mugs of ale. When Daikin walked in, every soldier stood and saluted. Lieutenants Loren, Rayvil, Linaria, and Tude stood before him, saluting.

"Baramay keep you, captain," Linaria said, her hazel eyes glistening as she looked steadily at Daikin.

The soldiers echoed her. "Baramay keep you, captain."

Daikin could hardly speak. When he did, his voice was strained. "I'm not your captain anymore."

Linaria stepped close to him and held out her hand. "You will always be our captain."

Daikin grasped her forearm. She slipped her arm around his neck and kissed him soundly. He was breathless by the time she ended the kiss. The other soldiers hooted with delight.

Daikin blinked at Linaria in surprise. He had never imagined she would do something so uncharacteristic. "Lieutenants don't kiss captains," he said, still startled.

"Then it's a good thing you're not a captain," she said, a sly smile on her lips. "We're equals now, you and I."

Daikin swallowed tightly, feeling a bit too warm. "I'll remember that."

"Good," she said.

The chief cook came from the kitchen, holding a sack of food. "You take care, captain. I doubt those cooks at the Southern Guard will feed you right. You take this with you, and if you ever get hungry, you just come back to my kitchen and I'll cook you a proper meal."

"Thank you," Daikin said as he took the sack. He gazed at the soldiers he'd served with and commanded for so many years. "Baramay bless all of you."

The soldiers saluted. Daikin returned their salute, wheeled, left the mess hall.

Walking briskly to the stables, Daikin saddled his chestnut stallion and tied his saddlebag securely. He led the horse from the stables and gasped as he looked out at the courtyard, lit only by torchlight. The entire Tarolin Guard stood at attention. *How can I leave them?* he thought, his heart nearly breaking. *But how could I stay?*

The soldiers saluted him, and he returned their salute. After a long last look about the courtyard, he mounted his horse and rode at a gallop through the gates, heading for his new post with the Southern Guard.

18

The seven days Gemna spent at home were almost more than she could tolerate, although it was good to see her brothers again. Maren had helped her and her brothers repair the damage to the house and barn, and Gemna was surprised Maren was so handy with a hammer. She showed Maren how to use a sword well enough he wouldn't injure himself with it. Her mother had embarrassed her continuously with insinuations of marriage and babies. Gemna cringed every time her mother spoke to Maren. Only the prospect of caring for Ilette had finally quieted Selene's blatant hints.

"Your father will be so surprised he has a new daughter," Selene said as she played with Ilette.

Gemna looked at Maren and grinned. He grinned back and winked. *Yes, Father will be very surprised,* she thought.

They got up at daybreak, preparing to leave. They left the wagon and the cow and most of the food with Gemna's family. She hugged each of her brothers, and then Ilette. Gemna's brothers had gleefully taken to the little girl and were already spoiling her, and Ilette seemed delighted with her new family. Gemna smiled to herself. *She'll be loved and happy,* she thought as she kissed the little girl goodbye.

Maren took Ilette and kissed her, smoothed her dark hair, then held her close. Gemna touched his arm. She saw in his dark eyes how hard it was for him to leave Ilette, and she wished she could make it easier for him. Slowly, he placed Ilette in Selene's arms and caressed the little girl's cheek. "Goodbye, dearling," he said. "Baramay keep you safe."

Selene smiled and hugged Ilette. "Oh, she'll be just fine. Come back and see her anytime."

"I will," Maren said, "as often as I can." He smiled, but Gemna heard a tremor in his voice and saw tight, tiny lines gathering at the corners of his eyes. He quickly turned and mounted his horse. Gemna mounted her horse, waved at her family, then Maren and she rode east down the lane.

Gemna was relieved to be traveling again. She loved her family, but being with her mother was like being smothered with a feather bed. Now Gemna felt free, as if she could breathe again.

They turned onto the North Road, toward the capital of Beltrin. The road wound through rolling hills, leafing woods, and greening meadows, all ravaged by winds and rains. Gemna's home had been only slightly damaged, but the farther north she and Maren traveled, the more devastation she saw. Rushing torrents had cut deep gullies in the hillsides, and mudslides had buried several huts. Trees were twisted and snapped; villages, flattened. The survivors had built huge pyres where fires burned drowned animals and people to prevent disease. The wide-spread ruin and loss of life everywhere Gemna looked made her sick.

"What could cause so much destruction?" she asked softly, a bitter-acid taste in her throat.

Maren shook his head. "The old woman called it the Witch of the Winds."

Suddenly, pain lined in his forehead. He clutched his temples and gasped, squeezing his eyes tightly shut.

Gemna reined her horse to a halt. "What's wrong?" she asked, bewildered. "What happened?"

"I tried — my head — I, uh, have attacks sometimes," he stammered, "sudden pains in my head."

"Do you have these fits frequently, or is this a new way to liven up our trip?" She tried to cover her apprehension with an annoyed tone, but her stomach was knotted with fear. Her heart pounded fiercely.

Maren rubbed his forehead. "They don't happen often."

Gemna blew out the breath that worry had trapped in her chest. "I was right. You do need a keeper."

Maren grimaced at her.

"You had an attack back at the barn, when you were taking care of the old woman, didn't you?"

"Well, uh, yes."

"Don't you have some medicine, some herb to prevent the spells?"

Maren shook his head. "There's no medicine to help me."

Gazing at him, she wondered what secrets he kept. She looked west where the sun was touching the tops of the trees. "It's nearly sunset," she said. "We might as well camp for the night. Tomorrow we'll reach Warren. We can stay at the mercenary guildhall, and I'll introduce you to the masters. I'll be glad to see them again."

They dismounted in the grassy meadow on the west side of the road. Maren seemed a bit shaky and pale. Gemna built a fire, and they settled down for the night. They enjoyed meat pasties, cheese toasted and spread on bread, and goldflower wine as light as a spring breeze and as clear as summer skies. Selene had insisted they take enough food for a company of mercenaries. For a sweet finish to the feast, Gemna stewed dried apples with a tiny piece of precious cinnamon, brought from the western lands. Maren slept soundly that night. Gemna didn't bother to keep watch, but several times she woke and checked his breathing, just to reassure herself.

She lay close by him. She almost reached out her hand to touch his face, he was so close, achingly close. Her thoughts lingered on every time he'd touched her, every expression of his face, the unexpected desire he provoked in her, even on the muscular curves of his body. She'd never known a man like him, never been so drawn to a man. Even in the guild house, she'd never allowed passion in her life, preferring swordplay to love play. Why did he stir such tender feelings in her heart, feelings she'd ignored so long, feelings as gentle as a summer wind, as sweet as goldflower nectar?

She clenched her hand, as if she could control the emotions growing in her. *I'm a sword for hire, sworn to his service until we reach Vorlik. After that, I'll probably never see him again.* Her chest tightened at the thought. She wasn't sure she could face never seeing him again. She closed her eyes and fell into a troubled sleep.

Morning brought black clouds and a driving rain that soaked them. The horses slogged through sucking mud. The wind turned frigid. The rain turned to sleet and freezing rain. Gemna's lips quivered with cold. Her hands were so numb, she had to weave the reins through her stiff fingers to hold on to the leather strips. Her chest hurt each time she breathed in the cold air, but she kept pressing on toward

Warren, city of the Beltrin lords and the mercenary guildhall. By the time Maren and Gemna reached the outskirts of Warren, her cloak was coated with ice.

Built on a squat hill, Warren had no wall surrounding it. Since Beltrin had no great material wealth, no army had ever attacked the land. The frugal Beltrin lords considered spending money for a wall foolish and unnecessary.

Unlike many cities, Warren had been built in an orderly fashion. Streets ran parallel and perpendicular from one end of the city to the other. Reflecting the sensible and thrifty outlook of the inhabitants, the houses were narrow, deep, two-story structures of white limestone or plastered mud brick. Plates of dark grey slate roofed the houses since wood was costly and thatch was used only in outlying villages.

In the center of Warren was the market square surrounded by small shops and taverns and a Temple of Baramay on the east and west, by mercenary school and guildhall on the south. On the north was Hearthstone, residence of the Beltrin lords. More a large house than a castle, Hearthstone was built of yellow-streaked limestone, a white banner with a wagon wheel and a long sword embroidered on it hanging above the door. There were colored glass windows on the second floor.

It was dusk when Gemna halted before the guildhall. Shivering, she dismounted before the solemn building without windows on the first floor. Maren followed her to the wooden door with a small, closed peephole. Knocking brought the sound of quick steps. A pair of shadowed eyes appeared at the small opening, peering first at Maren, then at Gemna.

"What call to knock?" a youthful voice asked in hushed tones.

"The call of the sword," Gemna responded properly.

"What is your call?"

"My call is Gemna."

The dark eyes glanced at Maren. "What is his call?"

"His call is Maren, my present master."

"What call have you here?"

Gemna sighed with weariness. Sometimes all the ritual of the guildhall was annoying. "The call to shelter, food, and rest."

The peephole closed, and a key turned in the lock.

Maren's teeth chattered, and his breath was like swirling fog. "Why did we have to stand out here in the cold while you went through that ritual?"

"That's the way of the guild," Gemna answered, her voice shaking as much as she was.

The door opened, and a figure shadowed by torchlight at his back bowed. "Enter, Gemna, sister of the sword. Enter, Maren, master of our sister. Shelter, food, and rest await within."

Stepping inside, Gemna greeted the door ward and clasped his forearm while he reciprocated. He was young, lanky, and sun-darkened. Maren and Gemna slipped out of their drenched cloaks and handed them to the youth, who hung the iced garments on nearby pegs.

"Thank Baygor that Ilette is at your house," Maren said to Gemna, his lips so cold his words were slurred. "This is no weather for a child to be out in."

Gemna nodded, rubbing her arms to warm up.

"My call is Rensome," he said. Green eyes twinkled in an affable face. He walked with a loose stride beside Gemna, Maren trailing down the wide corridor. "Supper's over, but there's still stew in the kettle, and bread and cheese on the table. The masters are in the mess hall if you want to greet them."

Gemna felt more comfortable here than she did at home. At the guildhall, she was an equal, not just a woman without husband and children as she was at her father's house. As she passed various doors and the stairs to the upper floor, she remembered the guild kin she'd trained with. They were more family to her than all her blood kin. Forgetting Maren's presence, Gemna walked through the entrance to the mess hall.

Half a dozen men and women occupied tables and benches. A hearth took up one wall, a huge kettle hanging over magenta embers. Rensome and Gemna wove their way to a hearth-side table where two battle-scarred men toasted each other with huge mugs of ale. One, whose craggy face reminded her of a fat and hairy cur, glanced over the lip of his mug at Gemna. Bounding to his feet with a wild whoop, he nearly smothered Gemna as he embraced her.

"See, Kagon, little Gemna's come back to us!" He laughed heartily. "And she's sopping wet!"

Gemna wiggled from his grasp, drew her knife, and neatly sliced the thong that laced his slit-front shirt.

Laughing louder, the giant-man ducked, twisted like a cat, and grabbed Gemna's wrist with a hand like the claw of a Formian bear. "You were always a fool for that defense, little sister." Chuckling, he released her. "What brings you to the guildhall, all drenched and shivering? Looking for work?"

"No." She grinned and replaced her sword in its sheath. Pointing at Maren, she said, "This is my master, Maren the minstrel of Hixus."

Maren bowed, though he looked puzzled.

With an exaggerated bow, the man said, "Welcome, Maren, master of our sister. I'm Ilmar, guildmaster of mercenaries, expert in weaponless combat. This is Kagon," indicating the other man, "swordmaster and my second. Welcome to our hall."

"Thank you, guildmaster."

"Gemna's a favorite of mine." Ilmar draped a thick arm around her shoulder. "We're always glad to see her. Will you be spending the night?"

Gemna nodded vigorously. "I'm not traveling any farther in this weather!"

"A merchant from the south hired nearly every swordsman available a few days ago, so there're only a dozen of us still here. There's plenty of vacant rooms right now," Ilmar said. "Of course, you can use one of them, Gemna. However," Ilmar gazed at Maren slyly, "your master isn't one of us, so he'll have to pay for his keep. Five gold for a single room or three for a cot in the barracks."

Wide-eyed, Maren looked to Gemna for assistance, but she remained stone-faced, staring at Ilmar. She knew exactly what Ilmar was doing, but she wouldn't interfere.

Maren cleared his throat. "I think five gold are too much for a room. One silver is fair."

Ilmar raised a shaggy brow, grinned down at Gemna, then looked back at Maren. "For Gemna's sake, I'll accept three gold for the room and a meal."

Maren's eyes met Gemna's, and she saw understanding twinkling in his eyes. Gazing at Ilmar, Maren almost smiled. "I could stay at a good inn, with meals and a bath included, for two silver."

"But the inn is full tonight, what with the weather stranding so many people. Two gold and two meals."

"Hah! I can sleep in the open for nothing, but out of courtesy I'll offer three silver."

"One gold and two meals."

"Five silver, two meals, refill our waterskins, stable our horses, and I'll entertain you tonight."

Ilmar grinned at Maren, then Gemna. "You've chosen a canny master," he laughed. "Agreed, Maren, but payment in advance." As Maren counted out the coins, Ilmar continued, "After you've dried by the fire, join us in a mug of ale. Are your horses out front?"

Gemna nodded her head.

"Rensome," Ilmar called.

The lad who'd let them in came running into the room.

"Stable their horses," Ilmar said. "Magrette, bring our visitors some food."

Between bites of herbed rabbit stew and hard rolls, Gemna blushed as Ilmar and Kagon spent the rest of the evening telling Maren tales of battles and Gemna's expertise. Maren played and sang a dozen songs, then ate another bowl of stew and sipped on a mug of ale while Ilmar, Kagon, and Gemna all talked of old times. After hours that seemed only minutes, Gemna glanced Maren's way, saw him yawn, and she realized how late it was.

"I think it's time for bed," she said.

Ilmar grinned lecherously. "Together? If Maren is trying to save the price of a room, it's too late."

The open-mouthed shock on Maren's face made Gemna laugh. Ilmar had always enjoyed teasing. Smiling innocently, she crooned, "Good night, Ilmar."

Rensome led them upstairs to two adjoining rooms, sparsely furnished with bed, washstand, and chair. "Sleep well, Gemna, Maren. Baygor protect you." He skipped down the stairs.

Left alone with Maren, Gemna turned to her door. "You haggle like a Beltrin merchant," she called over her shoulder.

"Your father taught me," Maren replied.

Gemna smiled at him warmly. "Good night, Maren."

He lingered a moment, gazing at her, then smiled. "Baramay give you pleasant dreams."

Long before dawn, the noise of activity woke Gemna. She dressed quickly and knocked on Maren's door. Soon, it opened. Scrubbed and fully dressed, Maren stood in the doorway. They walked downstairs to the dining hall and saw that everyone else had already finished eating breakfast. Taking a bowl of honey-sweetened barley groats and milk, a slab of ham, a boiled egg, and a soft roll, Gemna found two places across from each other. Rensome wedged in beside

Gemna and talked so much, Maren and Gemna finished their meal as fast as possible and stood to leave.

"Might as well sit back down," Ilmar said. "The storm is worse this morning than it was last night. Ice has coated everything, and the wind is like razors. I doubt anything could travel in this weather."

Maren turned to Gemna. "I think we should wait out the storm," Maren said, "but you know this place better than I do. What do you think we should do?"

Gemna smiled. "I say we stay warm and dry for another night."

"So," Maren turned back to Ilmar, "what will another night cost *me*?"

Ilmar grinned. "Just a few songs and maybe a story or two."

"Fair enough," Maren said.

Ilmar led Gemna and Maren to a small round table near the fireplace where they could sit comfortably. The guildmaster regaled Maren with stories about Gemna, which made her cringe.

"And you should have seen the look on her face," Ilmar said, "stuck up in the tree, her sword belt caught on a branch and unable to get down. We had to get a ladder and a saw to cut her down." He laughed and pounded the table.

"Why do you always have to tell that story?" Gemna said with a sigh. "I'd only been here one week when that happened."

"Because I love to see the look on your face when I tell it," Ilmar said.

Gemna sighed and shook her head, knowing that Ilmar would tell Maren every embarrassing tale about her. "Sometimes you're worse than my mother," she said.

Ilmar just laughed.

Most of the rest of the day Gemna spent close to the hearth, trying to soak up warmth from the blazing fire and listening to the howling wind blowing icy rain. Maren told the story of Radamin the Betrayer and sang numerous songs, and later, he told the tale of Timmree the Wizard and Cavolin of Vorlik. All the time he was telling about the Wizard who married a human lord, Maren kept glancing at Gemna, and his eyes seemed troubled. Gemna felt unsettled by his gaze, but when he sang "Old Mason's at the Barrel Again," he began to smile again and turned his gaze toward the crowd. Late in the afternoon, she took Maren to the practice room and worked on his sword skills.

"You'll never make a mercenary," she said, laughing and wiping sweat from her forehead, "but at least you won't hack off your own foot."

"That's good," he said between gasps for breath. "A one-footed minstrel couldn't wander very far."

After supper, Ilmar asked for more songs, and Maren obliged. Gemna noticed the wind had calmed a bit, but she still huddled close to the fireplace. For some reason, she couldn't seem to get warm enough. She closed her eyes and listened as Maren sang the plaintive "Tellowee's Lament" and the tender ballad "Sherlyn's Rose." Maren's baritone voice encircled her like a warm blanket, as if he held her in his arms. *I think I could listen to him sing forever,* she thought. Later, after she'd snuggled into her bed, she heard Maren strumming his lute in the room next door. She fell asleep to the sound of his voice singing "Sherlyn's Rose," and she'd never felt more content.

The next morning, Gemna woke to the twittering of snow sparrows. She gazed out the small window in her room. The storm had passed, and the sun shone on the ice-covered city, which glittered like thousands of diamonds. Dressing quickly and packing her belongings, she slung her sack over her shoulder, left her room, and knocked on Maren's door. "Are you awake?" she called.

He opened the door, fully dressed. His lute was slung over his shoulder, and he carried his knapsack. "Awake, hungry, and ready to be on our way."

They walked down to the common room, leaving their packs by the front door, and joined Ilmar and Kagon for breakfast. By the time they finished, Ilmar had told Maren four more stories about Gemna.

"Barg's Breath!" Gemna said, frowning at Ilmar. "You'll have Maren so convinced of my ineptitude, he'll want a different bodyguard."

Maren laughed. "No. I'm used to you now."

They all laughed.

Gemna pushed away from the table and stood up. "We need to be leaving," she said. "We have a long way to go yet."

Maren stood and bowed gracefully to Ilmar and Kagon. "Thank you for your hospitality and especially for the stories."

Ilmar grinned. "And thank you for the entertainment."

Ilmar enveloped Gemna in a bear hug and lifted her off the floor. "You take care, little sister," he said as he set her back on her feet.

Kagon did the same. "Come back and see us soon," he said. He turned to Maren. "Take care of our little sister."

"I thought she was supposed to take care of me," Maren said with a smile.

Kagon clapped Maren on the back, almost knocking him to the floor, and laughed heartily.

After refilling the waterskins, Maren and Gemna left the guildhall and found their horses saddled and waiting before the door. The weather was cool, but the ice was beginning to melt in the bright sunshine. The sky was clear, promising a mild and pleasant day.

Gemna looked up at Hearthstone, the Beltrin lords' residence as they rode toward it, and she chuckled.

"What's so amusing?" Maren asked.

"Those windows, the colored ones on the second floor," Gemna said.

Maren looked at her puzzled.

"They're called Ryan's Folly."

"Why?"

"The people of Beltrin are practical people and not given to ornamentation," she said, smiling. "However, many years ago one of the lords of Beltrin married a woman from Peltik, who scandalized the entire country. She dressed in bright silks and fancy hats and had lavish parties at Hearthstone. And she had those stained glass windows installed in her bedroom. Eventually, she became more subdued in her dress and behavior, but the windows stayed. Beltrini still chuckle over the ridiculous expense of the windows, and the lord's name is infamous now."

"Over colored windows?"

Gemna grinned and nodded.

Maren looked up at the brightly colored windows in the plain stone structure, then shook his head slowly. "Over colored windows," he said softly.

Gemna laughed. Together they rode north past Hearthstone and Ryan's Folly, as the sun crept above the eastern horizon.

19

As the hazy sky lightened to blue-pink, Gemna felt happy to be traveling again. Seeing old friends and teachers always brightened her mood, but it was good to be on the road with Maren again. She felt at ease with him unlike anyone she'd ever met, as if she'd known him all her life, and yet there was still some secret he kept from her. Some mystery surrounded him that she couldn't discover. When she looked in his eyes, her heart trembled, not only from delight.

They camped by the roadside that night. The air was chilly but not uncomfortably so. The stars overhead glittered like sunlight on snow. Gemna sat quietly beside Maren as he strummed his lute. She wanted to ask him about himself, where he came from, why he wandered, but something held her back, although she wasn't sure what.

She bedded down beside the fire and closed her eyes, but couldn't sleep. Finally, she cracked her eyes just a bit and gazed at Maren, sleeping on the other side of the fire. His head was pillowed on his arm. A few locks of his dark hair fell across his forehead. Firelight flickered across his face, illuminating every plane and curve, and making her heart quiver. For a moment she wondered what it would be like to caress his face, to kiss his lips, to hold him close.

Stop! she thought. *Don't even think about it! Some lines can't be crossed. He's your master. He can never be more than that. Even if you want him to be.* She rolled over, turning her back to Maren, and closed her eyes tightly until she fell asleep.

They rose before dawn and ate a cold breakfast before they mounted their horses and rode through flat plains and treeless meadows. By sunset they reached the Peltik border and stopped for the night at a cozy inn on the Beltrin side.

The innkeeper told of strange winds, vicious storms, and of many deaths in Peltik from winter fever. Gemna listened sadly as other customers verified the stories, and she didn't miss the grim set of Maren's mouth and the grief in his eyes. Nor did she miss the quiet despair in his voice.

"Briella would never have allowed this sickness to spread so widely — if she were alive," Maren whispered, knuckles purple-white as he clenched a mug of wine. "And I can do nothing to help!"

Gemna almost asked who Briella was and what she meant to Maren, but didn't. She truly didn't want to know.

Leaving early the next morning, they entered Peltik with caution. They passed a few farmsteads before they reached the towering forest just after midday. Gemna gazed up at the giant trees that seemed to touch the clouds, trees so huge it would take ten men or more joining hands to encircle one tree. Every time she saw the ancient trees, she felt breathless, awed, and very insignificant.

The quiet seemed to grow with every minute. Clouds darkened the forest and the air became stiflingly close. A wind whipped up suddenly and jagged streaks of lightning nearly blinded Gemna just before a deluge of tepid rain soaked her and Maren.

"There's an inn just ahead!" Gemna shouted over the wind and thunder. "Follow me!" She clapped her legs against the horse's sides, urging him to a gallop, with Maren close behind her.

By the time they reached the inn, they were drenched and shivering. A stable boy took their horses, and Gemna and Maren splashed through mud puddles to the inn door. Wind pounded rain against the walls the rest of the afternoon and all evening, forcing them to stay the night. Hail pelted the wooden roof. Even with the shutters latched, lightning flashed so brightly, Gemna's room would for an instant become like daylight. Normally, the storm wouldn't have bothered her, but the wind -- it was like someone laughing madly one moment, weeping wildly the next. Gemna huddled under the blankets, eyes open, until exhaustion finally pulled her down into sleep.

The storm continued all day, forcing Maren and Gemna to stay at the inn. Rain mixed with hail pounded against the roof and shutters. Thunder crashed outside so loudly, Gemna felt as if it were echoing in her head. By nightfall, the storm had diminished to a steady rain, and Gemna fell asleep to the gentle patter on her window.

The rain stopped and the skies cleared by late morning the next day. Gemna climbed out of bed, feeling refreshed and rested, got dressed, and packed her belongings, then went to Maren's room and knocked on the door. Maren opened the door and motioned her to come in. He looked as rested as Gemna felt.

"We should reach Lecida before nightfall," Gemna said, as she entered his room.

Maren stretched then sighed. "I really didn't want to get out of bed," he said. "That's the best night's sleep I've had since we left your home." He stuffed his worn clothing in his saddlebag.

"Thank Baygor the wind stopped howling last night." She shuddered.

Maren nodded. "It sounded like a woman shrieking. I think it was the Witch of the Winds the old woman spoke about." Suddenly, he gasped and sank to his knees, pressing his fists to his temples.

Gemna dropped down beside him, wrapped her arms around him, and held him tightly while he sobbed in pain. *The attacks are getting worse,* she thought, *and I don't know how to help him! There has to be some way to stop them!* She held him while he trembled, resting his head on her shoulder.

"Maren, isn't there some way to stop these attacks?" she asked, anguish tearing at her. "Isn't there anything I can do to help?"

"No," he said, his voice hoarse, his chest heaving as he panted for breath, "Nothing I can do to stop them. I don't know of any cure. And there's nothing you can do but what you've done already, and I'm grateful, so very grateful."

Gemna glanced toward the door. "I'll help you back to the bed. We can stay another night. That way you can rest and we can leave for Lecida tomorrow morning."

"No, I'm better." He raised his head from her shoulder and tried to move. "I...may need help standing though."

Gemna kept one knee on the floor while she put one foot down. He put his arms around her neck. Holding him firmly, she looked at him and nodded. Together they pushed to their feet. He swayed a bit, but she supported him until he was steady.

"What would I do without you?" he whispered, smiling weakly. "Baramay blessed me the day I met you."

"You're delirious," she said. "Do you really want to ride on today?"

"Yes."

She gazed at him, uncertain. "All right, but if you feel one of the attacks coming on, please, please, tell me."

"I promise."

"Let me take you to the common room. I'll get our things and saddle the horses. You eat something and settle up with the innkeeper."

He smiled at her. "Yes, master."

Chuckling, she helped him walk down to the common room and settled him at a table. Fetching their belongings, she walked to the stable, saddled their horses, and tied on their saddlebags and packs. Refilling their waterskins from the inn's well, she tied them to the horses, then went back inside the inn.

Maren was eating slices of warm bread with honey. The color had come back to his face, and he seemed recovered. Gemna grabbed one of the slices of bread and took a bite.

"Are you ready to leave?" she asked, still worried.

"Yes." He turned to the innkeeper who'd wandered over to their table. "Thank you," Maren said, fishing out several silver coins from his pouch and handing them to the man. "You keep a most comfortable inn."

The innkeeper took the coins, smiled, and bowed. "Come again any time."

Gemna offered her arm to Maren.

He gazed up at her. "What would I do without you?" he said as he took her arm gently.

His touch caused Gemna's heart to dance. She tried to think of something light to say, but couldn't. "Come on," she said, trying not to sound worried. "Let's go."

She guided him out to his horse, helped him mount, then mounted her own horse. "Are you sure you're well enough to ride?"

He nodded, clapped his legs against the mare's flanks, headed north toward Lecida at a slow walk, Gemna riding beside him.

Daylight was fading overhead as they neared the Beltrin Gate of Lecida, capital city of the lords of Peltik. Hanging above the closed gate were black wreaths and banners announcing a death in the royal house. Two guards, dressed in black and silver mourning clothes, stood on the balustrade above the gate, fatigue on their faces.

Pausing before the open portcullis, Maren called up to the gate guards, "Who has died?"

One of the guards leaned on a pike. "Lord Merovan, son of Lord Merrik, died five nights ago."

"I'm sorry," Maren whispered.

"Oh, it's worse," the guard said, despair in his eyes. "Merovan's wife and children died before him, and Lord Merrik himself died before them. Winter fever's taken all the house of Peltik. It's never been so severe and wide spread, at least as far as I remember."

The guard sighed, his back bowed with grief. "Some curse hangs over Lecida. Too many families in mourning; too many ghosts haunt the streets. I sent my family back to my father's farm in the south. I'd leave, too, but the city is closed and under quarantine by order of Counselor Vairin. I can't let you enter, and believe me, you don't want to come inside. Death walks these streets."

Maren turned to Gemna. "What should we do?" he asked.

"What can we do?" she said. "We'll have to go around the city and camp for the night."

The two of them rode between the giant trees and the city walls until it was nearly dark. Dismounting, Gemna took the horses' reins and tied them to a nearby tree. Gemna grief and frustration cross Maren's face as sounds of mourning echoed from the other side of the wall.

"People are dying inside the city, and there's nothing I can do to help!" he said.

Gemna turned toward Maren. "What do you mean, there's nothing you can do?" she asked.

Maren looked at her bewildered. "I don't understand."

"You have healing herbs with you!" she said. "That bark you made tea with — why don't you give it to these people for the fever?"

"Don't you think I want to?" Maren stared at the ground, his shoulders sagging. His voice sounded strained. "I'd do anything to help these people, but how would I get it to them? And I have enough bark left to cure maybe a dozen people at most. How can I choose who will live and who I'll turn away? Tell me, how would you choose?"

"Oh." Gemna swallowed her anger. "Maren, I'm sorry I doubted you. I couldn't choose either. Isn't there anywhere you can find more of the bark?"

"There's only one place the callum tree grows," Maren said quietly, "but it's too far away. I have no way to reach that land."

Studying his face, Gemna saw longing in his dark eyes, a longing she could only name home. *Where do you come from, Maren?* she wondered. *Where is home?*

"I'll tend the horses," Gemna said. "See if you can cook something for our supper."

Maren smiled and bowed to her. "Yes, master."

Gemna didn't sleep much that night. The wind brought the feverish cries of the sick and the grieving wails of the bereaved from inside the city, keeping her awake in spite of her fatigue. No matter what she did, she couldn't block out the cries of grief. By daybreak, she felt exhausted. She tugged on clean clothes, smoothed her hair, and bound it at the nape of her neck with a leather thong. When Maren woke and said good morning, she only nodded.

They rode to the northern edge of the city. The city gate was closed but strangely unguarded when they passed it and turned north on the wide road.

Are there so few guards left that they can't station one guard at the gate? Gemna wondered. She looked askance at Maren. His hands clenched the reins so tightly, his fingers where red. Lines marred his forehead, and his jaw was tight. Anger, frustration, and despair flickered through his dark eyes. *I know how you feel,* she thought.

They headed north through the giant trees. A brisk, cool breeze chilled Gemna's face and whipped through her hair. She pulled up her hood to keep the wind from her eyes. The wide road was deserted except for the two of them. They seldom spoke in the silence of the great trees. Something about the massive forest made Gemna reluctant to break the stillness. The only sounds Gemna heard were the wind, a few songbirds, the clomping of their horses' hooves, and the gurgling of an unseen stream.

Toward the end of the day, the forest thinned slightly. The gleaming peaks of the Circle Mountains became visible to the north, marking the border of Vorlik. Sunset painted the western sides like glowing embers while the eastern sides were blue-grey shadows.

Camping beside the road in the shelter of the towering trees, Gemna lit a fire. Maren prepared a soup from salted beef, some dried vegetables, and cracked barley. While the soup simmered, Maren took out his lute and tuned it. Gemna unsaddled the horses, staked them in a grassy area, and gave them each a bag of oats, then wiped them down and covered them with blankets. By the time she finished tending the horses, the soup was done. Maren handed her a bowl of soup and a spoon, then dipped one for himself.

Gemna sat cross-legged on the ground and blew on the soup to cool it. She sipped the broth cautiously so she wouldn't scald her tongue. The soup was hearty with a hint of pepper, and she ate it down without a word, drinking the last of the broth straight from the bowl.

"I take it you liked the soup," Maren said, grinning.

Gemna wiped her mouth on the back of her hand and grinned back. "Did I tell you you'd make someone a wonderful wife?" she said.

"Several times."

They both laughed. They each had another bowl of soup, which emptied the pot. Gemna washed the dishes, dried them, and put them back in a sack. Maren picked up his lute and began strumming.

Gemna sat down very close beside him. "Sing something."

Maren plucked a string. "Something lively?"

"No, something quiet, soothing. Something I've never heard before." She closed her eyes.

"All right." He strummed a chord. "I wrote this many years ago for... for someone I knew." He played a quiet melody touched by longing and sadness.

> Golden flowers scattered
> In a field of green,
> Laughing streams go skipping over stones.
> Gleaming mountains reaching
> To the clear blue sky,
> Songs of birds upon the wind are blown.
>
> Lovely are the woodlands.
> Silvery the moon
> Shining in a sky of midnight blue.
> Fair are all the meadows;
> Warm the golden sun.
> More beautiful than all of these are you.
>
> In our secret valley

I have loved you true.

All my heart to you alone I give.

Steadfast in my fervor,

Ever constant I,

You I'll love as long as I shall live.

His voice caressed Gemna's heart like velvet on her skin, warmed her like summer sunshine. The passion he poured into the song made her envy the woman he'd written about. She opened her eyes and studied him. His fingers plucked the lute strings softly. Dark brows pulled furrows in his forehead. His eyes stared at the ground. There were so many questions she wanted to ask him, so many things she'd like to know, but uncertainty closed her throat.

He looked up to see Gemna watching him. Resting the instrument on his lap, he asked softly, "What are you thinking?"

Gemna lowered her eyes to her folded hands. Warmth spread throughout her body, but she shivered. Finally, she looked over at him and blurted out, "I sense something in you I can't name, something that draws me yet disturbs me."

"Gemna," Maren said, smiling at her with tenderness, "you never need to be afraid me. Never."

"But who are you? What are you? Why are you here? Where's your home? Do you have a family? A wife? I know almost nothing about you."

"You know me," he said softly. "I'm Maren, a wandering minstrel who spends most of his time in Hixus."

"But that's all I know," she said, gazing at him intently. "Tell me about yourself. Please."

"All right." He set his lute down beside him. He bent one leg and propped his arm on his knee, turning toward her slightly. "My home's very far from here, a place you've never been. I have a sister named Amaly who lives there still. I've never married." He paused for a moment, staring at the fire, then looked back at Gemna. "I travel to meet new people and see new sights. Wherever I go, I sing a song, tell a tale, and bring joy to the lives of the people I meet. It's good to make people laugh and forget their worries for a while, to see wonder in the eyes of children and joy in the faces of adults. And that makes me happy."

Gemna played with a blade of dead grass. "Tell me about your sister. Is she younger or older? What does she do, all alone without you?"

"What's Amaly like?" Maren smiled. "She's seven years younger than I am, but she acts like she's my mother. Our parents died when we were young, and Amaly felt she had to take our mother's place as woman of the house."

"How did your parents die?"

Maren looked away and cleared his throat. "They were...murdered."

Gemna gasped. She started to reach out to him, touch him in sympathy, but she hesitated. In her family, everyone hugged each other in joy or sorrow. A touch could heal the soul, her mother always said. Gemna touched his arm. "Oh, Maren, I'm so sorry."

Maren gave her half a smile though his eyes were dull. "It was a long time ago."

"What about your sister?" Gemna asked, hoping to divert his attention.

His eyes gleamed. "She's almost as tall as I am, and she has golden skin, dark brown hair and eyes. She reminds me of our mother, at least the way I remember her. She loves animals, and they trust her. She frets over me when I'm home and worries about me when I'm gone. The last time I visited her, she scolded me for the first two hours for not sending word or coming home sooner. She makes silver jewelry for friends and family. She made me a pair of silver bracers."

"I've never seen you wear them."

"They're rather ornate. I've tried them on several times, but not in several years. I've never felt the time was right to wear them," Maren replied. "They don't seem appropriate for a minstrel."

"May I see them?"

"I'll get them." He turned to the pile of their belongings, opened his knapsack, and took out a rosewood box carved with an elaborate "M" encircled with flowers.

Gemna ran her fingers over the box. "This is beautiful," she said.

"She's good with wood, too."

Gemna leaned close and watched as he opened the box. Inside were silver bracers, etched with an eagle in flight and set with blue topaz for eyes. Both gleamed with the simple elegance of master craftsmanship.

Gemna gasped and touched the gleaming metal. "I understand why you've never worn them. They're magnificent! But you ought to wear them. Amaly wouldn't have given them to you if she thought you'd never user them. Why not put them on now?"

Maren took a bracer from the box.

"Look." Gemna pointed at the inside of the metal band. "There's writing. But not like any I've ever seen."

Maren squinted his eyes as he held the band up to the firelight. "I should know what it says, but I can't read the words." He shrugged and slid the bracers on his wrists.

Immediately, he shouted and clapped his hands his temples.

He's having another attack! she thought. She put her arms around him to hold him and keep him from hurting himself, but something thrust her away, and she was thrown to the ground. Startled, she stared at Maren fearfully. "What's happening?" she said. "What's wrong?"

He leaped to his feet, still screaming. Scrambling away from him, Gemna crouched beside a tree and watched in terror.

His shout became a wrenching shriek. He stretched his arms above his head and stared at the full moon shining directly overhead. Blue fire like lightning arced between the bracers, then crisscrossed, surrounding his body. A roar like a whirlwind engulfed him while a ray of dazzling moonlight shone on him. A red circlet of flame appeared about his brow. Blue fire warred against red flame, each striving for mastery. At last, the circlet of flame was broken and disappeared. The pain eased from Maren's face, and his screaming ended. Gemna heard him shouting words she couldn't understand.

"*Tasrin Baramay unalah salakin! Baramay paseelo a kaysaro habilah! Tasrin na Maren toolavraya!*"

The roaring stopped, the lightning disappeared, and the light subsided. Maren stood, hands reaching to the sky. "I'm free! Finally, I'm free!"

20

The morning sun was well above the Circle Mountains as Malbar left Abasette Castle with his squire and four guards to return to Vorlik. Miria's acceptance of Bren's proposal was in the leather bag slung over his shoulder. Miria and Malbar's father Captain Callas had explained Grimmin's plans to conquer Vorlik just before Malbar had left Drambit. He should be enjoying the coming destruction of Vorlik, but he didn't. Malbar ground his teeth in disquiet. Fear gnawed at his heart. He felt uneasy and unaccountably reluctant to be part of the charade.

He disliked Grimmin's scheme. Malbar was certain Grimmin couldn't be trusted, and as much as Malbar hated Bren and wanted him destroyed, Malbar sensed that the merchant — or whatever he was — was more dangerous than the entire Vorlikian army. Why would Grimmin conspire to conquer Vorlik? He was like a shadow across the sun. He made Malbar shiver with dread.

Malbar and his escort stayed the night at the inn near the border. When morning came, they approached the border keep. The Vorlikian solders stared at him but didn't attack him. The same sergeant who escorted him before came from the keep.

"Back again," the sergeant said.

Malbar nodded.

"I suppose I'll have to ride with you again."

"I suppose so."

"This could get to be a habit."

Malbar noticed a faint smile on the sergeant's face and almost smiled back. He had to remind himself the sergeant was his enemy.

Accompanied by the sergeant and seven Vorlikian guards, Malbar rode through the mountain pass and down into the plains of Vorlik. They stopped at the Western Guard barracks long enough to inform the lieutenant and secure additional troops for the border keep, then continued to Tarolin Castle.

It was early evening when Malbar reached the gate of Tarolin Castle and was met with respectful courtesy from the gatewards. Hiding his satisfaction, Malbar thought, *Cordwin must have punished the guards severely.* He rode into the courtyard, dismounted, and handed the reins to a stable boy.

The sergeant saluted. "I'll see you again when you're ready to leave, ambassador."

Malbar nodded and turned away, strangely troubled, then climbed the castle steps. Wearing the red and gold uniform of the Tarolin Guard, Cordwin met him at the entrance.

Malbar bowed. "I see you've been promoted," he said.

"Yes."

"What do I call you now?"

"Captain."

"Oh. What happened to the last one?"

Cordwin looked away from Malbar. "He chose to leave," Cordwin said quietly.

Malbar wondered what had happened, but said nothing.

Cordwin cleared his throat. "You've returned with word from Lady Miria?"

"I have a letter for the lord of Vorlik," Malbar replied formally.

Cordwin ushered him inside the castle and led him up the stairs. "You grew up with Bren, didn't you?"

Malbar nodded curtly, not wanting to remember.

"What was he like as a child? You see, I never knew him," Cordwin murmured.

"Neither did I," Malbar said bitterly. The memories were too painful. It was easier to block out all thoughts of Bren.

Shrugging his broad shoulders, Cordwin ushered Malbar to Bren's study, then stood close to the door.

Bren gave Malbar a wry smile. "So, we meet again."

"My Lady asked that I deliver this letter to you." Malbar took a sealed scroll from the leather bag and held the letter out to Bren, but refused to meet his eyes. Malbar didn't dare. He might betray how much he still cared for Bren, and how much being near him hurt. *No!* he thought, driving his nails into his palm. *I don't care about him anymore! I won't! I can't!* He clenched his teeth and waited silently.

Bren stood and walked around the table until he stood right in front of Malbar. "Will Miria marry me?" Bren asked softly as he took the letter.

Nodding reluctantly, Malbar said, "Yes."

Bren shouted and hugged him. "Drambit and Vorlik will be united, and all the old hatred will end. We'll be one people." He pulled back and gazed at Malbar. "Can't you and I put aside old hurts? Can't you forgive me?"

"I...don't know," Malbar said slowly.

"Would you...stand up with me?" Bren asked. "At the wedding."

Startled, Malbar didn't know what to say. How could he stand beside Bren as he married the woman Malbar loved? But there wasn't going to be a wedding. And Bren was going to die. That thought left an empty hole in Malbar's heart, no matter how much he wanted to despise and hate Bren.

"Do you remember our secret dell?" Bren asked, resting his hand on Malbar's shoulder. "Do you remember all the adventures we had together? I treasure those memories. We were the best of friends. I want us to be best friends again. Please." Bren leaned closer. "Please, Malbar. You're the only friend I have, the only friend I've ever had. I need you to stand beside me at the wedding."

Raising his eyes slowly, Malbar felt a cold knot in his stomach as he gazed at Bren. "I...I'll consider it," Malbar whispered.

"You'll stay the night again?" Bren asked.

Malbar nodded, his mouth tight, eyes staring at the floor. A voice urged him to remember their friendship, but he clamped his jaw tighter. Bren was his enemy now and would soon be dead.

"The tower room has been prepared for you," Bren said. "Anything you want, anything you need, just ask for it. Captain Cordwin will escort you to your room."

Bowing stiffly, Malbar exited the room. Their footsteps echoed loudly in the silence as Cordwin escorted Malbar to the tower room he'd occupied before. A woman wearing the red and gold uniform of the Tarolin guard saluted the Vorlikian captain as they arrived.

Cordwin opened the door and moved aside for Malbar to enter. "Do you want me to stay and taste your food and drink when it's brought?"

"Ah, no, thank you," Malbar replied with more graciousness than he had intended.

"If you want anything, call the guard. Or, if you prefer, have her send for me, and I'll take care of your needs." Cordwin bowed and left.

The meal seemed a feast. Malbar ate more than he should have. He loosened his belt and propped his feet on the table. *They eat well in Vorlik,* he thought. *I could get used to this.*

The breeze carried the sound of voices and music through his narrow window. Looking at the courtyard below, Malbar watched as soldiers and pilgrims assembled for the evening ceremonies. *They've a lot to celebrate,* he thought. *Some of our people would kill for a meal like this. Soon, our people will feast like this, too.*

Malbar lay down on his bed and clasped his hands behind his head. Listening to the faint chanting and music, he drifted to sleep. When he woke, the sky was midnight blue with diamond-dust stars. The air was only a light breath of flower- and earth-scented wind but carried a melody played on a flute. The musician was remarkably adept, but the song was sweetly plaintive. Rising, he strode down the spiral stairs to the door on the lower floor and called the guard.

Opening the door, the guard glared at him. She rested her hand on her sword hilt. "What do you want, Dramb—I mean, ambassador?"

Malbar gestured toward the window. "Do you hear that music?"

The guard nodded, her dark eyes narrowed and alert.

"Who's the musician?"

"Lord, I mean, Captain Cordwin."

"Cordwin?" Malbar couldn't hide his surprise. "A lord, a soldier, and a skilled musician, too? He is...extraordinary."

"Yes," the guard said, her head held high, "he is.

"That song, it sounds so mournful."

"Yes — mournful," she said softly, almost as if speaking to herself, "like a mourning dove."

Malbar looked at her questioningly, sensing there was more to the guard's words. "Why do you say that?"

"His wife was called Lady Mourning Dove." When Malbar cocked his head quizzically, the guard tensed, and her voice became like cold steel. "You mean you don't know? You don't recognize the name?"

"No," Malbar said, puzzled. "Who was she?"

"His wife was the Wizard Briella." The guard glared at Malbar. "Lord Bren killed her with a magic dagger given to him by Paxell."

Astonished, Malbar stammered, "Bren...killed...Cordwin's *wife*...and Cordwin still serves him?"

The guard nodded, the anger in her eyes diminishing slightly.

"But...why?" Malbar asked, bewildered. "How could Cordwin serve the man who killed his wife? How could anyone?"

"Because—" the guard halted, clenching her teeth. When she spoke again, her voice was softer. "Because Cordwin is a truly good and noble man, and a great and gracious leader. He knows that Bren was deceived and betrayed by Paxell. It wasn't Bren's fault."

Stunned, Malbar swallowed hard and nodded to the guard, then closed the door. Returning to his bed, he lay down and stared out the window at the stars in the night sky. Far into the night he listened to the sad, sweet music, wondering at the heart that could forgive a wife's murder.

He woke as the first golden-pink rays of the sun peeked over the eastern mountains. As soon as Bren summoned Malbar and handed the sealed letter for Lady Miria, Malbar set out for home. He didn't speak to his men or the Vorlikian sergeant who rode at his side. He wanted to reach home as soon as possible. Deeply troubled, Malbar tried to dismiss the warnings of his heart about Grimmin and the plan to conquer Vorlik. Tried to blot out the feelings he still had for Bren. Tried to forget the haunting melody he'd heard in the night and the man who played it. Tried, but failed.

21

The day before the culmination of the Spring Festival, Miria rode east at the head of a company of Drambini soldiers and a caravan of wagons, all escorted by a full squad of Vorlikian guards. She wore a bright blue dress to complement her fair complexion and golden hair. She was certain she would seem much less threatening than if she wore the traditional black and silver of Drambini lords. Surreptitiously, she noticed the faces of the onlookers who came to stare at her, their lord's wife-to-be. Some appeared curious; some, apprehensive; most, hostile. All bowed courteously if not enthusiastically as she rode past.

Captain Callas and his son Malbar rode beside her golden stallion; her maids, after them. She'd wanted Grimmin to ride with her, but he'd said he needed to arrive before her, so no one in Vorlik would suspect they were together. She missed him though, which surprised her. When she was near him, she felt as if she were standing on the brink of a cliff in a storm. Her skin tingled as she remembered his touch. Bren had never stirred such feelings in her.

It was late afternoon when she sighted Tarolin Castle for the first time. She wished her father could see her. She was finally going to do what he hadn't -- conquer Vorlik. It would've pleased Paxell, she was certain.

The caravan entered the courtyard to the sound of trumpets. Rows of guards in red and gold uniforms stood at attention. Miria saw Bren waiting at the top of the steps to the castle, other soldiers and dignitaries beside him. Bren was dressed in fine ceremonial attire: scarlet robe and cape, black boots, a sunburst medallion around his neck, and a golden crown on his head. He descended the stairs to help Miria from her horse.

Miria's stomach knotted with disgust, but she quickly composed her face to hide her rage. She smiled maiden-shy as Bren put his hands on her waist and helped her dismount. Her feet touched the ground; she leaned against him and gazed up at him. "Bren."

"Miria," Bren whispered.

"It's been so long," she said.

"Too long." His eyes locked with hers. For a long moment he didn't move. At last, he released her and bowed deeply. "Welcome, Lady Miria of Drambit. We are honored by your presence."

"Hail, Lord Bren of Vorlik," Miria replied formally. "We are honored by your courtesy."

Resting her hand lightly on his arm, Miria walked beside Bren up the steps of the castle. Malbar and Callas followed her while the Drambini soldiers waited in the courtyard. As they reached the top of the stairs, Bren turned and faced the courtyard, raising Miria's hand. The crowd cheered, but they didn't sound very convincing to her.

Bren led her inside the castle and introduced her to his advisors, four lieutenants, then to the captain of the guard. "This is Captain Cordwin," Bren said, "my uncle."

Miria studied Cordwin a moment. *So this is my father's worst enemy,* she thought, *the man he hated more than anyone else. I'll have to devise something special for him.* She lowered her eyes, then glanced up shyly. "Then you'll be my uncle, too," she said, touching his arm lightly.

Cordwin bowed stiffly, then saluted Bren. "I'll see that the Drambini troops are quartered and fed, their mounts stabled." He turned and went through the open doorway.

Bren let Miria, Callas, Malbar, and Miria's maids to apartments on the first floor. "These rooms are yours for now," Bren told Miria. "I hope," he paused and took her hand in both of his hands, gazing at her intently, "I hope that you find them comfortable. After our wedding, you'll have rooms on the third floor adjoining mine, rooms that belonged to my mother." Bren blushed, cleared his throat, and turned to Callas and Malbar. "We have provided rooms next to Lady Miria's rooms for both of you. I hope you will find them to your liking. If you need anything, please ask. I want to make certain you are comfortable here."

Malbar stared at Bren. "I'd prefer my previous accommodations."

Bren was silent a moment, then said, "Of course. Guard, please show the ambassador to the Green Tower."

He turned back to Miria and took her hand. "Would you allow me escort you to the evening festivities?"

Miria gave him her most inviting yet innocent smile. "I wouldn't want anyone else."

"I hope you dance as well as I remember."

"And I hope you are as enjoyable a partner." Miria's blue eyes widened as they gazed steadily into his.

Bren kissed her hand with the grace of a schoolboy and bowed. Miria opened the door and went in, followed by her maids. She smiled over her shoulder at Bren just before he turned and left. Moments later several of her serving men carried in trunks filled with her belongings, then departed for the servants' quarters.

Miria scanned her quarters while the maids unpacked her dresses. The apartment had a large sitting room with a limestone fireplace, a dark green settee, two plush chairs and footstools, and several tables. To the right was her bedchamber with a massive bed, a wash stand with bowl and matching pitcher, a table with a silver candlestick and two silver goblets, and a wardrobe of polished cedar. On the wall opposite her bedchamber was the fireplace. To the left of the fireplace was a bathing chamber; to the right, a small bedchamber for the maids. A tall vase with cuttings of pink apple blossoms and yellow forsythia sat on one of the tables in the sitting room. Thick furred rugs covered the stone floors.

Miria sank in one of the chairs, her feet on a footstool, and she smiled at the success of her first encounter with Bren. Such devotion. He hadn't taken his eyes off her. If she could keep him so enchanted, he'd be taken easily.

A knock at the door brought her to alertness. "Enter."

Captain Callas strode into the room and bowed.

"Yes, Captain?"

Callas glanced around the apartment. "Are we alone?"

Miria clapped her hands and turned toward the bedchamber.

The older maid came to the doorway. "Yes, My Lady?"

"Close the door and don't come out until I call you," Miria said.

"Yes, My Lady." The maid bowed and closed the heavy door.

Callas knelt beside Miria's chair and spoke in hushed tones. "Things are going exactly as we planned. Our soldiers are quartered in the trees west of Dancing

Glen so no Vorlikian will overhear or watch them easily. Grimmin delivered his barrels of wine two days ago, which he gave as a gift for the betrothal celebration. He also sent barrels to each of the border Guards."

Miria nodded. "Excellent. Hopefully, the poisoned wine should take care of all four border Guards. My forces will kill any Vorlikian troops that survive. And when all of Vorlik's forces are dead and Bren in our hands, we'll publicly execute the last lord of Vorlik. Then I'll rule both Vorlik and Drambit."

Miria leaned back languidly and savored the thought of Bren's death. She'd act the part of the devoted fiancée. Bren wouldn't realize he was trapped until too late. But before he died, she wanted him to know *she* was the one who had destroyed him, *she* had brought the downfall of Vorlik.

Dismissing Callas, Miria summoned her maids to help get ready for the evening. She bathed and scrubbed her hair with lilac soap. Wrapped in a thick towel, Miria lay on a thick fur rug before a crackling fire while the older maid brushed Miria's hair to shimmering gold. The younger maid rubbed Miria's body with lilac cream. When the maids were finished, Miria slipped on a linen robe and surveyed her wardrobe. She wanted to appear imposing but not haughty, modest yet playful, and above all entrancing.

"I think this one." Miria selected a medium blue woolen gown with high fitted waist and sheer long sleeves tied to the bodice with pink ribbons. Its low neckline and ankle-length hemline were embroidered with yellow and white flowers. The maids pulled the dress over her head and tied the bodice laces snuggly. She chose a sapphire and gold pendant that hung low enough to draw attention to her breasts.

"I want some flowers for my hair," she told the younger maid. "Ask the guard outside to direct you to someone who can find some. White flowers would be best. Pink if you can't get white. As many as you can find."

The maid bowed and hurried from the room. The other maid braided Miria's hair with a golden cord, wound it around her head like a crown, and secured the braid with dozens of golden hair pins. Next the maid used a kohl stick to line Miria's eyes, then rubbed cherry wine on her lips to stain them red. Finally, the maid brushed powdered silver on Miria's eyelids so they'd glitter in the firelight. The younger maid returned with two handfuls of tiny white snowstars, which the other maid scattered about the braid on Miria's head.

Miria stared at her image in the silver mirror on the wall in her bed chamber and nodded with satisfaction. She looked like an innocent young girl, sweet and shy, exactly how she wanted to appear. White teeth gleaming between her crimson lips, she said to her maids, "Leave me."

The maids curtsied and left.

Alone, Miria opened her jewelry box resting on a table beside her bed, took out the rest of her jewelry, then removed the bottom of the box to uncover a secret compartment. Inside were two glass vials of liquid, one colorless, the other a pale pink. She took the pink one from the box and opened it. Touching one drop to the back of her right hand, she massaged the liquid into the skin.

I hope Akavar is as good as Grimmin claims, she thought as she replaced the vial and closed the secret compartment.

She turned slowly before the mirror and scanned her reflection again, pleased with what she saw. Returning to the sitting room and settling in one of the chairs, she watched the sky dim with twilight and waited for Bren to call for her.

Sometime later, a knock startled Miria from her thoughts of revenge. "Enter."

When the door opened, Bren strode inside. He wore a white shirt with loose flowing sleeves, a red hip-length vest embroidered with gold oak leaves down the front and hem, black belt and golden sunburst buckle, black knee pants and boots. His dark brown hair was brushed straight back from his face and tied with a black ribbon at the nape of his neck. He started to bow, but his smile froze and his jaw fell open as he saw her. He looked as gawky and uncertain as he had when he was a boy.

"I'm glad you're here," Miria said, blushing and lowering her eyes to keep from laughing.

"I, uh, I've come to escort you to the dance. I hope you haven't been waiting long."

She looked up at him with a smile and made her voice soft and enticing. "Not long."

Bren walked toward her, took her right hand, and kissed it. Straightening, his head wobbled slightly; his eyes seemed out of focus. He licked his bottom lip and swallowed as if his throat were very dry. After a moment, he shook his head.

Miria caressed his cheek. "What's wrong? Are you ill?"

He blinked his eyes. "No, I, uh, I'm quite well, I think." His eyes focused on Miria. He kissed her hand again and spoke with breathless passion. "You glow with the radiance of Baramay's Circlet, and your hair is like spun gold. You're the most exquisite woman I've ever seen."

"Oh, Bren." Miria brushed her fingertips against his cheek, relishing the slight flush that spread across his face. "I didn't know you were so poetic."

Bren swallowed hard. "It's...it's time for the evening festival."

"Then we must hurry." Miria lowered her eyes modestly.

With her hand resting on his, Bren led her through the halls to the castle doors. They were greeted by a courtyard full of celebrants, gaily clad and bearing torches. Bren and Miria led the crowd through the castle gate to the meadow, just west of the castle, called Dancing Glen.

At the far north end of the meadow, tables had been set up with barrels of ale and wine and trays of cakes. A huge bonfire had been laid in the center of the meadow. Six-foot stakes with iron sconces encircled the area. Two thrones carved from oak and padded with red velvet cushions had been set on a dais near the tables for Bren and Miria. As the two lords stood before their seats, the women placed their torches in the sconces while the men thrust their torches into the bonfire. The stacked wood began to blaze.

A priest dressed in a blue and gold robe raised his hands to the sky and addressed the crowd. "Praise to Baygor. He has given us a new year. Life has come back to the earth; the cycle begins anew. Let us praise Baygor, for he has given each living thing the gift of offspring that life may continue. Praise to Baygor!"

"Praise to Baygor!" the crowd echoed.

Bren raised his hands and spoke to the crowd. "Now is the time of the dance. Now is the time to rejoice and be glad. Life is a circle year after year, from summer to autumn to winter and spring. So let the circle be joined. Let the dance begin."

Everyone cheered and shouted and clapped their hands. The women formed a ring around the fire, facing outward, while the men faced toward them. Even Captain Callas and Malbar joined in. The musicians began to play a centuries-old circle dance. Drums beat a slow yet compelling tempo. The flutes and harps played a quiet, seductive melody. The dancers skipped around the fire three times, stopped before a partner, and joined hands. Couples swung around, linked arms, and circled the fire. Palms touched palms, left to left, right to right. Hands clasped as the dancers skipped around the fire again. Forming concentric circles, the dancers repeated the steps with different partners.

Next was a lively folk dance. With Bren as her partner, Miria executed the intricate steps with liquid grace that brought admiring looks from everyone. Miria was delighted with the reaction she saw in their faces. The celebrants seemed to gaze at her with looks of surprise, as if they'd forgotten she was an enemy. She was like any other young woman dancing with her entranced suitor. Young men began asking her for a dance. Several older men smiled at her and nodded to each other. Women watched her with interest and envy; she overheard them commenting on her clothes, features, her dancing skill.

There were more circle dances, reels, and Vorlikian folk dances Bren had to teach Miria. For a while, she forgot she was surrounded by hated Vorlikians and just enjoyed the gaiety. Drambit seldom had any reason to celebrate. She smiled to herself. *Once Vorlik is mine,* she thought, *I'll have dances every month.*

22

Dressed in green shirt, pants, and tunic, Cordwin watched the celebration from the shadow of the trees north of the meadow. He had no desire to join in the dancing, but that wasn't why he remained apart, separate from the crowd. Many women had tried to draw his attention, but he wouldn't join in the merriment. He stared at the diamond-studded velvet sky. His heart was hollow, empty. No music could stir his blood; no fair face or delicate hand could tempt him to the dance. Caressing the silver and emerald ring on his hand, his thoughts dwelt in the past, on lost yesterdays.

"Briella." He whispered her name like a painful sigh, and fingered the silver dove pendant he always wore. "Why did you have to die? Everyone I've ever loved is gone. Clevil and Ellisa are dead. I barely know Bren. Even Daikin has gone away. Briella, I need you tonight."

Suddenly, the pendant began to glow blue, and he held it to his lips. The pendant felt warm, as if it were alive. He waited, hoping she would come to him again as she had other nights when he'd called her name. Suddenly, a breath of wind caressed his cheek and whispered his name. "Briella?" he said, expectation quivering in his chest.

"I'm here, my love," Briella's voice said softly. "I'm always with you. You're never alone."

He turned his back to the glow of the bonfire and leaned back against a tree, his heart beating like a blacksmith's hammer in his chest. He closed his eyes and felt her presence, breathed in the scent of lavender when there was no lavender in bloom. "I miss you," he whispered. "I miss you so much. At times I wish my heart would stop beating so I could be with you forever."

"Oh, no, please, don't say that! If anything happened to you—" Her voice halted. "Cordwin, I am here with you now, and I will always be with you. But your people need you. Bren needs you. You must protect your people. And I will be with you. Always."

He felt her touch his cheek, felt her lips kissing his, and he smiled.

"Go and be with your people," she said. "They need you."

The blue glow faded from the pendant. Cordwin tucked it inside his shirt next to his heart, and walked back toward the celebration, feeling more content than he had in months. His throat was dry, so he walked to the tables and asked for a cup of wine.

"Which shall it be, red or white, My Lord?"

Cordwin started to correct the man, then saw it was Leez, the taverner from Tarolin Town. Leez was a great bear of a man, kind-hearted and filled with the joy of life. "Which would you recommend?" Cordwin asked.

"Oh, the white," Leez said. "Sweet as honey, light as dewdrops. Warm you all the way down to your toes."

Cordwin smiled. "Then I'll have the white."

Leez drew a mug of wine and handed it to Cordwin. "The finest vintage Yarrow has produced in the last ten years."

Cordwin took a sip and let it rest on his tongue a few moments. The wine was as warm as a summer day, as light and clear as spring water, as sweet as tyneberries. He swallowed and licked his lips. "Oh, this is good," he said softly.

Leez grinned. "I have two more barrels after this one."

"I'll remember that." Cordwin ambled away, sipping the wine and savoring the burning tingle in his throat, the warmth and slightly dizzy feeling in his head. He stood watching the dancers, remembering the Autumn Fair in Tironza when he'd danced with Briella until he was nearly breathless. If only he could hold her in his arms, could dance one more dance with her... he shook his head. *Don't wish for the impossible,* he thought. *At least, I know she's with me, if only in spirit.*

A voice startled him. "You're not joining the festival, Lord — I mean, Captain Cordwin." A blond-haired man stepped from the shadows, holding a large mug, and he smiled engagingly. He was dressed all in black except for silver buttons on his jacket.

Cordwin stared at the man for a few moments. He seemed familiar, but Cordwin couldn't remember his name. "No," Cordwin said. "I don't feel like dancing right now." He continued to stare at the man.

The blond man bowed, smiling. "Grimmin, merchant from the south. I supplied the wine for the betrothal feast."

"Oh," Cordwin said slowly. "Yes. Grimmin."

"Quite a delightful festival," Grimmin said. "Lively music. Good food. Excellent wine." He lifted his cup in a toast to Cordwin and took a sip. "Lady Miria is quite beautiful, isn't she?"

Cordwin felt like snowflakes were melting on his skin. "She's a lovely young woman."

"She reminds me of Briella."

He glared at Grimmin. "No! No one is like Briella!"

Grimmin smiled. "Begging your pardon, captain. I meant no offense. Wizards are unique." He took another sip of his wine. "What do you think about this marriage?"

Cordwin forced himself to calm down. Exhaling slowly, Cordwin said, "Bren wants it. Hopefully, it will end the hatred between Drambit and Vorlik."

"Indeed," Grimmin agreed, "I'm certain this will be the end."

Something in Grimmin's tone disturbed Cordwin, but he couldn't pinpoint why. He knew he wanted to escape the merchant's icy blue eyes. "Excuse me, Grimmin, but I've had all the celebrating I care for. I hope you enjoy yourself. The dancing will last until early morning."

Grimmin bowed and smiled at him. "Good night, captain. May you have pleasant dreams."

Cordwin shuddered. For the first time he noticed how little the merchant had changed in all the years Cordwin had known him. Suspicion dug at his mind like a burrowing animal. He had no specific reason, just an uncomfortable feeling. Cordwin nodded to the merchant and turned toward Tarolin Castle. Disquieted by Grimmin, Cordwin trudged to the safety of his room. Stripping off his jacket, shirt, and trousers, he lay in his bed and stared at the dark ceiling. The dove amulet felt warm and comforting against his chest, relieving his apprehension. The fragrance of lavender filled the room, and he felt Briella's presence. Smiling, he closed his eyes and fell asleep while music and laughter drifted through his open window.

23

Miria noticed Grimmin smiling with pleasure as he watched her and Bren. The longer the two of them danced, the more Bren seemed her willing slave. Out of breath, Miria said, "I need to rest for a bit. Could you get me a cup of wine?"

Bren kissed her hand again. "Of course, My Lady. I'll be back in a few moments."

Miria sat back and smiled. *Yes, the plan is working well,* she thought. *One more day. Just one more day, and I'll have my revenge.*

Bren returned with two cups and handed one to Miria. "This is white spring wine from Yarrow, home of the finest wines in all Vorlik."

She took a drink, savoring the warmth in her throat, the tingling that spread throughout her body. The wine was exceptionally good. She could become accustomed to drinking this wine every day.

The dancing continued until the bonfire was reduced to a few glowing embers, and dawn colored the few feathery clouds bright magenta. The torches began sputtering out. Celebrants began wandering back to the castle or to tents set up all around the castle. Holding hands like any ordinary couple, Miria and Bren walked lazily from Dancing Glen, escorted by two Vorlikian guards, through the castle gatehouse and across the courtyard to the castle steps. Miria could barely lift her feet enough to climb the steps. By the time she reached the top step, she was glad her rooms were on the first floor, that she didn't have to climb any more steps. Bren escorted her to the door of her apartment and kissed her hand again.

"Baramay give you peaceful sleep," he said. "Tomorrow evening, we'll be betrothed, and the next day will be our wedding day. All my life I've dreamed of this. Miria... Miria, I love you."

"My sweet Bren." Miria leaned against his chest and gazed up at him with inviting blue eyes. She felt his heart hammering against his ribs and heard his breath come in short bursts. Akavar's potion had worked perfectly, binding Bren's mind and heart to her.

Bren kissed her hand again, and in a husky voice, stammered, "Un-until tomorrow."

Miria caressed his cheek. "Tomorrow."

He backed away, turned, and left. The two guards stationed themselves on either side of the door to her chamber.

Smiling, Miria watched him leave. She could almost feel his longing. Whirling, she entered sitting room with a light, skipping step and closed the door behind her. She sank into a chair and chuckled to herself.

"You were magnificent tonight," Grimmin said as he stepped from the shadowed doorway of her bedchamber.

Miria leaped to her feet, startled. "Quiet! There are guards outside my door!" she whispered.

Grimmin strolled toward her. "No one can hear us in this room." He caressed her throat, and she shivered with delight. "You were magnificent tonight," he repeated. "Any doubts the Vorlikians had about you were put to rest by your performance. Everything's ready for the second act tomorrow evening." He put his arms around her, crushed her to his chest, and kissed her until she was breathless. Lifting her in his arms, he carried her to her bedchamber, closing the door with his foot.

Miria struggled half-heartedly. "My maids will hear!"

"They won't wake up until morning. No one will come in here unless I allow it."

He set her on her feet and kissed her again. Slowly, he removed the flowers from her hair, then took out the golden hair pins until the braid came down. Unbraiding her hair, he ran his fingers through her thick golden tresses, lifting them to his face and inhaling the fragrance. Miria's heart danced with desire, and she wondered if the potion she'd rubbed on her hand to enslave Bren had affected her, too. She gazed into Grimmin's deep blue eyes and smiled. No, it wasn't a potion that made her blood race through her body.

Miria unbuttoned Grimmin's jacket and pushed it off his shoulders and down his arms. She slipped her hands under his shirt, caressing his smooth chest. He closed his eyes and tilted his head back for a few moments, then slowly exhaled a breath he'd been holding.

Grimmin moved behind her and began unlacing her dress. It slid to the floor. She wore only a thin linen chemise. He lifted her in his arms and kissed her again. "You are so beautiful," he whispered.

Placing her on the bed, Grimmin lay down beside her. "Tonight, we'll celebrate," he said, smoothing a strand of hair from her forehead, "just you and I."

Miria smiled up at him. "Tomorrow, we'll be rulers of Vorlik, and Bren will be our prisoner!"

24

Nearly paralyzed with fear, Gemna crouched behind the oak and watched as Maren stood with arms stretched to the sky. His whole body radiated power like heat from the sun. He seemed to glow as if he'd swallowed the moon. His eyes flashed with knowledge as deep as the roots of mountains. His voice roared through the silent night, causing even the great trees to tremble the way Gemna did.

She wanted desperately to flee, but she couldn't move. She stared at Maren in horrified fascination. Who was he? *What* was he? — It took all her will to force herself to stand. Her heart pounded in her ears as she edged her way toward her horse, hoping Maren wouldn't notice her. Before she was halfway there, Maren called to her.

"Gemna, wait!"

Terrified, she broke into a run, reached her mount, and leaped onto its bare back. Maren shouted a strange word as she clapped her legs against the horse's side. The animal refused to move.

Maren ran toward her. "Wait! Gemna, don't leave! Please!"

She jerked the reins and shouted, but the horse remained where it was. Maren grasped the bridle and reached up to her. Gemna slid off the other side and backed away, fear activating her mercenary training. She drew her sword and stood ready to fight. "Stay away from me!" she said.

He walked around the front of the horse, holding the reins. "Gemna, don't be afraid. You never need to be afraid of me. I would never hurt you."

"What are you?" she shouted, holding her sword with both hands to keep from shaking. "What *are* you?"

Maren dropped the reins and held out his hands. "Don't you know me yet? We've traveled together for weeks. We've shared our food, slept at the same fire, fought for each other and fought with each other." He took a step closer. "You saved my life," he said earnestly. "You held me when I was in so much pain, I thought I'd die." He took another step toward her. "Gemna, I haven't changed. What reason have I given you to be so afraid of me?"

"I saw you!" Gemna said. "I saw what happened! There's only one thing you could be, and that's a Sorcerer!" She spit on the ground.

Maren looked astonished. "How can you say that?"

Gemna pointed her sword at him. "Because you lied to me!" she said reproachfully. "Everything you told me was a lie! You're not a simple man from Hixus, no mere minstrel! What could you be but a Sorcerer?"

"I didn't lie to you. I just didn't tell you the whole truth. I couldn't then, but I can now. I'm a Wizard."

"A Wizard?" Gemna stared at him, not relaxing her guard. "A Wizard cares about people and uses his power to help them! Why didn't you heal that old woman? Why didn't you stop the killing winds and rains? Why didn't you treat the people in Lecida for winter fever? You could have! But you didn't! You let all those terrible things happen! What Wizard would do that?"

Maren hung his head and clenched his fists. "There was nothing I could do," he whispered. "Nothing!"

"And if you're a Wizard, why did you hire me?" Gemna said, taking one step back. "A Wizard's so powerful, he doesn't need anyone to protect him!"

Maren shook his head. "You don't understand. Please, come back to the fire and sit down. I'll tell you everything you want to know. If you still want to leave me, I won't stop you and I'll give you your payment for service. For the sake of all our time together, for everything we've been through, at least, listen to me. Please!" He knelt before her and held out his hand. "Please, Gemna, hear me out."

Gemna wanted to believe him, but how could she trust him? She thought about all their time together. He'd made her angry occasionally, but he'd never done anything to harm her. And he had been very protective and gentle with Ilette. "All right." She nodded but kept her sword in hand. "Make me believe you."

He stood, and she followed him to the fireside and sat opposite him.

Maren told of his meeting with her father and the news of Briella's death, how Maren's power had been bound by a Sorcerer, of the pain that struck him each time he tried to remember or search too deeply for answers. "Do you know how tormented I was by being unable to heal the sick of Lecida?" Maren asked, his face showing his anguish.

"But you're free now?"

"Yes." Maren held up his arms. The bracers gleamed in the moonlight. "My sister's gift broke the spell."

"Then you can do your magic?"

Maren nodded.

"Then what's stopping you from healing the people of Lecida now?" she asked pointedly.

Maren stared wide-eyed at her. A surprised smile spread across his face. "Nothing! Nothing's stopping me now! Finally, I can do something to help!" He leaped to his feet. "Wait for me. I'll return before morning."

She stood up, facing him. "But—"

He held up his hand to stop her, shaking his head. "Don't worry. I'll set a circle of protection around you while you sleep. You'll be safe." He touched her arm. "I won't let anything harm you."

Gemna felt too warm suddenly, her heart drumming in her chest. "I'm not worried," she said, "at least not about me. I've looked out for myself almost as long as you've been alive." Pausing, she let her eyes glide curiously over him before she spoke again. "Well, maybe not. Just how old are you?"

"Old enough," he said with an enigmatic smile. "I've a lot to do tonight. Watch but don't interrupt me. My work takes concentration."

Gemna nodded, sat down, and watched intently, silent and still as a stone.

From his sack Maren took out the pouch of herbs. Removing a piece of callum bark, he held the bark in his outstretched palm and reached toward the silver-white moon with the other hand. "By the power of Baygor who gives the increase, *tasrin callum enisan ahntahni barason.*"

He cupped his hands together. A blue mist swirled in them, growing larger. When it dissipated, his hands were heaped with callum bark.

Gemna gasped, speechless at her first sight of real magic. She slowed her breathing and calmed her pounding heart. She was actually watching a Wizard work magic! *Stay calm,* she told herself. *Be placid like a pool of water. Just sit and observe.*

"Barg's breath," Maren said softly.

"What?" Gemna asked, worried. "What's wrong?"

"Nothing," Maren said, his eyes wide with surprise. "It's just that the spell created twice as much callum bark than I expected, enough to treat the entire population of Lecida with plenty left over. And I feel somehow stronger than I did before I was ensorcelled."

"Maybe it's from the bracers," Gemna said.

"Maybe." He stared at the bracers a moment. "I need a pouch, a bag, something to put the bark in. Can you get me something?"

Gemna crawled over to her saddlebags and rummaged through them until she found a piece of cloth large enough to hold the bark and a longer strip to tie around the top. She held the large cloth while Maren carefully emptied the bark onto the cloth. He pulled the corners together and tied them with the strip of cloth.

Maren placed the bark in an inner pocket of his cloak, then took a tiny box from his other pouch. Opening it, he poured a small mound of bluish dust into his palm. He stood and walked twenty paces from the fire to the edge of the forest. He bent over and carefully sprinkled a thin line of the blue dust in a wide circle, enclosing the fire, Gemna, and the horses. Returning to the fire, he tossed in a small glass bead and said, "By the power of Baramay who made the world and all its elements, *tasrin lanifar cenarah barason!*"

The fire blazed even brighter, chasing the chill from the air.

He looked straight at Gemna. "You're safe here. Don't leave the circle for any reason. Once you leave, you can't enter again. But while you're inside the circle, nothing can harm you. Sleep peacefully, Gemna. I'll return as quickly as I can." He held his arms wide. Brown-black feathers covered his body as he shrank and became a large eagle. Powerful wings flapped as he launched skyward. He circled the campsite, and with a parting cry, flew south toward Lecida, dark wings beating against the night wind.

Gemna gaped at the dark sky even though she couldn't see Maren. Shaking with awe, she plopped down beside the fire. She glanced up at the sky again to assure herself he was gone, that she wasn't dreaming. There was no sign of the eagle, just the moon overhead like a saucer of milk. She stared at the flickering fire. The wood blazed fiercely but didn't turn to ash.

If I told Mother about this, she'd laugh and say I was crazy, she thought. *And I'm not certain I'm not. Maren, a Wizard! I never expected to see one, meet one.* She gazed up at the sky again, a sudden thought chilling her heart. *He doesn't need me now.* She swallowed hard, an ache in her chest. *He doesn't need a bodyguard. He can go anywhere he wants now. Why does he want me to wait for his return? Oh, my payment – he hasn't given me my payment. That must be it. What other reason would he have?* she wondered. Slowly, she rose and fetched a blanket from her saddlebags. *At least, it's only a few days ride back to the guildhall to find another master.* Tears came unbidden to her eyes, and she wiped the tears away. *But I don't want another master. I want to stay with him.*

Wrapping her blanket about her shoulders, she lay beside the fire, her head pillowed on her arm. The wind murmured through the thick branches, singing a soft melody of new life and awakening earth. Overhead, Baramay's Circlet seemed to hang protectively above Gemna, a promise that no evil could pass the confines of the circle. Gemna closed her eyes and fell asleep, secure and peaceful, undisturbed.

25

Dawn had colored the mountains and sky rose-pink when Gemna opened her eyes again. Although she'd added no wood to the fire all night, it still burned brightly. The air was chilly, but she wasn't. She yawned and stretched, working the stiffness out of her neck.

"Good morning!" Maren's cheery voice greeted her.

Bolting upright, she saw him step from behind his horse.

His hands balanced a large round of brown bread, a wedge of cheese, and a chunk of salted beef. A grin on his face, he walked to the fire and sat down beside her.

Gemna yawned again and rubbed her eyes. "Why are you so happy?"

He handed Gemna half the food. "The fever will soon be gone from Lecida. I took the callum bark to the regent of Peltik. He called in all the physicians and healers immediately, even though it was the middle of the night. I showed them how to use the bark, and within three days everyone should be well."

Gemna closed her eyes and whispered a prayer of thanks to Baygor.

While they ate breakfast, Maren told of things he'd seen, places he'd been in his wanderings, and of the Wizards' Vale.

It must be as marvelous as the legends say, Gemna thought with awe and wonder. She could almost see the red crystal house he shared with his sister, the ring of mountains protecting the vale, fields and meadows untouched by winter. What it would be like to live in such a place, where life, all life, was treasured as a gift?

Gemna's fingers brushed the cool metal of the bracers. "Your sister must be incredibly powerful to make things like these."

Maren turned his wrists slowly and examined Amaly's gift. "I had no idea she could do this kind of magic. Her talents have always been with animals and plants. I wonder what spells she used that were powerful enough to break a Sorcerer's binding?"

Gemna gazed at Maren, then looked away, troubled. She folded her blanket and walked to her horse. It was time for her to leave. There was a dull ache in her chest, no, it wasn't really an ache, more an emptiness, a sense of loss or loneliness. She didn't want to leave. She wanted to stay with him, now more than ever, but he really didn't need her. A shadow of despair clouded her heart. She tied her bedroll to her saddle, took her cloak from the saddle where she'd thrown it the night before, and clasped it about her neck. "I'll take my payment now."

"What?" Maren stared at her, his mouth dropped open.

"I'll take my payment now and be on my way."

Maren shook his head slowly. "You...can't... leave me," he said intently. "You haven't completed your contract!"

"You said I could leave if I wanted to, and you promised you'd pay me my wages."

He stepped closer and whispered, "Do you really want to leave me?"

"There's no reason to stay, Maren," she said softly. "You know that as well as I do. You hired me as a bodyguard; you don't need one now. You can protect yourself better than I can. After all, you are a Wizard."

"That didn't protect me from the Sorcerer."

"Maybe the bracers can. They broke the binding."

"But I don't know how they work!"

"You'll learn."

"You really want to leave me?" he asked quietly as he stepped toward her.

Gemna's throat was so tight with despair, she could hardly speak. "No," she said at last.

"Thank Baygor," he whispered. He caressed her cheek, sending a shock of delight through her. "I need you by my side, Gemna. I couldn't bear to be so far away from you. If anything happened to you, my heart would break. I... I love you."

Gemna inhaled sharply, too stunned to move. "What?"

"I love you," he said.

Joy, fear, and confusion swirled in her heart, but joy won out. "I love you, too," she confessed.

Maren breathed out a sigh and gently enfolded her in his arms. "From the moment I first saw you, I knew I would love you, that we would spend our lives together. I was so startled by the feeling, I couldn't believe it was true. But as our time together passed, I grew to love your strength, your compassion, your good sense. You are the only woman I want to share my life with, my life mate."

Gemna slid her arms around him, laid her head against his chest, and listened to his heart beating as fast as hers was. "I never wanted to love a man, didn't want to feel trapped into being like my mother. But I don't feel trapped. I feel freed and more alive than I've ever felt." She pulled back a bit and looked up at his face. "I love you, Maren."

He kissed her with gentle passion, but her whole body trembled with desire. By the time their lips parted, she was breathless.

Maren gazed into her eyes steadily for long moments before he spoke again. "I want to marry you this very moment, but I can't, not yet."

Puzzled, Gemna cocked her head. "Why?"

"Do you remember the story I told at the guild hall, the one about Timmree and Cavolin?"

Gemna nodded.

"Timmree is the only Wizard who married a human, and to do that, Baramay told her that she had to give up her powers and become human herself."

"I remember." Gemna studied his face, startled. "Would you have to do that to marry me?"

He nodded. "But I can't give up my powers, not yet. There's a war coming soon, a war between Wizards and Sorcerers that will determine the future of everyone. If the Sorcerers win, they will enslave the world. The Wizards have to defeat them. I have to fight, too, and I have to have my powers to protect you, your family, Ilette, and all the humans. I would do anything to protect you." He paused. "I would die for you."

"Then I'll fight by your side," Gemna said, "and when the Sorcerers are defeated and the world is safe, then, then we can marry."

"Yes," he whispered, "then, my beautiful Gemna, then we will marry."

He kissed her again, and they held each other for long, sweet moments, until Gemna pulled back.

"Are you still determined to go to Vorlik?"

Maren nodded. "I have to learn how Briella died. Your father said she was killed by a human, but that's not possible. Only a Sorcerer could kill a Wizard, so I know somehow Sorcery is involved. I have to know what happened so I can warn my people."

"Then let's go on to Vorlik, and you can learn the truth."

Quickly, they packed their belongings and saddled their horses.

Turning, Maren lifted his arms to the sky. "By the power of Baramay who made the world and all its elements, *nala tasrin lanifar nala tasrin traya!*"

The fire went out instantly. The partially burned wood was cold; not even an ember was left glowing. The circle of blue dust disappeared. Maren retrieved the glass bead from the wood.

Gemna glanced from Maren to the wood, then back again. "I'm not sure I'll ever get used to seeing magic."

Maren laughed. They mounted their horses and headed north toward the snow-topped Circle Mountains.

26

The forest ended abruptly as they reached the southern pass by noon. Sheer grey cliffs rose on either side of a road barely wide enough for two wagons to pass each other. A short way into the gap, the road narrowed to half its former width. The eastern half was occupied by the guardian keep with its three-story tower and barracks, both carved from the mountainside. Arrow slits were cut into the stone at regular intervals. An iron door opened from the tower into the pass. Four soldiers, clad in yellow and gold surcoats, halted them.

"Hail, travelers. Who are you and why have you come to Vorlik?" asked one soldier. Sandy-haired, lanky and freckled, he didn't look old enough to be a soldier.

"I'm Maren of Hixus, a wandering minstrel. This is Gemna of Beltrin, my bodyguard."

"You should've been here a week ago," said an older guard as he smoothed a tangle of mud-brown hair from his forehead. "Today's the last day of the Spring Festival in Tironza and Tarolin Castle, but you're in luck. Tonight, Lord Bren will be betrothed to Lady Miria of Drambit. There'll be a week of celebration, ending with the wedding and marriage feast. Your songs and tales will be in demand."

Maren tensed at the mention of Bren but managed to smile. "Thank you. I'll certainly visit Tarolin. Could we rest here before we continue through the pass? I could sing you a tune or tell you a tale in payment."

The brown-haired guard laughed. "Of course! We haven't had a minstrel in Vorlik since I was a boy." A curious look passed across his leathery face. He frowned, chewing the left side of his lower lip, uncertainty in his face. "You know, you remind me of that minstrel."

Maren kept the guilt-butterflies in his stomach from showing on his face. "We minstrels all look alike."

Gemna flashed Maren an accusing stare, but he ignored it.

The guard tilted his head slightly, then shrugged. "No matter, we'll enjoy your entertainment. Any news from the south?"

"Yes!" Maren said as he dismounted. "But I'll save it until your comrades can hear it, too. That way I won't have to repeat myself."

"A man who doesn't glory in the sound of his own voice!" The guard chuckled. "We're about to eat. I'm sure our sergeant would welcome you to join us."

"We'd be grateful."

Gemna dismounted, took the reins of both horses, and tied the reins to a post within easy reach of grass for the horses to munch. The guard led them to the door of the sconce while the other three soldiers remained on guard. Inside, the guard saluted a grizzled soldier who strode toward them.

"Sergeant Bassik, this is Maren, minstrel of Hixus, and Gemna, mercenary of Beltrin," the brown-haired guard announced. "They'd like to share our meal. Maren has agreed to entertain us."

"Hail, Maren and Gemna." Bassik bowed with surprising grace. His brown eyes sparkled with interest. "We welcome you."

The guard led Maren and Gemna to a narrow room with a long table and benches on either side. Five other guards already occupied the end closest to the kitchen. Some drummed fingers on the wooden table; some fiddled with their knives.

All glanced expectantly at the door that leaked delicious aromas. The guard introduced the travelers to his comrades who greeted the strangers.

"Any news from the south?" asked a guard with curly blond hair and pale blue eyes.

Gemna sat down, then Maren sat down beside her. He told the group about the pirate raids in the southern sea and the great battle that destroyed them.

"Wish I'd seen that!" the brown-haired guard said with wide-eyed excitement. "Sounds like it'd make a great song."

"Maybe I will." Maren told about the disastrous winds and rains that ravaged the southern lands, the winter fever in Peltik, and the deaths of Lords Merrik and Merovan and his family.

As they listened, the soldiers shook their heads.

The blond guard gazed at Maren, worry on his face. "I have family in the Freelands and in Peltik, and I haven't heard them from since last fall."

Sergeant Bassik entered the mess hall, and the guards all stood and saluted. "At ease," the sergeant said. He turned to Maren. "Did you say all the house of Peltik had died from winter fever?"

Maren nodded.

Bassik frowned. "Then Lady Miria of Drambit is the only heir to Peltik. She also has ties to Hargrim through her father's mother." He rubbed his chin, then looked at his comrades. "A rather powerful woman our lord is marrying."

"Food's ready," the cook called just then.

Maren and Gemna joined eight soldiers in the best meal the two had eaten since they'd left Selene's kitchen.

The guards talked almost as much as they ate. The brown-haired guard, the blond, and another guard with a bulbous nose had arrived at the keep only the day before. They'd attended most of the Spring Festival in Tironza and enjoyed their companions' envious stares as they told about women and drink and dancing all night.

Bassik gave them a toothy grin. "So that's why you three staggered in yesterday, all red-eyed and pale as milk!"

Everyone laughed, even Gemna.

Maren listened carefully to the easy banter. When he felt the time was right, he said, "There are strange tales of Vorlik even in the south. I've heard a Wizard lives here."

All the soldiers stopped eating and glanced at each other silently. Maren felt like winter had settled in the room.

Bassik cleared his throat with a swallow of wine. "A Wizard did live in Vorlik in the mountains west of here -- Briella Mourning Dove."

"How wonderful to have a Wizard's protection," Maren replied with awe in his voice.

His forehead pleated by a frown, Bassik stared at his plate. "She's dead now, much to our sorrow. She saved my only son from death when he was a baby. Every man here has some reason to be grateful to her."

The other soldiers murmured their agreement.

Feeling Gemna's eyes on him, he continued, "But I thought Wizards lived forever. How did she die?"

"Well, I'll tell you what I learned from Lieutenant Daikin at the Southern Guard's barracks," Bassik said. "I met him three days ago. He saw most of the events himself or heard them directly from those involved — Lord Cordwin and Lord Bren. You see, he's cousin to Cordwin and was captain of the Tarolin Guard until recently.

"Twenty years ago, Drambit..." Bassik muttered a curse under his breath and drove his knife into the wooden table. Looking up at Maren and Gemna, Bassik breathed out his anger slowly. "Sorry. I didn't mean to be so crude. Anyway, Lord Clevil and his wife were murdered, and their infant son Bren was kidnapped. There was no trace of the kidnappers. We didn't know it then, but Paxell of Drambit was behind it.

"Clevil's brother Cordwin became our lord. At his coronation Briella appeared and swore to serve and protect Vorlik all her life. She tended animals, served as midwife and healer, and set a Wall of Warding around Vorlik. She saved my son when the local healers had consigned him to Barg's kingdom." He halted, gulped half his mug of ale, and wiped his mouth with the back of his hand.

"But how did she die?" Maren asked, his voice cracking.

Bassik sighed and shook his head. "Bren killed her. Well, not exactly. You see, Bren had been raised in Drambit by Paxell. Seems Paxell told the boy that Briella and Cordwin had killed Bren's parents and stolen his throne. So when he grew up, he sneaked into Vorlik to avenge his parents. That's when he met Briella...and killed her."

"But how could he kill a Wizard?"

"Paxell had given him a magic dagger made especially to kill her."

"A magic dagger?" Maren asked, startled. "Where did he get a magic dagger?"

"No one knows."

"So Bren killed her with the dagger."

"Not quite. The dagger killed her, but Bren didn't."

"I don't understand."

"Bren said he was holding the magic dagger, and when he spoke Briella's name, the dagger moved all by itself. Briella died in his arms."

Maren had to struggle to keep weeping. "What happened then?"

"Briella had given Bren a magic sword before she died. He used it to magically travel to Cordwin in Tarolin Castle. Cordwin almost killed him."

Maren gave Bassik a puzzled stare. "Why?"

"Because Briella was Cordwin's wife."

"His wife?" Maren gasped. "Briella was married to Cordwin?"

"Well, yes and no. Cordwin had given her his ring and had sworn his vows to her, and she had spoken part of her vows but hadn't completed them. Daikin told me she stopped because she had a vision of Bren's arrival in Vorlik. You see, she'd had a vision when she appeared at Cordwin's coronation, a vision that she would die at Bren's hand and that Vorlik be attacked soon after her death. So when she saw that Bren had come back to Vorlik, she couldn't marry Cordwin since she would lose her powers as a Wizard and couldn't protect Vorlik. She gave up marriage to the man she loved because she'd vowed to protect Vorlik. She died, protecting us, all of us."

Everyone was silent, but the soldiers all nodded their heads.

Maren cleared his throat. "You said she was Cordwin's wife, but she didn't marry him."

"True," Bassik said, "but she'd agreed to marry him and had accepted his ring. All that was needed was for her to speak her vows. She nearly had." He paused. "Cordwin calls her his wife even now. He loved her more than his own life. Who am I to say he's wrong?"

"So what happened after that?"

"Bren and Cordwin rallied Vorlik's Guards to fight off a Drambini invasion. See, the Wall of Warding disappeared with Briella's death. Bren killed Paxell, and the Drambini army ran back to their hellhole to hide. So Bren's lord of Vorlik. And tonight he announces his betrothal to Miria, Paxell's daughter."

Maren was silent a long time and stared into his mug. At last, he'd heard most of what he'd come to learn, but he still needed to know how Paxell had obtained a magic dagger. He nearly jumped when Gemna touched his arm. He read understanding in her eyes and shared grief in the tight line of her mouth. He turned to the sergeant. "That's a tale of such love and woe as deserves a ballad," he said softly. "Perhaps I can compose one that will do justice to a love as deep and strong as Briella and Cordwin had."

"I'd like to hear it when you do." Bassik drained his mug, and in a much lighter tone, said, "You owe us a song, minstrel."

Maren swallowed hard and took his lute from the floor beside him. Quickly tuning the strings, he played "Tellowee's Lament."

How sweet the love you gave to me
And with joy you did fill my heart.
You pledged your faith with a tender kiss
And you vowed we would never part.

In the spring did we love, and you swore to be true
As we lay in each other's arms.
Oh, my love for you was ever true,
For you held me with secret charms.

Every thought I had was of you alone.
Every dream of my heart was for you.
Every wish I made, every hope I had
With your love was in me born anew.

In the summer we loved, and you swore to be true
As we kissed in the warm summer night.
Oh, my love for you was ever true,
And our troth I would gladly plight.

We spoke of vows and of golden rings,
And you promised to be my bride.
When the day arrived that we were to wed,
You said you had merely lied.

In the fall did you leave though you swore to be true,
And my heart was bereft of your love,
But your love for me was a travesty.
You proved false in your vows of love.

You were beautiful as the woodland flowers.
You seemed graceful and sweet and kind,
But beneath your face that I loved to touch
Was a dark and deceptive mind.

Now the winter has come, and your vows to be true
Are as cold and as dead as your heart,
But my love for you is still ever true,
And I'll love you though we are apart.

For a long moment the soldiers were as quiet as Maren. The brown-haired guard gave him a sad smile and nodded. The others murmured their appreciation.

Bassik sighed, gulped down the contents of his mug, and said, "Now let's have something lively."

Maren played "Old Mason's at the Barrel Again" but without the customary mug of ale. Almost against his will, Maren was cheered by the tune and the soldiers' enthusiasm. He continued with "Chellit's Cat," "The Barnyard Song," "Mellany's Inn," and "The Women of Karn." When he'd finished with "Rothanna and the Talking Fish," the guard with the bulbous nose clapped him on the back.

"That was wonderful, Maren!" Bassik said. "Now I don't feel so bad about missing the celebration in Tironza."

"I'm glad you liked it." Maren loosen the lute strings and slung the instrument on his back. "As much as I've enjoyed your company, I think we'd better leave if we want to reach the city before dark."

"Well, don't forget to come back."

"Oh, I'll be through this way again," Maren promised as he rose. He and Gemna stood up, went outside, and climbed into their saddles.

"I'll look forward to that," said the sergeant, who'd followed them from the hall.

Gemna climb up in her saddle. Maren mounted his horse, and he smiled down at Bassik. "Baygor keep you," Maren said

The guard's brown eyes twinkled. "Drink a toast for me at the celebration."

Maren laughed. "I will." He clapped his knees against his mare's sides and guided her through the narrow opening, Gemna following close behind.

The pass widened beyond the keep and began ascending, gently at first, then more steeply. The road wound through clefts, around jutting boulders, and into valleys, narrowing as it rose. As they reached the apex, the sun was midway between noon and sunset. The air was cold. Maren pulled two blankets from his pack, handed one to Gemna, and the other around his own shoulders.

Looking down into the plain of Vorlik, Maren remembered the last time he'd seen it. It had been autumn then. Now the fields were greening. Flocks of sheep dotted meadows. And at the center of all was Tironza, shining jewel of Vorlik. Suddenly, he felt Gemna inhale sharply. "Are you all right?" he asked, breathless and worried.

"Yes," she whispered. "I've never been to Tironza before, although Father has talked about it so often. I've never seen a city so... so...." Words seemed to fail her. "It's like a miniature carved from ivory, shining and perfect."

Maren looked down into the valley. "It is a beautiful city, the most beautiful I've ever seen, and I've seen many cities."

By the time they had reached the end of the pass, the sun touched the western peaks. Evening shadows lengthened as they arrived at the Southern Guard's barracks.

Maren dismounted. Gemna climbed down beside him. Maren called to a golden-haired man, wearing a yellow and gold surcoat, who lounged beside the door. "Hail, soldier. Sergeant Bassik said I might find Lieutenant Daikin here."

"He's inside." The young man stretched lazily and stood. "Who are you?"

"Maren, minstrel of Hixus, and Gemna of Beltrin, my bodyguard."

"I'm Cass." The soldier motioned them to follow and walked through the open doorway. The first room was filled with long, wooden tables and benches. Several men sat at one table, elbows propped and hands encircling large tankards. "Hey, Brice, where's Lieutenant Daikin?" Cass called.

A lean-faced man with deep blue eyes and dark arching brows looked up and grinned. "In the cellar checking out the wine sent from Tarolin for the celebration. First lieutenant's there, too. Oh, by the way, you owe me a bottle of brandy." Brice glanced at Maren, then turned to Gemna.

Maren was bothered by the way the soldier's gaze seemed to slide over her.

"And who have we here?" Brice asked in a weaselly voice.

Cass introduced them. "Maren of Hixus and Gemna of Beltrin."

"Married?"

"No," Gemna said, her tone like cold steel. "I'm his bodyguard."

Brice just grinned and raised his mug in salute.

Cass led them through the kitchen to a flight of steps. "Don't take Brice seriously. He thinks women can't resist him."

"I can," Gemna said sourly.

Maren chuckled.

Cass went down, motioning Maren and Gemna after. "Watch your head," the guard said and pointed at a lantern hanging from a rafter, lighting the small stone-walled cellar. Two men stood beside an open barrel and dipped small pewter cups into fragrant wine. Before they could taste it, Cass introduced the men.

"Lieutenant Kyris, Lieutenant Daikin, this is Maren, minstrel of Hixus, and his bodyguard Gemna of Beltrin."

Daikin nodded to Maren, but his green eyes fixed on Gemna. He gave her a sweeping bow. "Welcome, lady," he said.

Open-mouthed, Kyris stared strangely at Maren a moment before bowing. "Hail, Maren," Kyris said. "We'd appreciate some entertainment at our celebration tonight."

Maren bowed in return. "I'd be honored."

Suddenly, a voice whispered a warning in his mind. There was something Sorcerous nearby. He searched the two men standing before him for any glow of magic. Finding nothing, he scanned the cellar. His eyes rested on the barrel of wine; it glowed with a fiery-red aura.

The two soldiers lifted their cups.

"Stop!" Maren shouted. He leaped toward the two lieutenants and knocked the cups from their hands.

Jumping beyond Maren's reach, Kyris, Daikin, and Cass drew swords while Gemna did the same, ready to defend Maren.

Maren held up his hands. "The wine, it's poisoned!"

Kyris relaxed his guard only a little. "How do you know?"

Before Maren could reply, Gemna said, "Because he's a Wizard!"

"Gemna!" Maren gasped, astonished she'd blurted out his secret.

Daikin gaped at him incredulously. "A Wizard?"

"I thought I recognized you!" Kyris said, his eyes wide. "You were in Tironza when I was first stationed in the Southern Guard more than twenty years ago! You haven't changed at all!"

27

After dancing until nearly dawn with Miria, Bren had to attend ceremonies marking the last day of the Spring Festival only a few hours later. He'd dressed hurriedly in a red shirt, black pants, red and gold jacket, and the sunburst amulet. His eyes burned and kept watering. His feet felt like lead, making it hard to follow in the priest's footsteps. He was so tired, he wasn't sure whether or not he was supposed to recite something during the ceremony.

Bren covered his mouth to suppress a yawn as he walked behind the priest of Baygor. Maybe he could rest for a while before the betrothal or he wouldn't stay awake long enough for the betrothal toast. He wanted the day to pass quickly to night, ah, tonight, his betrothal night. Then tomorrow — no, one night at a time.

The morning ritual on the last day of the feast seemed much longer to Bren than on the previous six days. He glanced over at Cordwin, who seemed more alert than Bren was and whose eyes weren't bloodshot. *I guess he got more sleep than I did,* Bren thought, gritting his teeth to keep from yawning again.

The priest wore a blue robe, embroidered with golden sun and silver stars, and led a procession around the Dancing Glen seven times. Musicians played and pilgrims sang a hymn to Baygor. Acolytes constructed an altar of fifteen large white stones, speaking the name of each of the fifteen great constellations. On the altar the priest placed a handful of grain, a cup of wine, and a garland of apple blossoms. "For the gift of grain, for the gift of wine, for the gift of beauty, praise be to Baygor who gives us the gift of new life each spring, that the world may be renewed."

"Praise to Baygor!" the celebrants responded.

One of the senior priests opened an ancient book and read aloud the story of creation, ending with Baygor's gift to all living things. The younger priests went through the crowd, handing each celebrant a white snowstar or a blade of grass while the musicians played another hymn.

Raising his hands, the priest intoned a prayer. "Great Baygor, who set the sun in the sky to light the day, who set the stars in the night sky to add beauty to our lives, who gave every living thing the gift of offspring, we ask that you give us your gift again. Give the seed life; give the animals young. Great Baygor, stir the earth to life again and give us a bountiful harvest."

Taking the grain, the priest cast it into the air. The cup of wine he poured onto the ground. The garland he gravely presented to Bren, who set it on his head. With a shout of "Praise Baygor," the ritual ended, and the celebrants left to prepare for the betrothal.

Bren trudged back to the castle, rubbing his eyes and shaking himself awake. Cordwin walked beside him, and a dozen guards escorted them back to the castle. Everyone Bren passed was chattering like squirrels about the betrothal. Masters and mistresses ordered servants to fetch water for bathing and agonized over which perfume and what clothing to wear. All Bren wanted was a few hours' sleep.

Aromas wafted on morning breeze. Bren had hired extra cooks, mostly from Tarolin and Yarrow. They'd been working since before dawn in a specially constructed outdoor kitchen north of the castle. Four whole boars, four bulls, seven deer, and uncounted geese, ducks, and chickens turned on spits above glowing pits of wood and stones.

There was a wagonload of baked squash seasoned with honey and cinnamon. Bushels of carrots and turnips had been scrubbed and boiled. Loaves of soft bread were heaped into carts. Bag puddings steamed in huge kettles. Tables were lined with honey cakes and dried apple pies. Hazelnut cookies filled four wooden tubs. Rounds of cheeses, barrels of ale and mead, and kegs of wine were unnumbered. And a special treat for the betrothal cup had been provided by the merchant Grimmin: ten barrels of exceptional Yarrow wine, two years old and full bodied.

Bren's stomach growled as he inhaled the aromas. He hadn't eaten before the ceremony. He'd barely had time to wash and dress. *This will be the greatest betrothal feast in all the northern lands,* he thought, yawning. *Let's hope I don't fall asleep before I say my vows.*

He shuffled through the castle gate, up the steps, and up the stairs to his rooms on the third floor, Cordwin following him. "At least, I won't have to endure the priest's monotone speeches," Bren said, massaging his neck.

"There's the betrothal tonight," Cordwin said, "and I hope you look better by then than you do now. Your eyes are as red as if you'd been out drinking all night. Better get some sleep."

Groaning, Bren nodded and turned to his page. "Don't let me sleep too long. I can't miss my own betrothal."

Cordwin bowed and left.

Bren stripped off his jacket, shirt, and boots, then flopped down on his bed and covered with a blanket. "Don't let me sleep too long," he told his page again, his eyes closed. He didn't hear the page's reply.

It was late afternoon when the page shook Bren to wake him. Bren was still so tired, he couldn't keep his eyes open for more than a few minutes. The page shook him again, and Bren muttered a curse under his breath as he sat up and swung his legs over the side of his bed. He sat there, elbows resting on his knees and his head in his hands, his eyes closing again.

"My Lord, you must get up," the page said. "You have to bathe and dress for your betrothal."

Bren smiled to himself. His betrothal to Miria. He'd waited so long for this. All his life he'd dreamed of marrying her. Now at last his dreams were coming true.

The page had a large tub filled with steaming water beside the fireplace. Bren stood and stretched, then stripped off the rest of his clothes and stepped into the water. It was comfortably warm and was scented with dried lavender tied in cheese cloth. He sank down in the tub, leaned against the side, and breathed in the calming fragrance. He closed his eyes and pictured Miria, her hair shimmering like spun gold, her eyes as blue as sapphires, her skin as pale as porcelain and as soft as velvet. She was so beautiful, his heart ached just thinking about her.

"My Lord," the page pleaded, "you can't sit there all day. You have to prepare for the ceremony tonight."

The water had gone cold, and Bren shivered. He didn't realize he'd been musing so long. "Is there any hot water left?"

A cascade of almost too warm water pounded his head. He sputtered and coughed. Wiping his eyes clear, he started to yell at the page until he saw Cordwin holding a kettle. "Were you trying to boil me or drown me?"

Cordwin raised a dark eyebrow. "Neither. Do you realize it's an hour 'til you're supposed to be at Dancing Glen?"

"Oh." Bren's skin turned redder than it already was. "No, I didn't."

"Well, you do now, so hurry up. Unless, of course, you plan to attend your betrothal like that."

Bren smiled sheepishly. "I'll be ready on time."

"Do you have your pledge token?"

"I found a gold ring. It's simple and plain, but it was all I could find with so little time."

"Then I have something for you." Cordwin reached inside his jacket and pulled out a small velvet pouch. Loosening the drawstrings, he shook the velvet bag over his hand. A golden ring fell out, a golden ring with a blue-white diamond, sparkling and flawless. "Your father gave this to your mother on their betrothal day. Your mother wore it every day of her life. I thought you might want to give it to your bride."

Bren gazed at the ring, his throat tight. "Thank you," he said softly. "Thank you for everything you've done for me."

Cordwin slipped the ring back in the pouch, set it on the bed, and started to go, but seemed the change his mind. He turned back and faced Bren. "Be happy, Bren. Hold on to the woman you love and don't lose her." He turned on his heel and strode from the room.

Bren wished with all his heart he could bring Briella back to life. It was unfair he should be happy when Cordwin was so desolate. But life wasn't fair, not to Briella, not to Cordwin, not to Bren. He couldn't change the past; he could only try to make the future better.

He washed with soap scented with rosemary, comfrey, and rose petals, then rinsed and dried quickly in the cool room. He combed a few drops of attar of roses through his hair. With the page's help, Bren put on crimson shirt, crimson trousers with gold piping, black boots, and a gold and crimson short jacket over all. On his head he wore the crown of Vorlik. The sunburst medallion hung from his neck.

From the pouch, Bren took his pledge and slipped it on his little finger. He caressed the gold ring, wishing he had known his mother, wished he remembered anything about her. *I hope this ring means as much to Miria as it did to you,* he thought. He studied his reflection in his mirror. *I hope Miria will be pleased with me,* he thought, *and I hope she'll be as happy as I am right now.*

28

Daylight came much earlier than Miria wanted. As the late morning sunlight streamed through her window, she moaned and turned to the other side of the bed only to discover Grimmin was gone. She drew her hand over the linen sheet where he had slept. The sheet was cold, but still carried his scent. Miria smiled to herself, remembering the touch of his hands, the warmth of his body. She wished he were still there next to her.

Stretching and moaning again, she covered her head with the blanket and tried to fall asleep but failed. Sitting up, she called to her maids, who rushed to obey her.

"Today's my betrothal," she said with a smile. "I must look radiant."

The maids prepared a bath and scrubbed her hair until it shone like the sun. They rubbed her body with rose-scented cream, then dressed her in a blue satin dress with silver lace overlay. They drew her hair to the top of her head, set her silver circlet on her head, and made a cascade of curls mingled with blue ribbons trailing down past her shoulders. Opening her jewelry box, Miria took out a riviere of sapphires that had belonged to her mother. One of the maids fastened the necklace around Miria's neck while the other maid applied her makeup. Finally, the younger maid set blue satin slippers on Miria's feet.

"My Lady," said the older maid, "you are as beautiful as your mother. No man could resist you."

Miria studied her reflection in the mirror hanging on the wall, and she smiled. *As long as Bren can't resist me, that's all I care about tonight,* she thought.

She sat in a chair beside the sitting room hearth and waited. And waited. Miria drummed her fingers on the table in her sitting room. An hour passed, but no one had come to get her. *How much longer?* she wondered, irritation making her worried. *It's nearly evening. Why hasn't the ceremony begun?*

A knock at the door brought her to attention. Immediately, she hid her irritation and checked her appearance in her mirror. Her face was set in a shy but pleasant mask. Taking three slow breaths, she turned toward the door and said softly, "Enter."

Cordwin strode into the dimly lit room and bowed. He was dressed in a green shirt, dark green pants, and a green jacket with gold piping. His dark hair was combed neatly back from his face, and he looked pensive. "My Lady, it's time for the ceremony. By Vorlikian tradition, the nearest male relative of the groom has the honor of escorting the bride to the betrothal." He held out his arm and waited.

Miria stepped closer. She glanced up at him twice, hoping she appeared shy, before she looked at him steadily. Her voice just above a whisper, she said, "Cordwin, I can't undo what my father did, but I can be a good wife to Bren. I hope some day you'll accept me."

Cordwin's hand crept toward his throat and the silver dove amulet he wore. His face remained impassive. "I hope so, too. Shall we go?"

"A moment. I must get my pledge." Miria smiled at him, turned, and walked with liquid elegance toward her bedchamber. Certain Cordwin couldn't see her, she opened the chest that held the two vials. She opened the clear one and drank the contents. It had an oily-bitter taste, and she had to force herself not to gag. Replacing the empty vial, she slid the schorl ring, the signet of the lord of Drambit, onto her left hand. Grimmin had left it for her to complete the charade. For a moment, she felt angry at the thought of Bren wearing her father's ring, but calmed herself quickly and smiled. Bren would be wearing it only a short time.

Now she was ready. Tonight, she'd have her vengeance. Tonight, Bren would pay for her father's murder, and all of Vorlik with him. It was going to be so very sweet and satisfying to see him destroyed.

Composing her mask of modesty, she returned to the sitting room. Cordwin waited, woodenly staring out the open window. He snapped back to attention, tucked something inside his shirt, and again offered her his arm. Lightly resting her hand on his arm, she smiled. "Please, uncle-to-be, lead me to my betrothed."

Cordwin led Miria down the stairs to the entry hall and out the castle doors toward the Dancing Glen, but he felt no joy for the coming celebration. The sun set behind the western mountains, and the sky was deepening blue. The moon crept above the eastern mountains, full and yellowish-orange. Torch-bearing guards lined the steps to the courtyard and all the way to the castle gate. A gaily painted two-wheeled cart, pulled by a white horse bedecked with red and gold ribbons, waited at the bottom of the steps. Cordwin escorted Miria to the cart and helped her climb into the short bench seat on the right side, then climbed in and sat opposite her, but didn't look at her. Lieutenant Linaria, wearing her red and gold uniform, led the horse across the courtyard, out the castle gate to the East-West road to Dancing Glen.

Celebrants and spectators lined both sides of the meadow, waving and cheering, straining to catch a glimpse of the bride. Cordwin glanced at the crowds as the cart passed them on the way to the north end of the glen. The priest of Baygor stood under a pergola made of newly leafed grapevines. Bren stood beside him and stared down the torch-lit aisle. Linaria halted the cart. Cordwin climbed down, then he helped Miria descend the cart.

Miria seemed to sparkle as brightly as the sapphires at her throat. Moonlight danced on her golden hair and blushed her skin with an ethereal glow. Her blue gown made her eyes seem brighter, and the silver lace shimmered in the torchlight. Bren stared at her, speechless, seeming spellbound by the sight of her. Cordwin had to admit she was beautiful, but suspicion nagged at him. She seemed to lack some element in her soul. *Briella, I wish you were beside me right now,* he thought. *So many doubts fill my mind, I need you more than ever.* He reached for the dove pendent that lay next to his heart. It felt warm and comforting, and he felt calmer.

Finally, he reached the pergola where he put Miria's hand in Bren's. She glanced once at Cordwin and smiled timidly, but he felt no warmth in that smile.

The priest raised his hands. The crowd grew silent. "Hear now, people of Vorlik." The priest's resonant voice carried to all parts of the meadow. "This is the final day of the Spring Festival, marking the beginning of a new year and celebrating the renewal of life. Baygor gave all living things the gift of offspring that life will continue, renewing itself every year. All praise to Baygor for his most gracious gift."

"Praise be to Baygor," chanted the other priests.

"Praise be to Baygor," the crowd echoes.

Musicians played a hymn of thanksgiving while the priests all sang. At the end, the priest held up his hands again, and spoke to the crowd.

"What better way to conclude the Spring Festival than by the betrothal of our Lord Bren and his beloved, Lady Miria of Drambit?" He motioned for Bren and Miria to face each other. "Before you stand Bren, son of Clevil and Ellisa, Lord of Vorlik, and Miria, daughter of Paxell and Danneah, Lord of Drambit. Lord Bren of Vorlik, why stand you here?"

Bren looked straight at Miria. "To proclaim my love for this woman and my intention to marry her."

The priest turned to Miria and said, "Lady Miria of Drambit, why stand you here?"

She drew a slow breath and replied, "To proclaim my love for this man and my intention to marry him."

The priest turned toward Bren and lifted palms to the sky. "Bren of Vorlik, how do you declare your fidelity?"

"By vows and token of pledge."

"What is this token?"

"A ring."

"Place the ring on the first finger of her left hand and speak your vow."

Bren slipped the diamond ring on her finger and said in a quavering voice, "Miria of Drambit, I pledge my heart and my life to you. All that I am, all that I have, is yours. Baygor strike me if I prove false to my vow."

The priest turned toward Miria. "Miria of Drambit, how do you declare your fidelity?"

"By vows and token of pledge."

"What is this token?"

"A ring."

"Place the ring on the first finger of his left hand and speak your vow."

She hesitated a moment, then placed the schorl ring on Bren's finger. "Bren of Vorlik, I pledge my heart and my life to you. My every thought is of you. I honor you as is your due. Baygor strike me if I prove false to my vow."

Cordwin shuddered. Miria's voice sounded cold despite her warm smile. His eyes swept the crowd. Was he the only one who'd noticed? Maybe he was too suspicious. Maybe he'd let thoughts of Briella color his view of Miria. He shrugged off his doubts.

The priest raised his hands again, and in a loud voice, proclaimed, "Betrothed you are. Wedded you will be. May Baygor look with favor upon you and grant you a long and fruitful life together."

A cheer rose from the audience. Bren and Miria joined hands and walked to the cart. They climbed in and rode toward the castle through a shower of flower petals. Cordwin followed close behind, still feeling uneasy. Reaching the Audience Hall, Bren escorted Miria to their table, set in front of the dais where her throne had been placed beside his. The lieutenants of the Tarolin Guard came to the hall long enough to bow to Bren and Miria and wish them well, then left. The other guests filed into the hall for the banquet, while the common folk stayed at Dancing Glen to celebrate.

Tempting dishes of every sort imaginable were served to the celebrants. Wine and ale were poured freely for all. There were music and singing and laughing. Bren ate very little. His complete attention was focused on Miria, who also ate little. Everyone toasted the young couple, and more than one guest broke into spontaneous songs of congratulation to Bren on his choice of so lovely a bride.

Cordwin leaned against the wall near the entrance to the Hall, apart from the merriment. He tried to feel happy, but his heart ached. He felt the dove pendant warm and comforting against his chest, but reminded him he was alone. *Briella,* he thought, *I wish this were our wedding feast. Why couldn't we have had a lifetime together? I need you here with me.*

The celebration became too much for Cordwin. He strode from the hall but halted in the entrance hall. *Where can I go?* he wondered. *Where can I escape the music and laughter? I have to get out of the castle. Daikin, I wish you were here.* He ran up the stairs to his room and grabbed a hooded cloak against the chilly night, then walked back down, out the castle door, down the steps and across the courtyard to the stables. He stopped at Moon Shadow's stall. The white stallion was twenty-five years old and still strong, but Cordwin seldom rode him now.

Cordwin grabbed a handful of oats and held it out. "What do you say, Shadow? Shall we go for a moonlit ride? We haven't done that in quite a while." Shadow nuzzled the oats from Cordwin's hand. Cordwin patted his neck. "A ride's just what I need."

He saddled Shadow and pulled on the bridle. Cordwin led Shadow from the stable and swung up on its back.

Lieutenant Linaria blocked his way. "Captain, where are you going?"

"Anywhere but here," he said.

"Not without an escort," she said. "I'm coming with you."

He gave her a crooked smile. "You can try." He clapped his legs against Shadow's sides and galloped for the open gates. He heard Linaria shouting orders, but he didn't look back.

29

Malbar saw Cordwin leave the banquet and followed him unobtrusively. Cordwin walked to the stable and saddled his white horse, then led the horse to the courtyard and climbed into the saddle. *He's leaving the castle!* Malbar thought as he watched from the shadows near barracks. *If he escapes, Miria will be furious.* Malbar paused and smiled to himself, and for a moment considered not reporting Cordwin's absence. *But if I don't report this...* Malbar shuddered, frightened at what Miria might do. No, Malbar had to tell someone, maybe his father.

He watched as one of the lieutenants blocked Cordwin's way and argued with him. Cordwin rode around the lieutenant and out the gate. The lieutenant shouted orders as she ran to the stable. A dozen guards sprinted from the barracks to the stable, and a short time later they all led their horses from the stable, mounted, and rode after Cordwin.

Malbar frown. Some of the guards had avoided the trap. Now he had to report their absence as well. *Father will not be happy,* he thought as he stood in the shadows for a while. *I should've stopped Cordwin,* he thought. *He's the one person who could foil Miria's plan. He's the enemy... and yet, I trust him more than Grimmin. I should report Cordwin's absence,* he thought, *but I don't think he'll go far.*

He returned to the banquet, located his father, and told him Cordwin had left the castle walls, followed by the lieutenant and a dozen guards.

"Hound of Darkness!" Callas cursed under his breath. He looked worried. "Choose a score of men to find Cordwin. I want him in our hands before he's warned. Kill the guards."

Malbar nodded and casually walked around the room. As he passed the men he wanted, he signaled them to follow him. He watched his father amble toward Grimmin and nonchalantly speak to him. Malbar saw anger flicker over Grimmin's face, quickly replaced by his usual pleasant mask. Grimmin rose from his seat and left the hall for a moment, then returned. Against his will, Malbar feared for Cordwin.

Musicians played while the guests enjoyed the feast. After the guests had eaten their fill, many lined up for dancing, including Bren and Miria. Bren was entranced by Miria, her hair like spun sunlight, her eyes bluer than her dress, her smile as warm as a summer day. She was all he'd ever wanted in a wife. And tomorrow she'd be his. His heart pounded like a smith's hammer. He had difficulty believing all his dreams were coming true.

He touched her hand and gazed into her eyes. "Miria, I've waited for this day for a long time."

She smiled at him. "So have I."

"I'll do everything I can to make you happy. Anything you want, everything I have, is yours. I love you."

Miria gazed at him silently for a moment, then started to speak.

At that moment, Grimmin stood and held up his goblet. "Lord Bren and Lady Miria, let the servants bring in the Yarrow wine to drink your happiness."

Bren and Miria returned to their seats for the betrothal cup. A score of young women brought out pitchers of wine and began filling everyone's goblet, even giving the doorwards a cup.

"To Lord Bren and Lady Miria, may you find what you most desire in each other. Long life and happiness!" Grimmin cried, echoed by the crowd.

Bren lifted his golden goblet in salute to the guests, then turned to Miria. Pouring all his love, his passion into his words, he said, "Long life and happiness, my love."

He drank from his cup. Miria smiled demurely at him and lifted her cup to her lips. As he gazed at her, a halo of light circled her as if a ray of sunlight shone down on her, then her face became blurry. Shaking his head and blinking his eyes did nothing to clear his sight. He rubbed his eyes, but that didn't help. Ice crept through his veins. His hand became numb. The goblet clanged to the floor. Other cups crashed to the floor. The guests in the hall slumped against the tables. He tried to shout for his guards, but his tongue wouldn't respond. Near the door he saw Tarolin guards fighting with soldiers wearing black and silver. His vision turned dark, and he felt himself sinking into unconsciousness. He slumped in his chair, his head crashing against the table.

30

Cordwin rode east past Tarolin Town before doubling back north. He heard Linaria and a squad of guards galloping on the East-West road, trying to catch up with him. He almost laughed, thinking how furious Linaria would be when he returned to the castle. But it didn't matter at the moment. He needed to be away from the celebration. He rode slowly through hidden paths he and Daikin had found many years ago, until he approached the barrow ground from the north.

The full moon shone from the eastern sky, casting long shadows. White wildflowers gleamed like stars mirrored in a sea of grass and filled the air with light, sweet fragrance. A crisp, spring breeze brought with it the sound of music and laughter from the castle. The barrows were quiet and peaceful, the dead undisturbed by the merriment of the living.

Cordwin dismounted his horse and tied the reins to a tree growing beside a barrow. White rocks ringing Clevil and Ellisa's mound were like a string of pearls in the moonlight. Cordwin stood quietly beside the grave, reflecting on the days, seasons, and years of his life. Despair weighed heavy on him; memory was a dagger in his heart. He hung his head and wept. The chill breeze dried the tears on his face. "Clev, Bren's taking a bride tomorrow," Cordwin whispered. "Paxell's daughter Miria. I know her father was responsible for your death, but... but she's not her father. Bren loves her. It's time for someone to be happy again in Tarolin. My chance died with Briella."

He touched the dove pendent hanging against his chest. "You would've liked Briella. She was so alive. I loved her. I loved her as much as you loved Ellisa. I'd have lived and died with her. Clev, sometimes it hurts so much, I envy you."

He clutched Briella's amulet to his heart, and it warmed to his touch. The scent of lavender filled the night air, and he felt Briella's presence, his heart beating excitedly. He closed his eyes for a moment and felt her touch his cheek. "Briella," he said, delight flowing through him, "I needed you so much tonight. So much."

"Beware, my love!" she whispered. "Hide quickly! Danger rides toward you!"

Startled, he glanced quickly around and whispered back, "What kind of danger?"

"Listen," she said. "Listen."

The air became still, and the sounds of celebration had dwindled away. Suddenly, he heard the very faint clomping of horses' hooves and the clatter of armor. Creeping toward his horse, Cordwin stared toward the castle into the moonlit darkness. The sounds grew closer by the moment. Leading his stallion, Cordwin slipped quickly north to a tiny dell encircled by a tangled thicket. He hid his horse under a jutting stone ledge. Creeping to the rim of the dell, he looked over the edge then crawled to the edge of the road, hiding in the trees and brush that bordered the eastern side of the barrow ground.

Soon, he spotted reflections of shields and helms of riders. No Vorlik force would be galloping toward the castle at that hour. More soldiers rode from the castle gate and hailed the large company. Half the group turned toward the castle; the other half rode east. In the full moonlight he could see the soldiers weren't wearing the uniform of the Tarolin Guard.

Cordwin inhaled sharply, fear trickling down the back of his neck. Vorlik was in danger! Bren — Bren was still in the castle! Eight riders broke away from the company heading east. They rode straight for the barrow ground.

Cordwin watched the soldiers approach and realized they were wearing Drambini uniforms! They were looking for him, he knew it!

Thank Baramay I know this land better than they do, Cordwin thought. He'd played in the barrow ground with Daikin when they were both boys. The dell was difficult to see in daylight, nearly impossible to find at night unless one knew exactly where it was. The Drambini drew closer until Cordwin could hear their voices. He lay unmoving against a heap of damp, dead leaves and listened.

"Now the castle will be ours, and we'll live high!" said a gravelly voice.

"Sure, after the blood's washed away. Not much sport in killing drugged Vorlikians!" a younger voice said.

"There's always sport in killing Vorlikians, drugged or not!"

"True!" There were several harsh laughs.

"Most of the Western Guard were dead when we reached the barracks," the gravelly voice said. "The poisoned wine did most of the work. Took very little time to slit the throats of the ones still alive. Hope it'll be as easy in the castle."

A nasal voice snorted. "*If* all the Vorlikians drink the wine. I'm not sure their lieutenants let them toast their lord."

"If they didn't, we'll have a fight on our hands," the gravelly voice said. "And Lord Miria didn't want the Vorlikian lord dead, just drugged. She has special plans for him, revenge for her father's death. Oh, he won't die quickly, no, not quickly."

The Drambini all laughed.

"I wonder how our troops fared in the north and south," the younger voice said. "Of course, they probably haven't arrived yet. And the Eastern Guard should be ours by morning."

The gravelly voice chuckled. "We'd better find this Cordwin or our heads will line the castle wall. If he escapes, I don't want to be the one to explain to Lady Miria!"

"Me neither!"

"He's not here. He must've ridden east. Maybe he's hiding in that village down the road. Let's search the houses."

"And who knows what we might find there."

Snickering laughter faded as the riders turned east.

Horrified, Cordwin was almost too stunned to move. "Hound of Darkness!" he swore under his breath, digging his hands into the cold, damp earth. His suspicions had been proven true! Miria had betrayed them all! She'd planned it from the beginning! Bren was captured and going to be tortured! Most of the castle inhabitants were drugged or dead already by the sound of it! The Western Guard was slaughtered; the Eastern would be attacked by morning! The Northern and Southern would be taken unless he could warn them! He had to rescue Bren somehow! But what could he do? He was one man, alone. How could he save his people?

The signal fire at Yarrow! If anyone was alive to see it, perhaps he could still save Vorlik! *Lady Baramay, help me protect the people Briella loved as much as I do,* he thought.

He waited until he was certain the searchers were at Tarolin Town, then led his horse from the dell. Keeping to the shadows and out of sight of the castle walls, he reached the East-West Road. There was no sound of hooves, no movement at all.

Throwing his dark cloak over his white stallion, Cordwin guided it across the road. Once within the cover of Rindolar Woods, he peeked back at the castle. There were no shouts, no horn blasts. He hadn't been spotted. He wove his way through the edge of the woods, keeping just far enough in the shadow of the trees he couldn't be seen, but close enough he could see the road. He neared the castle and saw that the battlements were unmanned and the gates were closed.

Suddenly, a cloaked and hooded horseman blocked his path. Pulling up his horse, he tried to turn back but discovered he was surrounded. He reached for his sword and realized he wore only his dagger. Drawing it, he said, "I'll take one of you with me when I die."

"I hope not, captain." The horseman moved closer until he halted in a shaft of moonlight and pushed back his hood. Linaria's dark eyes glittered as she grinned at him. "I told you I was coming with you."

Cordwin sheathed his dagger. "Do you know what's happened?"

Linaria cocked her head. "What do you mean?"

Cordwin told her what he'd heard in the barrow ground.

"Barg's breath!" she said. "What should we do?"

"If they've taken the castle, we won't be able to get back in, not yet and not without help! Bren's alive from what the Drambini said, but I don't know for how long! We *have* to warn the other guards if we've any hope of saving our people! I'm going to light the signal fire at Yarrow to warn the Southern Guard. Send four guards north and four more east to the signal towers and light them. At least those Guards will be warned that something was wrong. You and the others come with me. All of you, be cautious! The lives of Lord Bren and all our people depend on us tonight!"

Linaria chose two groups of four soldiers and sent them back through the woods to try and reach the signal towers. Cordwin, Linaria, and the last four guards crept through the woods until they were a half mile south of the castle. Once they reached the Tironza Road, Cordwin spurred his horse to a gallop, Linaria at his side, the other guards keeping close behind.

Moonlight flickered through the budding leaves of the thick old trees, giving barely enough light to see the road in the darkness. Cordwin urged Moon Shadow faster as they left Rindolar Woods. Less than an hour had passed when he reached the sleeping village of Yarrow. He halted before the Singing Wheels Inn. "Wake the villagers!" he told Linaria, then he rode straight for the knoll behind the inn.

At the top was a ten-foot high tower of stacked logs and rails with leaves, twigs, and small branches in the center. Beside the tower was a small building. A guard stood outside, dressed in the red and gold uniform of the Tarolin Guard. The guard started, then saluted Cordwin as he leaped from Moon Shadow.

"Light the signal fire!" Cordwin said.

Without questioning, the guard took a torch from its sconce beside the door and shoved it into the tower. "Captain, what's happened?" the guard asked urgently as the tinder & leaves caught fire. Three other guards stumbled from the building, tying on their swords.

"We've been betrayed by Miria of Drambit!" Cordwin told them. "The castle is taken, and Lord Bren is their prisoner!"

The guards all gasped, and one whispered, "Baygor protect us!"

"I escaped only by chance," Cordwin said. "The Western Guard is dead! Drambini soldiers are riding toward the other Guards! I've sent guards to light the northern and eastern signals! I only hope the warning is in time!"

"What are your orders, captain?" the first guard asked.

Flames rose yellow-red in the milky sky, sending their light for miles in all directions. Soon, Cordwin saw other points of orangish light shine in the south and one to the east. Rindolar Woods blocked the view from the north, so he couldn't tell if the signal fire there had been lit. *We'll ride south,* he thought. *We can join Daikin and Kyris. We'll find some way to defeat the Drambini.*

Cordwin turned to the guards. "The Drambini at the castle will have seen the fire, too! They can be here in an hour, and they'll destroy Yarrow! Get everyone out of here as fast as possible and stay with them to protect them! Use every wagon, cart, horse, ox, whatever, but get the people out, now! Go to the caves west of here! I doubt the Drambini know about them! Tell the people to take nothing with them but blankets, food, and water! Remember, any delay could be too much!"

Mounting his stallion, Cordwin called, "Far-thell!" He signaled Linaria to follow and raced for Tironza and the Southern Guard. The moon was halfway between the eastern mountains and zenith as he left Yarrow. Praying to the gods to keep his people safe and that ancient Moon Shadow would have the strength to reach Tironza, he and the five guards rode through the shadow-laced landscape, passed bonfires set on hills. Cordwin called to the guards stationed at each bonfire to mount and follow him to Tironza.

By the time he sighted the outskirts of Tironza, the moon was not yet overhead. The city seemed quiet, its people sleeping. As he approached the burning signal tower near Tironza, a dozen mounted soldier in the livery of the Southern Guard appeared from the shadows.

"Halt and show yourselves!" one of the guards called, his sword drawn.

Cordwin pushed back the hood of his cloak and said, "What's your name, guard?"

The soldier's face was suddenly as white as the moon. "Lord, I mean, Captain Cordwin! I'm Brice. We saw the signal fires. We're ready for battle. But why are you and these guards here?"

"I have to reach the barracks and speak to Lieutenant Kyris immediately! Vorlik's been attacked!"

Brice looked stunned. "Where's Lord Bren?"

"At Tarolin! Only the gods know if he's still alive!"

"The entire Guard is watching the city's perimeter. Lieutenant Kyris knew there was danger before we saw the signal fires. He ordered us to stand guard all night."

Cordwin started. "How did he know?"

"I'll let him tell you himself." Brice turned to one of the other guards and nodded. The guard nodded back and ordered the rest of the Southern Guard soldiers back to their places.

Brice galloped beside Cordwin, with the other guards staying as close as possible, through the deserted streets of Tironza, occasionally meeting another guard patrolling the streets. They rode through the southern gate and straight toward the Circle Mountains. When they reached the barracks minutes later, the door opened. A dark figure blocked the dim candle light within.

Brice dismounted quickly. "Cass, would you see to our horses? We must speak to Lieutenant Kyris! He's still inside, isn't he?"

"Yes," Cass answered, saluting, "and so are Lieutenant Daikin and the visitors."

"Take care of Shadow," Cordwin said, worried by the wheezing sound of the horse's breathing. "It's a long run from Tarolin."

"I'll take care of him myself, captain," Cass said, taking the reins from Cordwin.

Brice led Cordwin and the other guards inside to the common room.

A fire blazed on the hearth, and numerous lanterns illuminated the entire room. Four people sat huddled around a small table near the hearth, their voices quiet and intense. Looking up as Brice and Cordwin entered the room, one leaped to his feet and strode toward them.

"Cord!" Daikin exclaimed, amazement in his green eyes. "And Linaria!" Suddenly, his face became serious. "What happened? Why are you both here?"

Cordwin clasped his cousin's arm and shook his head sadly. "You were right about the Drambini alliance. Miria's betrayed us all! The Western Guard is dead! The Drambini occupy the castle, and Bren's their prisoner! I don't know how long they'll keep him alive! The other Guards, including this one, will soon be attacked! I lit the signal fire at Yarrow, but I don't know if it was in time!"

"It probably wasn't, captain." Kyris rose from the table and saluted. "The wine sent to us, and most likely the other Guards, was poisoned. If it hadn't been for the minstrel, we'd be dead by now. He saved us."

Facing the table, Cordwin saw a dark-haired man rise and bow.

"Thank you for my friends' lives." Cordwin returned the bow.

The man inhaled sharply and whispered, "Briella's amulet."

Cordwin looked down at his chest. Candlelight reflected on the dove-shaped amulet about his neck. He stared at the stranger. "You knew her?" Cordwin asked.

The man's dark eyes were troubled, and his voice was tinged with pain. "Yes, I knew her well. My sister was her dearest friend."

Cordwin paused again. Astonished thoughts raced through his mind. How could this man know Briella? Unless... Cordwin swallowed tightly and asked, "Wizard, what's your name?"

"Maren, minstrel of Hixus," the dark-haired man said, "and this is Gemna, mercenary of Beltrin and my bodyguard."

Gemna rose and saluted Cordwin mercenary style. "We are honored, Captain Cordwin. My sword is at your command."

"I'm afraid we'll need your sword very soon," Cordwin said wryly. "The Drambini could arrive at any moment. Vorlik's only hope may lie in whether we can defeat this company. Maren," he faced the wizard, "can you help us?"

"Yes," Maren said. "Hopefully, I can stop the invaders without bloodshed. But if there is Sorcery involved, which I'm sure there is, it may be very difficult. I'll do what I can." He stood and started to leave.

"Where are you going?" Cordwin asked.

"To the other Guards. If they received the same poisoned wine, maybe I can keep them from drinking it, the same way I did here. Or if they drank it but haven't died yet, maybe I can save them. I'll return as soon as I've done what I can to save them." He hurried from the barracks, Gemna following him.

"Are scouts watching the Leflin road?" Cordwin asked Kyris.

"All the roads are watched," Kyris reported.

"Recall all guards to the barracks except a small force to guard the northern road. There may be refugees from Yarrow. The Drambini won't be far behind, some from the north, some from the Leflin road. Also, we need to organize the townsmen to help fight. The women can take care of the refugees. Baramay protect us and Lord Bren."

Maren walked into the moonlit night, took a small piece of callum bark from his pack, and cast a spell to multiply the bark. Blue light swirled in his hands until they were filled with the grey-green bark. He quickly placed the bark in the inner pocket of his cloak. "This should be enough to stop the poison," he said. "If I can reach the Guards in time."

Gemna moved close to him, so close he could feel her warmth. "You'll need someone to guard your back. Take me with you," she said. "You can do that, can't you?"

"I could," he said softly, turning toward her, "but it would be difficult, although I'm stronger since I broke the ensorcellment than I was before. Changing into an eagle takes little magic because I'm only changing myself. But if I take you with me, I have to use a different magic, more powerful and draining. I'm not sure I could reach all the Guards before I collapsed. Then I'd be of no use in defending Vorlik." He paused. "I don't want to leave you here, but..." He gazed deeply into her eyes, his heart racing. He cleared his throat. "Gemna," he said, savoring her name, "Gemna, I love you, more than my life."

She touched his cheek. He turned his head and kissed her palm.

"Do what you have to," she said. "Save as many as you can. I'll be here when you come back. Go, and Baygor protect you."

He nodded and handed his lute to her. "Keep this until I return," he said. He leaned over and kissed her lightly, then spread his arms and became an eagle, soaring silently on the night wind to the east. He glanced down at the ground and saw her standing in the moonlight, her face tilted up toward him.

31

It was an hour 'til midnight as Maren flew from the barracks northeast over Tironza, the moon shining brightly. The land streaked past below him as he beat his wings as fast as he could. He soared over farms and meadows, houses and hamlets, and he prayed he'd reach Yertz and the Eastern Guard before the soldiers drank the poisoned wine or at least in time to save them.

The moon was almost overhead when he spotted Yertz. As he neared the town, he saw something familiar, something that took him by surprise – several callum trees growing near the eastern edge of the city. He sailed down and landed on one of the branches. The trees were perhaps a decade old. *How did callum trees come to grow in Vorlik?* he wondered. *Briella! She must have planted them here. Maybe I can find someone to help me treat the guards! But who?*

He flew off toward the Eastern Guard barracks and landed just outside the door, changing to his natural form. Two guards, wearing a green and gold uniform, lay on the ground. One guard lay still. Maren felt his chest. The guard wasn't breathing; his heart was still. There was nothing Maren could do for him. The other guard writhed in pain, vomiting, an empty cup on the ground beside him. His young, lean face was a pale as the moonlight, but he was still alive.

Maren grabbed the cup and ran to a well beside the barracks. Drawing a bucket of water, Maren rinsed the cup out, crushed some callum bark, and mixed it in the water. He unhooked the bucket and carried it with him to the soldier. Filling the cup, Maren held it to the soldier's lips.

"Drink this," Maren said. "It will help."

The soldier sipped the water slowly, gagged, but kept it down and sipped more liquid. After a few moments, his breathing became more regular, and he stopped thrashing. He looked up at Maren with fear still in his eyes. "What happened?" the soldier asked in a hoarse voice.

"You were poisoned. Where are the rest of the guards?"

"Inside," the soldier gasped.

Slipping the bucket handle over his wrist and the cup in the bucket, Maren picked up the man and carried him inside to the common room. Long wooden tables with bench seats filled the room. Dozens of soldiers lay slumped over tables and sprawled on the floor. Some guards moaned and jerked spasmodically. Some lay deathly still. The room stank of urine and vomit.

Maren set the lean-faced guard down on the floor and checked the nearest soldier. Her breathing was so shallow, her heartbeat so faint, Maren barely felt it. He filled the cup with water from the bucket and forced the guard to drink some. *If I can get some callum bark water into each one,* Maren thought, *it will keep them alive long enough for me to make a true infusion to cure the poison.*

He checked each of the guards. Only a few were dead, but many were close to death. *How can I treat them all?* Maren thought, worried.

At that moment he heard horses galloping toward the barracks. *The Drambini!* he thought. *What can I do? If I try to put them to sleep, the guards would sleep, too, and I might not be able to wake them before they die! Baramay help me!* He gave a mouthful of water to the guard he was holding, then set him down.

Suddenly, the door flew open, and a man with salt-and-pepper hair and a blond-haired woman stood there, swords in their hands and wearing the green and gold uniform of the Eastern Guard. For an instant, the two glanced around the common room, their eyes wide, then they glared at Maren.

"Surrender!" the woman shouted.

"The guards — they've been poisoned!" Maren said. "I need your help to save them! Please!"

"Poisoned?" the man said, lowering his sword a bit. "How?"

"Wine," Maren said. "We have to give each guard some of the water in this bucket if we hope to save their lives! Please, you have to help me or they'll die!"

The two hesitated only a moment, then sheathed their swords and grabbed cups from the tables.

"Here, take this one," Maren said as he handed the cup to the man. "And rinse the other cup out first. It probably still has some poisoned wine in it. Then give each guard at least two or three swallows of the water. It should be enough to keep them alive while I brew a potion to cure them."

He hurried to the kitchen and searched until he found a large kettle and a clean wooden pail. Carrying them both to the common room, he dumped the water from the bucket into the pail and left it with the two guards, then Maren carried the kettle and bucket out to the well. It took four buckets of water to fill the kettle. He started to carry the kettle back to the kitchen, but the kettle was heavy and awkward. *I can't waste even a moment if I'm to save the guards,* he thought, *even if it does drain me.* He spoke a word of command. Rainbows swirled around him as he transported himself and the kettle to the kitchen.

He hung the kettle on the hearth hook and pushed it over the few embers still glowing on the hearth. Grabbing some firewood from the bin beside the hearth, he placed them on the embers, then said, "By the power of Baramay, who created the earth, *tasrin lanifar barason!*"

Fire leaped from the embers and surrounded the firewood, burning bright yellow-orange.

"What *are* you?"

Maren wheeled to see the blond woman standing in the doorway and gaping at Maren.

"What *are* you?" she asked again.

"I'm a Wizard, and I'm trying to save your friends' lives," Maren said.

The woman's eyes grew round with amazement. "A Wizard? Like Briella?"

Maren nodded. "How many guards are still alive?"

"Thirty-seven. Thirteen are dead, including our lieutenants."

"You're with the Eastern Guard?"

She nodded.

"What's your name?"

"Keldon."

"Keldon, who's your senior officer?" Maren asked as he took more callum bark from his cloak.

"I guess I am."

"Where were you when the rest of the guards were poisoned?"

"We each get a week off duty every three months to go home. Me and Jess were on leave visiting our families up north. But we saw the signal fires lit from Tarolin to Yertz and knew something was wrong, so we rode here as fast as we could."

"A good thing, too. Keep giving the soldiers the callum water. If you run out, draw another bucket, crush this bark, and add it to the water. I'll call you when this potion is ready."

Keldon nodded and hurried back to the common room.

Knowing the water wouldn't boil soon enough naturally, Maren cast a spell to increase the heat and boil the water faster. As soon as it did, he tossed the callum bark, ginger root, roborant, and peppermint into the kettle and stirred it with a wooden spoon until the infusion was green-gold. The clean fresh scent of callum bark tea filled the kitchen. He ladled the tea into a pitcher and called Keldon.

"Give each guard a cup of this tea," he said, handing the pitcher to her. "It will stop the poison." He filled another pitcher. "Give this one to Jess."

Keldon took both pitchers and hurried to the common room. Maren filled another pitcher and followed Keldon.

It took surprisingly little time to give all the guards a cup of tea with the two guards helping Maren. Immediately, the soldiers' color returned, their heartbeat was stronger, and their breathing eased. Maren refilled the three pitchers and told Keldon and Jess to give each soldier another cup of tea. Soon the guards were able to sit up but were still weak.

"What about the men at the border keep?" Keldon asked. "Are they all right?"

"I don't know," Maren said. "But I can find out. Keep giving them as much tea as they can swallow. I'll be back as soon as possible."

He strode outside, changed into an eagle, and flew straight to the border keep. Snow still clung to rocky ledges on the sides of the mountain pass, but the road was mostly clear. The moon was past midnight when he spotted four guards standing watch at the border keep. Maren landed before the guards and changed into his natural form. Startled, the guards shouted and drew their weapons.

Maren held his arms out to his side. "My name is Maren," he said. "I'm a Wizard, and I've come to warn you. I need to speak to the officer in charge."

The guards hesitated, then one guard ran inside the keep. Moments later, he returned with a grey-haired guard, tucking his shirt in his pants and blinking sleep from his eyes. "You're a Wizard?" the white-haired man said, brushing his hair back from his face. "Why have you come?"

Maren told him of Miria's betrayal, the poisoned wine, Bren's capture, and Cordwin's escape. "Drambini troops could arrive at the Eastern Guard barracks at any moment. I'll protect the guards as well as I can, but you need to assemble your troops and prepare for a battle. Ride to the Eastern barracks with every guard you can spare."

"We'll be there as fast as our horses can run," the officer said.

Maren changed back into an eagle and flew straight to the barracks. His eyesight was always keener as an eagle, and just before he reached the barracks, he saw a host of mounted men riding from the eastern edge of the village, men wearing black and silver uniforms. *The Drambini!* he thought anxiously. *The guards can't fight yet, and the border guards won't arrive in time. I have to do something, but what? What could I do that would keep the Eastern Guards safe?*

He landed, changed to his natural shape, and ran inside. "Drambini soldiers are coming!" he told Keldon. "I can only think of one thing to do to keep all of you safe, but everyone must be completely silent and still! Spread the word quickly while I begin my magic!"

Keldon told those closest to her, then they told others until everyone sat quietly and unmoving. Maren closed his eyes and cleared his thoughts. *Please let them believe the illusion,* he prayed. Holding his right hand raised over his head, his left hand facing palm out, he said, "By the power of Baramay who created all things, *tasrin devala ansolaya toolahdis barason.*"

He held his left hand facing the door to the common room, as if he were pushing against the air itself. The sound of horses drew near, and a loud voice called a halt. The door to the common room was flung open, and Drambini soldiers blocked the doorway. Maren whispered a word of command and held his hand out toward them. He clenched his teeth and concentrated until his head began to ache, and the muscles in his left arm and his chest started to cramp.

The first Drambini laughed harshly. "We don't need to slit their throats. Looks like they're all as dead as the one outside. They must have fouled themselves when they died because this place stinks like a cesspool. We'll get some of the villagers to clean this up tomorrow, and I'll send word to the castle that the Eastern Guard is dead. Let's go spend a comfortable night in the village tonight."

There was more harsh laughter as the Drambini soldiers turned away, mounted their horses, and rode back to Yertz.

Maren lowered his hand and sank down on a bench seat, sweat dripping down his face. His chest felt tight, and it was hard for him to breathe.

"What happened?" Keldon asked. "What did they see?"

Breathing in short, fast gasps, Maren said, "Exactly what they wanted to see: dead Vorlikian soldiers."

"What do we do now?"

"The guards from the border keep should be here soon. Keep giving the tea to all the guards, and here's enough callum bark to make another kettleful of tea. By the time they've finished it, they should be cured, but they still need to rest. Tomorrow they should be well. I have to go to the Northern Guard to see if they drank the wine, too." Maren sighed, tired but worried. "I may be too late to save them, but I have to try." He stood slowly.

"Maybe you should have some tea yourself," Keldon said as she held a cup out to Maren. "I mean, what good would you be to the Northern Guard if you don't have enough strength to do your magic?"

He gave a short laugh. "You're right. I need some tea." He took the cup and drank the tea. It felt warm going down his throat, soothing and invigorating, sending strength through his entire body. He looked at Keldon and smiled. "Thank you."

"Baygor protect you," she said.

Maren strode from the barracks, changed into an eagle the moment he was outside, and flew as fast as he could toward the Northern Guard.

32

Maren sighted the Northern Guard barracks when the full moon was halfway between midnight and moonset. *Barely three hours 'til dawn,* he thought. *I have to hurry or I won't make it back to Tironza in time to stop the Drambini army.* With his sharpened vision, he saw a dozen soldiers standing guard outside the barracks, fully armed and armored. Surprised, he landed just out of reach before them and shapechanged. The startled guards drew their swords and started toward him.

Maren held up his hands. "I'm Maren, Wizard and minstrel," he said. "And I've come to warn you."

The guards halted but didn't lower their weapons.

"Lieutenant Marissa," said one of the guards, holding out her hand. "And we already know the castle's been taken. Four Tarolin guards arrived several hours ago after they'd lit the signal fires."

Maren shook her hand. "Did they tell you the wine sent to you for the celebration was poisoned?"

"Yes." She laughed bitterly. "A good thing our first lieutenant decided to save it for the wedding toast tomorrow instead of for the betrothal or we'd all be dead, too."

"The Eastern Guard wasn't so lucky," Maren said. "Thirteen guards died before I could get there, but at least the rest are alive. There's a Drambini army coming from the west. They could arrive any moment, but I'll try to stop them. If I don't succeed, you'll have to fight them."

"We'll be ready," the guard said.

Maren changed to an eagle and flew west following the road. Gliding on the air, he searched for signs of movement but only saw a doe and her fawn nibbling grass at the edge of a stand of maple trees. Five miles from the Northern Guard barracks he spotted a glint of metal in the moonlight. Riding on the winds of night, he soared over the Drambini troops, fifty on horseback, nearly one hundred on foot.

They'll reach the Northern Guard by dawn, he thought. *How can I stop them?*

He circled above the Drambini, trying to think of some way to stop them. A vineyard on the southern side of the road caught his attention. The vines had just started to bud and send out pale green tendrils. *That will do,* he thought.

He landed in the center of the vineyard, shapechanged, and waited until the Drambini troops had nearly reached the vineyard. Holding his right hand toward the sky and his left hand palm up toward the road, he said, "By the power of Baramay, who created all living things, *tasrin bikhazi queesala barason!*"

The vines began to grow rapidly, twisting and curling, and thickened to the size of heavy ropes, reaching toward the Drambini. The vines wrapped around the horses' legs, hobbling them until they couldn't move. The soldiers tried to slash the vines with their swords, but the vines grew faster than the soldiers could cut them. Tendrils twisted around feet and legs, arms and hands, until the soldiers couldn't hack the vines, couldn't run, couldn't walk, couldn't move at all. The Drambini shouted and cursed until the vines covered their mouths, and all Maren heard was muffled cries of anger.

Maren leaned against a wooden post, tired but relieved. He'd stopped the army without harming anyone. The Drambini were alive, but unable to move. In the moonlight, they looked like statues made from living vines. *The Northern Guard can deal with them later,* he thought, *when the sun is up.* He flew back to the barracks and told Lieutenant Marissa what had happened.

"Be ready to come to Tarolin," Maren said. "We'll have to rescue Lord Bren and defeat the Drambini at the castle."

"We'll be ready," she said.

Maren shapechanged and flew straight south, over a small grove of callum trees outside the town of Tribbia, and on toward Tarolin Castle. He circled the castle, noting Drambini soldiers on the walls, a pile of dead Vorlikian soldiers on the eastern side of the castle. In the Dancing Glen west of the castle the celebrants lay on the ground, drugged and bound, and Drambini soldiers stood guard around the perimeter. He landed on the roof of the Audience Hall and peered into the torch lit hall. A handful of guards, wearing black and silver, stood against the stone walls. The room was filled with tables, heaped with the remains of the feast. Guests lay on the floor or slumped over the tables, their hands bound behind their backs, but he saw their chests moving as they breathed. *Still alive,* he thought gratefully. *I hope Bren is as well. Now to let Cordwin know and to stop the army marching on Tironza.*

He flew south, past Rindolar Woods, past the deserted village of Yarrow and its small cluster of callum trees. *Briella planted callum trees throughout the land,* he thought, amazed. *Why didn't we Wizards think of doing this before? And why restrict them to Vorlik? If they'll grow here, they should grow anywhere in the northern lands. When I leave Vorlik, I'll take callum seeds to the lands from here to Hixus.*

He passed fields and farms, vineyards and meadows until he spotted Tironza and the Southern Guard barracks. The four guards standing watch at the barracks entrance shouted in surprise when Maren landed and shapechanged before them.

"You *are* a Wizard!" said Cass, one of the four.

"I need to speak to Captain Cordwin and the lieutenants," Maren said. "And where's Gemna?"

"She's sleeping in the mess hall. I'll wake the others. They've only had a few hours' sleep." Cass opened the door and led Maren inside to where Gemna curled up on the floor close to the hearth, her hand clutching his lute, then Cass hurried away.

Maren knelt beside Gemna but didn't wake her, gazing at her sleeping. Firelight cast orange shadows on her. Her dark hair was unbound and lay around her face. She looked so peaceful, he smiled to himself. He bent over and reached out to shake her when she opened her eyes and slipped her arms around his neck.

"I'm not asleep," she said, pulling him down to kiss him. "You think I didn't feel you walking across the room?"

Startled, he smiled at her and kissed her, too. "I should know better. Time to get up. I have news to share." He stood up, and she did, too. She handed him his lute, and he slipped it over his head.

"I need you to be my bodyguard one last time," he said.

She looked surprised. "Why?"

"Because I've nearly reached the end of my strength and need to rest. I need you to watch over me while I sleep."

She glanced around the barracks. "But you're safe here."

"Yes, but I'm not going to sleep here. There's an army to stop yet, and for what I plan to do, I have to meet them far from here."

Gemna nodded. "I'll do whatever you need."

Cordwin, Daikin, Linaria, and Kyris walked into the mess hall just then, rubbing sleep from their eyes. They all sat down at one of the long trestle tables near the fireplace.

"What have you learned?" Cordwin asked.

He told them what had happened at the Eastern and Northern Guards, and what he'd seen at the castle. "I don't know where Bren is, but he wasn't in the Audience Hall. Probably in the dungeon. There were maybe two dozen bodies in Tarolin uniforms in the pile outside the walls."

"Two dozen." Cordwin frowned sorrowfully. "So many! And a dozen were with Linaria. That still leaves twenty-four guards unaccounted for."

"I doubt Miria would have thrown them in the dungeon," Daikin said, anger in his green eyes. "They're either dead or they escaped."

"Let's hope they escaped," Cordwin said. "What can we do about the army coming for the Southern Guard?"

"I'll take care of them," Maren said. "I'll send a signal when I need you."

"What do you mean?" Cordwin asked.

"For what I'm planning to do, you humans can't be nearby or you would be affected as well. As soon as you see a flaming arrow, come quickly. In the meantime, get your troops ready to follow us in case I can't stop the Drambini."

Cordwin nodded.

Maren stood and turned to leave, Gemna beside him.

Daikin stood. "She's not going with you, is she?"

"Yes," Maren said.

"But she's human! You said we couldn't be nearby!"

Maren turned and looked at Daikin, unsettled by the intensity of Daikin's voice. "I'll protect her. And she'll protect me. She *is* my bodyguard. We must do this alone."

Maren and Gemna strode from the mess hall and to the stables behind the barracks. They saddled their horses quickly, mounted, and galloped northwest beyond Tironza and the Southern Guard barrack, through moonlit meadows and woods until they reached the road to Leflin. Night birds sang to their mates, and small creatures skittered through the layers of fallen leaves and over small patches of snow hiding in the woods. The air was chilly enough, Maren could see his breath. They followed the road until Maren was certain they were far enough away from Tironza and the barracks. He halted, gazing at the meadows on either side of the road. "This is where I'll stop them," he said.

The moon was close to the western mountains; stars dimmed as dawn crept near. They dismounted and tethered their horses in a small clearing beside the road. Maren removed a small pouch from his cloak and sprinkled silvery dust in a circle encompassing the clearing.

Turning to Gemna, he said, "Watch over me while I sleep. Keep alert for any sign of the troops. If you hear anything, wake me. And stay inside the circle. Here." He removed his silver bracers from his wrists and offered them to her. "Wear these. They'll keep you safe."

Gemna shook her head. "No. I'd start to rely on them instead of my skill and instinct. But thank you."

"All right," Maren said reluctantly as he put on the bracers again. Worry gnawed at him. If anything happened to her... no, he wouldn't think about it. "I wouldn't want you to be hurt. I couldn't bear it if anything happened to you."

Gemna patted her sword. "I'll be all right with this. Sleep now, Maren. Baramay and I will keep you safe."

Nearly exhausted, Maren took a blanket from his saddle bag and bedded down on the grass, pillowing his head on his arm. He watched as Gemna sat at the edge of the circle, her hood up and her cloak pulled close around her, one hand on her sword, the other on the ground. *Baramay keep you safe,* he thought as he closed his eyes.

Maren felt as if he'd just closed his eyes when Gemna shook him. Dawn was creeping closer, but the land was still in the shadow of night. Birds twittered in the trees, welcoming the coming of a new day, but Maren feared what that day might bring.

"They're coming!" Gemna said, one knee on the ground. "Only a mile or two west of here. I felt hooves striking the ground, perhaps hundreds. I'd guess the riders are heavily armed and armored."

"Send a flaming arrow toward Cordwin's troops," Maren said as he sat up and rubbed his eyes. He felt better, but still fatigued. First light bathed the feathery clouds in the eastern sky in magenta and steel blue.

Gemna took her bow from her back and an arrow from her quiver. "Arrows, I have. Flames, I don't."

Maren grinned. "I can provide the flames. Wrap a piece of cloth around the arrowhead."

Gemna took a strip of cloth, left over from the clothing she'd made for Ilette, from her saddle bags and tied it around the arrow.

Maren held one hand toward the lightening sky and touched the cloth with his other hand. "By the power of Baramay who made all that is, *tasrin lanifar barason.*"

The cloth burst into flames. Gemna nocked the arrow, drew the bowstring back as far as she could, and let the arrow fly high toward Tironza. "I hope Cordwin saw that."

Maren nodded. "Now we'll deal with the invaders."

"You and me?" Gemna cocked her head. "Against hundreds? That doesn't sound like good odds."

"Ah, but I'm a Wizard."

"Really?" She grinned at him. "They don't have a chance."

He took his lute and tuned it. "I want to confront them here. Stay in the circle. You'll be safe from my magic. But if I stop playing and the troops are still coming toward me, get on your horse and ride to Cordwin as fast as you can. Don't look back. No--" he stopped her protest, "if I can't stop them, you have to promise that you'll warn Cordwin. Agreed?"

Gemna nodded slowly, looking troubled. "Agreed." She dropped to one knee and placed her hands on the ground. "They'll be here in minutes. Can you hear the hooves and clinking armor?"

Maren nodded, walked from the circle, and stood in the middle of the deeply rutted road, his eyes fixed on the top of the knoll where the road disappeared. Moments later, a ray of sunlight reflected from metal pikes, then on helms, and finally on black-and-silver shields as riders crested the knoll and trotted along the wide, worn track. A black-and-silver clad soldier pointed his sword at Maren and laughed. Others echoed his laughter, and the Drambini troops rode swiftly toward Maren.

Strumming his lute, Maren whispered a word of power. He began to sing "The Star Lullaby." His mellow, baritone voice echoed through the fields and meadows, building in strength though growing no louder.

At first the song had no effect. Maren sang louder, until his throat hurt. Gradually, the horses slowed to a canter, to a trot, to a walk, then to a halt. The riders' arms sagged, and they dropped their sword and shields. Their heads began to nod. They slumped forward on their sleeping horses' necks and fell to the ground with a clank, but even then they didn't awaken. The army lay sleeping on the dirt road as the sun crested the eastern mountains and shone its warm yellow light on the land.

Maren stopped playing, his lungs and throat aching, his fingers cramping. Moments later, Gemna appeared at his side.

"I saw it happen," she said, her voice barely audible, "and I still find this hard to believe. Is there anything you can't do?"

"I can't bring back the dead," Maren said. His hands were cold, and his fingers felt partly numb.

Gemna slid her arm around his back and leaned her cheek against his shoulder.

Suddenly, he felt dizzy, his legs buckled, and he nearly fell. Gemna caught him and wrapped her arms around his chest. He rested his head on her shoulder, feeling weak and drained. "I think I've reached the limit of my strength," he whispered.

"I'll be your strength," she said softly.

"My strength and my heart," he said.

She helped him back to the circle. Maren sank to the ground, exhausted. Gemna sat beside him and put her arms around him. Sweat trickled down his forehead, and his whole body ached. He closed his eyes and listened to his heart pounding. He felt Gemna's warmth and her compassion, and he thanked the gods that he'd met her.

"See?" he said. "I told you I still needed a bodyguard."

"What can I do to help?" she asked.

"I need some callum bark tea," he said. "But there's no time for that. Here." He pulled out the pouch with callum bark in it. "Crush this as fine as you can and mix it in some water. It will give me enough strength to go on for a while."

"All right."

Shivering, Maren lay down and wrapped up in his blanket, too tired to sit up on his own. He watched as Gemna wrapped a piece of callum bark in a square of cloth and pounded it with a stone. She opened her waterskin, poured in the powder, and shook it up. Sitting beside Maren, she slid her arm under him and levered him up until he could drink from the waterskin. The water was cold, but tasted sweet and slightly spicy. He gulped as much as he could. Strength seeped back into him. He gazed up at Gemna, her dark eyes filled with worry. He reached up and touched her cheek.

"What would I do without you?" he said.

She started to say something, then turned her head east. "Someone's coming," she said. "I can feel the pounding of the horses' hooves on the ground."

A short time later, Cordwin rode up, followed by Daikin, Kyris, and nearly all the Southern Guard.

"Captain Cordwin." Maren stood with Gemna's help, and he raised his hand in greeting. "You're a bit late. Gemna and I had to face the army alone, a hundred against the two of us. It was a difficult struggle, but they were no match for us."

Everyone stared at the slumbering army, then at Maren.

Suddenly, Daikin chuckled. "A hundred against two," he said, grinning, "a hundred against two." He threw back his head and laughed until his face streamed with tears. Cordwin smiled, then he began to laugh, too. Gemna and Kyris joined them. Maren's remarks were passed through the ranks, and the entire garrison laughed as well.

"Ah, Maren, you have a flair for words," Cordwin chortled.

Maren grinned. "That's why I'm a minstrel. And now, Captain, we need a plan to save Vorlik and Lord Bren."

33

Bren woke in a dark room, naked, lying on his back on a cold, damp floor. He was weak and groggy. His mouth was as dry as dust, and his head throbbed. Touching his forehead, his hand brushed a blood-crusted gash, and it began oozing again. His nose was assaulted by a vile odor of offal and sewage. Something furry brushed his face. Shunting it away, he heard a frightened squeak and scurrying feet. As he sat up, chains scraped against the stone, chains fastened by cold iron bands to his wrists.

Slowly, his eyes adjusted to the scintilla of flickering orange light peeping under a wooden door. He was alone in a windowless cell of stone walls and mud floor strewn with filthy straw. Blinking points of light revealed the ever-watchful eyes of rats. He was in the dungeon! But how did he come to be *there?*

Bren pulled and jerked on the chains. They were quite unbreakable. His head still muzzy, he tried to recall what happened. The betrothal ceremony, he remembered that. They'd said their vows, the priest announced the betrothal to the company, and they'd walked to the Audience Hall for the feast. Grimmin had proposed a toast to the marriage, then — he woke up here. What happened? Where was he? Where were Miria and Cordwin? He groaned as his head ached from injury and lack of answers.

The tiptoeing of small feet caught his attention. A sweet, quiet voice whispered his name, drawing closer to his cell.

"Bren, my love, my betrothed, my dearest, won't you speak to me?"

"Miria!" Bren struggled desperately to reach the door. "Miria, are you a prisoner, too?"

"No," Miria replied sweetly, "I'm still free."

"What day is it?"

"The morning after our betrothal."

"Do you know who's imprisoned me and why?"

"Yes, Bren, I know."

"Then who?"

"A moment," she said softly, "I have the key to your cell."

Bren heard the clink of the metal key sliding into the keyhole. With a rusty squeak, the lock opened. Painful light scorched his eyes. When they adjusted to the brightness, he saw Miria holding a torch in one hand and a ring of keys in the other.

She was dressed in the sky-blue gown she'd worn for their betrothal. The silver circlet of the lords of Drambit rested on her blond hair, made golden in the flickering torchlight. Her face was as fair as when they'd said their vows. His heart ached at the sight of her.

"Hurry, Miria!" Bren held out his wrists. "Unlock these, and we'll escape!"

"No, I don't have the key to your chains."

"Can't you find a tool to pry these off?"

"Yes, I could, but I won't," Miria answered with a smile.

"But... but why?" His voice trailed off as he stared at her. "I don't understand."

Glittering in the torchlight, a medallion caught his attention: the sunburst medallion of the Lord of Vorlik.

Surprised confusion crossed his face. "Miria, why are you wearing my medallion?"

"You can't wear it in a dungeon."

"What?" he asked, not understanding.

"I'm keeping it safe. You won't be needing it or your crown. You see, Bren," her smile grew wider, "Vorlik has a new lord, greater and more powerful than you."

Bren was bewildered. "Miria, are you crazy?"

Miria shook her head. "Oh, no, my dear Bren, I'm quite sane. Come, meet your new master." Sidling against the door, she bowed.

A man stepped into the yellow glare of the torch. He wore Bren's scarlet robe and fur-trimmed cloak. The gold and ruby crown of Vorlik rested on his blond ringlets. His dark blue eyes gleamed in his fair, youthful face.

"Grimmin!" Bren blurted out, staring with outraged disbelief. "Miria, I don't understand! He's only a merchant!"

Miria laughed, echoes redoubling the sound. "Oh, much more than that. He's Grimmin Slayer, Sorcerer of the Inner Circle, Lord of Vorlik -- and my husband."

Bren gasped. Cold fear crept into his stomach. Grimmin — a Sorcerer? And Miria's husband? "You betrayed me? You planned all this? You let me think you loved me and wanted to marry me? And all the while you were already married to *him*? To a *Sorcerer*? How could you? Why would you do this?"

"Do you really need to ask?" Miria's voice was soft; her lovely face, carved ice. "Revenge, Bren, revenge for Father's murder. You'll die for his death, but you won't die quickly, oh, no, not quickly." She flashed a cold smile at the Sorcerer, then turned back to Bren. "I promise you, you'll pray for death, beg for it, but your dying will be as long as we can make it. I'll celebrate every lash, every welt and wound we give you. I'll toast every drop of your blood that falls. Every time you scream in agony, I'll be in Grimmin's arms." She gave a high tinkling laugh, so incongruous with her words.

Grimmin smiled at her, then turned to Bren. His eyes were summer-blue and winter snow. His smile turned grim. "Your land is mine," he said. "Your guards are dead. The woman you wanted to marry is mine, was mine before she wrote to you. And I, too, seek revenge, for Sorcerers have very long memories. Long ago my ancestor was killed by the Wizard Timmree. She married the Lord of Vorlik. You're descended from her; you'll pay for her crime." He held out his hand to Miria. "Come, my love. Let's leave Bren to think about his death. We'll go to bed after washing off the stench of this place."

Turning, they left. Just before closing the door, Grimmin looked back at Bren, a cruel smile on his lips. "Think about this, too, Bren. We've taken your rooms for our own. I'll be holding her, caressing her, making love to her in your own bed."

Laughing at Bren's stricken face, Grimmin closed the door, sealing in the darkness.

"Miria!" Bren shouted, frustrated and enraged at his helplessness. He pulled against the chains, yanking them as hard as he could, but they only cut into his wrists. Something warm and wet trickled down his hands. "Miria! Miria!!!"

His shouts weren't quite loud enough to drown out the echo of Grimmin's laughter. The emptiness in his heart was as dark and deep as the blackness of the dungeon. He collapsed to the cold stones, desolate and hopeless.

"What have I done?" Bren cried, despair crushing him to the filthy stone floor. "First I killed Briella! And now I've let Miria destroy Vorlik! I've betrayed everyone! Everyone! Hound of Darkness, let me die! Just let me die!"

34

Malbar started to leave the cell where he'd interrogated Bren's counselors, trying to learn where Cordwin might go, when he heard Miria's voice calling Bren's name. He cracked open the cell door just enough to listen as she taunted Bren. Malbar could hardly comprehend what she told Bren. Grimmin — her husband and a Sorcerer? It couldn't be true! The longer he listened, the more desolate he became. He had to brace himself against the door as the horrors of what Miria told Bren sank like a dagger into Malbar's heart. As soon as Miria and Grimmin left the dungeon, Malbar staggered from the cell, cringing at Bren's despondent cries.

Devastated, Malbar sagged against the stone wall of the corridor, barely able to stand up. "Miria betrayed me!" he whispered, beating his fist against the stone until his knuckles bled. "Not only me, but all our people!" He felt as if a huge rock had slammed against his chest, as if he could hardly breathe. "She kissed me! She led me to believe she loved me and would marry me, but she was already married to another! A Sorcerer! Hound of Darkness, a *Sorcerer!* How could she let him touch her?" He lurched past Bren's cell. *We're all doomed,* he thought, *both Drambit and Vorlik! Bren, I betrayed you for her, but she betrayed us both, betrayed everyone! What have I done? What have I done?*

Tears blurred Malbar's vision as he stumbled from the dungeon, fled up the stairs to the Green Tower room, and slammed the door shut. He ran up to the bed chamber, sank to the floor beside the bed, and wept in shame. Memories flooded Malbar's thoughts, memories of the secret dell where Bren and he had played, of their treks into the wildlands of Drambit, the time Bren saved him from a wild boar, their pledge of brotherhood. Anger had driven him to throw away Bren's friendship, but for what? There was nothing left for him, nothing. "What have I done?" he said, guilt twisting in his heart like a knife. "And what can I do to stop Miria?"

Miria stretched contentedly beneath the linen sheets and thick quilt that covered Grimmin and her. Her eyes followed the contours of his golden body, lingering on his face and hair.

I must be crazy to want a Sorcerer, she thought. *But the blood of Sorcerers flows in my veins. Maybe that's what draws me to him.* She lightly brushed her fingers down Grimmin's smooth chest as he stirred and opened his eyes. She smiled. How delicious it was to have everything she wanted, just as he'd promised!

Grimmin smiled and propped himself on one elbow. "You look happy right now."

Miria stretched cat-like. "Oh, I am. I am."

"So am I. I've avenged myself and my people against the house of Vorlik. I've taken everything from Bren, even the woman he loves. How could I not be happy? But most of all," he caressed her cheek and ran his fingertips lightly over her lips, "you make me happy, Miria, more than I'd thought possible, more than I'd ever anticipated."

Drawing her against his bare chest and sinking his hand deep in her golden hair, he kissed her fiercely. "We're alike, you and I," he whispered against her mouth. He caressed the pale skin of her neck, and she shivered with delight. "We're strong-willed, we crave power, and we're passionate in everything. Not even in Derkhafen is there a woman like you. We could rule -- no, we *will* rule Baramayan, together."

Kissing her again, Grimmin flipped the coverlet off him and rolled to the edge of the bed. He sat up and stretched his arms. When he tried to stand, Miria's arms encircled his bare waist.

"Come back to bed," she pleaded, her hands caressing his chest. "Stay with me. There's nothing you have to do right now."

He pulled free of her arms and twisted to face her. "Only Bren's torture to watch and his execution to arrange." He toyed with one of her golden tresses. "Would you like to come with me?"

Her eyes narrowed, and her voice became colder than snowfall. "Yes. I want to watch him suffer for what he did to Father."

Grimmin chucked her under the chin. "Then perhaps you should dress. If Bren saw you like this, he'd be so aroused, he wouldn't feel any pain!"

Miria laughed and slid from the bed. "I wouldn't want that!"

Dressing quickly, the two left Bren's rooms. They descended the spiral stairs until they'd almost reached the entry hall. Callas and Malbar were on the bottom of the step.

"Greetings, My Lady," Callas said as he and his son bowed. "We were just coming to find you. I have reports from our troops. The Eastern Guard is taken; the soldiers are dead. There's no word about the Southern and Northern Guards as yet. I hope to receive word by nightfall. The village of Tarolin Town is occupied and under control."

"Well done, captain!" Miria said.

"I also have bad news." Malbar stood rigidly, his jaw tight. "Nearly half of the Tarolin Guard escaped, and Cordwin hasn't been found. He's probably the one who set the signal fires. The village of Yarrow was deserted when a company arrived this morning, as were several villages north and east. I think Cordwin may have fled to Tironza. It won't do him any good if our troops have taken the Southern Guard."

Grimmin frowned; his eyes narrowed. "I wouldn't be so sure about Cordwin. He has some power, some magic I didn't recognize. He should've been as enamored of Miria as Bren was, but he wasn't. How did he resist Akavar's potions? He's the one person who could rally the people against us. I think we've allowed the most dangerous animal to escape the trap."

Malbar remained silent, his eyes lowered.

"But on to more pleasant things." Grimmin grinned at Miria. "To the dungeon to see Bren. Captain Callas, I think a daybreak hanging would be an excellent way to start tomorrow."

"Oh, no," Miria said. "It has to be later in the day. I want every Vorlikian here and from Tarolin Town in the Dancing Glen to watch their lord die like a common criminal. And we have to have enough time to make Bren suffer first. I want him to be in agony."

Grimmin smiled at her, then Miria turned to Callas. "Would you take care of the details?"

Callas nodded. "There's already a dais in the Dancing Glen that would do perfectly for a gallows with a few additions. A delightful way to end their Spring Festival."

Miria giggled, then laughed freely. She looked at Malbar and smiled. "Let us go see how Bren is faring."

Malbar glanced at her, then stared down at his reports. "I need to wait for word from the north and south armies."

"But this is what you were waiting for," Miria said smiling. "Don't you want to enjoy his torment?"

Malbar didn't answer for a few moments. He slowly raised his eyes until he was gazing straight at Miria. "I must fulfill my duty to you before I allow myself such... enjoyment." He bowed stiffly. "My Lady." He turned and walk toward the main doors of the castle.

Miria watched him walk away, slightly unsettled.

"Shall we go, My Lady?" Grimmin asked.

"Yes, yes, of course," Miria said. "We've kept Bren waiting too long."

Grimmin took her arm and guided her down the remaining steps to the dungeon level, Callas following close behind.

35

Maren leaned on Gemna's arm and watched as Cordwin ordered the Drambini soldiers be stripped of their uniforms. The Southern Guard put on the Drambini uniforms, then bound the hands and feet of the sleeping Drambini soldiers.

"How long will the spell last?" Cordwin asked.

"Perhaps an hour," Maren said wearily.

"Leave the Drambini here," Cordwin told Daikin and the Southern Guard. "They'll be fine. It's not that cold. We'll have the townspeople bring out wagons to carry the Drambini back to the Southern Guard barracks until we return."

Although the callum bark water had renewed his strength a bit, Maren felt too weak to ride by himself. Gemna mounted her horse, and Daikin helped Maren climbed up in front of her. Daikin handed her the reins, then mounted his own horse and rode up beside Gemna while leading Maren's horse.

"We have to reach Rindolar Woods today if our plan is to work," Cordwin said. He looked toward the eastern horizon.

Maren glanced eastward. The sun was well above the horizon. "We won't reach the woods until late afternoon," he said. "Maybe not until early evening."

"That will give us time to scout the area. Hopefully, we'll meet up with other soldiers. Can you summon the Northern and Eastern Guards?"

Maren shook his head. "Not now. If I can rest a bit, perhaps until we reach Yarrow, then I'll be able to fly to the Guards and still make it back in time for the attack."

"All right. Mount up, everyone," Cordwin ordered.

Gemna held Maren close and whispered, "Sleep. I'll keep you safe."

Maren leaned against her and closed his eyes. He felt her warmth soaking into his back, her heart beat strong and steady. He breathed in the salty scent of her skin and earthy fragrance of her hair, and he felt safe and comfortable. Gradually, he fell asleep, hearing Gemna and Daikin talking.

Someone shook his arm and said softly, "It's time, Maren."

He opened his eyes, feeling rested and stronger. The sun was overhead, and the air was comfortably warm. The horse had stopped in the center of a deserted village. There was no sound except the light rustle of leaves in the gentle breeze from the northwest. A few tendrils of smoke flowed through the village from the embers of the signal tower on the knoll behind the inn.

Maren looked over his shoulder at Gemna. She smiled at him.

"Feeling better?" she asked.

"A bit," he said. "I hope I have enough strength to play my part."

Cordwin rode back toward them. "We've reached Yarrow," he said. "You must summon the Eastern and Northern Guards. Have the Northern Guard take out the Drambini holding the hostages at Dancing Glen, but they have to wait until we've entered the castle before they attack. Have the Eastern Guard meet us in Rindolar Woods before the attack."

"Lord Cordwin!" A man wearing the robe of a priest of Baygor ran toward Cordwin from the door of the grey stone inn and bowed. "Is it really you? I thought the Drambini had come back. Do you remember me?"

Cordwin gazed down at the copper-haired priest. "Aren't you the one who brought Briella's letter to me?"

"Yes. My name is Liska. I stayed close to the village so I could let the townspeople know when it was safe to return. But when I saw an army of soldiers in Drambini uniforms, I feared the worst."

"We're going to rescue Lord Bren tonight," Cordwin said. "Tell the townspeople it's time to come home. Hopefully, by tomorrow morning we will have driven the Drambini from our land."

Maren glanced beyond the priest to the inn. Towering behind the inn and the chapel of Baygor were small groves of callum trees. "Priest, those trees – Briella planted them, didn't she?"

The priest stared at Maren for a moment, then nodded. "She taught the innwife and me how to use the bark and leaves to heal. Briella said the tree was from her homeland, from the Wizard's Vale." He paused. "But you know that, don't you?" He bowed. "Welcome, Wizard. What is your name?"

"Maren."

"Baygor bless you, Maren."

"Would you have any callum bark tea?" Maren asked. "I find I need more strength than I have."

"I had just brewed a kettleful before we had to flee," Liska said. "It's cold, but it should still be potent. I'll fetch you a cup."

Liska ran to his small cottage beside the chapel and soon came back with a large wooden mug which he handed to Maren.

"I'm very grateful, priest," Maren said and drank the entire mugful.

"And I am grateful for what Briella did for us, all of us." Liska turned back to Cordwin. "I'll tell the villagers it's time to come back."

"Especially the innwife and anyone who has healing skills," Cordwin said. "We may need to summon them to the castle before the night is over."

"Yes, My Lord." Liska bowed.

"I'm a captain now," Cordwin said. "Bren is lord of Vorlik."

Liska smiled. "It is difficult to break a twenty-year habit. I'll fetch the people back to Yarrow. Baygor protect you all."

Maren slid down from Gemna's horse. She reached down and took his hand. "I'll be waiting in the woods near the crossroads," she said.

For a long moment, he held her hand, then kissed it. "I'll be there as soon as I can." He let go of her hand and shapechanged, flying eastward over the fields and meadows of new spring grass and wild flowers, past hamlets and farmsteads.

Within half an hour he reached the Eastern Guard. The soldiers had completely recovered from the poison and were eager to fight. The border guards were there as well. Maren explained the plan and told them where they were to meet Cordwin.

"What about the Drambini soldiers in Yertz?" Maren asked.

Keldon grinned. "The border guards took them out last night. And we kept their uniforms in case we needed them."

Maren smiled. "You will. Go as quickly as you can. The attack will begin as soon as everyone is in place tonight."

He shapechanged and flew to the Northern Guard. The lieutenant had already placed his men on alert when Maren arrived.

"We're ready to leave now," the lieutenant said. "We'll be in place by dusk."

"And the Drambini army I trapped last night?" Maren asked.

The lieutenant became solemn. "Many of them are dead. When we cut them free of the vines, they immediately attacked us. We had little choice but to defend ourselves. The rest were mercenaries. They surrendered. They're being held in the barracks."

Maren nodded. "You'll need to wear the Drambini uniforms."

"They're a little bloody."

"In the dark no one will notice," Maren said. "If they do, it will look as if you'd been in a battle and won. Come quickly. Cordwin will be waiting until dark for the attack."

"We'll be there."

Shapechanging, Maren flew back toward Tarolin. It was midafternoon when he spotted the castle walls. A gallows had been built in the Dancing Glen. All around the meadow the celebrants sat on the grass, hands tied behind their back. Two dozen Drambini soldiers patrolled the area, taunting the Vorlikians and eating food from the betrothal feast. *It will be dangerous for the people there,* he thought, worried. *They could so easily be hurt or killed in the fighting.*

He circled the northern edge of Rindolar Woods, its thick old trees just sending out pale green leaves, until he spotted Gemna and the Southern Guard camped far enough south of the crossroads they couldn't be seen from the castle. She was talking to Daikin when Maren landed beside her and shapechanged. She leaped to her feet, leaves crunching under her feet.

"How did it go?" she asked.

"Everything is set," Maren said, shivering as a cool breeze trickled through the woods. "Where's Cordwin?"

"Over there," she said, pointing eastward to a cluster of soldiers in Drambini uniforms sitting on logs dragged into a circle.

Maren strode toward Cordwin with Gemna at his side and Daikin following. Cordwin, Linaria, and Kyris stood when Maren approached. They all sat down, Maren to Cordwin's right. Gemna sat between Maren and Daikin.

"All is set," Maren told them. "The Eastern Guard should be here by dusk. They'll be coming through the woodland path so they won't be seen from the castle. The Northern Guard will be in place by the same time. Has there been any sign of the Tarolin Guards?"

Cordwin looked troubled and shook his head. "I don't know if any of them are alive or dead."

Everyone was silent for a few moments. Cordwin broke the silence.

"Briella could travel from place to place without shapechanging," Cordwin said. "She said it was difficult, but I traveled with her that way twice. Can you do that, too? Could you find Bren that way?"

"I can travel like that," Maren said slowly, "but it takes a great deal of power and strength, and I can only travel to places I've been before or at least seen. I've never been inside the castle although I've seen inside the Audience Hall. If I can reach the Audience Hall or find an open window I can enter, I can shapechange into something that won't be noticed easily, a rat or mouse perhaps, and work my way down to the dungeon. When I find Bren, I'll take him to some place safe, maybe the inn at Yarrow. The villagers should be back by then."

Cordwin picked up a stick and drew a sketch of the castle in the damp earth. "When we get inside the gate, we'll split into three groups," he said. "Daikin, your company will take the barracks. Kyris, send your men in twos to kill the guards on the walls. I'll take Linaria and the third company into the castle to find Miria and Callas. If we fail tonight, Vorlik is lost."

"I'll go with you into the castle," Gemna said.

Cordwin nodded.

"They've built a gallows in the Dancing Glen," Maren said. "My guess is it's for Bren. We have to rescue him tonight or it might be too late."

"Then we must succeed," Cordwin said.

"We should all sleep while we can," Maren said. "Post a few guards, but everyone else should rest. No fires."

"I agree," Cordwin said.

Maren stood and walked beside Gemna to where she had been. Daikin followed them. Maren turned and stared at him. "You should get some sleep, too," Maren said coldly. "There's plenty of room over by your soldiers."

Daikin frowned for a moment, then walked toward his soldiers.

Gemna's dark eyes fixed on Maren, and a slight frown tugged lines in her forehead. "Daikin's never done anything to you," she said. "Why don't you like him?"

"I don't like the way he looks at you," he said softly.

She stared at him for a few moments, then she touched his arm and smiled warmly. "We need to sleep. It's going to be a long night."

She handed him his pack and pulled a blanket out of her saddlebags. He took out his own blanket and spread it on the thick layer of fallen leaves beside Gemna's blanket. Maren lay down, facing her, and wrapped half the blanket over him, his back to the late afternoon sunlight. She smiled at him, then closed her eyes, and his heart felt as if he were still an eagle soaring in the sky. He closed his eyes, breathing in the scent of damp earth and the spicy fragrance of dry leaves, and slept peacefully.

Someone shook Cordwin from a dream of Briella. He tried to hold onto the dream, hold onto the feeling of her in his arms, of her lips touching his, but the dream slipped away like water through his fingers. Opening his eyes, he saw Daikin kneeling beside him in the orange-black shadows of sunset and grinning.

"Guess who decided to pay us a visit?" Daikin asked, his green eyes twinkling.

"You woke me to ask me *that?*" Cordwin finger-combed his dark hair from his face. "All right. Who?"

Daikin stood up, moved aside, and swept his hand toward a grizzled soldier in a torn and bloody red and gold uniform of the Tarolin Guard.

"Rayvil!" Cordwin leaped to his feet and grasped the lieutenant's hand. "You're alive! Did anyone else escape?"

"I did, captain." Lieutenant Tude walked up and saluted. Her uniform was splattered with blood, and she had a bandage tied around her left arm. "And so did twenty-four of the Tarolin Guard."

"What about Lieutenant Loren?"

Tude glanced down and shook her head. "He didn't make it out of the castle. No one else escaped."

"What happened?" Cordwin asked softly.

Tude was silent for a moment, then shuddered and cleared her throat. "We were in the barracks when I heard some shouting. I ran outside and saw Drambini soldiers attacking Loren and the guards on the wall. We all ran out to help but more Drambini came riding in the gate and from inside the castle. We fought and fought, but we were outnumbered. Loren—"

Tude halted, her hands clutched in tight fists. She took a short breath, then continued. "The first lieutenant ordered us to escape and get help. We forced our way through the castle gate and ran toward Tarolin Town, but Drambini soldiers were already there. We barely escaped and ran into the woods. Luckily, we knew the woods and the Drambini didn't. But everywhere we went, we saw Drambini troops. We killed a few Drambini, but mostly we've been hiding here. We almost attacked you until I recognized Daikin when he took off his helmet. We're ready to fight, captain. Just give us our orders."

Cordwin placed his hand on Tude's shoulder. "Well done, lieutenant, and welcome. Daikin, see that all the guards are given Drambini uniforms. They'll ride with us into the castle."

At that moment, the Eastern Guard rode into the camp. A woman in a green and gold uniform dismounted and saluted Cordwin. "Sergeant Keldon reporting with fifty soldiers of the Eastern Guard."

"Sergeant?" Cordwin said.

"I'm the highest ranking officer from the Eastern Guard," Keldon said.

Maren walked toward Keldon and shook her hand. "All the other lieutenants were dead so she had to take charge." He turned toward Cordwin. "If that's all right with you."

"Then I suppose I'll have to make you a lieutenant," Cordwin said. "A battlefield commission. You are officially First Lieutenant of the Eastern Guard."

Keldon smiled and saluted again. "Yes, sir. Thank you, sir."

Cordwin nodded and saluted Keldon in return.

"We brought ten Drambini uniforms," Keldon said. "The others were nothing but shreds."

"Good. Take one for yourself and give the others to whomever you choose. We have a few more you can have. You'll be in charge of leading the Eastern Guard against the Drambini in the Dancing Glen from the south when the Northern Guard attacks from the north. Above all, protect the people held hostage by the Drambini. As soon as it's full dark, we'll begin the attack."

Keldon saluted and hurried back to her troops.

The sun set, and the woods became as dark as a cave. Cordwin didn't dare light a fire, but soon moonlight drizzled through the nearly bare limbs of the great trees. He summoned the officers, Maren, and Gemna to the circle of logs.

"Keldon, move the Eastern Guard west through the woods and come in from the west," Cordwin said. "That way the Drambini will think you're reinforcements come from Drambit. Rayvil, wait in the woods across from the castle gates until you see a torch waved from the battlements. That will be the signal to attack. We'll enter the castle when the moon is halfway between horizon and zenith. Go and Baygor protect us."

Keldon saluted, the silver on the Drambini uniform gleaming in the moonlight. "Baygor protect us all," she said. She called her troops together, mounted, and rode west into the woods.

Rayvil saluted and took his troops eastward.

"The rest of you will follow me," Cordwin said.

"I'll leave now to search for Bren," Maren said. "It may take a while to locate him. Rats move fast, but it's a big castle and I'll have to be careful. I don't know if Miria bought poison from a Sorcerer or if there's a Sorcerer in the castle. If a Sorcerer *is* there..." He shuddered.

"Baygor protect you." Cordwin grasped the Wizard's arm. "I pray you find Bren alive."

Maren nodded.

"Be careful," Gemna whispered as she touched his other arm. "Baygor protect you, my love."

"Baramay keep you safe," Maren said softly. He changed into an eagle and flew away.

Cordwin waited until the moon was a quarter of the way across the sky, then he stood up. "Time to go now."

He climbed into his saddle and led the Drambit-garbed Vorlikians at a walk up the Tironza Road to the crossroads then turned toward the castle. He made certain his helm shadowed his face as he approached the gatewards.

"Halt and identify," one soldier challenged.

"Nathan of the southern army," Cordwin mumbled behind the helm. "I bring word to Lord Miria of the destruction of the Southern Guard. Also, I've brought a portion of the army back to Tarolin since they weren't needed to take Tironza."

The other gateward eyed him suspiciously. "It's late."

"Yes, it is!" Cordwin sounded irritated. "We've been traveling since midmorning, and before that we rode to Tironza like the Hound of Darkness was after us. I'm tired, soldier, and I intend to sleep in the barracks in a decent bed tonight! Now will you let me pass or do I have to dismount and teach you some manners?"

Faced with a bristling soldier, the Drambini guard allowed Cordwin and his men to enter.

"I'll mention your conduct to Lady Miria when I speak with her." Cordwin suppressed a chuckle as he rode past the guard. "I'm sure she'll give you what you deserve."

Once inside, they rode to the foot of the castle steps. Cordwin motioned Daikin and Kyris to his side with Gemna close behind. "You know what to do," Cordwin said. "Baygor protect us. May a friend guard your back."

"May you not die alone," the other two said, clasping his hands.

Cordwin glanced up at the castle doors. "Let's hope when we meet again, Tarolin will be ours."

36

Dressed in full uniform and cloak, Malbar waited impatiently in his tower room. He wanted to be certain Grimmin and Miria were in bed, and his father had finished making the rounds of the guard posts and was off to bed as well. Opening the door, Malbar peered into the empty corridor and listened for footsteps. He heard nothing. He slipped from his room, closed the door carefully, and walked cautiously down a hallway with Drambini guards. Swallowing tightly, he held his head up and strode purposefully down past the guards, who saluted him.

At last, he reached the dark stairwell. His stomach knotted with fear. Wariness prickled down his neck as he descended the stairs, pressing against the inner wall, worried he'd be discovered. He passed several guards patrolling the entry hall. They saluted, and he barely returned their salute, trying to appear as arrogant and uninterested as he could.

Finally, he arrived at the dungeon level. In the yellow glare of torches Malbar spied the single guard on duty, seated with his feet propped on a small table and his helmeted head slumped to his chest. A ring of keys lay on the table beside an empty wooden plate and mug.

A glimmer of a smile crossed Malbar's face as a plan came to him. He strode boldly toward the guard and growled, "Drunk and asleep on duty! I should have you whipped and thrown into a cell!"

The startled soldier leaped to his feet, knocking over his chair and table. Keys clattered to the stone floor.

Saluting Malbar, the guard blanched, his mouth open but couldn't speak.

Grasping the ring of keys from the floor, Malbar snarled, "Give me your sword! You aren't worthy to serve Drambit!"

"Lieutenant, please, don't—"

"Don't beg, you wretch!" Malbar snatched the man's sword from his outstretched hand. "You'll spend the night in a cell like that Vorlik filth! You might keep the Vorlikian company on the gallows tomorrow when Lord Miria hears about this! Think about that!"

The soldier turned ghostly pale and fell to his knees. "Please, sir, let me explain."

Malbar kicked the man in the chin, slamming the man's head again the stone wall. The man's eyes rolled back into his head, and he slid to the floor. Malbar dragged the limp body into an empty cell, pulled the door closed and locked it, and turned to Bren's cell. Twisting the key in the rusty lock and taking a torch from the wall, Malbar carefully pushed open the door.

Torchlight filled the room. Black bodies of rats scrambled for dark corners and hidden ledges. The smell gagged Malbar. He held the edge of his cape over his mouth and nose to filter out some of the stench.

Bren's naked body lay face down on the filthy straw. His back was crisscrossed with crusted blood from lash marks. Oozing flesh edged black on his back, buttocks, and soles told of heated irons. The rats had chewed an open sore on his leg. His bleeding hands looked as every bone in them had been crushed.

Malbar almost vomited at the sight. Clenching his teeth and tightening his throat, he controlled his stomach. He ran to Bren's side, weeping as he knelt and turned Bren on his side. Touching Bren's neck, Malbar felt a pulse, barely, but there. His vision wavered, and a grateful sob choked his voice. "He's alive."

Bren's face was swollen, purple, and blood-streaked from a broken nose and split lips. His hair was matted with blood and straw, and his jaw appeared to be broken.

"Pyccis," Malbar called Bren by his childhood name, "forgive me!" Tears streaked his face as Malbar lifted Bren in his arms, bracing his friend's body on his knee. "I'm so sorry! I'll get you out of here somehow!"

"Will you, indeed?" asked a quiet, unfamiliar voice.

Startled, Malbar rapidly drew his sword. Still kneeling and holding Bren, Malbar faced the stranger.

He was taller than Malbar and hidden by a dark hooded cloak.

"I'm warning you, I won't let you stop me," Malbar threatened.

"I've no intention of stopping you," the man said. "I came to rescue him myself."

Malbar gave him an I-don't-believe-you glare. "Of course."

The man slid the hood from his face. Dark eyes gazed into Malbar's with soul-searching, guileless eyes. They drew him the way Cordwin's did. Malbar lowered the sword slightly. Somehow he knew he didn't need it.

"My name is Maren," the cloaked man said. "I'm a Wizard."

Malbar choked. This was a Wizard? Malbar had always thought Wizards would seem darker, evil, dangerous, more like Grimmin. Stories said they were the same as Sorcerers. But Maren didn't feel evil, only powerful.

Maren's voice was quiet and comforting. "You care about Bren, I can see that. I can take him out of here without being seen, and I'll heal him. Isn't that what you want?"

Malbar wanted to trust him, but how could he? Malbar didn't trust his own father anymore. His voice cracked when he spoke. "Of course, it's what I want! I've betrayed Lady Miria, the woman I love, even my own father to save him!"

"Then trust me." Maren held his arms out to take Bren. "Let me help him."

Malbar looked down at Bren. There was so much Malbar wanted to tell him -- how much Bren still meant to him. He wanted to beg Bren to forgive him. But that could wait 'til later. Bren's life was more important. Malbar dropped his sword, and with both arms supporting Bren, forced himself to stand. He staggered to Maren and said, "H-he has to live. You promise he'll live."

Maren put his hand on Malbar's shoulder and gave it a gentle squeeze. "I swear if there's the faintest heartbeat, the slightest breath in him, I'll pull him back from death."

Looking down at Bren's battered face, Malbar slowly nodded his consent and placed Bren's limp form in Maren's arms.

"Take him far away from here," Malbar said, "away from this castle and Miria, and me."

"I can take all three of us to safety."

Malbar shook his head reluctantly. "I've betrayed everything for him. I may die for my actions, but—"

"You'll most certainly die, traitor," Grimmin said from the doorway, flanked by Miria and Callas.

Malbar hadn't heard them come.

"Grimmin!" Maren seemed to grow before Malbar's eyes.

"You've broken the binding." Grimmin's eyes were colder than the dungeon. "I felt your magic when you entered the castle. I followed it to its source and found you. I should've killed you in Hixus."

The Sorcerer leaped into the room but stumbled. A dagger sprouted in his shoulder.

"Go!" Malbar shouted at Maren, drawing another dagger and picking up his sword. He leaped between Maren and Grimmin. "Remember your promise!"

"You traitorous son of a whore!" Callas shouted. "You're no son of mine! I'll kill you myself!" He started toward Malbar.

Grimmin's iron grip jerked him back.

"No," Grimmin said with narrowed eyes and toothy smile. "I'll take care of this." He held out a hand and spoke the Sorcerers' language, a tongue so terrible, Miria and Callas fell to their knees and covered their ears. A blood-red ball of flame appeared in Grimmin's hand, and he threw it into the room.

Malbar stared at the ball of flame, knowing his death was moments away. He tried to run but couldn't move. *At least I saved Bren,* he thought. *Perhaps someday he'll forgive me.* He felt the heat of the flames growing closer, the light so intense he couldn't bear to look at it. He couldn't breathe.

Suddenly, he heard horns blowing. He felt a hand on his arm and heard words he didn't understand. The burning heat disappeared instantly, and swirling rainbows of light surrounded him. He felt dizzy and off balance, as if he were falling. He nearly fainted but fought to remain conscious. Suddenly, he was standing outside a two-story stone building. Maren was beside him, still holding Bren.

"I couldn't leave you to die," Maren said.

Tears filled Malbar's eyes. His legs buckled, and he sank to the ground.

Maren shouted for help. The door opened, and light streamed out. A man hurried out. He was wearing a simple brown robe, and his hair was like spun copper. He was followed by a stocky man with reddish hair turning white at his temples. The two men inhaled sharply as they looked at Bren.

"Great Baygor, who is this?" asked the man in the robe.

"It's Lord Bren! He's badly injured," Maren said, staggering slightly.

The robed man glanced at the stocky man. "Hollester, help the Wizard carry him inside."

The stocky man slipped one of Bren's arms over his shoulder and helped Maren support Bren's body. "You're a Wizard?" the man asked.

"Yes." Nodding at Malbar, Maren said, "Liska, help him."

The robed man bent down and helped Malbar stand, but Malbar's legs were so shaky, he could barely walk even with Liska's help. "You're injured," Liska said.

"Injured?" Malbar repeated, watching as Maren and Hollester carried Bren inside the building.

"There are burns on your face and hands."

Malbar looked down at his hands. The skin was red and blistered. The moment he saw the blisters, searing pain surged up his arms, and he gasped, gritting his teeth.

"Lean on me," Liska said. "Let me help you."

Malbar could barely see through his tears. "Why?" he asked. "Why would you help me? I'm a Drambini."

Liska smiled at Malbar and said, "Because the Wizard asked me to. Because he believes you are worthy of my help."

If only that were true, Malbar thought, guilt and shame filling his heart.

A plainly dressed woman with brown hair braided around her head stood in the common room, wiping her hands on an apron. She gasped as she looked at Bren's injuries. "What have they done to him?" she cried.

"Germaine, we need a bed, quickly!" Hollester said.

She led Maren and Hollester down a corridor. Liska supported Malbar and followed them. Germaine opened a door to a spacious room with a large bed. Maren and Hollester carried Bren into the room.

"Place him on his stomach," Maren said. "We need to treat the burns and lashes first."

Maren and the stocky man carefully placed Bren face down on the bed. Liska led Malbar to a cushioned chair and settled him there.

"Is he still alive?" Malbar asked frantically. "Will he be all right?"

Maren glanced up at Malbar. "We'll do everything we can," the Wizard said. He turned toward Germaine. "Do you have any of the healing salve from the callum leaves?"

She nodded, dashed away, and came back quickly with three jars and an armload of bandages.

Maren took one of the jars. "Spread it on thickly," he said, "then bandage the wounds. And we'll need some callum bark tea."

"I started some brewing," Germaine said.

"As soon as it's ready, bring in a cup. Hollester, we need a fire."

Hollester nodded and began laying kindling on the hearth on the wall beside the bed. Soon a blazing fire warmed the room.

Maren, Liska, and Germaine opened the jars and started spreading a creamy white salve on black-edged raw burns across Bren's back and buttocks and the soles of his feet. A fragrance of mint and wildflowers and something else filled the room, a fragrance Malbar had never smelled before, sweet and fresh as a meadow after a spring rain. Just inhaling the scent seemed to ease Malbar's heart. Liska and Germaine carefully wound bandages around Bren's body, and laid him on his side. Bren never opened his eyes, never made a sound.

Maren placed his hand on Bren's forehead. "He has a fever," the Wizard said, worry on his face. "He needs some callum bark tea."

"It should be brewed by now," Germaine said and hurried from the room.

Liska knelt beside Malbar and spread some of the salve on his hands and wrapped them with bandages, then spread a thin layer of salve on Malbar's face. The salve was cool against his burning skin, soothing, numbing, healing. Malbar closed his eyes a moment, grateful for relief from the pain. Opening his eyes, he gazed at Liska and whispered, "Thank you."

Liska smiled at him. "The burns should heal by tomorrow night, and there should be no scarring. Rest now. I'll bring you something to drink in a bit."

Germaine came back with a small kettle filled with green-gold tea scented like the salve, but more intense. "His jaw looks broken. How can we get him to drink this?" she asked.

Maren looked pensive. "I can heal the jaw so he can drink the tea."

"Can't you heal him completely?" Malbar asked anxiously.

"I could," Maren said slowly, "but he's so hurt that if I healed his body completely right now, the shock would be so great, his mind might never recover from the horrors he suffered. I must be cautious and gentle in healing him. First, the jaw, then the fever. After that, I'll heal his other injuries." He smiled at Malbar. "I made you a promise, and I'll keep it. Bren will live."

Maren closed his eyes for a moment, then placed his right hand on Bren's jaw. Bren moaned, but didn't wake. Maren held his left hand above his head and said words Malbar didn't understand. Blue fire flowed down Maren's arm and surrounded Bren's face, especially his slack jaw. The bone moved into place as the blue flames licked his skin. The Wizard's face was lined with pain, as if he were taking Bren's agony into himself, but Maren didn't let go. Sweat poured down Maren's face almost as if someone had dumped a bucket of water over his head.

Finally, the blue fire dissipated, and Maren slumped to the floor. "The jaw is healed," he whispered, gasping for breath, his face pale, his hair drenched with sweat. "Give him as much tea as he can drink. We have to break the fever. And I have to return to the castle to stop Grimmin."

"Then you drink some tea, too," Liska said, holding out a cup of the green-gold liquid.

Maren nodded and drank the hot tea as quickly as he could. Finally, he stood and turned to Malbar. "Bren will live, but his healing will take a long time. Not just his body, but his heart and mind. You and his family will have to heal his spirit, give him a reason to live."

"I won't leave his side," Malbar said earnestly. "Thank you. Thank you for his life."

Maren smiled, spoke a strange word, and disappeared.

37

Cordwin took the Battle Horn of Tarolin from a dead Drambini's fist. "He recognized me," Cordwin said as he stared down at the dead man. "He was one of Lady Miria's personal guards."

Gemna wiped her sword on the dead man's uniform. "So much for a surprise attack."

Footsteps pounded on the spiral stairs from above and below. Drambini soldiers raced toward them from the Audience Hall and from all parts of the castle. Cordwin drew his sword and shouted, "For Vorlik and Lord Bren!"

The Vorlikian soldiers echoed his shout and followed Cordwin as he and Gemna charged into the press of Drambini soldiers. Soon dozens of Drambini bodies lay on the entry hall, and the floor was slick with dark red blood. More Drambini guards came down the stairs, forcing Cordwin back, but he rallied his troops and charged again, driving the Drambini toward the Audience Hall.

At that moment he saw Miria, Grimmin, and Callas come rushing up the stairs from the dungeon.

Miria's blue eyes widened. "What's happening?" Cordwin heard her shouting. "Why are my soldiers fighting each other?"

Grimmin swept his hand in front of him in an arc. Helmets fell from all the soldiers' heads, unmasking the Vorlikians. "They're Vorlikians in disguise," Grimmin said. "Look!"

Miria looked startled. "Kill them!" she shouted. "Kill every Vorlikian you find!"

"Especially him, Cordwin of Vorlik!" Grimmin shouted, pointing at Cordwin. "I want his head!"

"For Lord Bren and Vorlik!" Cordwin shouted. "Baygor protect us!" He pushed through the fighting, trying to reach Grimmin, but lost sight of him in the crush of soldiers. He stabbed several Drambini and threw them to the floor. More Drambini came at him and pushed him back.

"Gemna, do you see Miria and Grimmin?" Cordwin called as he fought.

"No!" Gemna called over her shoulder. "Yes! Over there!"

Grimmin, Miria, and Captain Callas were fleeing up the spiral stairs.

"Follow me!" Cordwin shouted to his troops. He and Gemna cut a path through the Drambini ranks and raced up the stairs, half a dozen Vorlikians soldiers behind them. They caught up with Miria, Grimmin, and Callas on the third floor just past Cordwin's room. A weaselly man stood beside them in the flickering torchlight.

"Halt and surrender!" Cordwin shouted.

Grimmin stopped and turned, a sly smile on his face. "Akavar, take care of My Lady," he said. "I need a bit of amusement."

The weaselly man moved protectively close to Miria. Callas drew his sword and dagger, but Grimmin held no weapon.

"Now, you're going to die!" Cordwin shouted as he and Gemna ran toward them, their soldiers close behind.

Grimmin merely smiled. "Hardly. Feel my power, Cordwin." With a quiet, tenor voice that resounded throughout the hall, Grimmin spoke words that chilled Cordwin's heart.

Gemna froze beside him, as if held by invisible chains. Her sword slipped from her stiffening hand, and she struggled to speak. "Cordwin, I c-can't m-m-move."

"Neither can we, captain," whispered one of the guards.

Cordwin stiffened, then realized *he* could move. The spell didn't affect him! He stepped in front of Gemna to protect her. "What *are* you?" he asked, frightened. "You're no Wizard, so you must be a..." He couldn't bring himself to say the word.

Grimmin looked puzzled, his head slightly cocked. "My magic doesn't affect you. How curious. Do you have a charmed life?" Spotting the dove pendant, Grimmin nodded with a crooked smile. "Or just a charm. The Wizard's amulet — that's how you resisted all my potions and spells. No matter. I can still kill you. But I think I'll give Captain Callas the pleasure of slitting your throat. It will be most entertaining to watch."

Grimmin glanced at Callas and nodded. With sword and black-bladed dagger, Callas approached Cordwin. Callas' first blow against Cordwin's sword sent a shiver up Cordwin's arm. Callas was extremely skilled, blocking Cordwin's blows with his sword, then slashing with the dagger, but Cordwin avoided each blow and attacked furiously. Callas looked surprised, then worried.

Cordwin heard the clash of swords in the main hall, but he couldn't worry about what was happening with the battle below. He fought until Callas was backed against the corridor wall. Cordwin had Callas' sword arm trapped against the stones and was clutching Callas' other wrist. Suddenly, Cordwin heard the rush of wings and Grimmin cursing. A familiar voice startled Cordwin.

"Hail and ill met, Grimmin! Your life is now mine!"

Cordwin glanced over his shoulder and saw Maren standing behind Grimmin. "You know him?" Cordwin asked.

"Oh, yes," Maren said, glaring at Grimmin, who half-turned to face Maren. "We've met before. Haven't we, Sorcerer?"

Suddenly, Callas twisted his wrist free, and with the black dagger, raked a long slice down Cordwin's arm. Cordwin cried out in pain and staggered back. Grimmin moved as quick as lightning around Cordwin. He grabbed Gemna and wrapped his right arm around her throat. Gemna's eyes filled with terror as she gazed at Maren.

"Don't hurt her!" Maren cried and started toward Grimmin.

"Then don't move," Grimmin said, tightening his grip and smiling. "She is lovely, isn't she? Is she dear to you?" He ran his left hand slowly over her body. "Is she warm in bed?"

Tears filled Gemna's eyes, and she turned her eyes away. Shame and fear colored her cheeks.

"Stop it!" Maren demanded. "Let her go!"

"In time." Grimmin caressed Gemna's temple and cheek, and brushed his lips against her ear. He smiled at Maren, then said, "In time. Miria, come here."

Miria started to slip past Cordwin and Callas to Grimmin's side when Maren suddenly moved faster than Cordwin's eyes could follow. Maren wrapped his arm around Miria's throat.

"Let her go!" Grimmin said, glaring at Maren. "Let her go or by the Hound of Darkness I swear, I'll break this one's neck!"

"If you harm her at all," Maren said, his dark eyes staring at Grimmin, "you'll regret it more than you could ever imagine."

Grimmin seemed to hesitate, and worry crept into his blue eyes. "You won't hurt Miria. A Wizard wouldn't hurt a human, especially a woman."

"True," Maren said. "But if you harm Gemna, I will take Miria away from here, take her to a place you'll never find her and she'll never be able to find her way back to you. Never. I will hound your every step like the Hound of Darkness himself, and I will kill you. And remember, Wizards don't lie. Nor do they bluff."

Grimmin gazed at Miria for a long time before answering. "Let her go first, then I'll release this one."

"No," Maren said. "If I release Miria first, there's no reason for you to let Gemna go. You release Gemna first. Then I swear by Baygor, I'll release Miria."

"How can I be sure you'll keep your word?"

Maren stared intensely at Grimmin. "Wizards don't break oaths. You know that. Set Gemna free, remove the spell of holding, and let her come to me, and when she is by my side, I will free Miria."

Grimmin snorted. "And as soon as she's free, you'll kill me."

Maren smiled at Grimmin. "If I were a Sorcerer, Miria would already be dead and so would you. But I'm a Wizard, and I swear to you that if you free Gemna, you and Miria will leave unharmed and unhindered."

"No!" Cordwin shouted, anger burning in his heart. "You can't let them go! Not after everything they've done!"

"What should I do then?" Maren asked Cordwin. "Should I let him kill Gemna? Should I break my sworn oath? Did you learn nothing about Wizards from Briella? If I lie about this, about anything, then I am no better than a Sorcerer."

Abashed, Cordwin nodded reluctantly, but glared at Grimmin. "There will be a reckoning to come, but for the moment be grateful for Maren's protection."

Grimmin slowly released his grip on Gemna and spoke a few strange words. Gemna blinked and then flexed her hands and stared at them.

"Come to me," Maren told her. "Come quickly."

Gemna hurried to his side, turned, and watched Grimmin with narrowed eyes.

"Keep your word," Grimmin said.

Maren nodded and released Miria. She ran to Grimmin; he wrapped an arm around her.

"Don't try to ensorcell anyone here. If you do, I'll kill you now, Grimmin," Maren said. "Don't come back here. If you do, I will know. And you will die."

Grimmin glared at Maren. "Another time, Wizard, but we *will* meet again." He spoke an incantation. The next moment Grimmin and Miria vanished.

Instantly, Maren shapechanged into an eagle and raked his claws across Akavar's neck. Before Akavar could scream, Maren tore out the poisoner's throat. Changing back, Maren stood over the dead Sorcerer. "I didn't promise him anything."

Cordwin stared at Akavar's body, then turned his gaze to Callas. Fear bloomed in the Drambini's eyes. Cordwin picked up the black-bladed dagger Callas had dropped and attacked furiously with sword and the dagger. Callas was driven back until Cordwin plunged the dagger hilt-deep into the Drambini's chest. Callas sank to the floor, coughing and gasping until he stopped moving.

Maren put his arms around Gemna and held her close. "Gemna," he breathed her name like a prayer, "are you all right? Did he hurt you?"

For a moment, she said nothing, just lay her head against his chest. Finally, she looked up at his face. "I'm all right," she said, her voice slightly quivering. "But I swear, if I ever see that Drambini bitch again, I'll beat her bloody. I guess I'll have to leave the Sorcerer for you."

Maren smiled, then grinned, and finally laughed out loud. "Everything is all right now," he said. "We won."

Suddenly, Cordwin clutched Maren's arm. "Did you find Bren?" Cordwin asked desperately.

"Yes," Maren said. He glanced at the cut on Cordwin's arm.

"It's not serious, barely a scratch," Cordwin said as he cradled his arm. "Is Bren alive? Is he safe?"

"Yes, he's alive and safe, but badly injured," Maren said.

"But he's alive!" Cordwin said. "Can you help the others? Grimmin put some kind of spell on them."

Maren whispered a word of command to break Grimmin's spell, and the guards shook themselves, able to move again. Maren slid his arm about Gemna's waist and guided her down the stairs, Cordwin trailing behind.

The main hall was mostly quiet now except for the moans of the wounded. Bodies lay on the blood-slick stone floor. A company of Vorlikian guards lifted their dead comrades and carried them to the barrow ground. Two dozen Drambini knelt in the center of the main hall, weaponless, their hands behind their heads. Many more Drambini lay on the stone floor dead or dying.

Lieutenant Daikin stood just inside the castle entrance. "Has anyone found Physician Tothim yet? Or the counselors?" he called out.

"Not yet, lieutenant," a soldier said. "But we haven't checked the dungeon yet."

"Then look there. And take these Drambini with you while you're at it." Daikin glanced toward Maren, then Daikin raced across the entry way to Cordwin's side. "Cord! Let me help you."

"I'm only scratched," Cordwin assured him.

Turning to Maren, Daikin swallowed hard. "Will he recover?"

Maren nodded. "Yes, he just needs a bit of tending and rest."

Relief glittered diamond-bright in Daikin's eyes, and his voice was a quiet sigh. "Is that all? Thank Baramay! We freed the people in the Dancing Glen. The Drambini are either dead or prisoners."

"Put the prisoners in the dungeon," Cordwin said. "Then set the soldiers and servants to cleaning up the castle."

"I'll take you both to the inn at Yarrow," Maren said to Cordwin. "The healers are there. So is Bren. Daikin, if you need us, we'll be there."

In an instant the three stood in the common room of the inn. Hollester the innkeeper was adding wood to the hearth while Germaine the innwife ladled some callum bark tea into a cup. Surprised by their sudden appearance, Germaine gasped and spilled some of the tea.

Hollester looked at Cordwin's bloody sleeve. "My Lord! Here, sit down by the fire."

Cordwin shook his head. "Where's Bren? I need to see him."

"This way," Germaine said and led Cordwin down the hallway.

Maren followed, holding Gemna's hand. She seemed unusually quiet. Her face was pale, and she shivered constantly. "Grimmin's gone," Maren said softly. "You're safe now."

"I know," she said, shuddering, "I know. He was going to kill me, and you saved me, but I still feel his hands on me."

"He'll never touch you again," he said. "I swear before Baygor."

They entered the room and found Malbar lying on the wooden floor and Cordwin trying to strangle him.

"Cordwin, stop!" Maren said. He ran to Cordwin and tried to pull him off Malbar.

"No!" Cordwin shouted. "He's responsible for everything! He should die for what he's done! He deserves to die!"

"Yes! Yes, I do!" Malbar gasped, his face turning purple. "I deserve to die! Let him kill me!"

"He's the one who saved Bren!" Maren said, pulling Cordwin away and forcing him back.

Malbar crawled on knees and forearms toward the corner of the room and huddled there against the stone wall, coughing and choking.

Cordwin stopped struggling and stared at Maren. "He rescued Bren?" Cordwin said.

"Yes!" Maren nodded. "He was willing to die to save Bren! Grimmin almost burned him alive because he was rescuing Bren!"

"I don't care!" Trying to pull free of Maren's grip, Cordwin glared at Malbar. "Take him out of here! I don't want him anywhere near Bren!"

"No!" Malbar said, his voice hoarse. "I won't leave him! Kill me if you want, but the only way you'll get me out of here is if I'm dead!"

Maren felt Cordwin stiffen, then relax.

"Just stay away from me," Cordwin said through clenched teeth. He walked to the side of the bed and knelt beside Bren. "How is he?" he whispered.

"Badly injured," Germaine the innwife answered, her voice quivering, her eyes glistening with tears. "I've never treated anyone so badly injured. What they did to him... the tortures he endured...I don't know how he survived. He wakes up just long enough to drink the medicine, but falls unconscious again immediately, a blessing with all his injuries. I'm using everything I know about healing, everything Briella taught me, the callum bark tea and callum leaf salve. I pray he'll live, but I don't know if his hands will ever heal normally." She turned to Cordwin. "My Lord, let me tend your wound."

While Germaine washed Cordwin's arm, Maren eased Gemna into the chair by the hearth and knelt beside her.

"I'm cold," she whispered. "I'm so cold."

He rubbed her hands and legs, trying to warm her. "Is that better?" he asked.

Gemna smiled at him. "How could I not be, with you here beside me?"

Suddenly, Germaine shouted, "Maren! It's Cordwin! He's ill! Help him!"

Cordwin clutched at his throat, his body convulsing. His eyes widened with fear. His mouth tried to form words but failed.

Praying, Maren ran to Cordwin's side. Cordwin twitched and gasped for breath. Maren held him and tried to find the cause. He felt Cordwin's soul fleeing from his body. "No!! Lady Baramay, don't let him die! Help me, show me what to do!"

Maren felt Cordwin's life slipping away like sand from the shore, but Maren didn't give up. "Live! Live!!" he said. "I won't let you die! Lady Baramay, help me!"

Suddenly, the room filled with the scent of lavender. The dove amulet around Cordwin's neck, Briella's amulet, began to glow with blue fire. The light intensified, and the blue fire grew until it was almost as large as Maren. The fire formed a figure, a face. Like a blue ghost, Briella stood beside Cordwin. She took his hand and stroked his forehead. She turned lightning blue eyes to Maren. He stared at her, stunned.

"I knew this would happen!" Briella said. "I saw it years ago! The black dagger was poisoned! I'll keep his soul in his body! You destroy the poison in his blood! Hurry, Maren! Please hurry! He doesn't want to live! And he must live! He must!"

Maren touched the wound and felt the poison, like tar oozing through Cordwin's veins. Cordwin stiffened corpse-like. Maren spoke a word of command and poured his strength into Cordwin's body, straining poison from the blood.

"Hurry, Maren!" Briella whispered again. "Cordwin, Cordwin, my love, please live! Live for me! Oh, Maren, please hurry! He's dying!"

"*Tasrin lanifar hayna Baramay barason!*" he said and clasped Cordwin's arm.

Blue healing fire flowed from Maren and enveloped Cordwin, trying to burn the poison away. Cordwin's body arched and twisted; a shriek wrenched from his throat. Hands clenched like claws, he convulsed, and his eyes rolled back in his head. Sweat rolled down Maren's face; his muscles began to cramp from the strain. He felt the poison like lye eating away at Cordwin's body, surging through his veins. The pain was almost more than Maren could bear. Finally, Cordwin gave a long scream, the fire disappeared, and he went limp.

Cordwin still in his arms, Maren slumped to the floor, worn out, more exhausted than he'd ever been. But he found enough strength to gaze up at Briella and touch her hand. "Briella," he whispered, hardly believing what he was seeing. "You're really here! You're not just a phantom! Everyone said you were dead! I'd given up all hope of ever seeing you again! I don't understand! How is this possible?"

"I don't know." Briella looked down at him. "Perhaps only Baramay and Baygor know." She touched his cheek, and Maren felt as if her hand were made of the softest down, warm and cool at the same time. "Maren, I loved you — as a brother and a friend, but Cordwin holds my heart. Don't waste your life mourning for me. Your heart is already given to another. You already know that." Briella glanced at Gemna, then back at Maren, and she smiled gently. "Give yourself to the living and be happy, my dear friend."

She knelt beside Cordwin, kissed his pale lips. "My love, I'm here with you. I promised I'd watch over you, and I always will. Always." She glowed brighter, brighter, light swirling around her, then dwindled to blue threads of light that collected at the dove amulet. A moment later, the glow was gone.

For a moment, Maren stared at the place Briella had been, but his heart felt unchained. He looked over at Gemna and smiled. Now he could live and be happy.

38

Liska and Hollester carried Cordwin to the room next to Bren's. When they returned, Maren asked Hollester for a room for Gemna.

"I've one for her across the hall," the innkeeper said, "and another next to it for you. The rooms are small but comfortable and close by."

"Thank you. I desperately need to rest after the healing." Maren took Gemna's hand and started toward their rooms, but he turned back a moment.

"I'll try to heal Bren tomorrow as much as I can," he told Germaine, "but let him rest a while. Keep giving him as much callum bark tea as he can drink and apply the salve to his wounds. But if he becomes worse, call me immediately."

"I will," Germaine said.

He walked Gemna across the hall to her room and said, "Sleep peacefully, Gemna."

"Don't go," she said, her voice barely above a whisper. "Stay with me a while. I don't want to be alone."

Even though he was worn out from the healing, Maren's heart beat swiftly, and his mouth was suddenly dry. "For a while," he said. He followed her into her room and shut the door behind him.

The chamber was small, but a fire laid on the small hearth had warmed the room. Blue-white moonlight flowed through the windows. Flickering firelight cast shadows across the planes and curves of Gemna's face. Maren's chest tightened as he gazed at her dark glittering eyes.

Gemna slid her arms around him and kissed him. "I love you," she said.

"I love you, too," he said.

"You saved my life tonight," she whispered.

"And you've saved mine."

"Hold me tonight," she said. "I need to feel you beside me tonight."

Confused and baffled, Maren tried to think of exactly what to say to her. "Gemna, I want...I never..." he stammered, then paused and cleared his throat. "Wizards are... chaste...until they marry. But I feel...my heart...if we were married...but I can't lose my powers. I can't, not yet."

"You're a virgin," she said, a hint of amusement in her tone.

"I think that's what I said."

She ran her fingers through his dark hair and kissed the side of his neck. "My sweet Maren, it's been a long and hard day for both of us. Just hold me tonight while I sleep, nothing more. Let me feel you close, know you're near. That's all I ask. We can stay fully dressed. Except for our boots, of course." She smiled up at him.

Maren smoothed a stray lock of her hair from her forehead. "Then, yes, I'll hold you while we sleep."

They both pulled off their boots. Maren unclasped his cloak. Gemna took off the Drambini uniform she'd worn over her clothes, unbound her hair, then climbed under the covers on the bed and lay down. Her dark hair lay like an ebony halo around her face. Maren gazed at her, feeling as if he'd swallowed a whole swarm of butterflies. She smiled up at him and pulled the covers back. He slid in beside her and lay on his side facing her. She slipped her arm around him and kissed him gently but passionately. When she nestled against his chest, his heart began racing.

"I love you, Gemna," he whispered, breathing in the earthy scent of her hair. "You are my heart."

"And you are mine," she whispered back. "Rest now. Morning will come sooner than we'd like."

"Sweet dreams." He closed his eyes and listened to her breathing, felt her warmth and strength and softness, and his heart danced with happiness as he fell asleep.

He woke before first light, his arms still around Gemna, holding her against his chest. Gazing at Gemna's sensuous face and dark hair, he was amazed by the wild, exciting feelings swirling in his thoughts. He'd never felt so unsettled, so overwhelmed, so deliriously happy. Before he moved at all, Gemna opened her dark eyes and smiled at him. She brushed her fingers lightly over his lips and down his throat. Unexpectedly, his body reacted, embarrassing him.

Gemna grinned. "After all, you *are* a man," she said.

"But I didn't mean...I didn't intend..." He quickly disentangled himself from her, his face feeling hot. "I'm sorry," he said.

"I'm not," she said. "It's nice to know I can provoke a reaction from the man I love." She brushed his hair from his forehead, and she gazed intently at him. "But I think we'd better get up now."

Maren rolled out of bed and stood up, stretching. Gemna climbed out of bed and crossed the room to the wash stand. She poured water into the basin and started to take off her shirt.

"I think I'll leave now," Maren said, his eyes drawn to her against his will.

Gemna grinned. "I'll see you at breakfast."

Maren left and went to his own room. After he washed up, he went to Bren's room. Bren was sleeping on his stomach, a sheet covering his lower body. He was terribly pale, and his breathing was shallow and raspy. His burns and slashes were healing, but they were so extensive, Maren feared it might be days before the injuries were completely healed even with the salve and callum bark tea.

Malbar was huddled by Bren's bed, sleeping. Someone had wrapped a coverlet over the Drambini. The burns on his face and hands looked nearly healed. Next, he went to Cordwin's room. Cordwin slept quietly, his breathing regular, his color good. *I'm certain he'll recover, but I need to talk to him about Briella,* Maren thought. *What happened with the amulet, with her appearing, is unheard of! I have to understand this.*

Maren left and walked down to the common room. Gemna was there eating thick slices of buttered bread and jam and drinking a mug of white wine. Her hair was pulled back, bound with a black leather thong, and braided. She wore a black, laced up vest over a white shirt and black pants. Her sword lay on the table beside her. She smiled as he approached.

"You should try this wine," she said, licking crumbs from her fingers. "It's delicious. And this tyneberry jam is wonderful."

"Always thinking with your stomach," Maren said, laughing.

"Mercenaries never know when their next meal will come along, so they take advantage of any chance to eat."

Maren took a piece of buttered bread, spread the dark red jam on it, and took a bite. The bread was still warm, soft with a chewy crust, and the jam was tart-sweet. "It is wonderful," he said.

The innkeeper brought out a mug of the wine for Maren. "Can I get you anything else?" the innkeeper asked.

"Some cheese if you have it," Gemna said. "And some ham. And a few eggs. And some fruit if you have any."

"Of course," the innkeeper said, "although it's too early even for spring berries, but we might have an apple or two left from last year's crop." He bowed and hurried toward the kitchen.

Maren just laughed. "I'm going to the castle to see if I can help. Would you like to come with me?"

"How long will it take to ride there?" Gemna asked.

"We won't ride. I'll transport us magically."

Gemna looked surprised. "But I thought you said it was too difficult to travel that way."

"It is difficult," Maren said, "but I don't have to worry about fighting a battle now. Would you like to go with me?"

Her eyes grew large, and she nodded enthusiastically.

"When you're done eating, we'll go."

The innkeeper arrived at that moment with a tray of scrambled eggs, fried ham, a wedge of mellow white cheese, and two slightly wrinkled red apples. Gemna gazed at the food, then at Maren, and back at the food.

"Food first. Castle later," she said and dived into the eggs.

Maren laughed but helped himself to some eggs and ham.

When Gemna had finished, she buckled on her sword. Maren took her hand and led her outside. The eastern sky was lighter, and the mountain tops were colored pale blue with a hint of magenta. "Put your arms around me," he said.

"Gladly," she said with a sly smile.

"Hold on tight. You might want to close your eyes if you become dizzy."

"No, I want to see what happens."

"All right." Maren held her close and spoke a word of command.

Myriads of rainbows swirled around them. Gemna tightened her grip around Maren's chest until he could hardly breathe. Finally, they appeared in the entrance to Tarolin Castle. Gemna wobbled a bit and blinked her eyes several times.

"Barg's breath!" she said. "That was amazing!"

Dawn cast a golden-pink light through the open doors, and the air was damp and cool. Soldiers were carrying Drambini bodies from the hall, and scullery maids scrubbed blood from the stone floor. Daikin stood near the doors to the Audience Hall, speaking to Lieutenants Linaria and Tude.

"I want all the Drambini dead on a pyre north of the castle," Daikin said. "We'll burn them at daybreak tomorrow. And send a squad to prepare a mound for our dead. We'll mourn them as soon as Lord Bren is well." He looked at Maren and Gemna, and waved them over.

"What should we do with the mercenaries?" Linaria asked.

"I don't know," Daikin said thoughtfully. "They didn't join in the fighting against us. Keep them under guard. I'll decide later."

Linaria and Tude saluted and left the castle.

Daikin turned toward Maren. "How is Lord Bren?" he asked anxiously.

"Alive, but badly injured," Maren said. "His hands are so injured, I'm not certain even I can heal them."

"And Cordwin?"

Maren sighed, feeling tired. "He's alive, but he nearly died."

Daikin clutched Maren's arm, worry in his green eyes. "How? What happened?"

"The cut on his arm was from a poisoned dagger."

Daikin inhaled sharply. "Just as Briella said," he whispered. "But you healed him? He'll be all right?"

"His body is healed, but as for his spirit -- I don't know. So for now, I suppose you're in charge of Vorlik's safety."

Daikin nodded and slowly turned his gaze to Gemna. "And you, you're all right?"

Gemna nodded. "I heard you talking about the mercenaries. I might be able to help. I may know some of them. I can talk to them for you, help you decide what to do with them."

Daikin looked surprised, then pleased. "Yes, I'd appreciate any advice."

"Have you found the physician and healers yet?" Maren asked.

"Yes," Daikin said. "They are already ministering to the injured."

"Are there any who know how to use callum bark and callum leaf salve?"

"Several priests from the monastery have been trained in the usage of both. Briella taught Liska, who taught other priests. Now there is an entire order of itinerate healer-priests. But we could use as many healers as we can get."

"Briella was more farseeing than the rest of the Wizards," Maren said softly. "There's a healer-priest at Yarrow. If the innwife doesn't need him to care for Bren and Cordwin, I'll bring him to the castle to help here. I'm going to the western border and placing a Wall of Warding there. But you need to man the Western Guard as soon as possible. Grimmin and Miria escaped, but I know they'll attack again. And not just them next time. I fear that the next battle will be more bloody and devastating than we can imagine, with all the forces of the Sorcerers gathered against us. But I'll do what I can to protect your people." He turned to Gemna. "I'll be back as soon as I can, but it might not be until late tonight." He spoke a word of command and appeared back in the common room of the inn in Yarrow.

Germaine was in the common room, ladling callum bark tea from a kettle Liska was tending. They both started at Maren's sudden appearance.

"There's a great need for healers at the castle," Maren said to Germaine. "Would you be able to care for Bren and Cordwin by yourself if I took Liska to the castle?"

"Yes," she said. "If I need help, I have two daughters who I've trained in healing."

He turned to Liska. "Would you be willing to come to the castle with me?"

"Of course," Liska said. "Let me pack some more bark and jars of salve." He hurried out the inn's door to his cottage across the road. He came back with a bulging slingsack. "I'm ready." He paused. "At least, I think I am. Will we be going the same way you just appeared?"

"Yes."

The priest cleared his throat, excitement glittering in his eyes. "Then let's go."

"Hold tightly to me. If you become dizzy, close your eyes. It will make the travel easier for you."

Liska nodded and clutched Maren's arm. Maren spoke a word of command, and the next moment they stood at the castle's entrance.

Liska's eyes were wide with delight. "That was...amazing!"

"Ask for Gemna or Lieutenant Daikin," Maren said. "They'll tell you where to find the injured." He shapechanged into an eagle and rose into the sky.

The sun rose above the eastern mountains as Maren flew from the castle. He passed the Dancing Glen, where Vorlikian guards tossed the bodies of Drambini soldiers onto wagons, and the celebrants who'd been held hostage tore down the gallows that had been built for Bren. Flying on toward the western border, he saw the town of Leflin, where a funeral was being held around a large mound. Men, women and children ringed the grave and a priest of Baygor led a prayer for the dead. And just west of the town was a small grove of callum trees. *Briella gave so much to this land,* Maren thought.

He flew on past the Western Guard, where he saw numerous bodies in blue and gold uniforms lying on the ground. Anger filled Maren's heart. *I'm going to stop Grimmin,* he thought. *I won't let him do anything like this again. Somehow I'll stop him.*

Landing at the Drambini border, Maren shapechanged and searched the border keep, but all the guards were dead. Rage smoldered in him, and he swore that he would prevent such a tragedy again. He cast a Wall of Warding across the pass, still in deep shadow from the mountains, and extending a mile both north and south. *That will keep a Drambini army out,* he thought, massaging his neck and blinking his aching eyes. He felt his power was much greater since he'd broken Grimmin's binding, but there was still so much to do. Changing into an eagle, he flew to the northern pass and cast a Wall of Warding. Flying to the eastern border, he repeated the spell, then flew straight to the southern border and completed the barrier across the pass. He flew north to Tarolin Castle as the sun well past its zenith.

When he flew over the courtyard, Gemna was standing on the steps of the castle, speaking to a large group of men and women, surrounded by Tarolin guards. He perched over the castle entrance and listened to her.

"I know most of you," she said, standing tall. "You are brothers and sisters of the sword. You are honorable, but you were deceived into a dishonorable venture. Mercenaries take their oaths seriously, and no mercenary breaks a contract. But Grimmin lied to you. He tricked you into invading a peaceful land. That's not what we do. We guard. We protect. We defend. We don't attack." She paused. "Lieutenant Daikin offers you a choice. You can go back to the Guild Hall and tell the masters what happened, or you kan stay here and try to atone by helping to defend this land. If you choose to leave Vorlik, no one will stop you. If you choose to stay, you will be given a position in one of the five Guards of Vorlik. The choice is yours."

She turned toward the castle and climbed the rest of the steps. Maren flew down and shapechanged in front of her.

"You would make a good leader," he said.

She gave him a wink. "I think most of them will stay. Mercenaries value their honor."

"Would you like to go back to the inn now?"

"Yes!" Gemna grinned. "I haven't eaten since this morning."

Maren shook his head and rolled his eyes. "I need to speak to Daikin first."

"Last time I saw him, he was talking with the counselors in the Audience Hall."

They walked into the entry hall. The stone floor had been scrubbed until it gleamed. No trace of blood remained. Servants hurried on their way, carrying baskets of food or stacks of clothes and sheets. Two guards stood statue-still at the open doorway to the Audience Hall. Inside, Maren saw Daikin talking with several robed men and the three lieutenants. Daikin looked up as Maren and Gemna approached.

"All the passes are protected by a Wall of Warding," Maren said. "But the bodies of the Western Guard and the border keep lay where they died."

Daikin's jaw tightened, and his eyes narrowed and seemed to gaze beyond Maren. "Someday Grimmin and Miria will pay for their deeds." He looked back at Maren. "I'll send a troop right now to bury the guards."

"I think most of the mercenaries will choose to stay," Gemna said. "Treat them with honor, and they will be trustworthy."

"Good," Daikin said. "We need all the guards we can get."

"We're going back to Yarrow now to check on Bren and Cordwin," Maren said.

Daikin nodded, worry drawing lines across his forehead. "I'll be there tomorrow. Please, take care of them."

"Could you bring our horses?" Gemna asked.

Daikin smiled at her. "Of course. Until tomorrow."

Gemna clamped her arms around Maren's chest, and he enfolded her in his arms. "You don't have to hold on so tight," he whispered. "I do have to breathe."

She chuckled quietly and loosened her grip slightly.

Maren spoke a word of command. Rainbows of light enveloped the two of them, then they appeared in the common room of the inn in Yarrow. Several patrons gasped and gaped at Maren and Gemna.

"All is well," Hollester assured the frightened patrons. "This is the Wizard Maren. No need to fear him."

The patrons slowly went back to their meals, but glanced nervously at Maren.

"They've just come from the castle," Hollester whispered as he stirred a large kettle of callum bark tea over the fire. "They were held hostage in the Dancing Glen, and they're still edgy. I hope all is well at the castle," the innkeeper said.

Maren nodded. "And Bren and Cordwin?"

"Cordwin is sleeping, but he won't wake up. Lord Bren," he halted, running fingers through his thinning hair, "I fear for him. I don't know if the tea and salve will heal him. How does one heal a tormented soul?"

Maren laid a hand on the innkeeper's shoulder. "I'll do what I can." He turned to Gemna. "Let's see how Bren is doing."

Together they walked down the hall to Bren's room.

Late afternoon sunlight shone through the open window on Germaine in a chair beside Bren's bed. Her head nodded and her eyes were closed, snatching a few moments sleep. Malbar still huddled beside Bren's bed, head resting on the side of the bed. He opened his eyes when Maren walked in.

"Is he better?" Malbar asked desperately, climbing to his feet. "Will he live? You promised me he would live. Tell me he'll live, he'll be all right. Please!"

"I don't know yet," Maren said as he walked toward Bren's bed.

Bren lay sleeping quietly on his side. His breathing was raspy but regular, and his color was better except for the massive bruises on his face.

Maren laid his hand lightly on Bren's forehead. *The fever's gone*, he thought. *The callum bark tea is helping, but I doubt it will be enough.*

Germaine opened her eyes and yawned. Maren smiled at her, and she stood quickly. "I put salve on his hands, then splinted and bandaged them," she said. "And I salved and bandaged his feet and as many of his other injuries as I could. I hope that helps. But what they did to him..." She halted and wiped her eyes.

"You're a wise healer," Maren said. "The fever has broken. I think he's strong enough for me to try to heal him. He'll still need days of rest, but hopefully, he'll be completely well." He turned to Gemna. "I'm going to try to heal him the way I did Cordwin, but I won't have Briella helping me. I know I'm stronger than I was before Grimmin's spell, but I've never healed anyone this hurt before. I need you to watch over me, take care of me if I collapse."

Gemna nodded. "I'm still your body guard."

Praying silently for a moment, he took a deep breath, grasped Bren's hands gently, and said aloud, "By the power of Baygor who sustains and preserves life, *tasrin lanifar hayna barason!*"

Blue fire flowed down Maren's arms to Bren's hands, his shoulders, his face, his chest, enveloping his entire body. Bren screamed with agony, and Maren felt every pain Bren felt, suffered as Bren had suffered, felt every bone that was broken or crushed, every searing burn of a heated brand, every lash of a whip, every blow to his face and body. Maren could hardly breathe from the pain. He was absolutely astonished that Bren had survived. Gradually, Maren felt the bones in Bren's hands reforming, broken ribs knitting together, the open wounds closing and healing.

Finally, the flames disappeared. Bren sank back to the feather mattress, unconscious. The bruises on his face were gone, and his nose was straight and whole. The cut on his forehead was closed and healed. His breathing was easier.

"Unbind his hands," Maren whispered, too exhausted to speak louder.

Germaine carefully unwrapped Bren's mangled hands. "His hands! They're whole! And the rest of his injuries are nearly healed! You are truly amazing!"

Maren didn't reply. His vision turned dark, and his head ached. His hands shook. His legs trembled. He tried to speak, but he swayed and toppled. Strong, gentle arms caught him. A low, sweet voice called his name faintly, as though from across a valley or from the depths of time.

"I'm here, Maren," said the voice, Gemna's voice, quavering. "I'm here. I won't let you fall."

He blinked his eyes several times until he clearly saw Gemna's dark eyes in her olive face. "What would I do without you?" he said softly.

"Fall on your face."

He laughed. "Ah, Gemna. I think I need to rest now."

"I'll help you to your room," she said. "Put your arm around my shoulders."

His arm felt like lead, but he finally lifted it around her shoulders. It took all his will to move his feet while she guided him through the door of Bren's room, across the hall to his own room. Keeping her arm around his waist, she lifted the latch and nudged the door open with her foot. Sidling through the doorway, she helped him to the bed where he sank down, unable to stand up any longer. He reached up to undo his cloak, but his fingers were so clumsy, he couldn't. He felt cold and drained, and all he wanted was to sleep.

"Let me help," Gemna said, kneeling before him. She unclasped the cloak and removed it, then pulled off his boots and helped him into bed. "Rest now. You deserve it." She rose to leave, but Maren took her hand.

"Stay with me," he said. "I need to feel you near me. Please hold me tonight."

Gemna gazed down at him, then gave his hand a light squeeze. "How could I do less for you than you did for me?"

She let his hand go, walked to the door, and closed it, then slipped off her boots and climbed into bed beside him. He laid his head on her shoulder, and she wrapped her arms around him. She kissed his forehead and rested her cheek against his head.

"Sleep, my love," Gemna said. "I'll hold you until you wake."

Feeling her warmth, breathing in the scent of her skin, Maren closed his eyes and fell asleep into the safe comfort of her arms.

39

Cool air streamed through an open window as Maren woke. His head ached, and he felt weak, but otherwise he felt fine. Turning his head, he saw Gemna lying close beside him, her eyes closed. Stray strands of her dark hair had escaped the braid that trailed down her back.

Slipping his arm from under the heavy covers on the bed, he reached out and stroked her hair lightly. It felt as soft as velvet. He wanted to unbraid her hair and run his fingers through it.

She opened her eyes and gazed at him. Her eyes looked beautiful to him. *She* looked beautiful to him.

Gemna caressed his face and played with a lock of his hair. Relief filled her face, her eyes glistened, and her lips formed a tiny smile. "You slept so long. It's midafternoon the day after you healed Bren." She halted, blinking her eyes several times and chewing her bottom lip. "I couldn't wake you. I was becoming a bit worried."

"But you stayed with me," he said. "Watching over me, just as you have since the day we met."

"I promised to hold you until you woke up."

He smoothed the stray hair back from her face. "Your father named you well. You are a rare and precious gem."

Gemna's eyes widened, and her lips parted for a moment, but she said nothing. Leaning close to him, she kissed him so thoroughly, he was breathless and slightly dizzy when she pulled back. His pulse thudded loudly in his ears, and his throat was tight.

"Barg's breath, woman, if you kiss me like that again," Maren said, "I might break the Wizards' tradition of chastity before marriage!"

Laughing, Gemna rolled out of bed, stood up, and held out her hand. "Time to get out of bed."

Maren moaned as he sat up and massaged his neck. Finally, he took Gemna's hand and let her pull him upright.

"Wash up and change clothes," she said. "I'll meet you when I've done the same, and we can get something to eat."

Maren flexed his back. "What I wouldn't give for a hot bath."

Gemna smiled. "I'll talk to the innkeeper about that."

After she left, Maren lit a lantern and closed the window shutters. He stripped off his clothes, poured water into the basin on the wash stand, and scrubbed himself with the mint-scented soap. Shivering, he wrapped in a large towel, knelt beside the hearth, but only cold ashes covered the hearth stones. He sighed, then quickly dressed in clean clothes, pulled on his boots, and went to meet Gemna.

She was waiting for him in the hallway, leaning against the wall, her arms crossed.

"I want to check on Bren and Cordwin before we eat," Maren said.

They crossed the hall to Bren's room and opened the door. To Maren's surprise, Bren was sitting up in bed, and Germaine was feeding him a rich dark broth. Malbar sat on a chair beside the bed, eating some broth and bread and sporting a large red bruise on his face.

"Ah, you're up at last," Germaine said, smiling at Maren.

"How are your patients today?" he asked.

"Much better," she said. "These two are hungry, a good sign. And they've shown an interest in my two youngest daughters, not that it will do these two any good as long as I'm here." She stared intently at Bren and Malbar, and both of the young men blushed. "Bren's injuries are nearly healed, but it will be several days before he can get out of bed and walk again. As for Malbar, his injuries were completely healed, except for that bruise. He'll be fine. That is, if Lieutenant Daikin doesn't kill him." She frowned and sighed.

"Daikin?" Maren said. "Was he here?"

"Yes, he came to check on Bren and Cordwin, too. When he saw Malbar, the lieutenant reacted the same way Cordwin did." Germaine looked troubled. "I'm not sure Lieutenant Daikin will ever forgive Malbar."

Malbar stopped eating and looked grim. "Why should he forgive me? I can't forgive myself for what I've done."

"Time changes people," Maren said, gazing at the Drambini, "changes how people think and feel about so many things. I know you risked your life to save Bren. And Bren knows it as well. All of Vorlik will know of your bravery."

Malbar gazed up at Maren, then knelt before him. "All my life I was told Wizards and Sorcerers were the same, both powerful, dangerous, and evil. But I have seen Grimmin and I have seen you. And you are nothing like him. You are everything he isn't. You saved me. Only one other person has ever done that for me." He looked at Bren and bowed his head.

Bren nodded back, then looked back at Maren. "Vorlik owes its freedom to you, and I owe you my life. Anything you want, if it's within my power, it's yours."

Maren looked over at Gemna and smiled. "I already have what I want most in life."

Gemna smiled back at him.

"How is Cordwin?" he asked Germaine.

Germaine's forehead wrinkled, and worry filled her eyes. "I don't know. He hasn't awakened since he was poisoned."

Worried, Maren chewed his lower lip. *There must be something I can do for him,* he thought, *but what?*

Bren cleared his throat. "You've done so much for us, but is there anything you can do for my uncle?" He paused, worry in his blue eyes.

"Maybe — in time," Maren said softly.

Bren hung his head. "What have I done to him? To everyone?"

"You need to forgive yourself," Maren said. "We all have to learn to forgive ourselves."

Malbar looked at Bren. "And that's one of the hardest things to do, isn't it? Forgive ourselves. It's harder than forgiving each other."

"But we must," Maren said. "And we can. In time."

"In time." Malbar nodded.

40

Maren and Gemna left Bren's room and came face to face with Daikin in the hallway.

"I've been waiting to speak to you both," Daikin said. "Do you have a moment?"

"I was going to check on Cordwin," Maren said.

Worry lines marred Daikin's brow, and he rubbed the back of his neck. "I've been sitting with him for hours, but he doesn't move or wake or speak or anything. Will he ever wake up? Will he ever be Cord again?" He looked intently at Maren. "If there's anything you can do for him, anything at all, I'd be grateful."

"I swear by Baramay, I'll do everything in my power."

Daikin bowed. "Come eat with me afterwards. I have something I need to discuss with both of you."

"We'll be there."

Daikin walk down the hallway toward the common room.

Maren turned to Cordwin's room and opened the door. Cordwin lay in bed, his eyes closed, his chest barely rising and falling. He was pale, almost grayish, and thin. The brown stubble of a beard covered his chin and cheeks. Maren went to Cordwin's side and felt Cordwin's forehead. "No fever at least."

"What can you do for him?" Gemna asked.

"I don't know. Injuries of the body I can cure, but injuries of the mind?" Maren shook his head, feeling helpless. "I have to find something that will draw him back from the darkness he's fallen in. Some hope that will open his eyes and give him a reason to live. But at the moment, I don't have any hope to give him."

"But what about Briella? She appeared from the amulet."

"I know. I saw it, too. But I don't know how it was possible or what it means." He studied Cordwin's face, but saw no sign of consciousness. "Maybe he just needs time." Maren turned to Gemna. "We'll let him sleep and heal and wake when he's ready."

Maren took Gemna's hand, and they walked down the hall to the common room. Sitting at a long table by the fireplace, Daikin looked up as they walked toward him. Maren sat down across from Daikin. Gemna sat to Maren's left. Daikin motioned toward Hollester the innkeeper, who came right over.

"We need food for the three of us and some of your best wine," Daikin said.

Hollester bowed and hurried to the kitchen.

Daikin turned to Maren, distress in his green eyes. "Is there any hope, any sign that Cord will come back to us?"

"I don't know," Maren said, propping his forehead in his hands. "There must be something I can do. Something. Something." His voice trailed off into frustration.

Daikin was silent for a while, then said, "Now that Grimmin and Miria are gone, what are you going to do?"

Maren thought about it for a moment. "I don't know. I came here to learn what happened to Briella. I hadn't thought about what I'd do after that."

Daikin leaned toward Maren. "I have a proposal. Grimmin won't give up so easily. We both know he'll try to take Vorlik again. But we have no Wizard to protect us." Daikin paused. "Unless you decided to stay here. Make Vorlik your home and help us if — no, when Grimmin attacks again."

Turning toward Gemna, Daikin said, "And what about you? Would you consider accepting a position as lieutenant in charge of the mercenaries who choose to stay and join the Guards? You know how the mercenaries think, and they would accept and respect you as their leader." Daikin sat back. "You don't have to decide right now. Talk it over with each other. Let me know in a day or two. All Vorlik would be honored and grateful to you both."

Hollester arrived just then with a huge platter of food: roasted quail stuffed with rosemary, spring onions, and barley; steamed cabbage rolls filled with chopped carrots, apples, and parsnips; boiled tubers with parsley butter; hot crusty onion bread, and three plates. The delectable aroma made Maren's stomach rumble, and he realized he hadn't eaten since the day before. Two young girls followed Hollester, carrying three mugs, which they placed on the table.

"This looks marvelous!" Maren said as he reached for a quail. He took a bite and closed his eyes, savoring the delicate flavor. He looked up at Hollester. "Did your wife make this?"

The innkeeper nodded, smiling.

"She's not only a great healer, she's the best cook in all the lands I've traveled." Hollester grinned. "I'll be sure to tell her." He bowed and left.

While he was eating, Maren considered Daikin's offer. *It would be a chance to stay in one place and not hide I'm a Wizard,* Maren thought. *I could protect the land and its people from the likes of Grimmin. And I'd be close to Gemna. What more could I desire?*

Between bites, Daikin told them what he'd accomplished at the castle. "I've sent Lieutenant Tude and a dozen Tarolin Guards to take over the Western Guard and bury all those murdered by the Drambini. I also transferred half a dozen volunteers from each of the other three Guards to Lieutenant Tude's command. We burned the Drambini dead last night, but we're waiting until Bren is well enough to travel to Tarolin Castle before we mourn our own dead. I don't know what to do with the Drambini we still have in the dungeon. I'd like to kill every one of them," Daikin clenched his fists, "but Bren refuses to allow me to do that."

"He is the lord of Vorlik," Gemna said, sopping up the quail's juices with a piece of bread. "It is his choice."

Daikin growled at that and took a bite of a cabbage roll. "Yes, but I don't have to like it."

"Malbar might help," Maren said.

Daikin cursed at the mention of the Drambini.

"You may not like him, but he might be the best ally you have. Since he's a Drambini and the son of the captain of Drambit's army, he can deal with the Drambini troops in a way we can't."

Daikin glared at him. "Maybe. But if he steps one hair's width out of line, I'll still kill him!"

Maren cringed at Daikin's vehemence. "Give him a chance to prove himself. If you treat him fairly, you won't be disappointed."

"We'll see."

They finished the rest of their meal in silence. Finally, Maren stood up, stretched, and glanced at Gemna. "We'll give you an answer as soon as possible about staying in Vorlik," he told Daikin.

"We need you, both of you, to help protect our people. Oh, I forgot to tell you, I brought your horses with me. They're in the stable."

Maren nodded, then turned to Gemna. "I'll be right back." He went to his room, retrieved his lute and a blanket, then hurried back to Gemna. "Come with me," he said, holding out his hand.

Gemna took it and stood up. "Where are we going?"

"Someplace special."

He led her out the front door of the inn. Early evening shadows stretched across the main road to the chapel of Baygor. A light breeze brought the delicate fragrance of snowstars, the first spring flowers. They walked hand in hand around the side of the inn, past the kitchen garden in back to a small grove of tall trees with grey-green bark and wide hand-shaped leaves. He spread the blanket beside the western edge of the grove, where the light of the westering sun shone warmly, and motioned for Gemna to sit.

Maren ran his fingertips over the trunk of the largest of the trees, smiling. "This is a callum tree, the tree that gives us the healing bark and salve. Until recently, it grew only in my homeland, the Wizard's Vale. Briella planted these here for the people of Vorlik. She gave her life to protect them. Can I do less than she did?"

He gazed at Gemna. "I don't want to leave these people defenseless, knowing Grimmin will surely attack again. But there's something Daikin and Bren and Cordwin don't know."

He sat down in front of Gemna. "I told you the night I broke Grimmin's spell that there's a terrible war coming. A prophesy tells of a final war between the Wizards and Sorcerers that will happen here, in Vorlik. Grimmin's actions are a warning that the Sorcerers have already set their strategies in motion. I don't know how soon before they attack in full force, but I doubt it will be very long from now. I need to warn my people to prepare for war. It will take me less than three days to travel there, time to explain what's happened, and two to three days back. But I'd leave Vorlik unprotected for almost a week. Grimmin most likely wouldn't attack that soon, but I can't be certain." He took her hand and kissed it. "And how could I leave you for that long and with so much uncertainty?"

Gemna took both of his hands in hers. "Do what you have to do. If the Sorcerers are planning to attack Vorlik, we'll need all the help we can get. But can't you transport yourself to the Wizard's Vale the way you did when you brought Cordwin and me here from the castle?"

Maren shook his head. "The farther away a place is, the harder it is to travel that way. If I tried to reach the Wizard's Vale using that spell, I might not survive. But as an eagle, I can reach it in less than three days."

Gemna gave his hands a light squeeze. "Go. I will be here, waiting for you when you return. And when the war is over and we've won, you and I will be together for the rest of our lives. But stay with me tonight."

He smiled. "All right."

Slipping his lute from his back, he strummed "Our Secret Valley," the love song he'd played for her the night he'd been freed from the Sorcerer's binding, a song he'd written for Briella years ago.

"You I'll love as long as I shall live," he sang, savoring the final words of the song as he gazed at Gemna. "I wish you could see my home. There's a place in the Wizard's Vale we call the Teaching Glen. It's surrounded by callum trees that are as tall as ancient oaks. It's where I wrote this song. That's where Loremaster Gilfan taught all the Wizard children the history and legends." He paused, looking at the callum trees. "I remember listening to him tell us the beginnings story."

"The beginnings story?"

"The story about how Baramay and Baygor created all things."

Gemna smiled. "Oh, that story. I remember Father telling me that when I was little enough to sit on his lap."

"I always loved that story, that is, until Loremaster Gilfan came to the part about the Sorcerers."

Gemna looked puzzled. "What part? I don't remember anything about Sorcerers in the beginnings story."

Surprised, Maren told her how Baramay and Baygor had created the Wizards and how Canzet had turned to evil and became the first Sorcerer. Suddenly, he halted, recalling an ancient story. "The Witch of the Winds!"

"What?" Gemna said, startled.

"Logallah! Canzet's wife!"

Gemna looked puzzled. "Canzet's wife?"

"Yes! *She's* the Witch of the Winds! He transformed her into a wind spirit! The old woman said the Witch of the Winds had the keys of chaos and the power of light and darkness! But what does that mean? I have to find out! And I must warn the Wizards the great war is coming soon!"

A thought crossed Maren's mind, and he gasped. "Gemna, if Canzet could transform Logallah into wind, maybe I can find a way to change her to human again! The knowledge has to be somewhere." He paused, his eyes widening. "And if I can find that knowledge, maybe I can bring Briella back, and Cordwin and she could be together at last! I think I've finally found something to give Cordwin hope!"

Maren leaped to his feet. "I have to talk to him now! Let's go!"

Gemna stood and grabbed the blanket, and together they ran back inside the inn and straight to Cordwin's room.

Cordwin lay sleeping, unmoving, as he had been earlier. The room darkened as the sun began to set, shadows dancing on the walls in the orange light.

"Would you light a lantern?" he asked Gemna.

She nodded, quickly lit a thin piece of kindling in the fireplace, and lit the lantern, then set it on the small table next to the bed.

"Cordwin," Maren said, shaking the unconscious man lightly, but he didn't respond. "Cordwin, wake up. Wake up!"

Cordwin's eyelids flickered a moment, then he lay still again.

"You can't do this to yourself," Maren said. "Briella wanted you to live."

Cordwin's eyes opened slowly, and his lips quivered. "Briella," he said, his voice hoarse. "I dreamed about her. She held out her arms to me. I ran and ran, trying to reach her. I almost touched her." He sobbed. "Almost but couldn't."

Maren knelt beside him, eye-level. "You weren't dreaming. She was here. She saved your life."

Cordwin shook his head slowly, still not looking at Maren. "She's dead. I wish I were, too."

"No, you don't! And I'm not certain she'd dead!"

Cordwin's eyes widened. He turned and stared straight at Maren. "Are you crazy? She's as dead as my brother! Bren killed her! We found the dagger!"

"And where did you bury her?"

"I didn't! I couldn't!"

"Did you find her body?"

"No! I looked for her but—" Shock dropped Cordwin's jaw. "You don't mean..."

"I'm not sure what I mean! All I know is that when you were dying of poison, a blue light came from this," Maren lifted Briella's amulet where it hung on Cordwin's chest, "and she appeared and saved you! My sister Amaly made this. It may have powers I can't guess at. But I tell you, I've never heard of anything like this in all the history of Wizards! We don't disappear when we die any more than humans do!"

Cordwin looked at the amulet, then at Maren. Hope mingled with fear in his eyes. "Is it possible? Could she still be alive?"

Maren shrugged and spread his hands. "All I know is, she appeared, she saved your life, and she vanished back into the amulet. And she promised to be with you always." He paused a moment. "She wanted you to live. So live, for her sake. I swear by Baygor and Baramay, if there's any way to bring her back, I'll find it. Keep this amulet with you always and believe there is hope, because I truly believe it's possible she's still alive and there's a chance she'll return to you."

Cordwin nodded slowly, silently. His face lost its grayish tinge; his eyes glowed bright. Maren stood, and he and Gemna walked to the door. Just before he left, he looked back at Cordwin. Clutching the amulet to his chest, Cordwin looked up at them with tears in his eyes but a smile on his face.

41

"Back to your room," Gemna said as they left Cordwin's room.

"But I just got up a few hours ago," Maren said.

"Maybe, but you have a long day ahead tomorrow, and besides," she opened the door to his room and grinned, "you wouldn't want your bath to get cold, would you?"

Maren looked into his room as a small cloud of steam flowed out the open door. In the yellow light of a lantern he saw a large wooden tub filled with steaming water on the floor in front of the crackling hearth. Beside the tub was a chair with a folded towel and a cake of soap. "When did you arrange this?"

"While you were checking on Bren and Cordwin," Gemna said. "Hollester is heating more water for rinsing."

"You are wonderful!" He kissed her forehead. "A hot bath — exactly what I wanted."

"Take your bath and get some sleep." She walked to her own door, opened it, and a cloud of steam escaped. She winked at Maren and went inside.

Shutting the door behind him, Maren stripped off his clothes and sank into the tub of comfortably hot water. *This is probably the last hot bath I'll enjoy for several days,* he thought as he lounged in the tub. The warmth soaked into his muscles, relaxing him. His eyes began to droop, and he yawned. Shaking his head and blinking, he took the bar of oatmeal and mint soap and scrubbed himself until his skin was red and clean.

Someone knocked at his door.

"I have more hot water if you need it," Hollester's voice said through the door.

"Come in."

Hollester opened the door, entered, then nudged the door shut with his foot. "Are you ready to rinse off?"

Maren nodded and closed his eyes. Hollester poured the warm water over Maren's head and body. It felt good to be clean again. "Thank you," the Wizard said as he wiped the water from his face.

"My pleasure, sir."

"Maren. My name is Maren."

Hollester bowed. "My pleasure, Maren. Do you need more water?"

"No, but thank you."

"I'll remove the tub in the morning," the innkeeper said, then left.

Standing, Maren shivered as the water ran down his body. He quickly wrapped up in the towel and stood in front of the fire to dry off. He felt slightly unsettled, knowing he wouldn't see Gemna for at least a week. *I am so use to her being with me now, I don't know how I can be without her, even for a short time,* he thought. *I never imagined I'd come to love a human woman. Now I can't imagine loving anyone but her. Won't my sister laugh when I tell her?*

He slipped on a pair of linen underwear, then went back to the hearth and ruffled his fingers rapidly through his hair to dry it quickly. Climbing into bed, he pulled the covers close around his neck, closed his eyes, and fell asleep feeling very alone.

Maren woke as the first beams of the sun shot like arrows above the eastern mountain. Stretching, he climbed out of bed, dressed quickly, and packed all his belongings in his knapsack, then left the chamber and headed for the common room. Hollester poked the fire in the fireplace to life while Germaine carried breakfast to a round table in the center of the room. Daikin and Gemna sat there, and to Maren's surprise, Bren and Malbar were there as well. Bren wore the gold medallion of Vorlik. Daikin wore the livery of the Tarolin Guard. So did Gemna. They looked Maren's way as he walked toward the table and sat in a chair opposite Gemna.

"I wish I could take you with me," he said. "I'd love to show you my home."

Gemna smiled. "I'd love to see it. But I'll wait for you to come back to me."

Bren clasped Maren's hand and said, "Thank you for everything. Vorlik's safe because of you, Cordwin, and the Southern Guard." He cringed, and his shoulders sagged. "Without you, Vorlik would be in Miria's hands now, no thanks to me. All those people, dead because of me!"

"It wasn't your fault," Maren began.

"But it was!" Bren said bitterly. "I didn't know Miria was...I wouldn't let myself remember she was Paxell's daughter. I only wanted to believe she loved me!"

"So did I," Malbar said softly, staring at the table.

"I almost destroyed everyone!" Bren said.

Maren grasped Bren's shoulder. "If you know you were wrong, that you made a mistake, you've taken the first steps toward wisdom. Don't always trust blindly, but don't become cynical. There're people here who love you — Cordwin, Daikin, Malbar — you can always trust them."

His eyes lowered, Bren nodded.

"Oh, I brought you this," Daikin said. He held an ancient black leather-bound book with silver runes and whispered, "We found it among some things Grimmin left behind. I can't read it. Maybe you can."

Maren stared at the writing, hardly believing what he read: The Enchiridion Canzet. He trembled as he took the book cautiously from Daikin. "How did Grimmin forget this?" he whispered as he ran his fingers across the runes. "Do you know what this is? Do you know what it means to Grimmin? The secrets this book contains are so vast, all the power of the Sorcerers might join to get it back! It can't stay here; it might draw the Sorcerers to it!"

"But won't it draw them to you if you take it?" Bren asked.

"Perhaps," Maren whispered as he stuffed the book in his pack, "but I think I can hide from them."

"Will you come back to Vorlik?"

"Yes. And I'll bring other Wizards to serve and protect you. Look for me in a week. Far-thell and Baramay watch over you all." He turned back to Gemna and held out his hand. "Come see me off."

Gemna slipped her hand in his, and Maren entwined his fingers with hers. Together they walked out the inn's door. Maren scanned overhead. Dark clouds blown by a brisk northwestern wind covered the sky and threatened rain. "A storm will come soon," he said. "I'll have to leave quickly if I hope to escape the worst of it."

He turned and faced her, then leaned over and kissed her hair. In a voice like a summer zephyr, he said, "I love you. You are my heart."

"And you are mine," Gemna said, kissing his hand. "Go quickly and return quicker. I'll wait for you at the castle."

He embraced her, trying to preserve in his heart the memory of the moment. For an instant his resolve faltered and pressed her closer. "How can I leave you?"

"Because you must," she said. "Because so many people depend on you. Because you are a Wizard." She reached up and pressed her lips against his mouth firmly. "Now go before my heart breaks."

He shapechanged into an eagle and launched into the darkening sky. He had to tell the masters about Grimmin and show them the Enchiridion. He glanced back and saw Gemna standing in front of the inn. Happiness filled his heart, and he soared faster than he'd ever flown before.

A cold, spring rain began to fall, slicking down Gemna's dark hair and streaming down her face. Shielding her eyes with her hand, Gemna watched the dark winged shape that was Maren flying over Rindolar Woods toward Tarolin Castle and the northern pass through the Circle Mountains. She already missed him, but she still felt the warmth of his hand on hers, the sweetness of his mouth.

"Falling in love with a Wizard," she said, shaking her head. "Damn me for a fool." She watched Maren's eagle form fly north, then she laughed. "But a happy fool."

About the Author

 Deborah Millitello wrote her first SF story, her first poem, and her first play when she was in fourth grade, and she's been writing ever since. She loves gardening, growing herbs, berries, and orchard fruits, making jams and marmalades, baking, knitting, crocheting, good music, hot tea, and of course, reading. She lives with her husband Carl, who has put up with her writing obsession for over forty-six years. She lives in a small town in Southern Illinois and is retired.

Her first book, *Thief's Luck*, was published in 2006. Her second book, *The Water Girl*, was published in 2015. A collection of her short stories, *Do Virgins Taste Better? and Other Strange Tales* was published in 2016. *The Mourning Dove, Book 1 of the Baramayan Chronicles*, came out in September 2017.

.

Word Posse Fun Fact

I enjoy making unusual jams and marmalades. Some of my favorite jams are strawberry lemonade, lemon blueberry, peach pie, spiced pear, white peach ginger, and cherry vanilla. My favorite marmalades are Buddha's hand, tangerine, kumquat, blood orange, and grapefruit.